WELCOME TO THE
TIME OF LEGENDS

The Warhammer world is founded upon the exploits of brave heroes, and the rise and fall of powerful enemies. Now for the first time the tales of these mythical events will be brought to life in a new series of books. Divided into a series of trilogies, each will bring you hitherto untold details of the lives and times of the most legendary of all Warhammer heroes and villains. Combined together, they will also begin to reveal some of the hidden connections that underpin all of the history of the Warhammer world.

THE LEGEND OF SIGMAR

Kicking off with *Heldenhammer* and continuing in *Empire*, this explosive trilogy tells of the rise of Sigmar as he unites the tribes of men.

THE RISE OF NAGASH

Nagash the Sorcerer begins this gruesome tale of a priest-king's quest for ultimate and unstoppable power over the living and the dead.

THE SUNDERING

The immense, heart-rending tale of the war between the elves and their dark kin commences with *Malekith* and continues in *Shadow King*.

Keep up to date with the latest information from the **Time of Legends** at *www.blacklibrary.com*

More Time of Legends from the Black Library

· THE LEGEND OF SIGMAR ·

Book 1 – HELDENHAMMER
Graham McNeill

Book 2 – EMPIRE
Graham McNeill

· THE RISE OF NAGASH ·

Book 1 – NAGASH THE SORCERER
Mike Lee

· THE SUNDERING ·

Book 1 – MALEKITH
Gav Thorpe

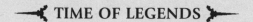

TIME OF LEGENDS

Book two of the Sundering

SHADOW KING

A Tale of the Sundering

Gav Thorpe

This one is for the loving fathers of the world!

A BLACK LIBRARY PUBLICATION

First published in Great Britain in 2009 by
The Black Library,
Games Workshop Ltd.,
Willow Road, Nottingham,
NG7 2WS, UK

10 9 8 7 6 5 4 3 2 1

Cover illustration by Jon Sullivan.
Map by Nuala Kinrade.

A CIP record for this book is available from the British Library.

US ISBN: 978 1 84416 817 0

Distributed in the US by Simon & Schuster
1230 Avenue of the Americas, New York, NY 10020.

Printed and bound in the US.

THE MOST TRAGIC tale from the Time of Legends tells of the fall of the greatest houses of the elves and the rise of three kings: Phoenix, Witch and Shadow.

There was once a time when all was order, now so distant that no mortal creature can remember it. Since time immemorial the elves have dwelt upon the isle of Ulthuan. Here they learnt the secrets of magic from their creators, the mysterious Old Ones. Under the rule of the Everqueen they dwelt upon their idyllic island unblemished by woe.

When the coming of Chaos destroyed the civilisation of the Old Ones, the elves were left without defence. Daemons of the Chaos Gods ravaged Ulthuan and terrorised the elves. From the darkness of this torment rose Aenarion, the first of the Phoenix Kings, the Defender.

Aenarion's life was one of war and strife, yet through the sacrifice of Aenarion and his allies, the daemons were defeated and the elves were saved. In his wake the elves prospered for an age, but all their grand endeavours were to be for naught. The warrior-people of Nagarythe found little solace in peace and in time would turn upon each other and their fellow elves.

Where once there was harmony, there came discord. Where once peace had prevailed, now came bitter war.

Heed now the tale of the Sundering.

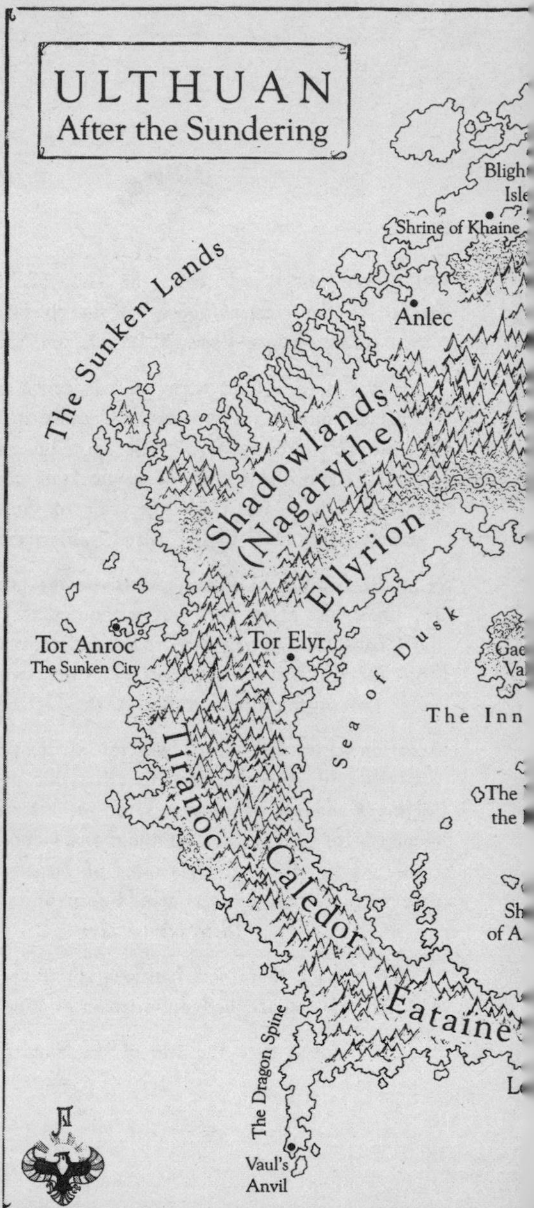
ULTHUAN
After the Sundering
The Sunken Lands
Shrine of Khaine
Anlec
Shadowlands
(Nagarythe)
Ellyrion
Tor Anroc
The Sunken City
Tor Elyr
Sea of Dusk
Tiranoc
Caledor
Eataine
The Dragon Spine
Vaul's
Anvil

The Isles
The Shifting Isles
hrace
Tor Achare
Forests of
Cothique
Averlorn
orests of
Averlorn
Cothique
Finuval
Plain
Tor
Yvresse
Sea
Tower of
Hoeth
Sea of Dreams
Saphery
Yvresse
Eataine
rn
The Shifting Isles

PART ONE

The Child of Kurnous; Strife in Nagarythe; A Trailing Shadow; The Treachery of Malekith

ONE

The Young Hunter

IN THE DAYS of the first Phoenix King, Aenarion the Defender founded the realm of Nagarythe in the harsh north of Ulthuan. Under his reign the Naggarothi – as Aenarion's people were called – studied long the arts of war and forged a formidable army to defeat the daemons of Chaos.

At Anlec, greatest fortress of the elves, Aenarion held court with his queen, Morathi, and they brought into the world their son, Malekith. Aenarion fell at the very moment of his victory and the rule of Nagarythe passed to his son. Prince Malekith formalised the promises of his father and secured the lands and wealth of the many princes who had fought by Aenarion's side. Yet, ever a warrior and a wanderer, Malekith departed for new wars in the colonies.

Second only to the great Caledor Dragontamer in Aenarion's esteem was Eoloran Anar, the Phoenix King's standard bearer. To his stewardship Malekith gave the lands of eastern Nagarythe in the hills and mountains of the Annulii. In Aenarion and Malekith's name Eoloran would rule, and there was peace and prosperity for an age.

Eoloran was a wise prince and was content to raise the power and privilege of House Anar without conflict, though he sent his son Eothlir to fight in the colonies for a time so that he might know something of war. His wife having died in the war with the daemons, Eoloran became reclusive, though always ready to answer the calls of the lesser nobles of Nagarythe. Other, more ambitious princes grew in renown and the deeds of Eoloran faded from memory except within the halls of Elanardris.

With Malekith gone from Nagarythe to conquer new realms for the elves, the seed was sown for division. Jealous of the power granted to Eoloran, though he did not wield it often, Morathi wove tangled politics to isolate the Anars from the rest of Ulthuan while all the while strengthening her grip upon Anlec and Nagarythe. It was not a topic Eoloran wished to discuss with his family, who were left to wonder what the ancient elf planned to revive his family's fortunes, or if he had any plan at all. He forbade any of the Anars from visiting Anlec and instead was content to petition his fellow lords with letters reminding them of their support from the Anars in centuries past and their ancient vows to one another. Eoloran's son, Eothlir, tried as best he could to maintain the status of House Anar, but he knew that there was a change coming. He could not define what it was that alarmed him; it was a flicker in the corner of the eye, a sound on the edge of hearing, a distant scent on the wind that cautioned him.

It was the Season of Frost, in the one thousand and forty-second year of the reign of Phoenix King Bel Shanaar. At the home of the Anars, the wind had turned north and brought with it the chill of winter down from the mountains. Snow flurries drifted from the highest peaks in long, fluttering streamers of white. The furthest reaches of the pine forests were dusted with snow as the bitter weather crept down the mountainsides day by day. Maieth was wrapped in a long shawl of dark blue wool as she stood in the gardens of the Anars' manse. Eothlir, her husband, placed an arm around her and smiled.

'There is a warm fire within, why do you stand outside in the cold?' he asked.

'Listen,' she said. They both stood in silence, and the only sound to be heard was the sighing of the wind. Then, faintly, there was a call, the croak of a crow.

'A single crow in winter,' said Eothlir. 'A bad omen, do you think?'

'Yes,' she replied. 'Though no more an omen than a houseful of sudden guests come here from Anlec seeking sanctuary.'

'It is but a temporary arrangement,' said Eothlir. 'One day Prince Malekith will return. He will rein in Morathi's excesses. We must be patient.'

'Excesses?' laughed Maieth, with bitterness not humour. 'Butchery and perversion are not "excesses"!'

'There are those who protect her, you know that,' said Eothlir. 'But there are as many who see her rule as tyranny and resist her.'

'When?' demanded Maieth, pulling herself free from her husband's arms to stare at him. 'For many years they have done nothing; we have done nothing.'

'She is the mother of the Prince of Nagarythe, the bride of Aenarion; it would be treason to move against her directly,' said Eothlir. 'For the moment it is sufficient that we rule our lands and keep them free of her taint. If she tries to take our power overtly, she will find greater resistance than she expects.'

'And what of Tharion, Faerghil, Lohsteth and the others who now sleep in our beds, afraid of returning to Anlec?'

asked Maieth. 'Are they not also princes of Nagarythe? Do you realise that they once thought that Morathi would never be so bold as to go against them directly?'

'Would you have me a traitor and usurper?' snapped Eothlir. 'Or worse, would you be a widow, and your son fatherless? In Anlec, Morathi holds sway, but here in the mountains her reach is short. She may try to pick us off one-by-one, but as long as we are united, she cannot move against us. Fully a third of Nagarythe's armies are abroad with Malekith. Another third owe allegiance to my father and his allies. Morathi cannot conjure soldiers from thin air, no matter her powers of seeing and scrying.'

'Your father holds half of the warriors in Nagarythe, and yet what does he do?' said Maieth with scorn. 'He hides here and writes letters. Are we not all sons and daughters of Nagarythe? Our armies should be camped outside the gates of Anlec, demanding restitution from Morathi for the wrongs she has done our people.'

'And what of Malekith, Aenarion's heir, our rightful ruler?' said Eothlir, grabbing his wife by the shoulders. 'Do you think he will look kindly upon those that raise arms against Anlec without his consent? Would he welcome those that threaten his mother? I tell you now, my father would die of shame to be thought of as a traitor, and so he rallies support in the only way he can.'

'Hush now,' said Maieth quickly, embracing her husband.

Turning, Eothlir saw a young elf, no more than thirty summers old, walking down the wide steps from the mansion. He was dressed in hunting leathers edged with dappled fur and bound with leather thongs, and in his hands he held a slender black bow and a quiver of arrows.

'More practice, Alith?' called Eothlir, disentangling from his wife's arms. 'You already know that there is not a lord in the mountains that can match your eye and hand.'

'I know nothing of the sort, Father,' said the boy sombrely. 'Khurion says that his cousin from Chrace, Menhion, can strike a pinefowl in flight at a hundred paces.'

'Khurion says many things, my son,' said Maieth. 'If we believe all that he claims, then his cousins, all four of them, would be the match for any army in the world.'

'I know that he exaggerates,' said Alith. 'However, I have made a wager with him, to call his bluff. In the spring I will contest with Menhion, and I shall uphold the honour of House Anar. Until then, I must practise further while the snows still hold back.'

'Very well, but be back before dusk,' said Eothlir.

ALITH NODDED AND walked away, slinging the quiver over his shoulder. He knew that his parents thought him distant, morose even. They whispered and fell silent when he was around, but he was observant and keen-eared and knew that all was not well in Nagarythe. The manse was full of refugee princes who had chosen not to support Morathi and her hideous cults.

He also knew, perhaps even where his father and grandfather did not, that this matter would be settled not with diplomacy but with force. He thought much of his family for avoiding direct confrontation with the rulers of Nagarythe, but he knew that one day he would lead House Anar and he was determined that the manner of the world in which he ruled would be better than that of today. Others would follow him not out of fear, but out of respect; it was never too early to earn respect, though often too late.

Leaving the formal gardens through a silver gate in the high hedge, Alith strode up into the hills that heaped up higher and higher upon the shoulder of Suril Anaris, the Mountain of the Moon. The whole mountain and its surrounds were the lands of the Anar, granted to Alith's grandfather by Aenarion himself. Though inhospitable in winter, they were abundant with game and fowl, and the lower meadows still made good pasturing for goats and sheep. These would be his lands one day, and so he walked them as often as possible, getting to know them as he knew the house where he had been born.

Today he went north and east, along the Inna Varith. The cold river flowed down from caves hidden upon the slope of Suril Anaris and fed the lands of Elanardris with fresh water until it disappeared back underground at the Haimeth Falls many miles to the south.

Picking his way along the winding bank, Alith watched the silver darting of fish in the clear waters, leaping and swimming through the rocky rapids. Needing to get to the northern side of the river the young elf leapt nimbly from rock to rock, heedless of the torrent sweeping past his feet, unmindful of the slicked stones upon which he stepped.

From here he found an old track that led further up into the hills, twisting around dark boulders and leafless bushes. It was some time before he came under the eaves of the pine forest, and set foot upon a frosted carpet of needles. Alith's light tread left barely a mark in the crisp mulch as he broke into a jog, speeding swiftly under the overlapping branches of the trees.

Alith was guided by an inner sense, attuned to the distant warmth of the sun behind the clouds, the wind upon his face and the subtle slope of the ground beneath him. As clearly as if he had a map, he cut eastwards through the woods, along the flank of the mountainside. In the branches above birds swooped to and fro while four-legged, whiskered hunters snuffled through the patchy undergrowth, unaware of his passing. His route brought him to an outcropping of rock that pushed several hundred feet up through the trees, and at its foot there was a low cave. Cloud had flowed down the mountainside and swathed the clearing with a fine greyness that dulled colours and muted sound.

Ducking inside the gap in the rock, Alith came to a wider cavern, dark but for the trickle of sunlight through the entrance. He reached out to his right and his hand came upon a torch of bound branches held within a sconce on the cave wall. He spoke a word; a spark lit within the torch's head and swiftly took flame. With this light, he walked further into the cavern.

The cave opened into a wide natural nave, shaped over thousands of years. Stalagmites and stalactites had met in ages past, forming glittering pillars much like the columns of a grand cathedral. It was not just a temple in appearance, for Alith had come to one of the shrines of Kurnous, the Hunter God. The glow of the flickering brand danced across dozens of skulls placed in niches around the cave wall: of wolves and foxes; bears and deer; hawk and rabbit. Some were gilded, others inscribed with delicate runes of prayer and thanks.

All were gifts to Kurnous.

Though worshipped much more in Chrace, whose hunters were renowned throughout Ulthuan, Kurnous was still acknowledged elsewhere in those communities that had not moved to the ever-growing cities. In Elanardris the Hunter God was held in high esteem, the ways of the wilds not yet swept away with the formality of Asuryan or the other gods.

It was a feral shrine, with a dirt floor scattered with dead leaves. The walls were painted with hunting scenes, of predator chasing prey. Some were ancient and faded; others were brighter and more recent. Alith knew that others came here, though he had never encountered another hunter visiting the shrine.

Alith had no such grand offering this day, though in the past he had fashioned such sacrifices for the Wolf of the Heavens. He knelt before the altar – a rocky plinth strewn with twigs, ash and detritus. There was a hole bored into the rock where he set the torch, and then he gathered up a mound of broken sticks and dried leaves. Snapping a single brand from the torch, he lit the small fire and breathed it into greater life. He spoke a few words of thanks and dropped the burning stem onto the miniature pyre.

Alith then pulled something from a pouch at his belt: a thin sliver of venison from the last deer he had slain, a dozen days ago. He skewered the meat on a forked piece of branch and set it atop the fire where it hissed and spat.

Alith then sat cross-legged before the altar and took his bow across his knees. With his hands upon it, he whispered a few words to Kurnous, thanking him for the kill he had offered and asking for grace in his hunts to come.

Head bowed, Alith sat for a while longer in silent contemplation. He tried to put aside his worries and focus on the hunt to come. He pictured himself stood atop the peak of Suril Anaris, the sun bright upon his face, the wilderness laid out before him. He pictured the trails the animals followed; the pools where they drank; the runs where they hunted. From within, the landscape of Suril Anaris opened up before him. There were still many dark patches: places where Alith had not yet travelled.

After paying due homage, Alith stood and left the cave, the venison still burning behind him. With another word of power he quenched the torch and placed it back in its holder ready for the next visitor; him or another, it did not matter. Stooping low, Alith ducked out of the cave – and then stood frozen.

Just ahead of Alith, in the thickening mist, stood a stag. It was a monumental creature: its shoulder higher than Alith was tall, with a spread of antlers wider than the young prince's outstretched arms. Its coat was white, save for a flash of black down its chest. The stag watched Alith with deep brown eyes, neither aggressive nor alarmed.

The young elf straightened slowly and stared back. The stag bent its head and shook its antlers, scratching at the ground with a hoof. Alith was convinced this was some sign sent by Kurnous, but could not fathom its meaning. The stag was becoming more agitated, and arched back its head and let loose a long bark. Alith took a step forwards, his hand outstretched in a placating gesture, but the stag suddenly looked to the west and then bounded away into the forest.

Alith turned his gaze to where the stag had looked and saw a figure beneath the eaves of the trees. He was mounted upon a black horse and swathed in a cloak of dark feathers. The rider's head was cowled and nothing could be seen of his face.

Unconsciously, Alith reached for his bow, and turned his head to grasp it from the quiver. As soon as he looked back, the rider was gone. Alith strung an arrow and dashed across the open ground to the edge of the trees where the rider's horse had been. There was no mark upon the ground, the frosted pine needles undisturbed by foot or hoof.

Two bizarre events so close together left Alith feeling unnerved, and he glanced around the rest of the clearing but could see nothing. Taking the arrow from his bow, he broke into a run and headed straight back towards the manse, all thoughts of hunting forgotten.

THE HEIR OF House Anar chose not to share his two strange encounters with his family, who had enough to contemplate without the fanciful tales of their son. The experience faded in his memory over the winter and spring until even he was not sure whether it had truly happened or been some kind of waking dream. Thoughts of strange omens and mysterious riders were replaced in the young elf's mind with more pressing concerns: love.

The day before midsummer, Alith savoured the warmth of the sun upon his skin. He wore a short sleeveless gown of white silk, his face, arms and legs exposed to the pleasant heat as he lay on his back staring up into a cloudless sky.

'That is not something I see too often,' said Maieth, sat on the grassy hill next to her son. Behind them the large manse of House Anar, capital of Elanardris, rose up from the slope of the mountain, its white walls bright in the sunshine. Elves were gathered in groups around the gardens, talking and drinking, taking sweetmeats and delicacies off trays from servants liveried in silvery grey.

'What is that?' asked Alith, turning to his side and resting on one elbow.

'A smile,' his mother replied with one of her own.

'I cannot be sad on a glorious day such as this,' declared Alith. 'Blue skies, the glow of summer; these things cannot be touched by darkness.'

'And?' said Maieth with an intent look at her son. 'There have been many such days this year, and yet I have not seen you this happy since you loosed your first arrow.'

'Is it not enough that I am content?' said Alith. 'Why should I not be happy?'

'Do not be so coy, my reticent child,' Maieth continued playfully. 'Is there not some other reason for this unbounded joy? Something to do with the midsummer banquet tomorrow?'

Alith's eyes narrowed and he sat up.

'What have you heard?' he asked, returning Maieth's gaze.

'This and that,' his mother said with a dismissive wave of her hand. 'I met with Caenthras just before I came up here. You must know him; he is the father of Ashniel.'

At the mention of the elf maiden's name, Alith looked away. Maieth laughed at his sudden discomfort.

'So it is true!' she said with a triumphant grin. 'I take it from your carefree happiness today, and the smitten expression you've worn whenever Ashniel has been around, that she has agreed to attend the dance with you?'

Alith's face was one of consternation as he replied.

'She has,' he said. 'Dependent on her father's permission, of course. What did he say to you, exactly?'

'Only that you run around in the woods like a hare, and dress like a goatherd more than a prince,' said Maieth.

Alith was crestfallen, and moved to stand. Maieth leant over and stayed him with a hand on his arm.

'And that he would be delighted for his daughter to court the son of the Anars,' she added quickly.

Alith stopped and paused before breaking into a wide grin.

'He said yes?' said Alith.

'He said yes,' Maieth replied. 'I hope you have been practising your dancing, and not spending all of your time with that bow.'

'Calabreth has been teaching me,' Alith assured his mother.

'Come,' she said, standing up and reaching down a hand to Alith. 'You should greet Caenthras and thank him.'

She pulled her son up by the hand. Alith stood hesitantly, eyeing the gathered elves as if they were a circling pack of ice wolves.

'He has already said yes,' Maieth reminded him. 'Just remember to be polite.'

TWO

Darkness from Anlec

FOR THE ELVES, who each live for an age of the world, time passes quickly. A year to them is as a day to men, and so their schemes and relationships develop slowly. Alith Anar, young and impatient, wooed Ashniel for two years, from midsummer to midsummer, through letters and courtship, dances and hunts. Entranced by the cool beauty of the Naggarothi maiden, the young Anar prince put aside his greater concerns and for a while was happy, or at least relished the promise of future happiness. So it came about that he listened little to the whispered worries of his parents and spent less time in the wilds, instead closeting himself in the study and library of Elanardris learning poetry to impress his amour or listened to tales from his mother, ancient legends of those two divine lovers, Lileath and Kurnous.

To pledge his love for Ashniel, Anar commissioned the finest craftsmen to weave for her a cloak of midnight-blue, studded with diamonds like stars, the constellations drawn in fine traceries of silver thread. Having read into the astronomical texts of the family, Alith had devised the design himself, representing the skies above Ulthuan on the day of Ashniel's birth. This labour he did in secret, even from his family, for he wanted to present Ashniel with this gift on the coming midsummer's night and would risk no warning of it reaching the ears of his loved one.

As evening fell on the night of the festival, servants came out with magical lanterns to hang upon the boughs of the trees in the gardens. The golden dusk was augmented by the yellow glow of the lanterns, which turned to pools of silver as the sun disappeared and the stars scattered across the skies. Chatter filled the air as dozens of elves walked the patios and paths of Elanardris's exquisitely designed surrounds, accompanied by the clinking of crystal goblets and the patter of fountains.

Alith flitted through the scattered crowds of guests like a shadow, his eyes seeking Ashniel. The cloak nestled under Alith's arm, wrapped in silken paper brought from the colonies to the west. The package was as light as a feather, but felt like a leaden weight. Excitement and fear vied inside Alith as he skirted around a plush lawn and headed back towards the paved area where food was being served.

As two guests parted for a moment, Alith spied Ashniel's pale face. Bathed in the lamplight she was beautiful, her expression one of poise and dignity, her grey eyes glittering. Weaving through the milling elves, Alith made straight for Ashniel and was but a few steps from her when a tall figure came up in front of him, forcing Alith to stop sharply. Glancing up as he was about to step around the obstacle, Alith saw the face of Caenthras, one eyebrow raised in suspicion.

'Alith,' said Prince Caenthras. 'I have been looking for you.'

'You have?' replied Alith, taken aback and suddenly worried. 'Whatever for? I mean, how can I be of service?'

Caenthras smiled and laid a hand on Alith's shoulder.

'Do not look so petrified, Alith,' said the lordly elf. 'I do not bear ill news, merely an invitation.'

'Oh,' said Alith, brightening up. 'A hunt perhaps?'

Caenthras sighed and shook his head.

'Not all of our lives revolve around the wilds, Alith. No, I have visitors from Anlec at my house who I wish you to meet: priestesses who will divine the future for yourself and Ashniel. I thought that if the augurs go well, we might discuss the details of the union of our two houses.'

Alith opened his mouth to reply but then realised he did not know what to say. He clenched his jaw to stop himself saying something stupid and simply nodded, trying to appear sagely. Caenthras frowned a little.

'I thought you would be pleased.'

'I am!' said Alith, panicking. 'Very pleased! That sounds wonderful. Although... What if the priestesses say something bad?'

'Do not worry, Alith. I am positive that the omens will be good.'

Caenthras glanced over his shoulder towards Ashniel and then at the package under Alith's arm. He nodded and pulled Alith closer, hugging him to his chest as he steered the youth through the crowd of elves surrounding Ashniel.

'My daughter, light of the winter skies,' said Caenthras. 'Look what I have found lurking nearby like a mouse in its hole! I believe it has something to say to you.'

Caenthras shoved Alith forwards and he stumbled a few paces and stopped in front of Ashniel. He looked up into those grey eyes and melted, the poem he had rehearsed again and again in the library slipping from his memory. Alith gulped, trying to recover his wits.

'Hello, my love,' said Ashniel, leaning forwards and kissing Alith on the forehead. 'I've been waiting for you all evening.'

Her perfumed scent, distilled from autumn wildflowers, filled Alith's nostrils and he was dizzy with the smell for a moment.

'I have this for you,' he blurted, stepping back and thrusting out the package.

Ashniel took the gift, ran her hand over the soft paper and gave an admiring look at the intricately knotted ribbon that bound it. With Alith's aid, she slipped the ribbon free and let the silk paper flutter to the floor. Alith took the neck of the cloak and flung it open, revealing its shining glory. There were appreciative gasps from the other elves and a pleased smile played upon Ashniel's lips.

Alith glanced around and saw that many more elves had gathered upon the patio and several dozen were watching the unfolding spectacle, his mother, father and grandfather amongst them. It occurred to him that perhaps he had not been so devious in his secrecy as he had thought.

'Here, let me,' said Caenthras, stepping forwards and taking the cloak from Alith. He swung the cape around Ashniel's neck and deftly fixed the crescent moon-shaped clasp upon her right shoulder. Seeing the gift upon Ashniel, the words sprang back to Alith unbidden.

'As the stars light the night, so you shine upon my life,' he said, clasping his hands in front of him, his eyes rising to the heavens. 'As the world turns under their gaze, my life unfolds under yours. Where bright Lileath gazes down upon us with her beauty, her radiance is as nothing compared to the light that shines from you.'

There were more gasps from a few of the assembled elves and whispered comments, complaining that Alith should not compare the beauty of a mortal to that of the

Moon Goddess. Alith ignored them, knowing that they were simply being prudish.

'My heart burns as the sun and I would have your soul reflect its light,' concluded Alith.

Ashniel's expression was one of refined amusement as she looked at the other maidens in the crowd, pleased with their jealousy. She cupped Alith's cheeks in her hands and smiled.

'Though Lileath spurned Kurnous, I shall not follow suit,' she said. 'The hunter has caught his prey with this most dazzling of traps and I cannot escape.'

There was a cheer, soon joined by more, and Alith and Ashniel found themselves at the centre of a jostling mass of elves eager to congratulate them and examine the fine cloak. Alith let it all wash over him, feeling a calm descend that he had not felt anywhere else except on the mountain tops with an arrow notched upon his bow. Contented, he took a glass of wine from a servant and raised it in toast to Caenthras, who nodded appreciatively and then disappeared into the gathered elves.

THE MOONS WERE barely above the mountains when Gerithon, the chancellor of the Anars, hurried from the house to speak with Eoloran and Eothlir. Alith excused himself from Ashniel and joined his father and grandfather.

'He insists that he speak with you,' Gerithon was saying.

'Then bring him through,' said Eoloran. 'Let us hear what he has to say.'

'Yes, let him speak his mind in front of us all,' said Eothlir.

With a resigned sigh, Gerithon walked back into the manse. For a moment Alith wondered if this visitor was perhaps the dark rider he had first seen in the forest several years earlier. Ever since that encounter Alith had spied the elf – or what he supposed to be an elf though he could not know for sure – several times more, watching the young prince from a mountain ridge or beneath the boughs of a wooded copse. Always the rider had disappeared before Alith could approach, and left no tracks for him to follow.

Alith had spoken of this strange watcher to nobody, fearing that it would cause alarm without bringing answers. But the elf Gerithon escorted from the manse was not the rider, or if he was then he wore a different guise, for he was dressed in the manner of one of the pleasure cultists.

The stranger was clad in swirling layers of purple robes, each diaphanous, but overlaid upon his body in such a way that where they overlapped they concealed his nudity and preserved a little dignity. His right brow was pierced with a silver ring from which hung an oval ruby, and a similar jewel hung from the left side of his nose. The hair that hung to his shoulder was dark but bleached white towards the tips, braided with beads of blue and red glass. Alith noticed that for all his decadent appearance, the newcomer wore a sheathed sword at his belt – a long, thin weapon with a crossguard fashioned into the likeness of two hands cupping the blade.

'My princes,' the stranger said with a low bow. 'Allow me to introduce myself. I am Heliocoran Haeithar. I have ridden from Anlec to speak with you.'

'There is no message from Anlec that we wish to hear,' said Eoloran.

Most of the party attendees and a few servants were gathering around the stranger and hostility filled the air. Heliocoran seemed oblivious to the situation and continued regardless.

'Her majesty, Queen Morathi, wishes to invite the house of Anar to an audience,' said Heliocoran. He looked around at the guests. 'And I extend that invitation to any prince present here, upon my own authority.'

'Queen Morathi?' spat Eothlir. 'When last I heard, Nagarythe was ruled by Prince Malekith. We have no queen.'

'It is unfortunate that the whispers of Bel Shanaar have been allowed to settle here and take root,' said Heliocoran smoothly. Upon close inspection, Alith saw that the envoy's eyes were odd, his pupils disturbingly small, while the green of his irises almost completely obscured the white. This was accentuated by a thin trace of kohl that brought the messenger's eyes into stark contrast in an unsettling fashion.

'We shall determine for ourselves what is truth and what are lies,' said Eoloran. 'Say your part and then leave.'

'As you wish,' said the herald with another exaggerated bow. 'The realms of the other princes are in concert against Nagarythe, and wish to make Malekith their puppet. He fears to return to Ulthuan under the present conditions. Dear comrades of our prince are held hostage against his loyalty. That is the truth of it. The Naggarothi have been betrayed by Bel Shanaar, he who usurped the Phoenix Throne from the heir of Aenarion. For these past many years Bel Shanaar has grown more and more vocal in his opposition to our traditions and customs, and Queen Morathi wearies of his hypocrisy. She calls out to all princes, captains and lieutenants still loyal to the true rule of Nagarythe, and bids them to travel to Anlec so that she might hold counsel with the greatest of these lands.'

His voice had become strident, but again dropped to a soft hush, and his manner became one of pleading confidant rather than bombastic herald.

'Innocent elves have been slain and imprisoned by the minions of Bel Shanaar, the Usurper Phoenix; persecuted for pursuing their leisures and beliefs, hounded for following the ancient rites of our people. If you allow this conspiracy to proceed unchallenged, Nagarythe shall fall and her power squabbled over by weaker bloodlines than stand here. If you would see your lands taken and your children chained and your servants and labourers whipped into misery, then stay here, stand idle and do nothing. If you would see Morathi preserve the inheritance of Malekith so that he might reclaim his rightful position as heir to Aenarion and ruler of Ulthuan, then return with me to Anlec.'

'Though I have no love for Morathi, I have none either for Bel Shanaar,' said Caenthras, stepping to the front of the ring of elves surrounding Heliocoran. 'If the warriors of the Phoenix King come to my lands, will Anlec send help?'

'That is for us to discuss in the council,' replied the messenger.

'What assurances do we have that this is not some trick?' asked Quelor, one of the princes allied to the Anars. 'Who says that bare cells and iron chains do not await us in Anlec?'

'Such division gives sport to the agents of our enemies,' said Heliocoran. 'To set Naggarothi against Naggarothi, that is the aim of our adversaries. Queen Morathi can give no assurances that the doubts sown by the spies of our foes cannot undermine. Instead, she appeals to your sense of duty and to the strength that flows within your veins. All here are true sons and daughters of Nagarythe, and each knows it is their right and their responsibility to uphold the honour of this realm. Lest you wish to be ensorcelled by the cowardly wizards of Saphery and see our dominions overseas taken by the merchants of Lothern and Cothique, heed Queen Morathi's warnings.'

'You do your position justice,' said Eoloran. 'Never have I heard such bile cloaked with such sweetness. You have said your piece, and now be gone from my lands.'

'You cannot stand aside in this battle, Eoloran,' said the messenger, and his tone was frank. 'For years now the house of Anar has refused to choose where its loyalties lie, and has gathered its friends close to protect it against the harms of this conflict. Now it is time to make your position plainly known. You may choose the correct path, and defend your lands against invaders from the other kingdoms, and your reward shall be in the sustaining of your line and the strengthening of your position. Yet you must stand against the misguided will and might of Bel Shanaar and his sycophants.

'If you choose to side with the usurpers, then you may well endure for a time, but dire shall be Queen Morathi's wrath on those who betray Nagarythe. You will be cast from power, scorned by those who once respected you and you shall spend the rest of your days as landless wanderers.'

'And so the threat is made,' said Eothlir. 'You would have it that we stand between a cliff and the ocean, and must dash ourselves against the rocks or else drown.'

'Then tell me, Eothlir, what does your heart say?' said Heliocoran. 'What have I said that you know to be untrue? Do you trust Bel Shanaar so much that you would throw in your lot with him?'

Gerithon hurried from the manse once more, looking agitated.

'There are armed soldiers outside, my prince,' he said. 'Three dozen, at least, that I could see. Their leader is arguing at the gate.'

'Why would a herald come armed for fighting?' said Eothlir, pointing to the sword at Heliocoran's waist. 'What is the meaning of these warriors before our doors?'

'These are not safe times,' said the herald. 'The agents of Bel Shanaar prowl the wilds like packs of feral hounds. You of all should know that we must protect ourselves. It would be most unfortunate if some foe were to waylay your family.'

'Get out!' roared Eoloran. 'Take your bribes and your threats and be away!'

Heliocoran flinched from the outburst as if menaced by a blade, and shrank back towards the house. With a snarl he turned and ran, pushing his way through the elves and hurling aside a serving maid who fell amid the splintered smash of crystal platters. No sooner had he disappeared into the manse than Eothlir was storming after him.

'With me!' he cried. 'He will open the doors and let in his soldiers!'

Alith did not chase directly into the house with the others, but instead ran for the east wing to his chambers. The high window was open and he leapt inside and flung open the chest at the foot of his bed where his bow and arrows were kept. With a straining gasp he swiftly strung his bow, and snatched up his quiver.

Wrenching open the door, Alith raced into the corridor and then along the wood-panelled passageway to the dining hall at the front of the manse. Shouts and the sounds of fighting echoed around the mansion. Striding to the windows, Alith saw that a group of black-armoured warriors had forced their way through the gate of the outer wall and were gathered about the colonnaded portico and were fighting to get inside, pushing at their companions to get through the door.

Opening the wide double doors that led to the entrance hall, Alith was confronted by the sight of his father and grandfather fighting back-to-back, wielding swords wrested from their foes. Meanthir and Lestraen lay bleeding upon the floor, possibly dead, and three of the envoy's warriors were also slain.

Taking up his bow, Alith shot one of the attackers in the thigh, saving his grandfather from a cut aimed towards his shoulder. In the space this created, Eoloran leapt forwards and thrust his blade past the guard of another warrior, cutting him across the arm. Other elves loyal to the Anars came rushing in from the opposite wing of the house, carrying swords and daggers taken from the walls of the great hall. Caenthras arrived, wielding a long spear, and drove its point into the back of one of the elves fighting Eothlir.

There came a deafening crash of glass from the eating hall and Alith turned to see dark-garbed soldiers breaking through the high windows, blades in hand. He shot the first to climb through, but two more jumped in swiftly behind the slain elf. Alith loosed another arrow but with a dull ring it merely caught a glancing blow on the golden helm of his target. Even as Alith whipped another arrow from the quiver across his back, the warrior turned and rushed towards him.

Jumping aside from the outthrust sword of his foe, Alith strung the arrow and loosed it in one fluid motion, the arrowhead punching through the elf's breastplate. Wounded, but not killed, the warrior gave a hoarse shout and swung his sword at Alith's neck. Alith swayed backwards but the point of the blade slashed across his tunic and a line of blood welled up from his wounded chest. Biting back a cry of pain, Alith whipped the tip of his bow into the face of his opponent, who fell back with a hand to his eye.

Tharion appeared at the doorway with a two-handed sword and chopped the elf's legs from beneath him, before giving a cry of alarm. Turning, Alith saw three more warriors advancing towards him, while a fourth made for the fire blazing in the great hearth. He saw the warrior snatch up a branch from the fireplace and take a step towards the tapestries hanging on the wall opposite the windows.

Without a thought, Alith nocked an arrow and took aim between the advancing elves. Breathing out slowly he loosed the arrow, which buried itself in the neck of the elf with the brand. The flaming branch fell from his dead grasp and thudded harmlessly on the stone floor.

The heir of Anar had barely time to loose another shot, which pierced the shoulder of his target, before Caenthras and Tharion were leaping forwards with their weapons, roaring ancient battle cries. Alith was struck by the ferocity of the two ageing princes; veterans of Aenarion's army and skilled warriors both.

Caenthras's spear took one of the dark-clad elves in the throat, who jerked like a puppet without strings before collapsing in a heap. Tharion parried a blow aimed towards his legs and spun his wrists to bring his heavy blade down across his foe's sword arm, severing it at the elbow. A backhanded strike hurled the elf back with his breastplate rent open, his lifeblood gushing over his black robes.

The clatter of hooves on cobbles attracted Alith's attention and he dashed to the windows. He saw Heliocoran wrestling with a tawny steed, trying to swing himself up into the saddle. As Alith climbed through the window, careful to avoid the slivers of shattered glass still protruding from the frame, Heliocoran mastered his mount. With much whipping of the reins, he turned his horse across the courtyard towards the main gates.

As the herald raced away, Alith's aim was obscured by the line of fir trees on either side of the roadway leading from the gate, and he leapt for the porch. Gripping the scrolled top of a column with one hand, he swung himself up onto the portico. From here, he could see the length of the courtyard to the gateway.

A soldier in the colours of House Anar stumbled from the gatehouse ahead of the messenger, blood dripping from a wounded leg. Heliocoran stooped low in the saddle and swept his sword across the warrior's chest as he sped past, felling him with a single blow.

Alith knelt on the roof of the portico and took aim. The clashing of swords and cries of battle below him drifted out of his thoughts as he focussed his mind and body on the dwindling figure of Heliocoran.

He imagined himself in the woods, stalking a boar or deer. He adjusted his line of shot for the wind sighing against the left side of his face, and raised his bow a touch so that his shot would not fall short of his rapidly fleeing prey.

Lit only by flickering lanterns, the herald was all but swathed in darkness and he was a moment from escape, but Alith could see his position clearly in his mind's eye.

With a whispered prayer to Kurnous, Alith loosed the arrow. The black-fletched missile streaked into the darkness, its point glimmering with firelight from the torches upon the walls of the courtyard. He heard a cry as it struck home. Heliocoran slumped upon his steed but did not fall, and then passed out of sight through the gatehouse.

Three of the fleeing messenger's warriors staggered out from the entrance hall onto the roadway beneath Alith, and he loosed three arrows in quick succession, taking them down with a single shot each. Eoloran, Eothlir, Caenthras and others ran out, stopping when they saw there were no more foes. Eoloran looked over his shoulder at his grandson.

'Did any of them escape?' Eoloran demanded.

'I hit Heliocoran, but I do not know if the wound is mortal,' Alith confessed.

Eoloran cursed, and signalled for Alith to climb down from his vantage point.

'That is the last of them,' said Eothlir. 'More will come. How soon, we cannot know. It seems that House Anar has chosen a side.'

Though his father's face was grim, this pronouncement brought pride to Alith's heart. Since he had been born, House Anar had been content to play no greater part in the affairs of Nagarythe. All of that had changed. Morathi had as much as declared war on House Anar, and Alith was pleased that his idleness would soon come to an end.

He was Naggarothi, after all, and battle was in his heart and glory called in his blood.

Now was the chance for him to prove his worth and earn the renown that surrounded his family; a renown he had felt had not yet been his to rightfully share.

He hid a smile as he lowered himself down to the tiled ground below.

THREE

The Prince Returns

NEARLY A YEAR had passed since the attack on the manse; many days filled with frenetic activity and tension. Eoloran and Eothlir were afraid that the warriors of Anlec would come upon them at any time, falling upon Elanardris before its defences were made ready. Riders made haste to all corners of the Anars' realm, to lesser princes and commanders, to muster their soldiers at the ancestral home and ready for battle. Other princes, from House Atriath and House Ceneborn, both long allies of the Anars, chose Elanardris to make clear their defiance of Anlec.

For all the fears of House Anar, the threats of Heliocoran did not materialise into action. All of the summer, autumn and spring, troops loyal to Eoloran came and camped upon the hills that surrounded the mansion, nearly ten thousand in all. The standard of House Anar fluttered atop the manse, white with a golden griffon's wing upon it, and from the banners of the regiments assembling at the call of their lord.

Yet Alith was disappointed. Fully half of their troops had not responded to the call to arms. Many had turned back the messengers and bid them return to Eoloran to convey their refusal to act against Anlec. This grieved Eothlir too, for Alith could see the strain written upon the face of his father when these messages were passed on.

Alith guessed, as did Eothlir and others, that these dissenters had succumbed to the bribes and threats of Morathi. None could say if their part was simply to step aside from their duties, or if there was some darker plot to be uncovered. Would Eoloran's own turn against him? Would they raise arms against their former master? It was this uncertainty that taxed the counsels of the Anars as they made ready. From where was the greatest threat – the legions of Anlec or traitors close at hand?

THE GREAT HALL of Elanardris was full of elven princes and lords, all trying to speak at once. Alith sat in the corner close to the empty fire grate and let the babbling pass him by. He heard his grandfather's voice raised, calling for quiet.

'I did not ask you all to come here for us to fight with one another,' Eoloran declared. He was sat at a table set across the hall, flanked by Eothlir and Caenthras, a few of the other Naggarothi princes stood behind him. 'Already there is enough division in Nagarythe, we need not add to it.'

'We demand that action is taken,' called out one elf, a lesser noble of southern Nagarythe called Yrtrian. 'Morathi has taken our lands and forced us from our homes.'

'And who is this "we" that can make such demands?' Caenthras answered sternly. 'Those who did not resist the cults that grew up under their noses? Those who stood idly by while Morathi's agents eroded their claim to lordship? Where were these calls for justice a year ago when Morathi declared the Anars traitors to Anlec?'

'We have not the means to defend ourselves,' said Khalion, whose domain bordered Elanardris to the west. 'We place our trust in the greater houses, which we have supported with taxes and warriors for many centuries. Now has come the time for that support to be returned.'

'Warriors and armies?' laughed Eoloran, silencing all. 'You would have me march to Anlec and throw down the rule of Morathi?'

There were a few calls for just such a thing to happen and Eoloran held up his hand to quieten them.

'There is no means by which our armies can match those of Anlec,' said the lord of House Anar. 'Not against a land filled with hostile cultists and those enthralled to Morathi's power. I have offered sanctuary to you all, and that offer comes with no price. Yet it also comes with no guarantees. For a year Morathi has been content to stay her hand, burdening our greater houses with the turmoil of lesser families, knowing that as she grows stronger, our ability to act grows weaker.'

Eothlir stood and scowled at the assembled nobles.

'If Morathi moves more directly against us, we will fight,' he announced. 'Despite that, we cannot, we will not, start a war with Anlec. The lands in the mountains are still safe haven for any that would escape the tyrannies of Morathi, and here we shall stand resolute. It is not for the Anars to cast away the hopes of the future through rash action. We have faith in Malekith and await his return. Under his rule, your titles and rights will be restored and you will be glad of the protection you received.'

'And when will that be?' demanded Yrtrian. 'Has any here heard word of Prince Malekith these past years? He cares not for our woes, if he even knows of them.'

This started a fresh round of shouting and recrimination, and Alith stood up with a sigh and eased his way out of the hall. Such had been the bickering for four seasons, since the confrontation with Heliocoran. The Anars had waited for the first blow to land, but it had not come. For a year they had patrolled their borders and taken in those fleeing the plight that had engulfed the rest of Nagarythe, and it seemed that the self-appointed Queen of Anlec was content to allow her enemies to hide in the mountains. Alith chafed at the inactivity but could see that there was little the Anars could do to mount an offensive against Morathi's stranglehold on power.

As he had often done during such bickering conclaves, Alith left the nobles to their arguments and went to his chambers to take up his bow and arrows. Seeking solitude, he quit the manse and headed up into the mountains. Alith did not know for what he searched, and trod the old game trails guided by whim, heading ever eastwards, deeper into the mountains.

His greatest lament was that he had seen little of Ashniel in the past year. Caenthras had been wary of allowing her to leave the confines of his mansion and Alith had been spared little opportunity to visit her as he played his part as heir of the Anars. In his bedchambers he had a chest filled with letters she had sent, but their polite affection gave him little comfort.

Conflicted between depression and anger, Alith sat himself down upon a rock close to a babbling stream and dropped his bow upon the ground. He looked up into the summer sky, where white clouds scudded across the sun. In just one year everything had changed, and yet nothing had, and he could see no way by which the current stalemate would be broken – not in any way that would be good for the Anars.

A flicker of white caught his eye and Alith snatched up his bow and stood. Amidst the tumbled rocks and bushes a little further down the brook he spied an antlered head dipping to the waters. It was the white stag he had seen outside the shrine of Kurnous.

Padding softly along the bank of the brook, Alith sneaked from boulder to bush to boulder, closing in on the magnificent beast. It stood at the water's edge, head held high. It looked towards him and Alith shrank back into the shadow of an overhanging outcrop. The stag seemed unperturbed and lazily walked down the mountain back towards the forest.

Alith followed at a distance, careful not to approach too closely lest he startle the beast, but always keeping it in view. Their path took them under the eaves of the pine trees, ever eastwards into lands that Alith had not yet explored. As he stalked the stag Alith realised there were few landmarks to guide his passage and feared for a moment that he would get lost in the endless trees. The fear soon disappeared when he came upon a clearing, not large but big enough for the sun to break through overhead. Whatever happened, Alith would be able to make his way westwards towards Elanardris.

The stag stood in the sunlight, basking in its warmth. The elf moved closer and saw that the black mark upon the beast's chest was no random pattern but a crude representation of Kurnous's rune. Clearly the stag was some omen or guide sent by the god of hunters.

As before, the white stag suddenly started and bounded away northwards. Alith rose up and gave chase but was barely into the clearing before the deer disappeared from view amongst the lengthening evening shadows.

Stopping, Alith glanced around the clearing and his eye settled upon a shadow just under the eaves to the west. Without thought Alith fitted an arrow to his bow and loosed the shaft at the apparition. The shadow swayed for a moment, seeping into the darkness, and the arrow sped into the woods beyond. The shadow reappeared, more clearly a figure. In a heartbeat Alith nocked and loosed another arrow, but with similar failure to hit his mark. The silhouette had simply merged with its surrounds as the missile had passed.

'Wait!' the figure called out in elvish, its voice deep, tinged with the accent of northern Nagarythe. 'I would not have you waste more of your fine shafts.'

Alith bent another arrow to his bow nonetheless and watched warily as the tenebrous apparition emerged into the sunlight. He was dressed all in black with a cloak and hood of feathers concealing his body and face. The stranger showed his open palms and then reached up to pull back his hood.

The elf had skin as white as snow and emerald eyes that shone in the sun, his face framed by long black hair free of any tie or circlet. His expression was solemn as he glided slowly forwards, his hands held up in a sign of peace. Alith's quick eyes noted the empty scabbard at the elf's belt but he did not relax the tension on his bowstring.

'Alith, son of Eothlir, heir of the Anars,' the stranger said, his voice low and quiet. 'My name is Elthyrior and I bear important tidings.'

'And why would I listen to an elf that skulks in the shadows and stalks me as if I were his prey?' demanded Alith.

'I can only offer my apologies and hope for your forgiveness,' said Elthyrior, lowering his arms to his sides. 'I have not spied upon you out of spite, but only to observe and keep you safe.'

'Keep me safe from what? Who are you?'

'I have told you, I am Elthyrior. I am one of the raven heralds, and I was guided to watch you by my mistress.'

'Mistress? If you are an assassin of Morathi, strike now and let us settle this.'

'It is Morai-heg that claims my loyalty, not the Witch Queen who sits upon an usurped throne in Anlec,' said Elthyrior. 'The crow goddess came to me in a dream one night many years ago, before you were even born. In the mountains she sent me to find you, the child of the moon and the wolf, the heir of Kurnous. The one that would be king in the shadows and hold the future of Nagarythe in balance.'

Alith pondered these words, but they meant little to him. In myth, there was no child of the moon and the wolf, for Lileath and Kurnous had parted without son or daughter. He knew of no other king than Bel Shanaar.

'I do not understand why you think I am the one you seek. What message does the crone goddess have for me? What fate has she seen for my line?'

Elthyrior did not speak for a moment and ghosted softly towards Alith until he was stood but two paces from the tip of the youth's arrow.

'My message comes not from the Queen of Ravens, but from Prince Malekith.'

CLOUDS HAD GATHERED at the peak of the mountain, obscuring the sun and chilling the wind. Alith fixed his eyes upon Elthyrior to discern any malign intent. The raven herald returned his stare without hostility, awaiting Alith's response. The two stood as such for some time, Alith warily eyeing Elthyrior.

'You have spoken with Prince Malekith?'

'Last night, on the northern border of Tiranoc at the Naganath River,' said Elthyrior.

'Surely we would have heard ere now that the prince had returned,' said Alith with a frown.

'In secrecy has he come back, or so he thinks,' said Elthyrior. 'Even now he marches north to reclaim Anlec.'

'Then the Anars and their allies will march with him!'

'No,' said Elthyrior with a sorrowful shake of the head. 'Morai-heg has shown me something of what will come to pass. Malekith will not reach Anlec. He is not yet ready to reclaim his lands from the rule of his mother.'

'Perhaps, with our help…' started Alith.

'No. The time is not yet right. All of those in Nagarythe that would see Malekith restored to the throne rest at Elanardris, but the hope that they hold will be dashed if they march now.'

'I cannot make this decision, why come to me?'

Elthyrior looked to leave but then stopped and turned back to Alith, his stare intent.

'I go where I am bid, though I know not all of the reasons,' the raven herald said softly. 'You have a part to play in these events, but what they are I cannot say. Perhaps fate itself does not yet know your role, or it will be for you to decide. I cannot ask you to simply trust me, for you do not know me at all. All I can give is the warning I bring: do not march with Malekith. But you cannot say these words came from me.'

'You give me this knowledge and then expect me to keep it hidden? My father and grandfather, they should hear this.'

'Your grandfather has little love for my kind, and none for me,' said Elthyrior. 'Words from my lips would be as poison to his ears, for he still blames me for the death of your grandmother.'

'My grandmother?'

'It is not important,' insisted Elthyrior. 'Know only that I am not welcome at Elanardris, and nor will be my words. The Anars must not march yet. Your time will come.'

Elthyrior saw the conflict in Alith and leant forwards with earnest intent.

'Can you swear that all who live under the banner of the Anars can be trusted?' asked the raven herald.

Alith thought about this, and though it pained him to realise, he could not in all honesty say that there were no agents of Anlec at Elanardris. There were simply too many elven nobles – and their households – for him to be sure of anything. Elthyrior recognised the consternation in Alith's face.

'If not for the reasons I have given, than for the secrecy desired by Malekith I ask you not to speak. This news will come to your family soon enough, but let it be from the lips of others. If the prince desires to come unheralded, it is for us to acquiesce to that wish. Every warning that our foes have may turn things against us. I tell you this only so that you might guide your family to the correct decision.'

Alith shook his head, casting his gaze to his feet for a moment while he collected his thoughts.

'When will…' he began, but when he looked up, Elthyrior had gone. There was no sign of the raven herald, only the shadows beneath the trees and a single crow swooping over the tips of the pines.

FOUR

Herald of Khaine

ONCE AGAIN ALITH found himself returning to Elanardris with a secret to keep, one which burned at him more than ever. Elthyrior's revelation that Malekith had returned had stoked the fires in Alith's heart and he longed to announce to his family that the war for Nagarythe had begun. Yet for all his desire, Alith was haunted by the sincerity in Elthyrior's face and tone. It was as a messenger bringing grave news rather than cause for celebration that Alith remembered the raven herald and so he kept his silence.

It was not long before Alith was relieved to hear a messenger from the lands westwards had come to Elanardris bearing the tidings of the prince's return. The manse was abuzz with activity as word spread to Caenthras and the other allied princes at the home of the Anars.

Three days after Alith's meeting with Elthyrior, Eoloran called the princes and nobles into the great hall to discuss their plan of action. This time Alith sat at the high table with his father and grandfather, though he was uncertain what he would say. Elthyrior's warnings to stay in Elanardris were at the front of his mind, but he sensed that the others were keen to march forth and meet with the returning prince.

'This is joyous news indeed,' exclaimed Caenthras. 'The day long hoped for has arrived and the cruel shackles of Morathi's reign can be cast aside. Though we have chafed at those bonds placed upon us by concern for the safety of our kin, now we can let loose our spirits and fight.'

There was much approval to this from the gathered elves, not least from Eothlir. Alith's father stood up and cast his gaze over the hall.

'For too long we have suffered, afraid of Morathi and her cults,' he declared. 'We have been slaves to that fear, but no longer! Word comes to us that Malekith marches for the fortress at Ealith, and from there he will retake Anlec. It is not only our duty but our privilege to aid him in this endeavour. This is a battle to reclaim not only our own lands, but all of Nagarythe.'

Again there was assent from the others and Alith struggled to remain silent. The mood in the hall was martial, the assembled Naggarothi given a vent for years of frustration. Alith could not think of the words that could turn such a rising tide of anger, not least in part because he felt it himself. He was torn between his own desires and the warning of Elthyrior.

Alith suddenly became aware that all eyes had turned to him and realised that he had stood up. He glanced at his grandfather and looked out at the hall filled with expectant faces. If he were to speak against his father, he would invite scorn, perhaps pity. They would not listen and would think him a coward. He was heir to House Anar and all expectation was that he would raise his own voice in defiance of Anlec.

He stood in silence a moment longer, tortured. There was a whisper of disquiet and frowns appeared on the faces in front of Alith. He swallowed hard, his heart beating fast.

'I too feel the desire for retribution,' Alith announced. There were nods of approval from the crowd and Alith held up a hand to forestall any optimism. 'This is a grave time, and calls for measured heads not fiery hearts. I have learnt much wisdom from my grandfather, not least the virtue of patience.'

There were a few heckling complaints but Alith continued.

'If Prince Malekith himself had called for our aid, I would proudly ride out on this campaign. Yet, he has not. It is presumptive of us to raise our blades against our fellow Naggarothi without invite from our true lord. If we take it upon ourselves to exact vengeance for the wrongs done against us, what difference would there be between those of us who hold true to the ideal of freedom and those who would enforce their tyranny with warriors?'

The grumbled complaints turned into derisive shouts. Alith dared not look at his father and instead focussed on one of the elves at the front of the crowd.

'Khalion,' said Alith, reaching out a hand. 'What has changed between yesterday and today? Do you not trust in our prince to restore your lands and bring back the rule of law we desire? Why would we be so ready to unleash the cloud of war now, when under the sun of yesterday we strove for peace? Our grief consumes us, eats at our spirits, but we must not feed it with the blood of our fellow elves. Only by leave of the prince did we claim our lands and we owe it to him to respect that authority. Draw blood and we may yet start the war we have so long wished to avoid. We must temper our feelings with caution, lest our actions have consequences beyond what we see.'

There was disgust clearly written on the faces of the elves and many waved dismissive hands and sneered at Alith.

'Care not for their scorn, Alith,' declared Caenthras, striding to stand beside him. The venerable lord glared at the other elves, cowing their disrespect. 'I value your reasoning and admire your courage and honesty. I do not agree with your arguments, but I think no less of you for voicing them.'

Alith let out his breath in a long sigh and sat down, closing his eyes. He felt a hand on his shoulder and looked up to see his father.

'The youngest of us might yet speak with the greatest wisdom,' said Eothlir. 'I know that none here will march forth unless it is beside the banner of the Anars, and so we face a tough decision. Long we have pondered what might become of us in these dark times. For my part, I would have us go forth to whatever destiny awaits, rather than hide here while it sneaks upon us. I am not the lord of the Anars, though.'

All attention turned to Eoloran, who was sat with one elbow on the table, his chin cupped in his hand. His eyes swept the room, spending more time upon Alith than any other. Straightening, he cleared his throat and laid his hands palm downwards on the table.

'My instinct has ever been to avoid conflict, that much you all know of me,' said the head of House Anar. 'Long we have endured turmoil and darkness, and it seems that stability and light can return to our lives. Though I hear your words, Alith, I am left with a singular fear. Malekith makes his bid now, and I cannot have it be said that the Anars stood by and watched it fail. It is beholden upon us to ensure the prince's success, for the peace and prosperity of all our people in the times to come. Long we have watched and waited, biding our time for the prince's return. That time has come. Unless you have some greater argument to make, I have reached my decision.'

Alith opened his mouth to speak but realised he had nothing else to say, no further argument he could put forwards to keep the Anars safe in Elanardris. He shook his head and sat back. Eoloran nodded and looked at his son and grandson.

'The Anars march at dawn!'

IT WAS WITH a sense of foreboding that Alith marched with the other warriors of the Anars. From across the hills and mountains the army had gathered, responding to swift-riding messengers despatched by Eoloran to muster just south of Elanardris. The host marched west, numbering some twenty thousand warriors, heading for the ancient citadel of Ealith.

The Anars went forth on foot, the rough terrain of their lands not suited to cavalry; since the time of Aenarion they had fought with bow and spear rather than horse and lance. The elves moved swiftly nonetheless, and would reach Ealith in four days.

Alith strode alongside his father at the head of a company of bowmen, the honoured guard of House Anar. For the most part they walked in silence, Eothlir's mood grim as was the atmosphere of the whole endeavour. Never before had the elves marched to war against other elves.

As twilight was spreading its shadow across the hills, Alith spied a crow flying overhead, towards the west. He followed its path and saw, just for a moment, a black-swathed rider silhouetted atop a ridge. The rider vanished into shadow in a moment, but Alith was left in no doubt that it was Elthyrior.

When the army stopped to make camp, Alith excused himself from his father, promising to bring back some game for their supper. Bow in hand, Alith picked his way quickly through the growing lines of tents and headed westwards.

Leaving behind the fires of the camp, Alith found his way lit by starlight alone. After some time, he reached the ridge upon which he had spied the dark rider and nimbly climbed its steep slope, jumping from boulder to boulder until he reached the summit. The white moon, Sariour, was rising and by her light Alith looked all about, seeking some sign of the raven herald. Some distance away on the far side of the ridge he caught sight of a black steed, standing docilely in a hollow. He took a step towards it but then stopped as he heard the sound of a whetstone on metal.

Turning around, Alith saw Elthyrior sitting on a rock just behind him, sharpening a serrated dagger. As before the herald was swathed in his cloak of raven feathers, his face all but hidden. Moonlight shone from his bright eyes, which followed Alith closely as he walked over and sat beside Elthyrior.

'I am sorry,' said Alith.

'Perhaps some things cannot be changed,' replied the raven herald. 'Morai-heg weaves across the skein of our lives and we must do the best we can with the threads she leaves us. None will hold you to account for the decisions of others.'

'I tried,' sighed Alith.

'It is of no matter,' replied Elthyrior. 'The path is taken; we cannot turn back, though your army must do so.'

'It is too late, my grandfather is resolute on marching to Ealith,' said Alith.

'He will not reach the citadel,' said Elthyrior. 'Malekith will take Ealith but it is a trap set by Morathi. Even now, tens of thousands of warriors and cultists close in on him. If you march to his rescue, you will also be caught. I warned that it was not yet time and nevertheless the Anars have stirred Morathi's wrath.'

Alith was incoherent for a moment, trying to comprehend what Elthyrior had said.

'Malekith trapped?' he finally managed to say.

'Not yet, and the prince is canny enough to avoid the snare,' said Elthyrior with a slight smile. 'I ride now to warn him of the danger. By dusk tomorrow, others will come from Ealith, sent by the prince. Be sure that your grandfather listens to what they have to say. Add your voice to theirs if need be. The Anars must turn back now or you will not see Elanardris again.'

Alith bowed his head and clasped his hands to his cheeks as he tried to think. When he sat up he expected Elthyrior to have gone, but the raven herald had not moved.

'Still here?' asked the young Anar.

Elthyrior gave a shrug.

'My steed is swift and I have time enough to enjoy the night air for a while.'

Alith took this without comment and stood up. He started down the slope and turned at a call from Elthyrior.

'I'll save you some time,' said the raven herald and tossed something towards Alith. He caught it out of instinct and found it to be a bundle wrapped in several broad leaves bound with strands of grass. Looking back to the ridge, he saw that Elthyrior had disappeared this time.

As he picked his way down the slope, Alith opened the parcel: two snow hares trussed together by their hind legs.

As Alith made his way back down the ridge, something to the north caught his eye. Looking closely, he saw the telltale flickers of many fires on the horizon. Not knowing the portent of this discovery, he hastened back to the camp, running directly to his father's tent.

Eothlir was deep in conversation with Caenthras, Eoloran, Tharion and Faerghil. They looked up angrily as Alith breathlessly burst through the door flap.

'The enemy are close,' blurted Alith, discarding the brace of hares upon the ground. 'There are campfires to the north.'

'Why have our pickets not seen them?' demanded Eoloran, glaring at his son.

'They lie beyond a ridge to the west,' Alith intervened to save his father's shame. 'It is only by chance that I saw them.'

'How many fires?' asked Caenthras.

'I cannot say for sure,' said Alith. 'Dozens.'

Eoloran nodded and gestured to Tharion to hand him a hide tube. He pulled a broad parchment from within and laid the chart out upon the table.

'Roughly where did you see this encampment?' Eoloran asked, beckoning Alith closer.

Alith looked at the map and found where he was currently stood. He traced his path westwards to his clandestine meeting with Elthyrior and located the area of the ridge he had been on. His finger then followed a line roughly northwards while he recalled the scene to his mind. The trail stopped upon a line of hills that stretched from north-east to south-west.

'They made camp somewhere at the base of these hills,' he said. 'I do not think they will have seen our fires unless they are looking for them.'

'Then we still have the element of surprise,' growled Eothlir. 'We should make ready to strike as soon as dawn rises.'

'What if they are a foe we cannot face?' asked Alith, recalling Elthyrior's dire warning.

'We must ascertain their strength first,' said Eoloran with a nod, more cautious than his son. He looked at Tharion and Eothlir. 'Assemble a small group of scouts and spy upon our foes so that we might know their strength and disposition.'

'Alith, you will guide us to where you saw these fires,' said Eothlir and Alith nodded, glad to have been included in his father's thoughts. 'Tharion, pick out the keenest-eyed warriors in your company and send them to me. Then ensure that all will be made ready to march come the rise of the sun.'

Tharion nodded and picked up his tall helm from a side table. He grinned briefly and then left.

'Beware of sentries,' said Eoloran. 'If the enemy are unaware of us, it should remain so. Count their numbers and observe them, but do nothing else without my command.'

He stared intently at Eothlir to ensure his point was understood, and Alith's father nodded in agreement.

'Do not worry, lord,' said Eothlir. 'I'll not scare them away and deprive you of the chance to lead the Anars in battle again.'

EOTHLIR ASSEMBLED A handful of elves at the edge of the Anar encampment. Swathed with dark cloaks, they set out before midnight, following Alith's lead. He took the small group westwards up the ridge, heading slightly north of where he had met Elthyrior. Though he doubted that the raven herald had remained close by – or that he would be seen against his wishes – Alith thought it best not to risk any discovery.

From the top of the ridge the campfires could clearly be seen. Alith took the time to count them. There were more than thirty fires, two of them exceptionally large. The undulating nature of the foothills meant that the enemy camp would be out of sight until the party was almost on top of it, and so Eothlir marked the direction by the stars in the clear sky and headed north-east.

After a short time the second moon ascended in the west, a sliver of bright green that spilled its sickly light over the Annulii foothills. The elves travelled swiftly over the rugged hillsides, no more distinct than the shadows of the rocks and trees around them. Sariour had set and the shadows had deepened by the time the sounds of the enemy camp came to them on the wind.

The enemy made no pretence of secrecy; piercing shrieks sounded occasionally, accompanied by roars of approval. Harsh laughter drifted towards the scouts and Alith cast an anxious glance towards his father, worried by what they would find. Crouching low, the group crested a low hill and saw the Naggarothi camp laid out before them.

A mass of black conical tents encircled an immense pyre, in the light of which Alith saw cavorting figures, their shadows flickering upon earth slick with blood. Figures flailed and cried out in agony upon the flames. Alith saw a huddled mass of elves bound with spiked chains, kicked and tormented by their captors.

As he watched, one of the prisoners was taken from the group and dragged crying towards the pyre. There she was tossed to the ground at the feet of a male elf stripped but for a daemonic metal mask and ragged loincloth made of skin. Alith recognised him immediately for what he was – a high priest of Khaine, the Lord of Murder. He held a long blade in his hand, shockingly similar to the one Elthyrior had been sharpening, and for a moment Alith feared that the raven herald had led him astray. However, the elf in the mask was taller than Elthyrior, his hair dyed white and beaded with raw bone.

Alith watched reluctantly as the priest's victim was dragged to her feet. The Khainite slashed her across the arms and chest and cultists hurried forwards with bowls made from skulls to fill with the blood that spilt from the wounds. They clawed and bit at each other as they tried to catch as much as possible, before raising the obscene cups to their lips and taking deep draughts.

Weak, the captive fell to her knees. The priest grabbed a handful of her hair and cut the skin from her scalp, tossing the bloody trophy onto a pile behind him. Screaming in pain, the maiden was again hauled to her feet, her feeble struggle no match for her captors as she was spitted upon a spear and driven into the fire. Another great cheer rose up from the camp, chilling in its adoration of the slaughter.

'We cannot see them all from here,' said Anadriel, an elf-maiden who Alith had known for as long as he could remember. For years she had helped those who had displeased Morathi escape the clutches of the cults and brought them to Elanardris. Her sharp features were set impassively, and Alith could only guess how many times before she had witnessed the horrors unfolding below. 'We need to move closer.'

Eothlir nodded, signalling for Anadriel to lead the way. They followed a snaking trail down the hillside, plunging into a grove of trees. Anadriel led them surely between the thin trunks, heading for the light of the fires.

All of a sudden she stopped, her bow in hand and an arrow ready. Alith glanced ahead and saw two figures silhouetted against the firelight. He slowly bent an arrow to his bow and joined Anadriel, glancing to the left and right to see if there were any others close at hand.

'You take the one on the left,' she said, her eyes fixed on the staggering cultists, a male and a female. It was clear what the couple intended, and disgust welled up inside Alith as he watched the pair trot hand in hand into the woods, their bodies smeared with blood.

'Now,' sighed Anadriel and Alith let go the bowstring. The arrow sped surely between the tree trunks and took the male elf in the throat. Anadriel's shaft hit the eye of his companion. Both fell without a sound. Undiscovered, the party moved forwards again until they were hidden in the shadows of the tents.

Alith turned at the sound of metal scraping and a brief, wet noise. His father had a cultist's body cradled in one arm, his knife bloody in the other hand.

'Swiftly, the distraction of the ceremony will not last forever,' said Eothlir, lowering the corpse to the ground and dragging it further into the darkness.

They made their way stealthily through the tents until the words of the high priest could be clearly heard. Eothlir despatched Anadriel and Lotherin to the left and right to count the enemy's number.

Alith felt a hand on his arm and realised that he had made to stand, his bow in hand. Eothlir gave him a shake of the head.

'Tomorrow,' he whispered. 'Tomorrow we make them pay.'

'What of those yet to be sacrificed?' demanded Alith. He felt an almost physical pain at the thought of what was about to happen. Eothlir simply shook his head again, eyes averted.

Alith forced himself to listen to the tirade of hatred spilling from the high priest.

'Hearken to me, the Herald of Khaine. As the libations of the King of Blood pour over us, let us remember that which Khaine calls upon us to do. Cast out the impure and make testament to their weakness with the offerings of their flesh. Raise your voices in praise of their deaths, and take strength from the Lord of Murder so that you might strike down those who would scorn our bloody master!'

A vicious baying and howling welled up from the assembled elves. The high priest raised his left hand above his head and in the grip of his fist a gory heart dripped blood down his arm.

'Mighty Khaine, look upon these offerings and be placated. Grant us your power so that we can slay the traitor who has disowned you, and slaughter his misguided followers upon the pyres of your glory.'

More screeching accompanied this proclamation as the cultists worked themselves into a shrieking horde.

'Let he who has turned his back upon you be cut down and his organs thrown upon the fires in repentance for his misdeeds. Let the ill-begotten heir of your chosen son perish in the ashes of vengeance. Let crimson retribution spill from his corpse to wash away the perfidies of his deeds.'

The priest tossed the heart into the crowds, who fought over their prize like a pack of wild dogs. The Herald of Khaine's voice was calmer though it still carried easily across his followers.

'We are many, they are few,' he told the Khainites. 'Even now the hated foe thinks he is on the brink of victory. Little does he suspect the agony that awaits. His is a false victory, devoid of Khaine's blessings. Even as he rejoices in his empty triumph, he crows at the heart of a trap. None shall leave Ealith alive. Death to Malekith!'

'Death to Malekith!' chorused the crowd, at the crescendo of their frenzy, slashing at their chests and arms with daggers, matting their hair with their own gore. The mob descended upon the remaining captives. Alith turned away, filled with a mixture of loathing and dread. The blood-curdling cries of the Khainites reverberated around the camp, thousands of voices raised in blood-thirsty praise that made Alith's skin crawl. The wind gusted towards him and the stench of charring flesh wafted between the tents, causing him to gag.

There was a flutter of shadows to the left and Lotherin returned, his face grim. Alith noticed a cut upon his cheek and blood upon his hands.

'Ten thousand Khainites, perhaps many more,' Lotherin told Eothlir. 'There is a further camp to the west, where there are trained warriors of Anlec: perhaps another five thousand spears and bows.'

Eothlir nodded at this news, his expression distant. Anadriel rejoined them shortly after and confirmed Lotherin's estimate. There were several thousand cultists attending the rituals and many thousands more scattered across the camp in narcotic stupors.

'I have seen enough,' said Eothlir, signalling for them to move back out of the camp. 'Tomorrow we must be ready for battle.'

ALITH PROWLED HIS grandfather's tent like a trapped wolf, pacing back and forth as he listened to the army commanders making their plans. The words of Elthyrior gnawed at him, their sinister warning vague but nagging. As Eoloran outlined the disposition of the Anars' companies, Alith's exasperation took hold.

'Wait!' he barked, and suddenly felt the stares of the others fall upon him. He calmed himself before continuing, looking directly at his father. 'You heard the words of the Herald of Khaine. Malekith is trapped at Ealith and we cannot hope to reach him. What purpose do we serve by throwing ourselves into the grip of our foes?'

'What other course would you suggest?' asked Caenthras, his voice cold with scorn. 'To slink back to the mountains to await Morathi's ire? We must push forwards and link up with Prince Malekith, unite our strength.'

'And if that strength is spent in this one fruitless endeavour?' countered Alith, trying to present himself as reasoned rather than fearful though the elven lord's anger had shaken him. 'On a hunt, one might get a single shot to fell the prey. The hunter learns when to shoot and when to wait. If we loose our shaft too soon, our target knows us and can react.'

'And if one dithers, the opportunity for the killing strike may be missed,' growled Caenthras. He took a breath and cast his gaze at Eoloran, who was scowling at the noble's outburst, before returning his stare to Alith. 'Forgive my anger, Alith. For long years we have waited, seeking the moment when we can attack. To hesitate invites disaster. I would not be content to sit in my hall and see that moment pass by, nagged by doubts that we stood idle when we should have acted. And on what would we base our strategy? The boastful rhetoric of an intoxicated priest? We cannot be sure that Malekith's position is as forlorn as the Herald of Khaine would have his followers believe.'

Alith smarted at the intimation in Caenthras's words but held his retort, knowing that Elthyrior had presaged the Herald of Khaine's words but unable to reveal this knowledge. Caenthras turned his attention back to Eoloran and rested his fists upon the table on which the map charts were spread.

'Though perhaps we cannot aid Malekith directly, we can still help. An attack now will distract the foe, drawing the eyes of some away from the prince. If we do nothing, the thousands that camp north of us will march on Malekith's position, closing the trap. Should we not intervene? Should we not do what we can to weaken that trap?'

'Your strategy has merit,' said Eoloran. 'The fewer forces Malekith must face, the better his chances for escape.'

'I have another fear,' added Alith. 'Who guards Elanardris while we fight here? Who is to say that Morathi's next blow will not fall upon our homes rather than us? What victory is there to win tomorrow only to return to our lands to find them in the clutches of our enemies?'

This argument bit home and a look of anguish passed across Eoloran's face. His gaze flickered between Alith and Caenthras, and then rested upon Eothlir.

'My son, this is not my decision alone,' Eoloran said heavily. 'Though I am lord of the Anars, I am steward for their future under your rule. You have been silent. I would hear what you have to say.'

'Give me a moment to think,' said Eothlir.

He walked slowly from the pavilion and left the others in silence. Caenthras pored over the charts on the table, avoiding the gazes of others, while Alith took up a stool and sat to one side. The quiet was heavy with anxiety and Alith longed to leave, having said his piece. He forced himself to remain, though he could sense the resentment of some of the elves present, not least Caenthras. Fearful of alienating the father of the one he loved, part of Alith hoped that Eothlir judged in Caenthras's favour and would allow Alith to make amends. Though Caenthras had seemed supportive before, Alith did not know how the proud elf would take the decision going against him.

The tent flap opened with a snap and all looked up. There was purpose written on Eothlir's face.

'We fight,' he declared. 'We cannot stand by while atrocity is committed, though only fate knows at what price. The crimes of the cultists cannot go unpunished. For good or ill, there is a time when we must look to others and a time when we must look to our own. Prince Malekith must be restored to the throne for the future of Nagarythe and we must play whatever part we can.'

'I concur,' said Eoloran. 'Tomorrow we slay the Khainites and then we shall look again at what course of action we must take. Are we agreed?'

Caenthras nodded his assent immediately. Alith stood slowly and looked at his father and grandfather.

'None will fight harder than I,' he declared. 'We will avenge.'

WITH THE DAWN sun glinting on speartips and armour, the army of the Anars broke camp and marched north. It was Eoloran's strategy to come upon the cultists as swiftly as possible, before they moved further west towards Malekith at Ealith.

The Khainites would be ill-disciplined and eager to attack, so the lord of the Anars split his host into three parts. At the fore he sent swift-moving scouts who would circle to the flanks of the enemy and remain out of sight until the battle began. Alith was tasked with leading the right wing of this attack while Anadriel commanded the left. Eoloran was very specific that these flanking forces would target the disciplined Anlec warriors and draw them out of the camp. It was imperative that they were pulled away from the main fighting line but were not allowed to engage the scouts directly. Alith was to withdraw as soon as the enemy came close, dragging their foes away from the Khainites.

Meanwhile, Eothlir and the spear companies would form the main advance to take up a defensive position on the hills overlooking the enemy camp. The remaining archers, under Eoloran, would rain down their arrows upon the cultists and goad them into an unfavourable attack up the slopes.

Alith was tense with anxiety and excitement as he marched northwards at the head of five hundred elves. The rugged terrain and dawn twilight concealed the force and soon they moved out of sight of the main part of the Anar host. Alith realised that this was real and not some story; that he was in charge of a company of elves marching into battle. Unlike his grandfather and father he had never commanded other elves, and the experience was very different to the lone hunts he enjoyed so much. For the first time he truly felt as a lord of the Anars, gripped equally by the glory and the heavy responsibility.

His thoughts turned to Elanardris and his mother, knowing that she would be at the manse wondering what became of her family. He was determined to return with pride. His mind swiftly moved to Ashniel. Would she be impressed? Alith was convinced that she would be. She adored her warrior-father, and Alith's experience in battle would surely increase his standing in her eyes.

As the sun rose and the scouts moved swiftly north, Alith allowed himself to daydream a little, picturing the scene of his triumphant return. Ashniel would be stood on the steps of the porch at the manse, a flowing dress tugged by the breeze, her hair streaming. Alith would run up the long path and they would embrace, her tears of joy wet on his cheeks. So gripping was the fantasy that Alith stubbed his toe on a rock, bringing him back to the present in a flash of pain. Chiding himself for his immaturity, Alith checked on his warriors and saw that none had seen his stumble, or were polite enough to feign disinterest. Realising that soon he would need all of his focus and skill, Alith gritted his teeth, gripped his bow tighter and strode onwards.

THE THOUGHTS OF Alith's father were very different. He was no stranger to battle, having spent several hundred years in the colonies before returning to Elanardris to start a family. This time was different. His army did not face savage orcs and goblins or bestial creatures from the dark forests of Elthin Arvan; his foe this day was one he had never thought he would face. Even in the dark times that had shrouded the latter years of Morathi's rule, Eothlir had never envisaged fighting against his own people. The fight at the manse had been instinctual, reacting to attack. Now he found himself leading several thousand of his subjects to purposefully slay other elves.

The thought was disquieting, not least because Eothlir felt no inevitability about the battle ahead. He could have convinced his father to return to Elanardris with their weapons still sheathed, but he had chosen not to. As the tramp of booted feet sounded around him, Eothlir was perturbed by the notion that he wanted this conflict. He worried that the same desire for bloodshed that drove the Khainites to their depraved acts nestled somewhere in the dark recesses of his spirit.

His concerns brought to mind a tale his father had once told him. Eoloran had only spoken of the event once and refused to be drawn on it again. The event Eoloran had related had taken place shortly after the Phoenix King had drawn the Widowmaker from the altar of Khaine, the infamous weapon that was said to hold the power to slay gods and destroy armies. Eoloran always refused to speak of the Sword of Khaine by name, often calling it simply the Doom or 'that infernal blade'. There would be a haunted look in his eye as he spoke of the Widowmaker, a distant memory of sights that Eothlir would never see, even in nightmare.

The particular story recalled by Eothlir concerned fighting at Ealith, the same fortress that Malekith currently held. A great army of daemons had appeared in the mountains and swept down across the hills, over the lands that would one day be ruled by the Anars. The raven heralds, Aenarion's swift-moving eyes and ears, had brought word to the Phoenix King at Anlec and he had set forth with his host to confront the legion of Chaos.

At Ealith Aenarion made his stand and during an endless night of fighting through which the skies shimmered with ghostly lights and the ground itself burned underfoot, the daemons hurled themselves at the citadel's walls. Though the greater part of the Chaotic host was destroyed, Aenarion was intent on their utter annihilation. Atop his great dragon Indraugnir, the Phoenix King led his army from the fortress, Caledor the Mage at his side, Eoloran and a hundred other great princes behind him. Eoloran had described the battle-fever that had gripped him, the jubilant singing of Khaine that rang in his ears from 'that infernal blade'. He remembered nothing else but the constant slash of sword and thrust of spear, and a joyous love of death in his heart.

Eoloran had spoken of that time with shame, though the cause in which he had slain with such happiness and abandon had been the most righteous: the survival of the elves. Eothlir could never truly understand what the war against the daemons had meant for an entire generation, but if the self-loathing he felt was but a tenth of their woe he could imagine the horrors that disturbed their dreams.

Another memory came to mind, much more recent: the recollection of the Herald of Khaine's vile sermon and the sacrifices heaped upon the pyre. Unless Eothlir would see such slaughter across all of Ulthuan, this blight had to be stopped. It had consumed Nagarythe and it was clear to Eothlir that such barbarity would spread if left unchecked. The thought fortified his resolve and so he pushed aside his worries until a time when he could allow himself the luxury of doubt and compassion. He realised he must fight without joy or anger, for such temptations could awaken the ancient call of Khaine that still rang down through the centuries from the time of Aenarion.

Today he would slay his fellow elves; tomorrow he would mourn them.

ALITH AND HIS small company crept through the hills surrounding the Khainite camp, wary of sentries. Their caution proved unnecessary, for not a single figure was standing watch and as Alith came to the brow of a hill he could see that the encampment was quiet, the depraved cultists within sated by the debauchery of the previous night.

There was more activity further north and west, amongst the pavilions of the Anlec warriors. Their captains strode between the tents, bellowing orders to assemble their archers and spear companies. At first Alith thought that perhaps they had detected Anadriel's scouts and were responding. After short observation, his fears calmed as the soldiers of Anlec formed up in disciplined ranks in the wide spaces at the centre of their camp, parading and drilling for their officers. Their activity was nothing more than the regular movement of troops in camp.

Circling eastwards, Alith allowed the Khainite camp to disappear from sight, though the smoke from its fires ensured that the archers knew where it was at all times. The sun broke strongly over the mountains to the east, casting its dawn glow across the hillsides. Despite the sunlight, the air was still chill and the breath of the archers misted in the air.

Judging that he had come north of the Khainites, Alith headed directly westwards, towards the Anlec camp. His caution returned as they neared. In scattered groups the Anars' warriors flitted from bush to rock to tree, remaining out of sight. It was not long before they were crouched just beneath the summit of a steep hill, ready to move forwards and overlook the Anlec tents.

Signalling to a couple of his warriors – Anraneir and Khillrallion – Alith sneaked to the brow of the hill and looked out over the formations of the Anlec army. They were still practising their spear and bow drills, moving with precision and speed in a well-rehearsed choreography of simulated battle.

Alith waited nervously for a while, not knowing whether Anadriel was yet in position. He watched the skies as much as the enemy and was relieved when he saw the flitting shape of a hawk dashing from the west, climbing and swooping over the foe's camp. The hawk circled for a while and then flew low, its wingtips brushing the grass of the hillside. With a cry, it settled upon the leafless branch of a bush not far from Alith's right hand. He held up his arm and the hawk swept forwards to land on his wrist, its talons gripping his flesh firmly but not piercing the skin.

'We will attack now,' Alith whispered to the bird, which bobbed its head in acknowledgement before beating its wings and launching into the air once more. Alith watched it skirt around the Anlec encampment and then disappear into a small copse of short firs on the westward side of the camp.

Alith nodded to Anraneir and Khillrallion. They turned and slithered down the hill to pass the word to the other archers. Soon the company of elves were all hidden in the long grass at the hilltop, readied arrows at their bowstrings. Raising himself up to a half-crouch, Alith took a final look at his target.

The outskirts of the camp were no more than a hundred paces away, where several sentries stood with spear and bow, their eyes gazing across the hillsides.

'Now!' barked Alith, loosing his shaft at the closest sentry. The arrow took Alith's victim low in the chest, punching through the silvered breastplate he wore. He collapsed with a shout as more arrows whistled through the air, cutting down the other guards.

The warriors of Anlec were professional fighters and responded quickly. They formed into marching columns, archers to the front, and split into companies. A vanguard of roughly a thousand warriors advanced at a quick march, cutting through the lines of tents along wide paths left for just such a reason. As they did so, Alith and his warriors shot their arrows high into the air, allowing them to fall at a steep angle amongst the ranks of the warriors. Though dozens fell to the deadly shafts, the column continued its implacable advance.

Behind the vanguard, more companies were surging out of the camp towards Alith. Bass horns sounded from the Naggarothi warriors, sending a chill across Alith's skin. Those same notes had once signalled the attack of daemons, calling the loyal followers of Aenarion to war. It seemed perverse to Alith that he and his warriors were now deemed the aggressors, fighting against the armies of Anlec. The tramping of boots sounded heavily in the morning quiet, accompanied by the jingling of mail and the scrape of metal.

There were other pained shouts from the far side of the camp and Alith glanced across the expanse to see the arrows of Anadriel's company filling the air to the west. The Anlec vanguard continued on its course while the companies behind hesitated at a shout from their commander, unsure whether he was responding to a feint or a real attack.

'Keep shooting!' ordered Alith, standing fully to loose a stream of arrows into the Anlec warriors.

The vanguard had reached the edge of the camp and the archers split from the spears. Soon, black-shafted arrows were singing their way through the air back towards the Anar scouts. Alith heard shouts of pain and looked to his left to see several elves lying in the thick grass, arrows protruding from their bodies. Two were not moving, two more quickly pulled free the shafts and bound their wounds.

The spearmen were no more than seventy paces away and the storm of arrows from the camp's defenders became relentless. A dozen more were wounded as the cloud of shafts fell amongst the Anar scouts.

'Carry the dead, help the wounded!' yelled Alith, letting loose a final shot at the advancing spearmen. 'Head north-east, draw them from the Khainite camp.'

Under the barrage of arrows, the scouts slinked back down the hillside and cut to their right. At a run, they broke from their cover and followed Alith down the dell and up the mound on the opposite side. Here Alith called for them to halt, once more out of sight of the archers in the camp, and they turned their bows upon the spearmen as they crested the hill in front.

The spearmen fell back from the hilltop, and reappeared shortly after, flanked by their supporting archers. As he called for his scouts to retreat once more, Alith wondered how Anadriel was faring and if the Khainites had yet responded. Focussed on the enemy ahead of him, he realised that it was going to be a long morning.

* * *

THE HAWK CIRCLING high above signalled to Eothlir that Alith and Anadriel were about to start their attacks. All was ready above the Khainite encampment as well. He was stood beside Eoloran looking down on the Khainites. In his left hand Eothlir carried the furled banner of House Anar, in his right he held the golden blade Cyarith, the Sword of Dawn's Vengeance. The weapon felt warm to his touch, feeding upon the rays of the morning sun that broke over the mountains, its keen edge glittering with magical energy.

Behind Eoloran stood Caenthras, a curling ram's horn decorated with bands of silver in his hand. At a nod from the lord of the Anars, Caenthras raised the instrument to his lips and let forth a long pealing note, high in pitch. Three times more he sounded the blast, the notes echoing from the hillsides and reverberating across the camp below.

Eothlir waited a few moments while the stupefied elves roused themselves at the sound of the horn. He saw the Herald of Khaine striding from a pavilion with blood-stained walls, his burnished mask gleaming. The priest was gesticulating wildly, summoning his followers from their slumber. When a good number had gathered around their leader, Eothlir let slip the knot upon the standard and the great flag unfurled. He lifted it high so that the symbol could clearly be seen.

Planting the banner into the soft turf of the hilltop, Eothlir took a step forwards. Caenthras blew another long, high note to ensure that all eyes were upon the hillside.

'Behold the mighty Eoloran Anar, lord of these lands,' shouted Eothlir. 'You are trespassers in this realm. Lord Anar demands that this ragged mob departs immediately and slinks back to the dark holes that spawned it. He renounces the accusations of cowards who would slaughter those that cannot protect themselves, and dares his unworthy foes to match their blades against true warriors. He is not without mercy and will hear the pleas of all who beg forgiveness for the crimes they have committed. All who recant their false faith will be granted the peace of Isha.'

Eothlir took a step back as Caenthras sounded the horn once more to signal the declaration was complete.

'That should get their attention,' said Eoloran with a grim smile. 'I think the "peace of Isha" part in particular will get them going.'

Eothlir could not help but smile himself, knowing that the taunts would have precisely the effect he had intended. He glanced over his shoulder and saw the thousands of the Anars' warriors standing ready out of sight. Archers were lined up just below the crests of the surrounding hills, the spear companies arranged behind. Banners slapped in the morning air and the sun shone from the keen edges of speartips and the points of arrows. Dressed in dark blue, the host looked like a deep lake glittering in the sunlight.

'Here they come,' muttered Caenthras.

Eothlir turned his attention back to the camp to see several hundred Khainites racing from the tents towards the Anars. He shook his head slightly, almost embarrassed by the ease with which the ploy was working. Truly their foes had given up any right to be considered sane and civilised folk.

Eoloran turned and marched down the hill, signalling for the archers to move forwards. He crossed to join the right wing of the army as the first of the Khainites reached the foot of the slope in front.

These were the worst fanatics, utterly heedless of their own lives as they charged forwards, knives and swords in their hands, their skin patterned with bloody handprints, their hair slicked into gory spines. Their headlong rush did not falter as the thousands of archers appeared at the summit of the hill.

Eothlir heard his father give the command and watched without emotion as a black cloud of shafts filled the air. The arrow storm dropped down the hillside, falling upon the cultists in a dark mass. Not a single charging Khainite survived that first volley.

The Herald of Khaine was mustering a more coherent force. His hoarse screams could be heard on the wind as the high priest and his underlings moved along the unsteady line of Khainites, sprinkling them with blood from the sacrifices, exhorting them to slay the offenders of the Lord of Murder. As during the ceremony of the night before, the cultists were baying and howling and screaming, offering praises to Khaine or simply giving wordless voice to their seething rages.

Drums joined the cacophony of bellows and shrieks, pounding out a rapid beat that thundered from the hillsides. Just hearing their martial rhythm caused Eothlir's heart to thump faster, his pulse singing in his ears. That there was some magic woven into the incessant drumbeats was inescapable as he felt his anger rising and had to fight the urge to charge forwards. A glance showed that Caenthras and the others were suffering similar temptation.

'Hold fast!' Eothlir called out. 'Await my command!'

He raised his right arm outwards and held out Cyarith at shoulder level, as if it were a barrier to the thousands of spearmen waiting behind him. His hand trembled for a moment, the grip of the ancient sword growing ever hotter in his palm as his excitement fuelled its magic further. Eothlir could feel the sword drawing in energy from the air around him, and he licked his dry lips.

The Herald of Khaine strode forwards at the head of thousands of his followers. The drumbeats continued and were joined by the pattering of bare feet on hard soil. The cultists' screeching had become a singular chant – 'Khaine! Khaine! Khaine!' – which caused Eothlir's skin to crawl as dark energies churned in the skies above. Though the air was clear, the redness of the dawn light deepened, turning to a crimson shroud above and around the elves. Eothlir's magical senses thrummed to an invisible pulsating, in tune with the rapid beating of his heart.

Advancing faster than his warriors, the Herald of Khaine stopped a dozen paces in front of them. He theatrically drew two knives from his belt and Eothlir almost flinched at the sight of the sacrificial daggers. Though impossible for even an elf to see at that distance, Eothlir could feel the runes of Khaine etched into the blades, a burning mark in his mind.

Crossing his arms so that he held out each blade to the opposite shoulder, in one fluid motion the Herald of Khaine drew their edges across his chest. Blood welled up from the wounds as he flung his arms out to the sides. Droplets of crimson fluid flew from the tips of the blades and hung in the air.

A sickness gripped Eothlir as he watched the droplets dissipate into a growing red mist, a cloud of blood that increased in depth until the Herald was obscured from view. The cloud continued to expand, rolling up the hill-side towards Eothlir and cascading down the slope to envelop the Khainites.

'Shoot!' Eothlir called out to his father, realising that soon the enemy would all be hidden.

Eoloran did not question the command of his son and signalled for his archers. In long lines they loosed their missiles upon the chanting mob below. Many Khainites fell to the volley, pierced by the Anars' arrows, but soon the survivors were swathed in the red mist. The archers continued to shoot into the roiling mass as it boiled towards them, though with little hope of finding their marks.

Eothlir realised that soon the whole hill would be engulfed by the enchantment and the archers rendered useless. Without waiting for any order from his father, he turned to the spearmen upon the slopes behind.

'Advance to your positions, quickly!' he bellowed, raising his sword above his head and swinging it forwards as if he could drag the spear companies into position. Horn blasts signalled the advance and soon the steady march of thousands of booted feet sounded on the hillside.

The crimson fog was at the summit of the hill and within moments Eothlir could taste blood upon his tongue as the unnatural cloud swallowed him into its ruddy depths. Trickles of blood ran down his face and stained his silver mail, gathering in pools between the fine links. His grip upon Cyarith became slick and, looking down at his hand, Eothlir realised that so tight was his fist, his nails had drawn blood from his palm, his own blood mixing with the roiling cloud around him.

Dark figures appeared in the fog around him, ruddy shapes silhouetted by the rising sun behind them. With a sigh of relief, Eothlir saw familiar faces – Thorinan, Casadir, Lirunein and others loyal to the Anars. Elegant white shields to the front, black-hafted spears levelled forwards, the warriors of House Anar gathered around their commanders.

HUNDREDS OF ARCHERS lined the hilltops surrounding the Anlec camp, more than a match for the bows under Alith's command. The scouts were dispersed along a ridgeline looking west towards the Anlec warriors, taking what cover they could amongst the scattered bushes and high grass.

A tap on the shoulder drew Alith's attention to Anraneir, who pointed to the south. Alith could see a strange hue in the distance, a red miasma that swathed the hills surrounding the Khainite encampment. He did not understand what he saw, but knew it did not bode well.

At that moment, Alith heard the tramping of boots resounding from beyond the hillside opposite. Though the source of the noise was hidden from view, after a while it was clear that the sound was moving southwards. With his apprehension rising, Alith realised that the Anlec spearmen were heading out of the camp towards the main Anar army, content that the archers protected them.

'It seems our prey does not wish to bite on the bait any more,' said Anraneir.

Alith nodded, his brow knotted in thought. The plan had been to draw away the Anlec warriors, but it had failed. There was little that a few hundred bows could do against such a host if the enemy considered them no threat.

'We have to get their attention,' said Alith, backing down the slope of the hill and gesturing for Anraneir to follow him. 'When the prey eludes the hunter, the hunter turns to Kurnous.'

Anraneir looked on in puzzlement as Alith drew an arrow from the quiver at his back. The young noble rang a finger thoughtfully along the shaft from feather to tip, his finger lingering on the sharp arrowhead.

Alith then spoke the word of fire used in the shrines of Kurnous and the arrow's head sprang into flame, burning bright yellow. Angling his bow high into the air, Alith fired the flaming arrow in the direction of the camp. The flickering of the fire sailed high into the air and then disappeared out of sight.

'Spread the word to the others,' said Alith. 'Target the camp with fire.'

Anraneir smiled appreciatively before hurrying along the line of scouts to pass on Alith's orders. Alith took out another arrow and repeated the process of lighting its head, before shooting again. Soon flares of light arced out from along the hillside, descending into the camp beyond the enemy archers. Alith could not tell how many shafts found a mark, but after several volleys, thicker, blacker smoke rose into the air.

'It's working,' Anraneir laughed, returning to Alith's side.

Crawling forwards to the brow of the hill, Alith saw that the Anlec archers were advancing, arrows nocked to their bows. If the scouts simply retreated directly away from their advancing foes, they would soon be out of range of the camp.

'Circle to the north, keep out of sight,' commanded Alith, stowing his bow and crawling back to Anraneir. 'Though I have danced very little, I know enough that one should take the lead.'

'And what a merry dance it shall be,' said Anraneir.

THE RED MIST obscured all sight beyond twenty paces, and Eothlir was tense as he peered into the shifting depths, seeking some sign of the enemy. Their howling and shouting was getting closer, but the sound was muffled by the unnatural fog.

'Silence!' Eothlir bellowed and within moments the lines of spearmen had fallen still, so that not a clink of armour or whispered word broke the quiet.

Eothlir listened carefully to the approaching noise of the Khainites. It seemed loudest to his left.

'Look to the west!' he warned.

No sooner had the words left his lips than a dark mass appeared in the gloom, quickly resolving into running figures. Thousands of Khainites poured up the slope, yelling and panting, wielding wicked daggers and swords with serrated blades. Their faces were twisted into leers of hatred and masks of total fury as they charged.

The cultists hurled themselves at the Anar spearmen, leaping from their feet a few paces distant and descending with flashing blades. Shields were raised to ward off the blows and the clash of metal echoed dully through the mist. Anar battle cries and praises to Khaine filled the air along with the chime of blades meeting.

Eothlir could not see clearly what was happening, but soon his concern was drawn directly ahead as more Khainites came rushing up the slope.

'Take prisoners if you can,' growled Eothlir. 'My father would question those who plot with Morathi. Take the Herald of Khaine alive, if possible.'

The cultists were barely a dozen paces away and sprinting towards the Anars. Eothlir raised Cyarith in one hand and slipped a dagger from his belt with the other. When the cultists were no more than six paces away, the Anar prince leapt to the attack, Cyarith cutting the head from one Khainite while his knife slashed across the bare chest of another.

Dodging a blade aimed for his face, Eothlir parried another attack and drove the point of his sword into the throat of a third cultist. A moment later, the spearline crashed into the Khainites all around him, unleashing the chaos of battle.

The wall of speartips scythed down the foremost cultists and the Anars pressed on, stabbing with their spears and smashing aside their wounded foes with their shields. The controlled ferocity of the phalanx was more than a match for the raw aggression of the Khainites, who were thrust back by the counter-attack.

'Keep to the high ground!' bellowed Eothlir, worried that the momentum of the spearmen would carry them too far down the slope.

Keeping their line, Eothlir's company backed off to the crest of the hill. The Khainites renewed their assault, ducking beneath the spears to hack at the legs of their enemy. Eothlir parried, chopped and slashed with Cyarith, cutting down any cultist that approached. The wounded of both sides were quickly mounting, as injured elves fell into the grass crying out in pain. The Khainites were unheeding of their losses and pushed on, driven by their bloodthirst. The spearmen were resolute in the face of the deranged murderers, stepping forwards to fill the holes in the line left by the fallen.

Caught in the maelstrom of blades and screams, Eothlir could do nothing but fight for his life. He chopped the arm from a raging cultist and drove his dagger into the groin of another. Blades shrieked from his armour as he punched a Khainite in the face, his gauntlet breaking bone. A wide swing with Cyarith severed the leg of yet another foe, who tumbled down the slope still screaming obscenities.

Eothlir felt a wave of dismay, almost like a chill breeze upon his flesh. It came from the right, accompanied by shrill cries of pain and lamenting wails. Cutting through more cultists, Eothlir pushed his way towards the disturbance. As he shouldered aside one of his own warriors, the melee opened up and Eothlir saw the Herald of Khaine.

The blood-drenched high priest was surrounded by a pile of several corpses, his long daggers held out to each side. Scarred runes upon his flesh burned with dark flame and his daemon mask writhed and snarled with magic. Leaving ghost-like red shadows in his wake, the priest leapt forwards and slashed with his right-hand blade, the dagger slicing clean through a shield and sending the arm holding it flying through the air. No blade or armour could hold against those Khaine-cursed daggers, and more elves fell to their wicked attentions in moments.

A spearman dragged himself to his feet behind the Herald of Khaine, leaning heavily on his weapon. With visible effort, the warrior thrust his spear into the priest's back until the point lanced from his stomach.

The Herald of Khaine fell to his knees, but only for a moment. Surging upright, he turned, ripping the spear from the elf's grasp. A hand flicked out and a dagger appeared in the spearman's face, sending him screaming to the floor. Snapping the shaft transfixing him, the Herald of Khaine ripped free the spear and cast the two parts upon the ground. Blood gushed from the wound and spilled onto the ground at the priest's feet.

'Accept this offering, my most beloved of lords!' the Herald cried out, lifting his bloodied hands into the air.

Black flame enveloped the Herald of Khaine's fingertips, spread down his arms and then coruscated across the priest's wounded body. His flesh cracked and burned, but as the flakes fell away they revealed untarnished skin, and the grievous wound was no more.

As the magical fire flickered and faltered, the Herald stepped forwards and stooped to pull his knife from the dead spearman. In moments the Herald was attacking again, cleaving a bloody path through the Anars' warriors.

Eothlir slashed his way through the throng of cultists surging forwards in the gory wake of their leader. He cut at arms and legs, plunged Cyarith through breastbones and hewed through necks in a constant whirl of blades.

'Face a true son of Nagarythe!' roared the Anar prince as he burst from amongst the falling bodies of his foes.

The Herald of Khaine whirled to face Eothlir, white flame burning in the eyeholes of his mask. The glare of that unnatural gaze froze Eothlir with terror for it seemed as if he looked into the eyes of the Bloody-Handed God himself.

'Your agony will be most pleasing to my lord,' crowed the Herald, his voice harsh, edged with the ring of metal. 'None triumph in battle without his blessing, and your fate is sealed.'

The Herald of Khaine dashed forwards, breaking the link between his eyes and Eothlir's. Out of instinct, the prince ducked and threw himself to the right, narrowly avoiding the priest's daggers, which screamed as they cut the air.

Rolling to his feet, Eothlir knocked aside the next blow with the blade of Cyarith and lunged forwards with his knife. The Herald swayed away from the jab and backed off, stepping quickly on the balls of his feet. He wove his knives in a complex pattern, their fluid movement mesmerising. Eothlir kept his eyes fixed upon his opponent's mask, ignoring the horror that crawled up his spine from the entwining sigil drawn in the air by the knife blades.

Eothlir dropped his left shoulder and then spun to the right, Cyarith flicking out to catch the wrist of the Herald. The priest's hand spun through the air still clutching its baleful dagger. Eothlir jumped back as the Herald struck back as quick as a serpent, the tip of his knife flashing less than a finger's width from Eothlir's throat. Edging sideways, Eothlir looked for an opening to attack the Herald's good arm, hoping to disarm him of the weapons that gave him so much power.

Just as he saw his opportunity, Caenthras dashed past, roaring with anger. He held his spear two-handed – Khiratoth, the Ruinclaw – and drove its point clean through the Herald's chest. Blue fire erupted from Khiratoth, tearing the Herald of Khaine apart, the priest's body exploding into a pall of smoke-wreathed destruction. Without a backwards glance, Caenthras charged through the dissipating remains of the priest and into the cultists, who had momentarily stopped their attack, dismayed at their leader's demise.

Caught unawares by Caenthras's sudden attack, Eothlir hesitated a moment, trying to clear his head. Though some cultists broke and ran from Caenthras, many crowded forwards, growling and snarling, hungry for vengeance. Eothlir gathered his nerve as the spearmen around him closed ranks and prepared to face a fresh assault.

* * *

DESPITE ALITH'S BEST efforts, the Anlec host had pushed his scouts out of bowshot from the camp. The enemy stood just out of range, serried ranks of spearmen glowering from the opposite hilltop. The sun was nearing midday as the two forces faced off against each other, their commanders waiting to see what happened next.

'So, we have their attention, what do we do now?' asked Anraneir.

'Something is troubling me,' replied Alith, giving voice to a doubt that had been slowly growing within. 'I see bows and I see spears, but I see no horses. The armies of Anlec are based upon archers, spearmen and knights.'

'So, where are the knights?' asked Anraneir, looking over his shoulder as if to see enemy cavalry approaching at that moment.

'Perhaps the Khainites ate their steeds,' laughed Khillrallion.

'I would guess that they have moved ahead towards Ealith, to threaten Malekith,' said Alith.

'What if they return?' Khillrallion said with a grimace. 'We cannot outrun knights.'

'We must remain here so that the Khainites receive no reinforcement,' said Alith. 'For better or worse, there is little we can do about the situation. If we withdraw, the warriors will simply move south and attack my grandfather's army.'

'It would be wise to have a plan for what happens if their cavalry show up,' said Anraneir.

Alith looked around, seeing only the scattered bushes and trees of the Annulii foothills. Though these were his family's lands, he did not know them with the intimacy of the mountains. He might well have been in Saphery or Chrace for the little local knowledge he had.

'This might help,' said Anraneir, proffering a rolled-up parchment. Alith took it and let it fall open, revealing one of Eoloran's maps.

'Where are we now?' asked Alith, wishing that he had paid more attention at the war council.

With a sigh, Anraneir pointed to the north-west and then to the map.

'Ealith lies that way, we're on the edges of the foothills, here,' the scout explained. 'If we need to hide from cavalry, I suggest the Athrian Vale, north and east of here. If enemy cavalry approach, we can be under the eaves before they're upon us.'

'Provided that we get enough warning,' added Khillrallion.

'Good point,' said Alith. He nodded at Anraneir, handing back the map. 'Take five scouts and head north to keep watch for unpleasant arrivals.'

Anraneir placed the map back in his pack and set off at a trot, calling out names. Alith tapped his fingers on the broad silver buckle of his belt, seemingly deep in thought. The spearmen opposite had remained in place and gave no sign that they intended to attack.

Alith turned suddenly towards Khillrallion.

'Any suggestions for what to do now?' asked Alith.

Khillrallion thought for a moment, a smile creeping across his lips.

'I know some good songs…'

WHOEVER COMMANDED THE Anlec force, Alith admired his patience, if not his loyalties. Noon came and went and the black-armoured warriors stood guard against an attack from the scouts, standing in silent ranks while the air grew hotter and hotter. It would have been foolish to chase the lightly-armoured elves, for there was no hope of catching them. Instead, the Anlec officer was content to wait. The enemy's contentment unnerved Alith. He fretted that he was missing some kind of trick, and worried that his opponent knew something Alith did not – such as when the cavalry would be returning.

Every now and then, Alith led his scouts forwards a little way, shot some arrows at the Anlec ranks and then withdrew to a new position. He did this mainly out of boredom, though he justified it to himself with the notion that such harassment would be sapping the morale of his foes. The truth was that his scouts were left with perhaps half a dozen arrows each, and if the enemy decided to come after them there was little they could do except run.

As midday passed into mid-afternoon, Alith looked constantly to the south for some sign of his father and grandfather; he gazed to the north for warning of approaching cavalry. He was confident that the main force would be victorious over the Khainites, but as time passed he longed to see the banners of the Anars appearing over the hills.

'Look,' said Khillrallion, nodding to the south.

'Finally,' Alith sighed as he saw the telltale silvery shimmer of armoured warriors crossing a distant hilltop.

The enemy commander had also noted this development. Ignoring the scouts, his companies turned quickly southwards and deployed to meet this new enemy. Alith was about to give the order to close in behind the Anlec columns when a shout drew his attention to the north.

'Riders!' yelled Anraneir, running along a ridgeline to the north. 'Hundreds of them!'

'North-east!' bellowed Alith, rising to his feet. 'Run!'

The scouts sprinted down the slope, leaping nimbly over bushes and rocks. Keeping a swift but steady pace they headed towards the woods of Athrian Vale, casting glances to the north. Alith spied a cloud of dust on the horizon, growing nearer with some speed, though the riders themselves were yet hidden from view.

'Faster!' he urged his warriors, picking up speed.

* * *

THE TREES OF Athrian Vale came into view as Alith reached the crest of a tall hill. In the vale below, a stream meandered down from the distant mountains. Slender pines crowded to the river's banks and spread out across the deep valley where the waterway widened, an expanse of trees large enough to conceal the fleeing elves.

Alith could feel the ground trembling from thousands of hoofbeats, a rumbling that grew louder and louder as he sprinted towards the first few trees scattered around the border of the woods. The jingle of harnesses was audible too, as were shouts. Ducking beneath the branches of a tree, Alith risked a glance to his left and saw long lines of riders cresting a hill barely two hundred paces away.

Swathed in the dust thrown up by their galloping mounts, the riders appeared through the murk. These were not the sinister black-armoured knights of Anlec. They were dressed in bright blue and white, with armour of silvery mail. Their banners bore blazons of white horses and horses' heads and their helms were decorated with gaily-coloured feathers.

'Ellyrians!' laughed Alith, sliding to a stop on the fine carpet of needles beneath the gloom of the trees. He knew not how they came to be here so far from home, but grinned widely at the sight. He turned and jogged back to the edge of the wood to watch the reaver knights of Ellyrion sweep down the hillside. Other scouts stood close at hand looking at the same spectacle.

The riders carried leaf-bladed spears in their hands and the bright tack of their steeds glinted in the sun. As they came closer, Alith could see their faces, and the sight sent a shiver running through his body. They were grim of expression as they lowered their spears for a charge. Others had bows in their hands and loosed arrows at the fall gallop, the shafts falling towards Alith and his scouts.

'Into the trees!' he yelled, bounding towards the nearest trunk and leaping up into the branches with the surefootedness of a cat. Climbing higher through the pricking needles, he ran to the end of one branch and crouched there.

'Friends!' he shouted out, cupping his hands to his mouth to be heard over the panting of steeds and the thunder of hooves. 'Stay your weapons!'

Dozens of reavers converged upon the tree, bowstrings bent and arrows nocked. A knot of knights came forwards beneath a long pennant displaying a silver horse on a circle of blue, the banner decorated with a white mane.

'House Anar!' shouted Alith though he did not know whether the name would be of any import to the Ellyrians.

A rider with a golden helm topped with a horsehair crest rode from the circling elves, his spear couched beneath one arm, a gold shield embossed with a rearing stallion on the other.

'I am Prince Aneltain of Ellyrion,' the elf called out, shielding his eyes against the sun to peer at Alith.

'Alith Anar,' replied Alith, standing up warily. 'Announce your allegiance and explain your presence in our lands.'

'I have sworn loyalty to the Phoenix King and have just this past night ridden to war alongside Prince Malekith, rightful ruler of Nagarythe. I head for the Pass of the Unicorn to take word back to Prince Finudel, my liege.'

Alith leapt nimbly from the branch and landed in the long grass not far from Aneltain. He raised a hand in welcome as the mounted elves closed in around him, circling menacingly.

'I am son of Eothlir, grandson of Eoloran Anar,' Alith announced. 'We fight the same foe as you.'

Alith turned and pointed to the south.

'Even now, the warriors of House Anar fight the traitors of Anlec. Your presence would be most welcomed by my grandfather. Later you can tell us how Prince Malekith fares at Ealith.'

Aneltain leaned over and said something to one of his knights, who brought out a curling horn of gold and sounded a series of notes. At the ringing command, the Ellyrians broke away from the trees and formed into long columns once more, leaving Aneltain alone with Alith. The Ellyrian prince nudged his horse closer to Alith and bent down in the saddle to speak to him. Closer, Alith could see a fresh cut upon the prince's cheek and the dirt of hard travelling on his cloak.

'Ealith was a trap,' Aneltain said with a woeful shake of the head. 'Malekith retreats westwards to take ship at Galthyr. You would do well to return to your homes. We will speak more of this once the enemy at hand are destroyed.'

Before Alith could utter any answer Aneltain had wheeled his horse away and broken into a gallop, heading for the front of his army. Another clarion burst set the knights moving forwards, cantering away to the south, heading for the army of the Anars.

LAUGHTER FILLED EOLORAN's pavilion, a sound that Alith had not heard for some time. Aneltain and his Ellyrian captains toasted the victory with silver cups of wine. Eothlir was smiling also, though Eoloran's expression was pensive.

'You have the thanks of House Anar,' said Eoloran, raising his own goblet towards Aneltain.

'As you have already told us a dozen times, Eoloran!' replied the Ellyrian prince. 'You owe us no gratitude, for without your host we would have faced the Khainites alone. It was by fortune, or perhaps the weavings of Morai-heg, that Prince Malekith asked me to lead some of my number directly south. Had he not done so, the knights we destroyed not far from Ealith would no doubt have been a match for your army.'

Alith wondered at these words, having already heard from Aneltain that Malekith had sought the Ellyrian out after the battle for Ealith and directed him to ride back to Ellyrion along the Unicorn Pass. It seemed more than coincidence that Elthyrior had promised Alith others would come to confirm his warning that Malekith was trapped. He had no doubt that the rightful ruler of Nagarythe was aware of what the Anars were doing and had sent aid in their direction. As before, Alith chafed at having to withhold this information, knowing that to announce what he knew would betray the pact he had made with Elthyrior.

'Do you think Malekith will reach Galthyr?' asked Caenthras, looking up from the map table where he had been staring at the charts since Alith had arrived. 'By what route will he march to the port? In whose hands will he find it?'

Aneltain shrugged.

'I cannot answer those questions, any more than you can,' said the prince. 'I entered Nagarythe for the first time only days ago. These are not my lands; I know nothing of their people. I will say that if any of us can escape the clutches of the cultists, it is Malekith. His army is strong and the march not overly long. The prince himself is the greatest warrior and most skilful commander I have ever seen. His personal fleet waits at Galthyr and I hope that the city's rulers remain opposed to Morathi.'

'That is a rare hope in these times,' said Eothlir, becoming serious. 'Yet it is heartening to think that it is not the Anars alone that would resist the power of Anlec.'

'Will Malekith return?' asked Caenthras, staring intently at the Ellyrians.

'Not before spring, I would say,' said Eoloran. 'Though he has not suffered true defeat as yet, this attack seems to have been... hasty, I would say. One does not merely walk up to Anlec and knock on the gates to be allowed entry.'

'We must do what we can to pave the way for that glorious return,' said Eothlir. 'Morathi knows Malekith's intent now, and all surprise is lost. We have raised our weapons against Anlec as well, and we do not know when the return blow will come.'

'We should harass a few more of Morathi's armies, keep her busy while Malekith regroups,' said Caenthras. 'When Malekith returns, he should not face a united, well-composed foe.'

Alith was worried by these words and the look of consideration on Eoloran's face. The Anars had suffered little in the battle that day; Elthyrior's warning had to relate to matters not yet known to Alith.

'That would be unwise,' said Eothlir, much to Alith's relief. 'Now that we have truly stirred up the wasps' nest, we should seek sanctuary in Elanardris.'

'From what little I heard from the raven heralds, that would seem the best course of action,' said Aneltain.

The mention of the raven heralds drew Alith's attention immediately, and also that of his grandfather.

'Raven heralds?' said Eoloran, his eyes narrowed with suspicion. 'What dealings have you had with those dark riders?'

Aneltain was taken aback and gave a defensive shrug.

'They act as Malekith's scouts and brought us to Ealith by secret ways,' replied the Ellyrian. 'Word came to us at the citadel that armies from the north and west and south were converging at Ealith to trap the prince and destroy his army. I fear that House Anar will fare no better if you remain out in the open.'

'Already we have helped Malekith,' Alith said, directing his words towards his father and grandfather. 'The army we have crushed today will not threaten Malekith, and we have bought him time to make his retreat, as was Caenthras's suggestion. Our losses are comparatively few as yet, but if we remain here that might not hold true for long. And who can say what forces will march on our homes once Malekith has slipped away?'

Eoloran sat down behind the map table and rubbed the side of his nose, as he was wont to do when deep in thought. He closed his eyes, seeming to block out the rest of the world as he contemplated his decision.

'We return to Elanardris,' he said, eyes still closed.

Alith stopped himself from crying out with relief. The anxious energy that had filled him since his meeting with Elthyrior drained away and he suddenly felt very tired. He excused himself from the continuing discussions and made his way to his tent, exhausted but happy. Elanardris would remain safe and soon he would see Ashniel again.

FIVE

Clothed in Darkness

IT SEEMED TO Alith that the winter wind was more bitter than any that had come before. It brought swirls of snow down from the mountains, but it was not just the cold that clawed at Alith, it was the feeling of being trapped.

From the high mountain path, the young Anar looked south and west across Elanardris. He could see the manse, the gardens swathed in snow. Smoke drifted from the house's three chimneys, billowing southwards on the stern breeze. Beyond the manse, the meadows and hills were laid out in a pattern of dark walls and hedges cutting through the white blanket. The white-walled farmhouses and guard towers could barely be seen, located only through their brightly tiled roofs and the telltale wisps of smoke.

Beyond that, almost at the horizon, the hills of Elanardris gave way to the undulating plains of central Nagarythe. Here the cloud-swathed sky was shrouded by a darker smog, the fires of a huge encampment. The army of Anlec squatted like a brooding black beast on the borders of the Anars' realm, waiting for the snows to cease. At this distance, and through the snow flurries brought down from the north, even the keen eyes of Alith could make out little detail. The enemy camp spread like a stain over the white hills, lines of black shapes that stretched from north to south.

The druchii, his grandfather had called them: dark elves. They had turned from the light of Aenarion and the lord of gods, Asuryan. Eoloran no longer regarded them as Naggarothi. They were traitors to the Phoenix Throne and betrayers of Malekith, their rightful prince.

Their foes thought the same of the Anars. They considered Eoloran's refusal to acknowledge the authority of Anlec as a slight against Aenarion's memory. Alith knew this from the interrogations of prisoners taken after the last battle, when the druchii had attempted to force their way up into the hills. It had been a foolish, desperate assault before Enagruir tightened her wintry grip on Nagarythe. The druchii had been stopped by Eoloran and Eothlir – again, for there had been three such attacks since Malekith had returned – and the dark elves were content to wait for conditions to improve and their numbers to swell further.

Alith's loneliness had been increased by the lack of contact with Ashniel. Far from giving him the triumphant homecoming Alith had imagined, Ashniel had been moved by her father to one of the lord's castles higher in the mountains, far from the enemy. Occasionally Alith would receive a short letter from her, in which she professed her regret at their parting and her wish that they would see each other again soon. Alith had little enough time to reply to these letters, for he spent most days up in the mountains keeping watch on the druchii host. Try as he might, he had little leisure to spend composing poetry and declarations of love and knew that such missives as he managed to send were brusque and clumsy.

As these morose thoughts occupied Alith, a lionhawk, her plumage white to camouflage her against the snows, swept down with a shriek from the mountain clouds. She circled around Alith and the group of scouts around him, and then settled on his wrist. Alith listened to her chirping and cawing for a moment, nodding in understanding as the bird relayed the message from Anadriel.

He stroked the lionhawk's head in thanks before raising his arm and allowing her to fly back to her nest. She would come again when called.

'A rider, on the Eithrin Ridge,' Alith announced to the twenty elves accompanying him. They were all dressed in robes of white trimmed with dark bear fur, enchanted with the greatest blessings of stealth and secrecy known to the dedicants of Kurnous. Even this close, it was hard for Alith to see where elf stopped and snow began. 'Anadriel is moving in from the south-west; we shall intercept this spy from the north-east. Quickly now, we don't want Anadriel to steal our glory!'

Many times the scouts had intercepted druchii warriors attempting to spy upon the Anars' army and defences. As far as Alith knew, not a single one had escaped to take news back to the druchii commanders. This one was different. It was obvious that nobody would be able to cross the Eithrin Ridge unobserved, especially on horseback, and so the druchii had concentrated their forces to the west and north. Alith's instinct told him that this uninvited visitor was not a spy, and wondered if Elthyrior had finally been caught out.

However, there was no solid reason to suspect that this stranger was the raven herald. Alith had heard nothing from Elthyrior since their parting before the battle with the Khainites, and guessed only that he had reached Ealith safely and persuaded Malekith to send Aneltain south. Elthyrior could be dead, a captive of Morathi, or hidden in whatever lairs the raven heralds used to avoid the attention of their enemies.

As wintry spirits, the scouts made their way across the snow-covered rock, heading towards Eithrin Ridge. They flitted through the sparse trees, deftly running across the snow, moving sure-footedly over patches of sun-glittering ice. As they made their way down the mountainside, the shadow of Anil Narthain fell upon them and the air grew colder. Alith blew on his fingers as he jogged, keeping them warm so that he would not fumble with his bow if the stranger proved to be a threat. The snow crunching underfoot, Alith and the other archers ghosted southwards, eyes fixed ahead for any sight of the interloper.

It was mid-morning before Alith crested a rise, coming out into the winter sun, and saw the intruder. It was not Elthyrior. Although the elf was some distance away, Alith could see that he was shorter than the raven herald, and he was dressed in a grey cloak beneath which could be seen flashes of golden scale and white robes. The intruder was leading his horse, striding across a long snowdrift that had built up on the flanks of the Eithrin Ridge. Alith signalled wordlessly to the others to spread out and circle to the east to come at the stranger from several directions.

For a short while Alith lost sight of his quarry as the rocky slope dipped sharply and then rose up again. Pulling himself up the steep wall of the snow-filled crag, Alith caught sight of the stranger again, standing some three hundred paces away. He had stopped and was looking around quickly, and for a moment Alith wondered if the intruder had spied one of the scouts.

A keening cry overhead announced the presence of Anadriel's lionhawk, and only moments later six figures that before had been invisible stood up. Standing in a semi-circle some hundred paces from the stranger, they were dressed in the same style of clothes as Alith's warriors and had arrows bent to their bows. Alith rose to his feet and dashed across the snow, fitting an arrow to his bowstring.

The stranger had raised his arms and thrown back his cloak, revealing no scabbard at his waist, only the long knife that any traveller in the wilds would be sensible to carry. He was exchanging words with Anadriel and Alith caught the end of a reply.

'...need to speak to Eoloran and Eothlir,' the stranger called out.

Anadriel saw Alith and his scouts approaching from the opposite direction and lifted a hand in brief greeting. The stranger turned slowly to look at Alith. His expression was calm, confident even. He pulled back his hood with deliberate slowness, revealing reddish-yellow hair tied with golden thread. He was certainly not from Nagarythe.

'Name yourself,' Alith called out, stopping some fifty paces from the elf, his arrow aimed at the stranger's chest.

'I am Calabrian of Tor Andris,' the elf replied. 'I bear messages for the lord of the Anars.'

'We know the manner of messages that Morathi would send,' said Alith. He lifted up his bow and arrow. 'You know the manner of our replies.'

'I come not from Anlec, but Tor Anroc,' Calabrian said patiently. 'I carry missives from Prince Malekith.'

'And what proof do you offer?' demanded Alith.

'If you would allow me to approach, I will show you.'

Alith relaxed his arm and brought down his bow. Letting go of the arrow, he waved for Calabrian to come closer. The messenger lowered his arms and stepped up to his horse. He drew something from his saddlebags and held it up. It was a scroll case. Calabrian walked purposefully, glancing at the other scouts, the case still held clearly in view. Alith signalled for him to stop a few paces away and stepped up to him with an outstretched hand. Calabrian placed the casing in Alith's grip and took a few paces further back, his eyes unwavering from Alith's face.

The seal on the case was certainly that of Prince Malekith, and was unbroken. It was light, and so Alith doubted it contained a concealed weapon. Just to be sure, he tucked the case into his belt rather than return it.

'That message is for Eoloran Anar alone,' said Calabrian, stepping forwards. In an instant, Alith was ready, bowstring taut, the arrow pointed towards Calabrian's heart. The messenger stopped. 'I have other assurances, but only Eoloran will understand them.'

'I am Alith Anar, grandson of the lord you seek,' Alith assured the other elf. 'I will take you to the manse and there you will meet Eoloran Anar. Be warned, though, that if your claim proves to be false, you will not be treated well. If you wish, we will take you to the border of Elanardris directly and you can return to your master unharmed.'

'My mission is vital, the prince made that very clear to me,' said Calabrian. 'I offer myself to your judgement and mercy.'

Alith regarded Calabrian for a long time, seeking some hint of deception. There was none that he could see. A glance over the messenger's shoulder showed that Anadriel was inspecting Calabrian's horse and saddlebags.

'She will find nothing out of the ordinary,' said Calabrian, without looking around. 'A few personal items and those things needed when travelling in the grip of winter; that is all.'

Alith did not reply but simply waited for Anadriel to complete her search.

'All is well,' she called out eventually. 'No weapons of any kind.'

'These are dangerous times to be travelling unarmed in Nagarythe,' said Alith, his suspicion returning. 'How is it that you could pass without fear through the Anlec host that sits upon our doorstep?'

'I came not directly from the south, but crossed the mountains from Ellyrion,' explained Calabrian.

'A dangerous crossing,' said Alith, unconvinced.

'Yet it is one that I had to make,' said Calabrian. 'Though I do not know the detail of Prince Malekith's message, he left me in no doubt as to its importance and urgency. When I have Prince Eoloran's reply, I must return by the same route.'

There was earnestness in Calabrian's expression that convinced Alith.

'Very well,' said Alith, lowering his bow and returning the arrow to its quiver. 'Welcome to Elanardris, Calabrian of Tor Andris.'

ALITH WAS NOT surprised when Calabrian had insisted that only Eoloran, Eothlir and Alith were allowed to be present when Prince Malekith's message was opened. The messenger had requested that he be brought to the manse in secret, and made it plain that he only trusted the Anars and feared that agents of Morathi were present in Elanardris. Alith left him with Anadriel on the slopes north of the manse while he consulted his father and grandfather.

So it was that in the darkness of the cloud-swathed night, Alith led Calabrian to the summer house that stood in the eastern stretch of the garden. A single lamp burned within as Alith entered and gestured for Calabrian to follow. A ewer of spiced tea sat steaming on the low table in the middle of the single-roomed building, fluted cups arranged around it. The smell was sharp and Alith crossed quickly and poured himself a hot drink, warming his hands on the delicate cup.

Eoloran was stood at the window, gazing to the south, swathed in a fur-lined robe of deep blue, calfskin gloves upon his hands and his breath misting in the cold. Eothlir was sat on one of the benches that lined the white walls of the summer house, the scroll case in his hands.

'You said that you would offer further assurances as to the veracity of your claims,' said Eoloran, still looking out into the darkness. 'Make them known to me.'

Calabrian cast an appealing glance towards Alith, who poured a drink for the messenger. Sipping gently, Calabrian turned to Eoloran.

'Malekith instructed me to say "The light of the flame burns brightest at night",' said Calabrian, intoning the words with deep solemnity.

Eoloran spun around and glared inquisitively at Calabrian.

'What does it mean?' asked Eothlir, taken aback by his father's reaction. When Eoloran replied, his voice was quiet, distant.

'Those words were first spoken by Aenarion. It was before Anlec was built, just after the daemons had ravaged Avelorn and slain the Everqueen. I remember it well. He had vowed vengeance for the death of his wife and the slaying of his children, and in grief had decided to draw that accursed blade. I argued against him. I warned Aenarion that… that weapon was not for mortals to wield. I could see that his rage would consume him, and said as much. Those words were his reply. He left atop Indraugnir that night and flew to the Blighted Isle. When he returned, the Aenarion I had known was no more and a life of bloodshed followed. How do you know this phrase?'

'You will have to ask Prince Malekith,' said Calabrian, setting his empty cup on the table. 'He bade me to learn the words but offered no explanation. I trust that you believe my story?'

Eoloran nodded and gestured for Eothlir to pass the scroll case.

'Only Aenarion and I were present when those words were spoken, but it seems reasonable that Aenarion might use them again in the presence of his son,' Eoloran said.

Taking the case, Eoloran examined the seal and, satisfied that it remained intact, broke the circlet of black wax with his thumb. He pulled open the end of the tube and slid out a single piece of parchment. Placing the case carefully on the table, he opened the scroll.

'It is a letter,' said Eoloran. He scanned the elegant script for a moment and then began to read aloud, his voice breaking with emotion.

For the eyes of Eoloran Anar, beloved of Aenarion, true protector of Nagarythe. First I must thank you, though words cannot do justice to the debt I owe you for your support. I have heard that you marched to my aid at Ealith, and though that endeavour was ultimately to fail, I escaped and that is due in no small part to the presence of your army. I understand the great risk that you took in showing such support and assure you that you will be honoured and repaid when I reclaim the rule of Nagarythe. Truly you were a friend to my father and, I hope, an ally to me.

Eoloran paused, clearing his throat, a tear forming in his eye. He swallowed hard, brushing away the memories with a wipe of his hand across his brow. He continued in a clearer voice, his calm demeanour returned.

Alas that I must entreat further aid from you at this time. What I ask is dangerous in the extreme and I will not hold it against you should you feel unfit to comply. Please respond through my messenger, Calabrian, who can be trusted with the deepest of secrets. However, I must ask that you tell no more of your people than necessary of what I now request, lest word of it reach the ears of Morathi, by conventional means or via other, more deceitful paths. I march upon Anlec with the first thawing of the spring. Even now, my army assembles in Ellyrion, far from the prying eyes of my mother and her spies, while other forces loyal to the Phoenix King draw their gaze southwards. I am confident that I will reach Anlec, but the defences of the city are little short of impenetrable.

I ask that you take such warriors as you deem utterly trustworthy and infiltrate Anlec, there to stand ready for my attack. I cannot say at what time the stroke shall fall, so you must set out for the city come the first sun of the spring. No army can breach the gates of Anlec, but should they be opened before me I stand ready with a host of warriors the likes of which have not been seen upon Ulthuan's shores for an age. I wait with anticipation for your speedy reply and wish you the blessings of all the gods.

I remain your loyal ally and grateful prince.

'Then there is the rune of Malekith and his seal,' Eoloran finished.

'That is a considerable request,' said Eothlir as Eoloran passed the parchment to him.

'We are going to help, aren't we?' said Alith.

'Yes we are,' replied Eoloran, surprising Alith with the speed of his answer. It was unlike Eoloran to take such a decision with so little consideration. 'Had the prince commanded us to hurl ourselves at the walls of Anlec, I would comply. For the sake of Nagarythe, and all of Ulthuan, Morathi cannot be allowed to continue as ruler.

The prince must be restored if we are ever to know peace again.'

Eoloran stood in thought for a moment, rubbing at his chin. He looked at Calabrian, who had stood meekly listening to the contents of the letter he had carried on such a dangerous journey.

'How much of Malekith's intent do you know?' asked Eoloran.

'No more than you,' the messenger replied. 'I left Malekith in Tor Anroc and knew nothing of his plan to move his army to Ellyrion. Nor of his intent to assault Anlec.'

'Then I shall write a reply to your master, and you will be taken across the mountains to Ellyrion,' said Eoloran. 'With Anar guides to lead you, I am sure that your return journey shall be less fraught than the one that brought you here.'

'Who shall we send with him?' asked Eothlir. 'Perhaps more importantly, who shall we take with us to Anlec? And by what means will we get there unheralded?'

'Anadriel and the other scouts who met Calabrian already know of his presence here,' said Alith. 'They are all trustworthy, kin to the Anars each of them. Anadriel knows the mountains as well as I, perhaps even better. I can think of no better guide, nor a more skilful warrior.'

'I would have you take Calabrian, Alith, and then return to the manse to keep our lands safe for our return,' said Eothlir. 'To risk every lord of the Anars on this one quest seems careless, and to abandon Elanardris would be perverse.'

'No,' said Eoloran, cutting across Alith's protest. 'Alith has proven himself in battle, and a finer eye cannot be found in Elanardris. If he is to have a future as a lord of the Anars, he fights with us. There are many who can see to the defence of Elanardris in our absence, and if Malekith marches on Anlec I would say that our foes' priorities will quickly change!'

Alith was profoundly grateful for his grandfather's opinion, but remained quiet lest an outburst change Eoloran's mind.

'For the moment,' said Eoloran with a look at Alith, 'he can run down to the house and bring me back parchment, ink and a quill.'

'Of course,' said Alith, bowing his head in thanks. As he left the summer house, he heard his father's voice quiet but angry, but his words were lost as Alith headed down the path towards the manse.

THE WINTER DAYS dragged on as heavy cloud sat upon the mountains, the snow sometimes coming in blizzards and at other times in more gentle flurries. Anadriel took Calabrian across the mountains to where the borders of Nagarythe, Chrace and Ellyrion met, and sent him south to Malekith.

By secret paths and unknown vantage points, the scouts of the Anars spied upon the enemy camps, noting their numbers and positions. All of this was passed to Eoloran to chart the disposition of his foes. With Alith and Anadriel, the lord of the Anars plotted the route by which a small group of warriors could evade the enemy and leave Elanardris unseen. Twice more Calabrian dared the dangerous route across the mountains to confer with the Anars, bringing assurances from Malekith that his attack was ready and returning with the renewed promises of Eoloran. Then the winter's grip tightened, blizzards ruled the peaks and there came no further word from the prince.

Thirty warriors were chosen by Eothlir, as those most trusted and most capable. All had served the Anars for centuries, several of them distant cousins to Alith.

Amongst them were Anadriel, Anraneir, Casadir and Khillrallion. Eothlir began to refer to these warriors as the Shadows, as it would be in secrecy rather than strength that they would succeed.

The Shadows met each other every few days, to discuss the route from Elanardris to Anlec. Khillrallion tested the pathways out of Elanadris and returned several days later to confirm that he had not seen another elf in all of that time. While these practical steps were taken, Eoloran turned his hand to a different form of subterfuge: promulgating a falsehood to his allies that would explain his coming absence.

Through Caenthras, the ruler of the Anars spread the word that he had been in contact with Prince Durinne of Galthyr, a port in the west of Nagarythe. Eoloran let it be known that the two were arranging to meet, and would confirm their alliance and mutual support in the spring. Caenthras took this news with enthusiasm, and would often speak of how he wished for Malekith's return. Eoloran kept his silence on this matter, uncertain of Caenthras's reaction should he know the truth. The old warrior had been invigorated by the fighting against the Khainites and was clearly chafing at the imprisonment imposed by the besieging army. It was Eoloran's fear that Caenthras would march out to join Malekith if he knew the truth, leaving Elanardris unprotected, though it pained him to lie to his friend.

Each day Alith would awaken and look to the skies, hoping to see the first sun of spring. In Nagarythe, the winters were deep and harsh, but once the north wind turned to the west and the clouds broke, spring and then summer would come quickly. The sign that Malekith was ready to attack grew closer with every morning.

ALITH WAS CURLED up on a bed of leaves at the back of a cave, at one of the watch positions overlooking the druchii army. A slight noise caused him to wake instantly, reaching instinctively for the naked sword that lay beside him. Someone was silhouetted against the slightly paler circle of the cavern entrance. A smokeless lamp glowed into life to reveal the face of Anraneir. He was smiling broadly.

'Come, sleepy one, and look at this,' he said, stepping aside.

Alith sprang up and strode to the opening, guessing Anraneir's cause for happiness. There was an almost imperceptible warmth on the breeze, which came from the west. Looking to the east he saw the first red rays of the sun cresting over Anulir Erain, the White Mother who was the tallest of the mountains south of the manse.

'The first spring sun!' laughed Alith. Anraneir hugged Alith in his joy, and the young Anar shared his enthusiasm. The sun signalled a very perilous time for them both, but the prospect of action after such a bleak winter was exciting.

'We should head back to the manse today,' said Anraneir. 'Your grandfather will no doubt wish to leave tonight,'

'Best wait for Mithastir to replace me here,' said Alith. 'Someone still needs to keep an eye on the enemy. You should go now, since it would raise questions why you are here and not at your post.'

'Of course,' said Anraneir, deflated by Alith's practicality. With a waved hand and a whispered word he dimmed his lantern and disappeared into the gloom.

Alith sat cross-legged on the ledge outside the cave, gazing down at the pinpricks of campfires far below. He whispered a chant in praise of Kurnous as he waited for Mithastir to arrive, thanking the Lord of the Hunt for bringing the early spring. Alith took it as a good sign from his patron.

* * *

Singly and in pairs, the Shadows gathered in a small copse of trees known as the Athelin Emain close to the southern border of Elanardris. Alith was one of the first, and waited in the darkness for the others to arrive. As the moons glowed from behind thin clouds, Eoloran and Eothlir finally made their appearance, clad in dark cloaks like the rest. It was the first time Alith had seen his father and grandfather dressed in this fashion, entirely unlike the statesmanlike robes or shining armour he was accustomed to seeing. The ruler of the Anars gathered his warriors beneath the boughs of a great tree, the dim moonlight streaming through the naked branches to cast dappled shadows on the ground.

'We must pass the druchii line before sunrise,' said Eoloran, looking at the thirty Shadows. 'We all know the path which we take, and the danger should we be discovered. I offer you one last chance to return to your homes. As soon as we set foot beyond these trees we are committed to this journey, all the way to Anlec and whatever fate Morai-heg has reserved for us. Some of us, perhaps all of us, may not return from this fight, and it may be a fool's errand that we run.'

There was silence from the others. Alith was eager for them to start out, to put an end to the waiting and planning.

'Good,' said Eoloran with a grim smile. 'We are as one mind. Lauded shall be those that march with me today, and great shall be the gratitude of the Anars and Prince Malekith.'

With that, Eoloran turned south and the Shadows began their perilous quest.

It was not long before the Shadows encountered their first difficulty. Casadir had moved ahead of the main group as lead scout and returned just as Eoloran and the others were leaving the cover of Athelin Emain. They had planned to head directly westwards before turning north, but Casadir brought alarming news.

'The druchii have shifted the southern boundaries of their camp,' he reported as the others gathered at his surprise return. 'Cultists have moved south of the road.'

'Can we go around them?' asked Anadriel.

'Certainly,' replied Casadir. 'Though if we wish to remain out of sight we would have to travel through the fens of the Enniun Moreir. Who can say how many days that would add to our journey?'

'Arrive at Anlec too late or risk discovery, that is no small choice,' said Eothlir. He looked at his father. 'I would put my vote on speed and directness. The risk of being seen is one that we can control, while the delays are beyond our measure to manage.'

'I concur,' said Eoloran. 'It would be of little use to arrive too late and be trapped outside the walls with Malekith.'

'Perhaps there is even an opportunity here,' suggested Alith. He turned to Casadir. 'How large would you say is the cultist camp? How close are they to the others?'

'Two hundred cultists, maybe less,' said Casadir. 'They are camped on the lee side of the hills, on the banks of the Erandath, some distance from the bridge at Anul Tiran.'

'What are you thinking?' asked Eothlir as Alith stayed silent for a moment.

'We can address two problems with one solution,' said Alith. 'I say we kill the cultists in their camp, and take on their guise. Clothed as cultists we can move freely along the roads rather than avoid them, speeding our journey by many days.'

'What if the alarm is raised?' asked Eoloran. 'What you suggest risks a battle that we cannot win and an end to our journey before it has begun.'

'The cultists will be unprepared and we will use stealth as our weapon,' replied Alith, nodding as a plan resolved in his mind. 'From what we saw of the Khainites, they have no military discipline. They expect no attack, and more than likely will be lying in their tents stupefied and unaware.'

'I saw very little movement,' added Casadir. 'It would be very simple to come upon them unseen, if we choose confrontation.'

'Kill them in their sleep?' said Eothlir. 'What you suggest fills me with a deep distaste. We are not assassins, we are warriors.'

'And what of those that have fallen beneath their blades already, and those that would be sacrificed in the years to come should Malekith fail?' growled Alith. 'Too long has justice been absent from Nagarythe. It is all well and good to march out gloriously with banners flapping and clarions blaring, but in this war there are battles to be fought unseen by others. Are we not the Shadows for a reason?'

Eothlir's expression showed his uneasiness, but he turned to his father rather than reply. Eoloran shook his head slowly, unhappy with the decision he faced.

'You did not see what we saw in the Khainite camp,' Alith said. 'Though you may think it cold-blooded murder that I propose, we at least will have the dignity to give our victims a clean and painless death. They will not be tossed screaming onto fires nor have their living bodies desecrated by abuse! Does the hunter regret every life he takes, or does he know that it is the way of the world that some die so that others may live? He cannot pity the stag or the bear, no more than we can pity those that have chosen to prey upon their own kind.'

'You make a powerful argument, Alith,' replied Eoloran. 'To move cloaked in the guise of the enemy would be a great advantage, especially when we come to Anlec.

Though we have pondered long on our journey to the city, this gives us a means by which we might enter unknown. We must accept that there is darkness in all shadows, and take strength from the promise that such deeds as we are about to commit are so that others may not know such sacrifice.'

With attack decided, the Shadows broke into groups of three and set out, circling around the cultist encampment. It was past midnight when they had come to their positions, and all about the camp was quiet. The orgy of celebration Alith had seen with the Khainites was absent, but clouds of narcotic vapours drifted from bone-wrought braziers. That the cultists were in a drugged stupor seemed likely.

Coming to the closest tent, a high pavilion of purple cloth, Alith moved to the front at a crouch, dagger in hand. There was no movement from within and only the sound of slow breathing. With a glance around to ensure he was unobserved, Alith opened the flap and slipped inside.

There were seven elves within, all entwined in nakedness upon a huge carpet made of several furred skins sewn together. A lamp with red glass glowed in one corner, bathing everything in vermillion. Two of the elves were male, the others female, the bare flesh of all marked with runes drawn in blue dye. Amongst the swirls and shapes, Alith recognised the rune of Atharti, a goddess of pleasure.

They were utterly still as Alith crouched above the closest. He could smell the fragrance of black lotus, a powerful narcotic that gave vivid dreams when smoke from its burning petals was inhaled. Drawing up his scarf across his mouth and face, Alith leaned forwards and brought his blade up to the sleeping maiden's neck. The dagger shone in the ruddy light and Alith paused.

To kill in the heat of battle was one thing, but to purposefully slay a defenceless victim was unlike anything Alith had ever done. His hand began to tremble at the thought and a sudden fear gripped him. Then the memories of the Khainite ceremony resurfaced in his mind and his hatred for what he had witnessed quelled all revolt.

With a smooth, almost gentle motion, Alith drew the knife across the side of the elf maiden's neck, slicing the artery. Blood spurted from the wound, a crimson shower that soaked the fur underfoot and pooled on Alith's black boots. Fighting down his disgust, Alith moved to the next, and the next, and the next.

It was soon over and without another glance at those he had slain, Alith left the tent and moved on, blood dripping from his dagger.

'By whose leave do you travel on the road?' demanded the Anlec captain, his sword half-drawn from its sheath. Behind him stood several dozen warriors armed with barbed spears and covered from neck to knee in long coats of blackened mail, their faces hidden behind heavy aventails that covered their noses and mouths.

It was not the first patrol the Shadows had encountered on the road to Anlec, and each meeting had been a fraught experience for Alith and the others. Dressed in the garb of Athartists and Khainites and other cultists, the Anars had hidden their weapons in swathed bundles upon their packs and had no means to defend themselves if their enemies attacked.

The whole journey had been nerve-wracking, the masquerade a thin defence against inquiry. The group of elves had travelled along the main road to the capital for seven days, avoiding other parties where possible. Though they looked the part of cultists, they knew nothing of the rituals and workings of the cults and were forced to avoid others on the road. This had led to several instances of the Shadows being forced into the wilds at night so that they were not asked to share camps.

The number of soldiers on the road had been a problem as well. It was clear that Malekith's plan to draw attention to the south was working and the Shadows had passed by thousands of warriors marching towards the border with Tiranoc. For the most part these companies had been too preoccupied with their own fates to notice a small group of cultists, but there had been several times, such as this, when bored officers had decided to investigate.

'I did not know that the roads were barred to those who travelled to pay homage to Queen Morathi,' said Eoloran, bowing apologetically. Alith could imagine the self-loathing his grandfather felt at having to utter such words, but pride was the least casualty of their subterfuge.

'There's war afoot, you should know that,' snarled the captain. 'The roads must be clear for the queen's armies.'

'We would offer no obstruction, my noble friend,' said Eoloran, keeping his gaze downcast. 'In fact, we travel to the temples of Anlec so that we might entreat the gods to bless the endeavours of Morathi's favoured warriors. We are not fighters, and we owe everything to the great soldiers of Nagarythe who would protect us against the persecution of Bel Shanaar.'

It was a well-rehearsed turn of phrase, which Eoloran had devised after much thought, and it seemed to be working on the captain.

'There is little room in the city for vagabonds and wanderers,' he said. 'I warn you that there is a levy upon the people of Anlec to provide more warriors for the army. I see nothing of value in this motley band, but it is the queen's decree that all stand ready in defence of our realm.'

'You are right, we know little of war and battle,' said Eoloran. 'Yet, should our enemies threaten, none will fight harder than I in the defence of Nagarythe and her great traditions.'

Alith was forced to turn away and cough to conceal a short laugh at his grandfather's wordplay. Certainly the Anars would fight hardest to restore Malekith to the throne.

The captain mulled over this answer for a time. Having wearied of the lack of sport provided by Eoloran, he waved the Shadows aside, forcing them onto the muddied grass bank that lined the road. With glowers at the group as they passed, the soldiers formed up and marched on, leaving the Shadows in peace.

Eoloran urged them onwards, keen to put distance between the Shadows and the soldiers, and only after some time did he speak more freely again.

'I judge that we are no more than a day from Anlec, and we must be on our wits,' he warned. 'So far it seems that Malekith's ploy is working, for if the druchii suspected any attack on Anlec, all roads would be closed. We must enter the city before the threat is known, lest the gates be barred against all entry prior to our arrival. I feel that events will quickly come upon us. We must put haste before caution. We must reach Anlec before nightfall tomorrow.'

ANLEC WAS MORE of a fortress than a city, though massive in size and home to tens of thousands of elves. It was the greatest citadel in the world, built by Aenarion and Caledor Dragontamer to hold against the tide of daemons that had assailed Ulthuan. Immense walls encircled the city, bolstered along its circumference by twenty towers, each a small castle in its own right. Black and silver banners flapped in the spring wind from a hundred poles and the glint of weapons could be seen as hundreds of guards made their patrols along the battlements.

There were three gatehouses, each grander than the manse of Elanardris and protected by war machines and dozens of soldiers. The gates themselves were immense portals wrought from blackened iron and enchanted with the most powerful spells of Caledor. Walls extended like buttresses from beside the gates, creating a killing field into which bolts and arrows and spells could be cast upon any attacker. A ring of outer towers, each garrisoned by a hundred warriors, protected the approaches. Perhaps most daunting was the great moat of fire that encircled the entire city, which burnt with a magical green flame and could only be crossed at three mighty drawbridges.

It was across one of these bridges that the Shadows walked, the heat and crackling of the flames to either side. The sun was setting behind Anlec; the city rose out of the gloom like a black monster, spires and towers its horns and claws.

Once this place had been the beacon in the darkness, the fortress of Aenarion the Defender. Now the sight of its black granite buildings sent a shudder of fear through Alith and he cast a glance at Eothlir and Eoloran. Not for many centuries had they come to the city, ever since Morathi had usurped rule from the chancellors and councils left by Malekith. The stories of the dark rites and bloody rituals were enough to make the skin crawl, and the sight of the city left Alith's father and grandfather with pale, pinched faces.

They crossed the killing ground swiftly. Alith glanced up at the high walls to either side and lamented silently, fearful for any warrior doomed to assault Anlec. No doubt many thousands of loyal elves would lose their lives when Malekith attacked. Pushing these sombre thoughts from his mind, Alith heartened himself with the knowledge that the Shadows had arrived. It would be their purpose to ensure the gate opened to save those warriors from such a bloody fate. Seeing Anlec firsthand strengthened Alith's resolve and he took no small measure of pride in the idea that the Anars would play such a pivotal role in the war for Nagarythe.

Fires could be seen through the yawning maw of the open gate, flickering from the dark stone of the flanking towers and the huge arch of the portal. A chill swamped Alith as the Shadows passed into the gatehouse, as if all light had been extinguished. He suppressed the urge to glance backwards as the city swallowed them.

SIX

Anlec Restored

THE NIGHT WAS torn by the screams of sacrificial victims and the screeching entreaties of wild cultists. Alith stood at the window of the abandoned garrison tower and looked over Anlec. Fires of different colours broke the darkness, while bloodthirsty mobs ran amok in the streets below, fighting each other and dragging off the unwary to be sacrificed to the dark gods of the cytharai.

The Shadows had made their lair in a deserted building not far from the northern arc of the city wall. Once it had been home to hundreds of soldiers, but they had been moved south to confront the threat from Tiranoc. Like many parts of Anlec, the area was eerily quiet, the cultists preferring to keep to the centre of the city where the great temples were found. There was strength in numbers as the cults vied with each other for dominance.

There were chambers below the tower that the Anars had not ventured into since their first exploration, appalled by bloodstained floors and barbed manacles, broken blades and wicked brands. Shuddering at the thought of the torments that had been visited upon fellow elves, they had closed the doors and kept to the upper storeys.

'I had no idea that we could fall so low,' said Eoloran, appearing at Alith's shoulder. 'In this place of all, where once there was such dignity and honour, it pains me to look upon what we have become.'

'We are not all the same,' said Alith. 'Morathi has spread weakness and corruption, but Malekith will bring strength and resolve. There is still a future worth fighting for.'

Eoloran did not reply and Alith turned to look at his grandfather, to find that he was gazing at Alith with a smile.

'You make me proud to be an Anar,' said Eoloran, touching Alith's shoulder. 'Your father will be a great lord of the house, and you will be a fine prince of Nagarythe. When I see you, memories of the ancient past disappear and pain goes away. It is for the likes of you that we fought and bled, not these wretches that cavort through Aenarion's city.'

Eoloran's words warmed Alith's heart and he grasped his grandfather's hand.

'If I am so, it is because I have your example to follow,' said Alith. 'It is the fine legacy that you will leave us that stirs me, and I call myself Anar with such pride that I cannot put it into words. Where others faltered and fell into the darkness, you have stood unflinching, a shaft of light for all to follow.'

Eoloran's eyes glistened with tears and the two embraced, drawing comfort upon each other's love and putting aside the horrors that lay outside.

Breaking away after some time, Eoloran turned his eyes back to the window and his expression hardened.

'Those that have perpetrated these atrocities must be punished, Alith,' he said quietly. 'But do not confuse punishment with revenge. It is fear and anger, jealousy and hatred that feed these cults, stirring those darkest emotions that lie within us all. If we stay true to our ideals, the victory will be ours.'

For nine days the Shadows concealed themselves within the heart of the enemy. For the most part they stayed out of sight, but singly and in pairs they dared the city on occasion, to gather information and food. The daytime was less perilous than the night, for the orgies and sacrifices of the night before left the cultists sated for a while and the streets were quieter.

While the cultists ruled the night, the garrison of Anlec held sway in the daylight, patrolling the streets vigorously to ensure that total anarchy did not consume the city. It became clear that Morathi held the various forces in balance, indulging the cults to retain their support, yet reining back their excesses enough to ensure that some semblance of order was maintained.

It was late afternoon on the ninth day when Alith and Casadir took their turn to go out into the city and find out what news they could. Garbed in their elegant robes, swords concealed beneath the folds of cloth, the pair headed for the main plaza outside the palace. There was a guard of soldiers upon the steps that led up to the huge doors of the citadel, and a throng of elves was massing in the square.

There was a hum of conversation, an edge of fear to the atmosphere that drew Alith's attention.

'Let us split up and see what we can hear,' he said to Casadir. 'I will meet you back here in a short while.'

Casadir nodded and headed off to the right, passing in front of the steps. Alith turned left, towards the market stalls that had been set up on the edge of the square. He moved along the stalls, seemingly browsing the sellers' wares yet he was alert to the hubbub around him.

Amongst the usual fare of a market there were more sinister goods on sale. Ritual daggers inscribed with evil runes, talismans of the cytharai and parchments filled with incantations to the underworld gods. As he eyed a silver amulet forged in the shape of Ereth Khial's sigil, Alith heard a passer-by mention the name of Malekith. Turning, he followed the group of elves across the square. Amongst the languid strolls of the other elves, these five moved with purpose towards the street of temples that lay to the west.

'Riders came in early this morning,' one was saying. Though the air had not yet thrown off the full chill of winter, she was dressed in a diaphanous veil that was wound loosely about her body, her pale flesh exposed for all to see. Upon her back were scars in the shapes of runes, and her flesh was pierced with rings of gold. 'My brother was at the south gate and overheard what was said to the guards. The riders told the garrison that Prince Malekith advances on Anlec with an army.'

This was greeted with twitters of fear from the other elves.

'Surely he won't attack the city?' said one.

'Are we safe here?' asked another.

'Perhaps we should flee,' suggested another.

'There is no time!' said the first, her voice shrill. 'The riders say that the prince is but a day's march away. His wrath will fall upon us ere sundown tomorrow!'

A thrill of excitement pulsed through Alith on hearing these words. He longed to follow the group further but they had turned up the steps that led to the shrine of Atharti and he had no desire to enter that damned place. Cutting down a side street, Alith circled quickly back towards the square and there he found Casadir waiting for him.

'Malekith is close,' Casadir whispered as Alith came up to him. 'I heard a captain of the guards sending his company to the walls to make ready the defence of the city.'

'He is but a day away,' said Alith as the two of them walked together back towards the abandoned barracks. 'Or so some believe.'

'Morathi is keeping this news secret for the moment,' said Casadir. 'She fears that there will be panic if the people find out that the prince is about to besiege Anlec. Perhaps we should spread the word, and hope that we can cause fear and confusion and hinder her plans.'

'That might be a good idea, but I would speak with my father first,' said Alith.

'I will linger a while longer and see what else I can learn,' said Casadir. 'I will return to the tower before dusk.'

'Be careful,' said Alith. 'As this news spreads, I fear hysteria will grip many of the cultists. The sacrificial fires will burn high this night.'

Casadir nodded reassuringly and disappeared into the gathering crowds. Alith headed for the Shadows' lair at a brisk pace, keen to move quickly but fearful of attracting attention. If Malekith was indeed but a day away, his approach having been kept secret by Morathi's warriors, the Anars had little time to prepare their plan of action. Though the prospect filled Alith with excitement, he felt an underlying dread that the Shadows would fail and the prince would be destroyed upon the city's walls.

As ALITH HAD predicted, the night was punctuated by much rowdy behaviour, the beating of drums and the blare of horns as word spread of Malekith's approach. Amongst the mayhem of the cultists' tribulations and celebrations, the tramp of marching feet reverberated around the city as the garrison turned out and such forces as were near at hand were brought back to Anlec. The Shadows kept to their dark tower whilst this hysteria gripped the druchii, fearful of being set upon in the streets.

Alith spent a sleepless night with the others, alternating between keeping watch for intruders and discussing the coming events with his father and grandfather. When the rosy haze of dawn crept across the horizon, barely glimmering over the stone wall of the city, Alith was in the highest chamber of the tower with Eothlir and Eoloran. In the light of the dawn and by the fires of torches along the ramparts, they could see a great many warriors standing ready to receive an assault.

A singular question had vexed Eoloran since their arrival at Anlec and he gave voice to it again as the sun crept onto the sill of the window.

'From which direction will Malekith attack?' he asked, though posing the question to nobody in particular. 'We must know which gate needs to be opened.'

'I have heard conflicting reports,' said Eothlir. 'Some believe he marches direct from Tiranoc and comes from the south, while others have said that he comes from Ellyrion in the east.'

'From his messages, we know the prince intended to muster his army in Ellyrion,' said Alith. 'The east seems the most probable direction.'

'That does seem likely, but such is the confusion that I have even heard tell that he comes from the west, having landed at Galthyr. While I suspect that you are right, Alith, it is not beyond the bounds of reason to wonder if his plans have changed, either through his own decision or forced by the actions of the druchii. A wrong assumption would not only cost us our lives but could damn Nagarythe to this torment for many more years to come.'

'Then we must see for ourselves what is the truth,' said Alith.

'And from where would you look?' said Eothlir. 'The walls are full of warriors and no tower save for the citadel is high enough to see any distance.'

'When faced with only one path, no matter how dangerous, that is the route we must take,' said Alith. 'I will scale the citadel for a vantage point that will give us sufficient warning of Malekith's approach. We need time to order ourselves and reach whichever gatehouse he assaults, and for that we need to know his intent as soon as possible.'

'If only there were some way we could send or receive word from the prince,' said Eoloran. 'A bird, perhaps?'

'I fear that Morathi's eye will be alert to such things, and we risk revealing ourselves for only an uncertain gain,' said Eothlir. He paced to the window and back, obviously distressed. 'It seems unwise to send out a solitary spy, Alith.'

'Better that only one is caught than all, and I would not ask any other to risk themselves,' said Alith. 'Do not be too disheartened. Anarchy still holds sway over much of the city, though I am sure before long Morathi will instil a greater fear in her followers than Malekith. The shadows are still deep at this early hour and a lone figure moves unseen where many would attract attention.'

'I am still not certain,' said Eoloran.

'Then you'd best bind me and leave me here, for I intend to go!' snapped Alith, who then fell silent, taken aback by his own determination. He continued in a more measured tone. 'I promise I will not take any unnecessary risks, and if I hear word that confirms Malekith's plan I shall return immediately and dare nothing. All eyes are outwards at this moment, none will see a solitary shadow.'

Eoloran said nothing and turned away, giving his assent yet not able to say as much. Eothlir stepped in front of Alith and placed a hand upon the back of his son's head. He pulled him closer and kissed his son upon the brow.

'May all the gods of light watch over you,' said Eothlir, stepping back. 'You must be quick, but in your haste do nothing rash.'

'Believe me, I would like nothing more than to return whole and unharmed!' said Alith with a nervous laugh. He waved away his father's concerns and headed for the door.

Alith stripped off the cumbersome Salthite robes he had been wearing and adorned himself with a simple loincloth and red cloak, such as might be worn by a Khainite. He wrapped a ragged sash around his waist in which he placed a serrated knife. Thus disguised, Alith slipped from the tower without a word to his fellow Shadows.

The street directly outside was empty and the tower itself concealed the view from the walls. Hugging close to the side of the street, where tall-roofed buildings had once housed thousands of warriors, Alith headed for the centre of the city.

Feeling that he would arouse less attention on the main roads than if he were seen skulking through alleys and side streets, Alith took the most direct route to the central plaza, coming at the palace of Aenarion from north-west. Here were many of the homes of Anlec's rulers, most empty while their noble owners commanded troops on the wall or were with their soldiers far to the south. Leaping over garden walls and flitting past bubbling fountains, Alith looked for a means by which he could gain entry to the citadel.

Where once the spire of Anlec had stood alone in the centre of the city, the passing centuries had brought more buildings, each getting closer and closer to the palace. Though the square south of the citadel was open, generations ago the houses of the nobles had joined to the northern wall of the palace and it was here that Alith headed.

As easily as he had once jumped from rock to rock on the mountainsides of his home, Alith leapt into the bare branches of a tree close to the porch of one of the manses. From here he jumped onto the roof. Sliding past an open dormer window, Alith stooped low to avoid being seen and ran along the angled tiles at the ridge of the steep roof. There was some distance between the manse's gable and the wall of the citadel and Alith took the leap at a run, hurling himself over the drop. His fingers found a hold on the age-worn stones of the wall and, after a moment of scrabbling, his naked toes also found purchase. Spider-like, Alith shimmied to the top of the wall. After peering over to ensure he was unobserved, he slipped through the tall crenellations onto the rampart beyond.

His vantage point was no better than that elsewhere and he could see no further than the curtain wall of Anlec. He needed to climb higher if he was to get a good view of the surrounding plains and witness the arrival of Malekith.

Keeping to the western side of the citadel, still shrouded from the rising sun, Alith climbed up turrets and minarets, sidled along ledges and clawed his way up steepling roofs until he was far above the city. Pausing beneath the sill of an arched window, Alith glanced down and saw figures on the streets below, made incredibly small by distance. There was a great throng in the central plaza and the street of temples was full of people. Elsewhere there were very few elves. Alith could see over the walls, but only to the dark west, the direction least likely to reveal Malekith. He needed to look east, to confirm that Malekith's army indeed approached from that direction.

Crawling along a narrow gutter, Alith came to the edge of a roof overlooking the top of an open turret below.

Three warriors stood guard at the door beneath him, but their eyes were looking outwards, seeking the same thing he was. Ignoring the soldiers, Alith pulled himself across the gap above their heads and silently climbed higher.

The sun bathed Alith with its warmth as he rounded the golden pinnacle of a minaret. The sensation gave him a sudden flash of memory. He remembered lying on the lawn of the manse with his mother, talking about Ashniel. It was with guilt that Alith realised he had not thought of Ashniel since leaving Elanardris, so possessed had he been of the coming mission. The memory heartened him, for if they succeeded today, Malekith would regain his throne and Ashniel would no longer be bound to her safe retreat in the mountains.

Spurred on by his desire, Alith looked around for surer footing and saw a balcony not far above him. With a spring, he grabbed hold of the curving stone supports beneath the balcony and pulled himself up to an elegant balustrade. A huge windowed door stood open, leading into a darkened chamber.

Alith heard voices and froze.

After a moment, he relaxed as the voices receded into echoes. Standing to one side of the door so that he could not be seen from within, Alith had the chance to look out properly. Everything to the south and east was laid out before him. The roads running from the gates travelled directly away from the city as far as the horizon, broken only at the raised bridges across the fire moat.

For some time Alith stayed there, seeking some clue that would confirm Malekith's approach. As time dragged on, doubt gnawed at Alith's resolve, his expectation slowly leeched from him as the sun rose higher and higher. On occasion there would be the sound of footfalls within the citadel and Alith held his dagger ready in case someone came upon him.

Even as the last of Alith's hope was waning, he spied a flashing to the south-east. Shading his eyes, he looked more carefully. It was the unmistakeable glint of sunlight on metal. Dust rose on the horizon and Alith watched in awe as the host of Malekith marched towards the city.

Alith had never seen so many warriors. Thousands upon thousands of knights, spearmen and archers advanced, spreading far to either side of the southern road. As the army came nearer and nearer, Alith saw white chariots pulled by fierce lions, and the banners of other realms flapping above the endless ranks of warriors: Ellyrion, Yvresse, Tiranoc and Chrace. Front and centre were the silver and black standards of Nagarythe, the warriors of Prince Malekith. At this distance, Alith could see nothing of the prince, though his black-armoured knights were visible. Winged creatures circled in the clouds above the army: three pegasi and a mighty griffon with riders on their backs.

It was clear that Malekith marched for the southern gate, his army forming up towards the drawbridge in that direction. Relieved, Alith was about to start his long climb down when raised voices from within the citadel attracted his attention. He risked a glance into the chamber and found it was empty. However, through an archway at the far side of the room he could see an inner hall and his heart skipped a beat when a tall figure crossed into view.

She was tall, majestic, her black hair spilling down her back in languid curls. She wore a purple gown of gossamer cloth, which wreathed about her white skin like smoke. There was a strange shadow about her, a barely visible miasma of darkness that seemed to teem with a life of its own. Alith fancied he saw tiny glaring eyes and fangs appearing in that shadowy mist. In her hand the matriarch held an iron staff topped with a strange horned skull and her hair was bound by a golden tiara set with diamonds and emeralds.

Morathi!

Alith was spellbound by her beauty, though he knew in his heart that she was utterly wicked. Her back was to him but the curve of her shoulders and hips stirred a passion inside Alith that he had not known he possessed. He longed to lose himself in that lustrous hair and feel the touch of that smooth skin beneath his fingers.

The sound of voices broke the enchantment and Alith realised the sorceress-queen was not alone. Black-robed figures passed back and forth across the archway, their heads shaved bald and tattooed with strange designs. He could not hear the words being said and against the promise he had made his father, Alith slipped into the chamber to come closer to the hated Witch Queen.

From this new position Alith could see more clearly into the central hall. He recoiled from what he saw. Beyond Morathi burned a multi-coloured flame, which recalled to Alith the tales of the Flame of Asuryan that had blessed Aenarion at the dawn of time. Yet there was nothing holy about these fires, their licking tongues strangely jagged and angular. A half-formed shape dwelt in the middle of the twisting flames. Though indistinct, made up from but also not part of the flames, it looked like the face of a bird, perhaps an eagle or a vulture, shifting between two different appearances. Its eyes glittered with power and to Alith the flames looked like a pair of immense wings furled around some otherworldly creature.

'Their time will come,' intoned a solemn, deep voice that resounded around the hall. The words came from the flames, but did not seem to be elvish, though Alith understood them easily. It was if the words came from a language that bound all other languages together, utterly recognisable and yet totally different.

'The winding road forks many times,' warned another, with a cackle.

'And we see where all paths lead,' said the first voice.

'But not when,' responded the second.

Alith was confused, for both voices seemed to come from the flaming apparition, yet they had about them the tone of an argument.

'And in return for this undertaking, I shall expect to be rewarded.' Morathi cut across the bickering, her voice as luxuriant as her body. 'When I call, I will be answered.'

'It makes demands,' said the screeching voice.

'Demands,' echoed the deeper voice with a guffawing laugh.

'I do not fear you,' said Morathi. 'It is you that came to me. If you wish to return to your infernal place with no bargain made, I shall not stop you. If you wish to return with what you came for, then you will treat me as an equal.'

'Equal?' the creature's shrill voice bit like splinters inside Alith's ears and he winced at the sound.

'Equal in all things, we are,' said the deep voice, reassuring and gentle. 'As partners we make this trade.'

'Remember always that there are things a mortal can do, places a mortal can go, that are beyond your reach, daemon,' said Morathi. A trickle of dread ran down Alith's spine at the mention of daemons and he was gripped by the urge to flee. Shaking, he mastered his fear and forced himself to listen on. 'It was our kind that bound you to the prison that holds you. Should you wish to reach beyond that prison, it is with mortal hands that you must work.'

'Always so arrogant,' mocked the sharp voice. 'Mortals imprisoned us? You would do well to know that no prison can keep us for all time, and no barrier holds us wholly back. There will come a reckoning with mortals, oh yes. A reckoning.'

'Shut up, you stupid old crow,' said the other voice. 'Do not listen to his idle chatter, queen of the elves. Our deal is set, our pact is made. Your followers shall go into the north and teach the humans of the sorcerous ways and in exchange the power of the Everchanging Veil shall be yours.'

'I mark this pact with blood,' said Morathi. Her staff tip lashed out towards one of the sorcerers and he was suddenly swathed with blood from hundreds of small cuts, his screams echoing around the hall. With a contemptuous sweep of her staff, Morathi hurled the still-shrieking acolyte into the fires. The flames burnt brightly for a moment, almost blinding, while harsh laughter resounded from the walls.

'Your fate is woven,' said the daemon. With another flash the flames disappeared, leaving the hall in darkness.

Alith blinked to clear the spots from his vision. It was a moment before he realised Morathi had turned and was heading towards the archway. In a panic, Alith sprinted back out onto the balcony and threw himself over its rail, grasping hold of the supports as he dropped. He clung there, grimacing, as he heard the tap of narrow-heeled boots clicking on the stone above. When Morathi spoke next, her voice was almost on top of Alith and his skin crawled at being so close to the sorceress-queen.

'How remarkable,' Morathi said. 'I thought the fires beyond him. It seems as if my son has grown up finally.'

'Do you not feel its presence, majesty?' hissed one of the sorceresses. 'The circlet upon his helm, it burns with the ancient powers.'

'Yes,' said Morathi with a sigh. 'Has he the will to wield that power though? We shall soon see. It is an artefact from before Ulthuan was raised from the seas. Be wary, my darlings, or we shall all suffer the consequences.'

'Prince Malekith has crossed the fires, your majesty,' said another acolyte. 'What if he takes the city?'

'Send your familiars out to spread the word to the others, our agents in the mountains and the cities,' purred the queen. 'A single battle does not win a war. Should he enter Anlec, he will come to me.'

Footsteps receded into the citadel and Alith let out his breath in an explosive gasp, almost losing his hold on the pitted stonework. There was too much to think about and not enough time to consider everything. Alith focussed on what was important: the Shadows had to open the southern gate, and quickly.

THERE WERE FEW elves on the streets of Anlec, and those that were spared no second glance to thirty Naggarothi garbed in short mail coats and cloaks of black who marched along the road with bows in hand and grim looks on their faces. Shouts and cries echoed down from the walls, but from within the city it was impossible to know how the battle progressed. Now and then Alith saw one or other of the pegasus-riding mages sweep down to the ramparts unleashing magical fire or forks of lightning. The screams of the dying grew in number as an elven prince atop the back of a majestic griffon crashed into the soldiers upon the walls. His icy lance and the claws of the monster gouged great wounds in the druchii regiments. All else save for the clouds of arrows that passed back and forth was hidden from view.

'Wait!' hissed Eoloran as the Shadows came into sight of the wide plaza behind the south gate. The open square was filled with elves howling and screaming: Khainites. Their priests and priestesses moved amongst the shrieking mob, sprinkling them with handfuls of blessed blood, exhorting them to slay the city's attackers for the glory of Khaine. Hateful oaths to slay Malekith echoed from the gate and surrounding buildings. Some of the Khainites fell to their knees, wailing and snarling, dousing themselves with blood from silver chalices, slicking their hair and painting runes upon the flesh with the blood of their companions. Bodies littered the flagstones where the most frenzied worshippers had fallen upon their fellows with knives and bare hands. The skin and flesh had been torn from them, their organs plucked free and devoured by the demented cultists.

Looking up towards the high towers of the gatehouse, Alith could see a great deal of activity. Archers were gathering from the surrounding walls, pouring their arrows into some foe close at hand.

'We must take the gatehouse!' hissed Alith, taking a step.

'We will be butchered,' replied Eothlir, grabbing Alith by the arm and dragging him back as the other warriors took shelter in the shadow of the wall.

'Malekith's soldiers will all be killed,' said Alith, snatching his arm from his father's grasp.

'And so will we,' snarled Eoloran. A bell rang out three times from the direction of the citadel. A moment later a loud grinding echoed across the courtyard. Eoloran pointed towards the gate towers. 'Look!'

The huge gates of Anlec swung open with a rattle of heavy chains. On the gate towers, naked slaves were bent to two great wheels as their druchii masters lashed their backs with barbed scourges. Like a dam being opened, the Khainites flooded out of the city, whooping and screaming with murderous delight.

The gates closed with a shuddering thud as the last of the Khainites passed through. The courtyard was empty and silent, save for the distant battle cries and clash of war from beyond the walls.

'Now is our chance!' said Eoloran, waving Alith and the others forwards.

Bows and arrows readied, the Shadows ran swiftly across the gate square. As had been discussed before setting out from their hiding place, Alith and Eothlir led half of the Shadows towards the eastern tower while Eoloran took the rest towards the western tower. Eoloran's group disappeared through the doorway whilst Alith was still a dozen paces from the other tower.

A figure clad in chainmail appeared at the doorway right in front of Alith. The druchii's eyes widened with shock a moment before an arrow from Anadriel took him in the cheek, hurling him against the stone of the tower. Alith leapt past and was engulfed by the torchlit gloom.

The stair spiralled to the right and Alith dashed up the steps in bounding leaps, the other Shadows closely on his heels. No other druchii came down and as Alith burst from the door at the top he found himself looking out across the plains of Anlec and the army of Malekith.

He had only time to register rank upon rank of spears and knights and archers before movement to his left caught Alith's eye. There were dozens of warriors on the wall next to the tower and the closest were turning towards him.

Without thought, Alith aimed and loosed his first arrow, which punched through the gilded breastplate of the closest warrior. As he nocked and shot his next, Eothlir and the other Shadows fanned out around him to add their own missiles to the volley. Within moments, two dozen druchii lay dead and wounded upon the stones.

'The gate wheel,' said Eothlir, pointing up to the next level of the tower above the parapet.

'Five with me, the rest hold the door,' ordered Alith, running to a flight of steps atop the gatehouse wall. He rammed his bow into its quiver and drew his sword as he bounded up the final few steps to the roof of the tower.

The slavemasters were ready and a cracking whip lashed out to greet Alith as he ran onto the open space. Pain bit through his left arm and he glanced down to see the sleeve of his shirt in tatters, a bloody wound on his forearm. Snarling, he ducked beneath the flailing barbs that snaked out towards him and launched at the whip's wielder. The druchii drew a knife with his free hand but

Alith was too quick, driving the point of his sword into the slavemaster's bare chest.

More burning pain screamed across Alith's back as another wicked blow tore at his cloak and flesh, ripping through to the muscle. He stumbled but Casadir was there, dashing past to cut the whipmaster's arm at the elbow. A reverse slash took the elf's head clean off.

The emaciated slaves at the wheel threw themselves at their tormentors, battering and swinging with the chains of their manacles. As Anadriel helped him to his feet, Alith spared a glance across to the other tower and below. He could see black-armoured bodies tossed over the parapet by the Shadows. Much further down, in the killing ground between the outcrops of the walls, a phalanx of spearmen pressed towards the gate, their shields raised against the arrows falling upon them.

'The gate!' shouted Alith, grabbing the nearest slave and pushing him back towards the capstan. 'Open the gate for your freedom!'

Alith lunged onto the nearest bar of the wheel and heaved, the weeping slaves taking their places around him. Fire burned along Alith's spine and he bit back a scream of pain as he bent all of his strength to the task. With a clank-clank-clank the chains tightened and gears turned.

'Keep going!' yelled Casadir from just behind Alith. 'The gate's opening!'

The wheel gathered momentum and within moments ran freely as the gate beneath swung open on its own weight. Alith flopped to the ground with a curse. Casadir dragged him sideways from under the feet of the following slaves as the wheel continued to spin.

With a thunderous crash, the gates slammed against the walls.

Shouts of joy and laughter echoed up from the spearmen below and Alith pulled himself up with Casadir's help and staggered to the parapet. Thousands of warriors streamed into the city. On the wall, Eothlir stood upon the battlement, the unfurled banner of the Anars held high in his hand.

As Casadir bound Alith's wounds with the remains of his cloak, a cry of dismay came from the other Shadows atop the tower. Looking down into the square inside the gate, Alith saw that the druchii beastmasters had unleashed their monstrous creatures upon the army of Malekith. Two enormous hydras advanced on the spearmen, smoke and fire billowing from their jaws.

As the first of the monsters closed on them, the spearmen formed a shield wall, their weapons jutting like silver spines. With a clatter of wheels on stone, the chariots of Chrace charged through the gate and swung around the spearmen. Drawn by white lions, the chariots headed straight for one of the hydras; their prince, a tall elf wielding a gleaming double-headed axe, led the charge.

To the right, more cages were opened and a stream of unnatural beasts loped, skittered and slithered across the stones. Taken from the Anullii and the wastes across the sea north of Ulthuan, the Chaotic monsters lurched forwards, driven by the goads and whips of the beastmasters. More spearmen moved up beside the Naggarothi, their blue banners marked with the symbols of Yvresse.

Alith turned his attention back to the Naggarothi warriors as the flicker of flames and the roars of the lions echoed across the courtyard. The other hydra was almost upon the spearmen. The creature drew back its heads and a shouted command cut across the cacophony filling the square. As one, the spearmen dropped down, raising their shields above their heads. Fire spewed from the hydra's heads, lapping against the shields of the warriors. Some fell, wreathed with smoke and fire, their cries shrill. As the flames dispersed a bank of charnel smoke drifted away from the scorched warriors.

'Kill the handlers!' gasped Alith, drawing his bow.

A shower of arrows fell upon the beastmasters behind the hydra and each fell, pierced by several shafts. As the Shadows turned their missiles upon the other druchii emerging from the cages, Alith watched the hydra.

Suddenly free of the goading whips and spears of its handlers, the hydra slowed. Three of its heads bent back to examine their unmoving corpses, the other four rose into the air, nostrils flaring as they caught the scent of basilisks and khaltaurs. Fiery venom dripping from its maws, the hydra heaved around its bulk and spied its enemies from the mountains. With hisses issuing from its many throats, the hydra lumbered into a run, heading for the other monsters.

'Alith!' Eoloran called up from below. 'Come down here.'

Casadir tightened the knot on the makeshift bandages around Alith's torso and then took off his own cloak and fixed it around Alith's shoulders. With a nod of thanks, Alith trotted down the stairs. The pain had subsided but his back was numb, and twice he almost stumbled as he hurried down the steps.

Coming out onto the rampart, Alith found his father and grandfather in conversation with a majestic elf lord clad in golden armour. He was dark of hair and eye, taller and broader than both Eoloran and Eothlir. He turned as Alith walked out of the tower, a smile on his lips.

'Alith, I would like you to meet a very special person,' said Eothlir, laying an arm across his son's shoulders and pulling him forwards. 'This is Prince Malekith.'

Alith bowed out of instinct, his eyes not leaving the prince's face. Malekith leaned forwards and took Alith by the arm, pulling him upright.

'It is not you that should bow, it is I,' said Malekith, and then he did so, sweeping aside his cloak and lowering himself to one knee for a heartbeat before standing again. 'I owe you a debt that will not easily be repaid.'

'Free Nagarythe and I will consider us even,' said Alith.

'Alith!' snapped Eoloran, but Malekith waved away his rebuke with a laugh.

'He is of the Anars, that is for sure,' said the prince. He turned his gaze back to Alith and his expression was earnest. 'I agree to my part of the bargain. The tyranny of Morathi will end today.'

The prince's attention was drawn to a captain of the spearmen who was striding up the steps to the wall. Malekith waved him forward.

'This is the noble Yeasir, commander of Nagarythe and my most trusted lieutenant,' said Malekith. Yeasir nodded his head in greeting, somewhat uncertainly. Malekith clapped a hand to the shoulder of his second-in-command.

'Well done!' the prince exclaimed. 'I knew you would not let me down.'

'Highness?' said Yeasir.

'The city, you fool,' laughed Malekith. 'Now that we are in, it is only a matter of time. I have you to thank for that.'

'Thank you, highness, but I think you deserve more credit than I,' said Yeasir. He looked at the Anars. 'And without these noble warriors, I would still be stood outside, or perhaps lying outside with an arrow in my belly.'

'Yes, well I have thanked them enough already,' said Malekith. 'It would be best not to give them too much credit, otherwise who knows what ideas they might get.'

'How did they come to be here?' asked Yeasir.

'Malekith sent word to us many days ago,' said Eoloran. He went on to explain the plan devised with Malekith and how the Anars had infiltrated the city.

'Well, you have my gratitude, prince,' said Yeasir with a deep bow. He turned to Malekith with a frown. 'I must admit to being somewhat hurt that you did not feel that you could trust me with this counsel, highness.'

'Would that I could have,' said Malekith airily. 'I trust you more than I trust my own sword arm, Yeasir. I could not divulge my plan to you lest it affect your actions in battle. I wanted the defenders to know nothing was amiss until the gates were opened, and foreknowledge of the Anars' presence may well have meant that you held back until the gates were already flung wide. We needed to keep the pressure on so that all eyes were turned outwards rather than inwards.'

Malekith then turned to Eoloran.

'If you would excuse me, I believe my mother is waiting for me,' the Naggarothi prince said, now empty of all humour.

PART TWO

Exile in Tiranoc; An Usurper's Folly;
Hope Restored; A Banner Falls

SEVEN

A Bitter Parting

Conversation and laughter spilled across the lawns of the Anars' manse in harmony with the pattering of fountains, against a low backdrop of flutes and harps. Three pavilions of red and white, hung with golden chains studded with precious gems, dominated the gardens. Within and without these huge tents, the guests of the Anars strolled and talked, enjoying the midsummer sun.

Nearly twenty years of relative peace had seen the fortunes of the Anars wax again and many of the wealthiest and most powerful nobles of Nagarythe attended Alith's ascension gala. It was his coming-of-age, an occasion of great celebration for the family and their allies. Even Prince Malekith had sent his warmest regards, though his business in the court of Anlec had prevented him from attending, a distraction he professed to regret deeply.

Eoloran had not been surprised by the prince's absence, and Alith also knew well that while Malekith had restored his rule, the problems of the Naggarothi were not yet wholly behind them. Many of the cultists' leaders had escaped capture and hidden, in Nagarythe and other realms of Ulthuan. There was an occasional murmur of uprising, though such demonstrations as happened were local and easily curbed by Malekith's warriors.

The threat of Morathi had receded but not disappeared. Malekith had promised mercy for his mother and the former queen was a prisoner of the Phoenix King in Tiranoc. Though Bel Shanaar forbade her visitors save for her son, and she was kept guarded in chambers lined with magical wards, there were some that believed Morathi still orchestrated the actions of the cults from afar.

Such worries and suspicions were far from Alith's mind on this momentous day. Not only was he a true lord of Elanardris and a prince of Nagarythe, he was also about to make a declaration that he had longed to make for many years.

As the afternoon sun sank towards the horizon, the attendants of the manse marshalled the guests into the main marquee. Censers puffed wisps of fragrant smoke into the air, filling the space with the fresh perfume of mountain flowers. Bunches of white-petalled hill roses and ruby-bloomed caelentha decorated the poles that held up the high roof. Servants swayed effortlessly through the throng with platters of silver, laden with the most exquisite delicacies of Ulthuan and her distant colonies.

A stage of white wood had been erected at one end, gilded with the griffon's wing crest of the Anars. Upon a high-backed chair, Eoloran looked out upon the sea of guests that filled the tent and spilled out onto the grass beyond. His visitors were dressed in their finest clothes, with feathery hats and glittering crowns, bejewelled armlets and necklaces, gowns embroidered with silver thread and hemmed with gilded stars.

Eothlir stood to his father's right hand and Alith to the left. Caenthras stood beside Eothlir while Alith was flanked by Ashniel. She looked resplendent in a gown of soft yellow, which was gathered up in silken billowing clouds about her arms. Golden chains bound her hair in a complex of braids and a single oval diamond hung on a golden necklace around her alabaster neck. She exuded serenity amongst the hubbub of the elves, maintaining an air of cool and noble poise. Alith continually glanced sideways at his love, feeling her beauty lap upon him like the gently cooling waves of a lake's shore.

When all the guests were assembled, Eoloran stood and raised his hands in greeting.

'My most noble friends, welcome to Elanardris,' he declared with a smile. 'It is my honour to have such fine company to witness the ascension of my grandson to adulthood. Many times he has proven his worth, and it is right that we now give praise to his achievements.'

There was a whisper of assent and a forest of hands rose in the air holding crystal goblets and golden cups filled with dark wine. Eoloran took a chalice from a low table set before his throne and raised it in both hands above his head.

'I am Prince Eoloran Anar, lord of Elanardris,' he intoned, his voice quiet and assured. 'My blood hath passed into my son Eothlir, and from he into his son, Alith. My grandson hath come of age this day and upon him now fall the duties of a lord and prince of Ulthuan.'

He took a sip of the wine and lowered the chalice.

'As we gave blood to defend our people alongside great Aenarion, now we take of this wine in remembrance of the sacrifice he made,' Eoloran said solemnly. He drank once more. 'Blood we have shed again to restore peace to these lands, and Alith gave of himself in that conflict. Though we all wish it that such brave deeds are never needed again, my grandson has shown he has the mettle and the spirit to prevail against the darkness that would threaten our homes and our society.'

The mood in the marquee had become sombre as the crowd of elves nodded sincerely, while a few wept silently at the memory of what had befallen Nagarythe. Eoloran allowed his audience to hold their thoughts and memories for a while, his head bowed in meditation as he also contemplated the dark acts he had committed in his life. Straightening, he smiled again.

'Yet it is not for the past that we mark this day, but for the future. Alith is, as are all our children, our legacy to each other and the world. As I pass over this chalice, so I pass my hopes and dreams to the generations to come, and wish them the peace and happiness we have also enjoyed. Into their stewardship we place our great civilisation, from Elanardris to Anlec, Tiranoc to Yvresse, Ulthuan to the far colonies. Into their guardianship we entrust the prosperity of our people, from farmer to prince, servant to king.'

Eoloran turned and proffered the chalice to Alith, who took the goblet with slow ceremony.

'Upon this day of my passing from childhood to adulthood, I accept the duties that fall to me,' Alith said. 'As I have enjoyed the privilege and harmony to learn and grow beneath the boughs of my father and grandfather, I now extend the protection and wisdom of my position to those that will come after.'

Alith then lifted the cup to his lips and took a mouthful of wine. He savoured the deep, rich taste before swallowing, taking in the import of the ceremony just as he imbibed the liquid. No more a child, he was a true lord of House Anar. Pride filled him. Pride that he was Anar, and pride that already he had shown himself worthy of the title of prince.

Alith realised he had closed his eyes. Opening them, he saw expectation in the faces before him: his father and grandfather, Caenthras and Ashniel, and the dozens of elves who had come from across Nagarythe to witness this. Lowering the goblet, Alith smiled and applause filled the tent, with no few shouts of happiness and encouragement.

Caenthras stepped up, hands raised for silence. As quiet descended eventually, the elven lord looked at Alith, his expression thoughtful.

'Let me congratulate Alith on his ascension,' said Caenthras, crossing the stage to embrace the newest prince of the Anars. 'And also let me invite him to say to you all that which we have spoken about between ourselves for many years.'

Suddenly self-conscious, Alith stepped away from Caenthras and turned to Ashniel. He took her left hand in his, still holding the wine in his other.

'On this day of my ascension, it is now time for me to declare to the world that which has been plain for all to see,' said Alith. He looked out towards the audience, joy washing away his nervousness. 'A year hence from this day, House Anar and House Moranin will be joined not just by alliance and friendship, but also by marriage. It is my intent to marry Ashniel and she will become a princess of the Anars as I become a prince of the Moranins. A more profound love I cannot imagine, nor a more fitting dedication to the future than to pave the way for the new heir of the Anars and many more generations to follow.'

'I bless this union between our houses,' said Eoloran.

'I am proud to call Alith a future son,' added Caenthras.

Alith took another sip of wine and held the goblet to Ashniel's pale lips. Her eyes glittered as she looked at him. Her fingers curled around his hand, cool to the touch, and tipped the cup so that the wine wetted her lips and no more. Lifting the chalice away, Ashniel kissed Alith on the forehead, leaving the lightest smudge of red on his brow. She turned with delicate precision, kissed her father upon the cheek and then addressed the crowd.

'There are not the words yet created to express my feelings at this moment, though poets have bent their skills to such labour for a lifetime to fashion them,' she said. 'In the Anars there is great strength, and in my house also. The blood of princes runs deep in Nagarythe, in our bodies and in the land. The generations to come from this lineage will be fair and noble, brave and strong, compassionate and wise. All that is great in the Naggarothi will be made greater yet.'

Alith hooked Ashniel's arm under his and they walked down the short steps from the stage, to be surrounded by the surging elves, who pushed forwards to congratulate the couple and shower them with embraces and kisses. The sides of the marquee were thrown back and the gentle summer breeze stirred the perfumed mists and cast the petals of the flowers into the air above them.

ALITH WAS AWAKE immediately. He did not know what had woken him, but a moment's listening brought sounds of a commotion from the main part of the manse. Evening sun streamed through the unshuttered window; a last defiance against the swiftly approaching Season of Frost. Alith did not remember falling asleep, though upon the table beside his bed lay half-open a lengthy tome by Analdiris of Saphery, analysing the warrior-poetry of Elynuris the Accepter.

Pushing aside the grogginess from his unplanned nap, Alith pulled himself from the bed and straightened his clothes. He heard his father call his name. As he opened the door, Alith found two servants bustling down the corridor, lanterns in their hands.

'What is it?' demanded Alith, grabbing the arm of Cirothir as he jogged past.

'Warriors are marching along the road, prince,' said the servant. 'Your father awaits you at the front of the manse.'

Alith hesitated, deciding whether to fetch his bow. He decided against it, twenty years of peace having eased the paranoia that had once gripped the Anar household. In all likelihood, the soldiers were merely a guard of honour for an important guest. Grabbing a cloak from the chest at the foot of his bed, Alith hurried to the foyer and out onto the courtyard.

Eothlir was there with several other retainers. Eoloran was currently away from the manse, signing a treaty with one of the other noble houses, while Maieth was with Ashniel at the manse of the Moranins making arrangements for the wedding. Father glanced at son with raised eyebrows.

'I have had no word of any important visitor,' said Eothlir. Alith noted that his father had a short sword strapped to his belt. It seemed Eothlir was less willing to forget the troubles of the past.

The clatter of hooves echoed into the courtyard and riders came to a stop just beyond the gateway. Alith could see a column of a few dozen knights, with black pennants on their silver lances. Their leader swung down to the road and crossed quickly to the side of the gate, where Gerithon was standing. There was a short exchange between the two and Gerithon bowed and turned towards the manse with an outstretched arm.

The figure strode purposefully along the pavement, his black-enamelled armour glistening like oil, his dark cloak swirling in his wake. Alith relaxed as the figure came nearer and removed his helm: it was Yeasir, Malekith's captain and commander of Nagarythe. Eothlir seemed set at ease as well, and stepped forwards to meet the Anlec officer.

'You should have sent word, we would have arranged a more suitable welcome,' said Eothlir with a smile, extending his hand. Yeasir's face showed no joy at the encounter and he shook Eothlir's hand only briefly.

'I am sorry,' the lieutenant said, his eyes alternating between Eothlir and Alith. 'I do not bear good news.'

'Come inside and we will hear you,' said Eothlir. 'Your soldiers are welcome to make their camp in our grounds.'

'I fear you will not be so hospitable when you hear what I have to say,' said Yeasir, clearly uneasy. 'I am here to place you under house parole, on the order of Prince Malekith, ruler of Nagarythe.'

'What?' snarled Alith, stepping forwards, stopped only by the outstretched arm of his father.

'Explain yourself,' demanded Eothlir, forcing Alith back. 'Malekith counts House Anar amongst his allies, even his friends. For what reason does he command this arrest?'

Yeasir's expression was pained, and he sent a longing glance back towards his knights.

'I assure you that Malekith has no ill intent towards House Anar,' said the captain. 'If your offer still stands, I would gratefully accept the welcome of your manse.'

Alith was about to tell Yeasir that he had already overstayed such welcome as he deserved, but Eothlir caught his eye and shook his head.

'Of course,' said Eothlir with a nod. 'Your knights may stable their horses and take rooms in the servants' wing. Gerithon!'

The steward came trotting down the path, casting worried looks over his shoulder at the fearsome riders outside the gate.

'Our visitors are to be extended every hospitality as guests,' said Eothlir. 'Please inform the kitchens and make ready such spare bedding as we have available. Commander Yeasir will be accommodated in the main house.'

'Of course, my lord,' said Gerithon, bowing. He hesitated before continuing. 'And how long might your guests be staying?'

Eothlir looked at Yeasir, who sighed.

'Probably for the winter, I'm afraid,' he said, avoiding Eothlir's stare.

'Is it me, or has the weather turned chill quickly this year?' said Alith, wrapping his cloak tight around his body. 'Or perhaps it is something else in the air that makes me shiver.'

Alith stalked back towards the house but a shout from his father caused him to stop and turn.

'Wait for us in my chambers,' Eothlir called out. 'Once everything has been attended to, we will join you there.'

Alith gave no nod or word of assent and merely strode away, his mind full of turbulent thoughts.

WHILE ALITH WAS seething with anger, Eothlir was the picture of patience and understanding. The pair were on the balcony outside Eothlir's chambers with Yeasir, looking at the mountains rising up wild and sharp beyond the ordered nature of the garden. Eothlir and Yeasir were sat on divans, a low table laden with decanter and goblets between them, though nobody had taken a drink. Alith stood staring at the Annulii, his hands fiercely gripping the balcony rail.

'I understand that this must come as something of a shock,' Yeasir was saying. 'No doubt it is some ploy to embarrass or discredit House Anar, and we will be able to put the matter aside in a short time.'

'Who would accuse the Anars of being cultists?' said Eothlir. 'What evidence did they present?'

'I cannot say, for I do not know,' replied Yeasir. 'Prince Malekith vowed before the Phoenix King himself to hunt down the cults, and even his own mother languishes in imprisonment because of that oath. Accusations have been made against the Anars and he is bound by his honour to treat them as equal with any other. You understand that to display any favour or prejudice in this matter would undermine the prince's rule?'

Eothlir acceded grudgingly to this logic with a shallow nod of the head.

'This is a deliberate attack on the Anars,' growled Alith, gazing out towards the mountains. He turned and directed his glare towards Yeasir. 'It is plain that this is some move by the cults to avert the prince's gaze away from them. They seek to divide those that would see them destroyed. Whoever made these accusations is a traitor, performing the deeds of a master other than Malekith.'

'Though I have no name to give you, Prince Malekith assured me that his source is being investigated no less than your family,' said Yeasir.

'What can we do to make this pass away swiftly?' asked Eothlir as Alith turned away again.

'I must conduct a thorough search of the manse and grounds,' said Yeasir. 'As we all know, there is nothing of an incriminating nature to be found, but that must be proved to the prince and his court. Without further evidence, this baseless allegation can be disregarded just as many others have been since the cults scattered on Malekith's return. Many have used such false accusations to settle old scores.'

'I cannot give permission for this,' said Eothlir, and raised a hand to quell Yeasir's argument. 'My father is still lord of the Anars and you must await his return before any search is made.'

'I understand,' said Yeasir. 'Thank you for seeing the difficult position in which I find myself.'

'Gerithon will convey you to your quarters shortly and you are welcome to join us for dinner,' said Eothlir, standing up.

'I think I will go hunting,' muttered Alith, pushing past Yeasir and storming out of his father's chambers.

EOLORAN WAS MOST unhappy by the turn of events he encountered when he returned to Elanardris, though he realised he had no option but to acquiesce to Yeasir's search. The knights were exceptionally thorough, examining every room and corridor and alcove in the manse, searching for amulets and idols that would betray the Anars as worshippers of the cytharai. They scoured the wine cellar and the library, and pulled up the carpets from the halls to seek hidden trapdoors.

Yeasir busied himself with measuring the dimensions of the manse and its rooms, to locate any dead spaces or voids that might conceal a shrine to the lower gods. Despite his personal dislike for events, Alith was impressed and intrigued by Yeasir's diligence. Several days after the search had begun, as he was setting out through the gardens to go hunting, Alith saw the captain on the southern lawn, pacing up and down the rose beds that bordered it. He held parchment in one hand on which he scribbled measurements with a piece of charcoal.

'What do you expect to find out here?' said Alith, crossing over the grass. Yeasir stopped suddenly, surprised.

'I, well, I am looking for concealed entrances,' he said.

'You think we have some grotto beneath the garden, festooned with the bones and entrails of our victims?'

Yeasir shrugged.

'If I cannot conclusively say that you do not, the doubt remains. I am convinced of the innocence of your family, but Malekith needs proof not assurances. The Anars are not the only noble family to have come under suspicion, and some of the things we have found I would spare you description. Complacency now, when so much has been achieved, would only strengthen those that would undermine the true authorities of Ulthuan.'

'The prince has placed a great deal of trust in you,' said Alith, sitting cross-legged on the grass.

'A trust that has been earned over hundreds of years,' said Yeasir, rolling up the parchment. 'He named me commander of Nagarythe in return for the loyalty I have shown him. I was with the prince when he saved Athel Toralien from the orcs. I marched with him across Elthin Arvan and have commanded armies in his name, both in the colonies and here in Nagarythe.'

'I hear that you went with Malekith into the north, as well,' said Alith lightly. Yeasir frowned and looked away.

'That is true, but none of us that came back speak of what happened there,' said the captain. He looked northwards and closed his eyes for a moment. When he opened them, Alith saw fear unlike any he had witnessed before in a Naggarothi. 'There are things on the edge of the Realm of Chaos best left forgotten there.'

Alith considered this with pursed lips.

'I have heard it said that the northlands changed Malekith,' he said after a while. 'He is more serious now, less inclined for adventure and battle.'

'Some adventures and some battles make us realise what it is we want from life,' said Yeasir, fiddling with the charcoal, staining his fingertips. 'Prince Malekith came to the conclusion that his place was here, on Ulthuan, as ruler of Nagarythe. It seems he was right to return when he did.'

'If only he had returned to us sooner,' Alith said with a sigh. 'Perhaps we might have avoided much bloodshed and anguish.'

'The prince was not ready to return earlier, and would not have been able to do what he needed to do,' said Yeasir. 'I am thankful that I was not in Nagarythe to suffer under the rule of Morathi, but that darkness has passed.'

'Has it? What of the cult leaders that escaped justice? What of those depraved worshippers who fled Anlec and Nagarythe?'

'They will be hunted down and brought before Malekith. It is his decree, and I have never seen him fail in something he has set his mind to, even when others thought it impossible.'

Yeasir was about to say something else but stopped.

'What is it?'

'Thank you for talking with me, Alith,' said the captain. 'I know the business that brings me here is unpleasant, but I would have you bear me no ill will for following the orders of our prince.'

Alith considered this for a moment and saw the earnest expression of Yeasir. He remembered the commander's profuse gratitude on the walls of Anlec and realised that Yeasir believed he owed his life to the Anars. He was an elf of much honour, Alith decided, and if he trusted the judgement of Malekith then he would have to trust Yeasir as well.

Alith stood and extended a hand to the captain, who took it gratefully.

'We are both Naggarothi, and we are not enemies,' said Alith. He glanced towards the clouds gathering overhead. 'I must go hunting before the weather turns against me. When you are done with our gardens, I will take you up to our hunting lodges so that you might see that we have nothing to hide there either.'

'And perhaps catch myself one of the famed Elanardris deer?'

'Perhaps, if your eye is as good for shooting as it is for prying!' laughed Alith.

THE LAST DAYS of the short autumn were drawing to a close, and dark clouds settled around the peaks of the Anullii, pregnant with snow. Yeasir had concluded his exhaustive searches and had not found any evidence of cult activity by the family or their followers. The commander sent word to Anlec along with a complete list of his findings, or lack of them. As Yeasir apologetically explained to his hosts, until he received fresh orders from

Malekith he was still bound by the command to keep the Anars under watch. Alith had become almost unaware of the silent knights stationed around the manse and grounds, and they interfered little in his daily life.

The wind was veering to the north with each day, and soon the snow would come again. In the mid-morning just a few days before winter's arrival, Alith was in the side room of his chambers reading Thalduir of Saphery's account of birds in the Saraeluii, the huge mountain realm of the dwarfs that marked the eastern bounds of the colonies in Elthin Arvan. He studied the intricate watercolour paintings, marvelling at the diversity of birds of prey. He hoped that one day he would travel to Elthin Arvan and hunt beneath the wide woods and across the towering mountains of the colonies.

The rattle of carriage wheels in the courtyard broke his thoughts and he placed the delicate silk-bound book upon the table beside him. He stood and went to the high window that overlooked the front gardens of the manse. Several carriages marked with the crest of House Moranin had drawn through the gateway. Excited that Ashniel might be among the passengers, Alith quickly changed from his hunting leathers, which he dressed in when at leisure to do so, and threw on a more formal robe of soft black wool and a wide belt of whitened leather. He tied back his long hair with a thong of woven silver thread and headed downstairs.

On coming out of the main foyer, Alith saw Ashniel gazing from the window of one of the coaches, and he waved. She saw him but her look was blank and a grave doubt began to fill Alith's heart. She drew the curtain closed.

Alith made to walk over to her, but Caenthras stepped down from the lead coach and intercepted him.

'Go fetch your father,' the elven lord said gruffly. 'Bring him here.'

'A lord of House Anar receives guests in the proper manner, he does not hold his councils on the porch,' Alith replied. 'If you would wait a moment, I will have a servant inform my father of your arrival.'

'Your petulance is unbecoming,' said Caenthras. 'Take me to your father.'

Alith still fumed inside at Ashniel's indifference, but acquiesced to Caenthras's demand and led the prince into the house. He knew his father was in the library.

Caenthras followed Alith in silence as they mounted the winding stairs that led up to the second storey of the manse. Alith seethed, wanting to demand what was happening, but he held his tongue, fearing to anger Caenthras even further. Perhaps, a small part of him said, he had misread the situation. His head knew this to be foolish, that something grim was afoot, but Alith said nothing.

Eothlir was sat at a broad desk of white-stained wood, which was littered with maps held down with goblets, plates and other assorted items. The library was not large, barely a dozen paces across, but every wall was lined floor to ceiling with shelves holding scrolls and bound tomes of varying age and subject.

Alith had spent little time here as a youth, no more than required by his tutors, for his passion lay under the open skies and not with written lore. He had preferred his lessons to be practical not theoretical, and had constantly taxed the patience of his teachers with his disdain for poetry, politics and geography. These days he found a little more comfort indoors and the library had a great many maps and diaries from travellers to the colonies. He fondly imagined that at some time he would go to those strange lands with Ashniel by his side.

Eothlir's expression was welcoming as he looked up at the disturbance, but this changed to one of concern when he saw the stern look of Caenthras.

'I fear I am not going to like what you are about to tell me,' said Eothlir, picking up a ewer of water and proffering it towards the lord of the Moranin family. Caenthras declined the drink with a shake of his hand.

'You are not,' Caenthras said. 'You know that I hold no house in higher regard than yours, save for that of Prince Malekith.'

'That is nice to hear, but I think that you are about to demonstrate otherwise,' said Eothlir.

'I am,' said Caenthras. 'My loyalty lies with Nagarythe and my family above all others, and so when I am faced with a decision it is that loyalty which steers my thoughts.'

'Enough, my friend,' said Eothlir. 'Say what it is you have to say.'

Caenthras still hesitated, his eyes fixed on Eothlir, giving not even the slightest glance to Alith who was stood beside his father.

'Ashniel has been invited to attend at the court of Anlec, and I have accepted on her behalf,' said Caenthras.

'What?' snapped Alith. Eothlir did not reply, but shook his head in confusion.

'There have been many wounds between Anlec and the east of Nagarythe, and this is a great opportunity to heal those injuries,' continued Caenthras. 'Think of what good can come to the eastern princes with our voice heard in Malekith's court.'

'And what of the wedding?' said Alith.

Only now did Caenthras look at Alith. His expression was stern.

'Ashniel travels to Anlec before the winter comes,' said the elven lord. 'You are free to join her there in the spring if you wish. Not before then, for she has many duties that need attending to upon her arrival, and I fear she has much to learn about court life in the capital. She does not need the distraction of your presence for the moment.'

'That is unacceptable!' snapped Alith. 'She is to be my wife and yet you have made this decision without consultation with me.'

'She is my daughter,' replied Caenthras, his voice quiet and dangerous. 'Even when you are wed she is my responsibility. I would not have Ashniel waste her life in the woods and mountains when she could achieve so much more in Anlec.'

'One day I will be lord of those woods and mountains,' said Eothlir. 'So will my son. Have you such disdain for us that you prefer the company of the fashionable elite of Anlec? Those who not twenty years ago were all too ready to bend their knee to Morathi and her cults?'

'Times have changed, Eothlir,' said Caenthras, calming his voice. 'Malekith is the new power in Nagarythe, and perhaps one day across Ulthuan.'

'You would see him made Phoenix King also?' asked Eothlir.

'It is the only natural conclusion to events that I can see,' continued Caenthras. 'If you back his claim as heir of Aenarion, then you must feel, as do others, that it is his right not to rule just Nagarythe, but all of Ulthuan.'

'I feel your logic is flawed, Caenthras,' said Eothlir. 'I have no concern who wears the Phoenix Crown and the feather cloak. It is stability and prosperity in Nagarythe that I fought for, not some wider goal.'

'Then it is you who has been deluded,' said Caenthras. 'Or perhaps your father, from whom you have taken all your misguided counsel. Maybe there is more to the accusations of treachery than I first gave credit. What loyal son of Nagarythe would not see Malekith crowned as Phoenix King? Would the Anars see themselves as successors, perhaps?'

'Be careful what you next say,' said Eothlir, standing. 'It seems House Anar has few enough friends at the moment, but House Moranin would do well not to be added to the list of our enemies.'

'And so the ploys of Morathi come full circle, and innuendo and threats have become your weapons, is that right?' spat Caenthras.

'Morathi was correct in one thing,' said Eothlir with a sneer. 'The time to fight was upon us, and those battles have not yet all been fought. There can be no bystanders. I tell you that House Anar has nothing to do with the cults and if you turn from us, you only fan the fires of falsehood that have smouldered in Nagarythe since Malekith's return.'

'I have come out of courtesy for your family, and for you, whom I once named friend,' said Caenthras, controlling his anger with considerable effort. 'I thought you would offer me the same respect. I will not speak against you, Eothlir, but I cannot aid you. I hope that one day, in not too many years, we can meet again and put this behind us and be companions once more. I wish you no ill, Eothlir, but I cannot countenance moving against the will of Anlec.'

With no further word, Caenthras spun on his heel and stalked from the room. Eothlir's face was a mask of anguish, torn between ire and woe. Alith stared out of the doorway at Caenthras's retreating back, his teeth grinding.

'See that they leave without incident,' Eothlir said, before waving Alith away and sitting down to bury his head in his hands.

Alith hurried after Caenthras, who returned to his caravan and gave the signal for them to depart. The young Anar watched the coach of Ashniel, hoping to see her draw back the curtain and give him some indication of her feelings, but it was not to be. The coach rattled from the courtyard without the slightest glimpse of her.

Alith silently cursed House Moranin, and he cursed the cowardly Caenthras even more. With a snarl he strode towards the house, the servants and soldiers in the courtyard fleeing before his foul mood like sheep from a stalking wolf.

As WHEN HE was a child, Alith sought sanctuary in the wilds of Elanardris, despite the misgivings of his father and the bitter weather. He would walk out into the cold peaks sometimes to hunt, on other occasions simply to be away from any other soul.

On this day he was sat on a rock at the bank of a thin stream, skinning and cleaning a mountain hare he had shot. As he stooped forwards to clean his blade in the almost-frozen water, he caught the reflection of a black shape in the sky: a crow.

'It has been a long while,' said Alith, straightening.

'Yes it has,' replied Elthyrior, sitting down beside Alith. As before, the raven herald was draped in his cloak of shadowy feathers, his face hidden in the depths of his hood. Only his green eyes showed. 'And you know that my appearance is not a glad tiding.'

Alith sighed and finished cleaning his knife, slipping it into his belt as he turned towards Elthyrior.

'And what new threat arises?' he said. 'Perhaps the dwarfs have built a fleet of ships made from rock and cross the ocean to sack Ulthuan? Or maybe the Sapherian mages have turned themselves all into rampaging goats?'

'Your attitude is unbecoming for a prince of Ulthuan,' snapped Elthyrior. 'Allow the grace of your bloodline to show through.'

Alith sighed again.

'I am sorry, but I have much in my mind of late. I suppose you warn me not to go to Anlec?'

Elthyrior sat back in surprise.

'How could you know this?'

'Nothing else has changed recently that would warrant your return after twenty years,' explained Alith. 'Always you come when there is a decision to be made, to warn against one course of action or the other. It is the way of Morai-heg to lay these dilemmas before us and laugh as we try to navigate our way through the tangled web she has woven.'

'Do you know why you cannot go to Anlec?'

'Bad things will happen, though of an enigmatic nature I am sure.'

Alith stood and looked down at Elthyrior.

'What can I say to you? I cannot promise that I will not go to Anlec. Ashniel is there now, and if you tell me it is unsafe for me there, I cannot believe that it is safe for my betrothed. Your words make me more inclined to go to her, not less.'

'Ashniel is lost to you, Alith,' Elthyrior said sorrowfully, standing and placing a hand on Alith's shoulder. 'Anlec is not the place you think it is.'

Alith laughed and cast aside Elthyrior's gesture of sympathy.

'You expect me to believe you? You think a few rumours would break the bond that lies between us?'

'Soon there will be more than rumours,' said Elthyrior. 'Since Malekith's return I and others of my order who are loyal to Nagarythe have followed the spoor of those cultists that escaped. They have not been idle, in Nagarythe and elsewhere. Though they are more hidden than ever before, there are ways to find them and learn their secrets. The accusation of the Anars is part of a grander scheme, though what its aim is remains unknown to me. Though word has not yet reached Elanardris, there have been attacks and uprisings in several parts of Nagarythe. The cultists have returned, but this time they declare not for Morathi but for Eoloran of House Anar!'

'That cannot be! You know that we are free of any taint.'

'And yet they protest at the arrest of your family, and so give truth to the lie. Anlec is not safe for the Anars, and I fear that Elanardris will be a haven for little longer.'

'Yeasir…'

'Perhaps,' said Elthyrior. 'He should be watched closely. I do not think he knows truly his part in this, he is but a piece on a game board for a more powerful player.'

'Who is this player? Morathi?' Alith waved away his own concern. 'She is held captive in Tor Anroc, I cannot believe that she still wields the power over the cults that she once had.'

'You know of the saying, "As the parent, so too the child"?'

'You cannot surely suspect Malekith of being the architect of this deception?'

'I cannot *surely* know anything,' laughed Elthyrior, a bitter sound. 'This is a game played with deceit and misdirection. It is played in shadows and with the minds of elves. Yet, I am not a player, I can only follow the moves as they are made and report them to others.'

'So do you know who any of the players are?'

'Morathi, for certain, though at a distance,' said Elthyrior. 'Malekith certainly moves some pieces, though for his own ends or those of some other cause I cannot say. Others in his court are also tied to the strings of their puppets, though it is hard to follow the threads back to the hand that controls them. As I have warned before, you cannot afford to trust anyone save yourself.'

'So what am I to do? It seems as though there is little we can do to defend ourselves against accusation if the cults treat us as their own. It seems we are pieces being played, and have no control over the game or its rules.'

'Then you must find a player on your behalf, and change the board in your favour.'

Alith turned away and gazed at his rippling reflection in the icy water.

'The Phoenix King,' he said. 'There is no greater player in Ulthuan.'

Elthyrior gave no reply and when Alith turned he saw that the raven herald had, as usual, disappeared without warning. A long caw echoed from the mountainsides and then Alith was left alone with the wind and the babbling of the stream.

ALITH BROODED ON Elthyrior's words for several days, weighing up the courses of action he could take. Each day brought the risk that news would come of the cults' uprisings in defence of the Anars, and Alith feared that such tidings would stir Yeasir to firmer security. As midwinter approached, he also knew that travel from the mountains would be all but impossible and, stirred by this vague deadline, called his family together to discuss with them his thoughts.

Unobserved by Yeasir, his soldiers or any of the servants, Alith gathered his family in the chambers of his grandfather. Eoloran was sat beside the crackling fire, while Eothlir and Maieth stood hand-in-hand gazing out of the ice-freckled window.

'I am leaving Elanardris,' Alith announced as he closed the white-panelled door to the chamber.

'For where?' asked Maieth, crossing the room to stand in front of her son. 'Surely you do not think to travel to Anlec in such harsh weather.'

'It is not for Anlec that I am bound,' Alith told them. 'The Anars are being used, and we do not have the means to reveal this deception. I will go to Bel Shanaar and ask for his intervention.'

'That would not be wise,' said Eoloran. 'It is not the business of the Phoenix King to involve himself in matters internal to Nagarythe. Other princes and nobles will not take kindly to interference from Tor Anroc. He knows little of what happens here, and is an uncertain ally.'

'An uncertain ally is better than no ally at all,' said Eothlir. 'House Moranin has all but deserted us, no doubt for the benefit of Caenthras's reputation. Our friends have been few for many years. I think Alith is right that we need to seek strength as times turn against us.'

'Some will say such a move is in defiance of Malekith's rule,' said Eoloran. 'Should we not have the confidence of our prince, then we have nothing.'

'We do not know the counsels Malekith receives,' said Alith, moving to sit in the chair opposite his grandfather. He leant forwards earnestly. 'While we can keep our faith with Malekith, are you so sure that what he is told is the truth? Do not his own oaths of honour make him susceptible to lies told by others? If Bel Shanaar is an uncertain ally, Malekith has not yet proven himself a certain master.'

'What of Ashniel and the wedding?' said Maieth. 'Caenthras has not ruled out the union between the houses. If he were so turned against us, he would not allow Ashniel to be married. There is hope there, Alith. It is my fear that you would risk that alliance by involving the Phoenix King. Caenthras is a strong advocate of Nagarythe's independence from the Phoenix Throne.'

Alith shook his head sadly, and gave voice to a conclusion that had troubled him since Ashniel's departure.

'There will be no wedding,' said Alith. 'Though he says one thing to us, I believe that he has turned Ashniel against me. He treads upon the line between friend and foe, not wishing to associate openly with the Anars but willing to keep alive what connection he has should he find the need for us again. In Anlec, I would be the fly trapped in the web. I cannot go there, and in refusing I snub House Moranin and give Caenthras greater excuse to be displeased with us. I wonder how long it is that his goals and ours have been at odds, and it seems that he has positioned himself to benefit whatever the outcome.'

'I am so sorry, Alith,' said Maieth. She crouched beside her son with a tear on her cheek, and stroked his hair. Alith leaned forwards and kissed her on the head and pulled her up.

'I feel as though I had been blinded but now I see the light,' he said. 'Though I loved Ashniel, I realise that my feelings were never returned. This was ever a match of politics, made by Caenthras and dutifully carried out by Ashniel. I saw her when she left and there was not a sign that she was sad at our parting. What I saw as calm nobility was no more than cool aloofness.'

Alith found his embarrassment rising and became angry, standing up and balling his fists.

'How much she must have thought herself clever, seeing the ignorant Anar come at her slightest call, like the hawk to its master,' he snarled. 'She has played me for a fool, and I filled my part all too well for her. I have read again those letters that she sent me, and think on the conversations we have had, and ever the affection was from me to her, while her own love was but an imagining I had conjured for myself! I am sure she amuses her maids in Anlec with tales of her tame prince, telling them how I will come running to her in the spring with the gentlest flick of my reins!'

Maieth embraced Alith, running her hand down his back. He allowed himself to enjoy the comfort of her love for a while and then gently pushed her away.

'Though I have been wronged, it is not out of spite that I turn to the Phoenix King,' said Alith. 'I believe that there is genuine danger for the Anars, and it will come soon.'

'What sort of danger?' asked Eothlir. 'How do you know this?'

'First I must tell you that I cannot say from where I gained this information,' said Alith. He held up his hand when Eothlir opened his mouth to object. 'I have given my word, but if you trust me then have faith that what I am to tell you is true.'

'Always we will believe you, Alith,' said Eoloran with a concerned look. 'Tell us what it is that you know.'

'There have been demonstrations against Malekith's house arrest of the Anars,' said Alith.

'So there are those who we can count upon as allies,' said Eothlir. 'I do not see–'

'By cult leaders,' Alith interrupted sharply. 'The cultists make a pretence that we are of their ilk, and thus we will be condemned alongside them. For whatever reasons further their cause, the cults speak openly in praise of the Anars and there is no defence we can make that will stop the accusations that will surely follow.'

'I do not see how Bel Shanaar can help us,' said Maieth. 'Why will he not believe our enemies as well?'

'There is no guarantee that he will not,' said Alith. 'That is why it is I that must go to him. Better that we put some case before the Phoenix Throne than no case at all.'

Alith waved for his mother to be seated and when she had done so, he stood behind her, his hands on her shoulders.

'I have given this my deepest consideration,' he told his family. 'It is not wise that all three lords of the Anars, present and future, are trapped in Elanardris. One of us must leave here so that whatever happens, the cause of the family can be championed beyond these walls. We cannot send a servant to do this, no matter how trusted, for whoever entreats the Phoenix King to help must carry the full authority of the house. I am the most free to leave without question, for Yeasir and his guards are content to allow me to go hunting without escort. They will not expect a swift return and so I can gain a day, perhaps two, ahead of any pursuit that might be sent after me. No one else enjoys that freedom from scrutiny. When my absence is noted, it can be said that I have perhaps fled for Anlec, unwilling to wait until the spring to see Ashniel.'

Alith paused and gave a meaningful look to his father and grandfather. 'I am also the most expendable, should things go ill in one way or another.'

'You are not expendable to me!' said Maieth. 'You are my son and I would see you safe before all other considerations.'

'None of us are safe, Mother,' replied Alith sternly. 'It is not in me to hide here and await the inevitable. The last time we were pressed by the power of Anlec, it was only through the strength of our alliances that we were able to resist our foes. This time the Anars will be forced to stand alone unless we can find help from another source.'

Eoloran and Eothlir exchanged a long look with each other, reading each other's thoughts from their expressions. It was Eoloran who spoke first, standing and gripping Alith's arm.

'It is pointless to express regret on things that we cannot change, and I cannot fault your reasoning. I will write letters of introduction to produce for Bel Shanaar. We know each other of old though many hundreds of years have passed since we last spoke. I believe that the Phoenix King will give you fair hearing, though I cannot guess his response.'

'Do not go openly,' warned Eothlir. 'Morathi dwells in Tor Anroc and though imprisoned I am sure she has her spies at hand. If the Phoenix King is to aid us, then it must be kept secret as long as possible. I understand why Malekith returned to us without announcement, as the element of surprise is one of the greatest weapons we can yet rely upon.'

'When do you plan to leave?' asked Maieth. 'Tell me you will not be going immediately.'

'A day or two at the most,' said Alith. 'Though Yeasir has not yet heard of the cultists' support for us, he will soon and then we cannot say how he will react.'

'Yeasir and his few dozen knights are little threat to us,' said Eothlir. 'Should we need to be rid of his scrutiny it is easily accomplished.'

'No!' said Eoloran. 'We must be beyond reproach, even when no one will believe us. Yeasir is here under lawful authority and we have accepted as such. We must do nothing that adds further fuel to the fires of suspicion.'

'How will we hear from you, or contact you?' asked Maieth. 'Is there a messenger we can trust?'

'There is one who I may be able to use, but I cannot name him now,' said Alith. He directed his gaze to Eoloran. 'If he does come, you will know him and you must trust him, as I do. I cannot say any more.'

Maieth threw her arms around Alith once more, stifling a sob.

'I will write that letter,' said Eoloran, bowing before leaving the room. Eothlir laid his arms about the shoulders of his wife and son, and the three of them stood sharing the silence for a while longer.

IT WAS THREE days before Alith was ready to set off for Tor Anroc. His hunting trips roused no suspicion in the warriors from Anlec, and under the cover of these excursions Alith was able to stockpile a small amount of food and clothes in one of the watch-caves in the mountains. On the seventh morning after meeting Elthyrior he was set to go.

He said no goodbyes to his family as they had already said their farewells several times. Alith was eager to leave now that his mind was set – for practical reason of the deteriorating weather and also driven by the urge to act against the forces aligning in opposition to House Anar. He did not depart early, keeping to his usual routine of heading into the mountains mid-morning. Grey clouds swathed the sky though the snow had lightened in the past few days. As he left the manse, Alith saw Yeasir with his knights drawn up for inspection in the courtyard. Alith waved cheerfully and cut eastwards through the gardens, leaving by the gate in the high hedge that bordered the lawn.

FREE FROM THE eyes of Yeasir and his warriors, Alith turned south-east and made directly for the cave where he had stashed his provisions. It was past midday by the time he had climbed up to the empty watch post and the snow was falling heavily. The air was filled with flurries of white and Alith was unable to see more than a dozen paces ahead. The wind tugged at his grey hood and cloak and swept his long hair across his face as snowflakes settled on his fur-lined hunting coat. His boots were crusted with ice as he strode purposefully across the snow drifts towards the south. Glancing back, Alith saw the falling snow obscuring the faint footprints his light tread had left. Smiling at being free once more, Alith hiked his pack higher onto his shoulders and pressed on.

The snow continued relentlessly for the whole day and into the night. Alith spared himself only short breaks from his walking, taking shelter beneath overhangs and in craggy defiles to drink spice-seasoned water from his flask and eat a little of the carefully wrapped rabbit and bird meat he had cooked over the previous days. As twilight fought through the thick clouds he looked for somewhere to stay for the night.

After much searching, Alith located a small knot of trees further down the mountainside. He climbed into one of the larger pines and quickly wove a rudimentary roof from the branches above. With the worst of the snow kept away, he sat with his back to the trunk, his legs along the branch, and fell into a light sleep.

ALITH WOKE BEFORE dawn and was suddenly aware that he was being watched. Opening his eyes just a fraction, he saw a large crow perched on the end of the branch. With a wry smile, he opened his eyes fully and looked around for Elthyrior.

The raven herald was squatting in the snow a little way off, rousing a small fire into life. A thin wisp of smoke drifted up through the branches. Elthyrior looked up as Alith stood.

'I am happy to see that my warnings do not fall upon deaf ears,' he said.

'I am sorry if I was harsh when we last met,' said Alith, dropping down from the tree. 'Often one knows that something is amiss but refuses to look upon the truth. I knew that all was not well with Ashniel, but would not believe myself. One should not shoot the messenger if the tidings are bad.'

Elthyrior waved Alith closer.

'I wish that I could bring better news on occasion, but it is not the task of the raven heralds to be bearers of happiness,' he said. 'In war and hardship our order was founded, and so our eyes and ears are ready for that which brings misery not joy.'

'It must be lonely,' said Alith, crouching beside the fire. A thought occurred to him. 'Is it safe to have a flame? The smoke might be seen.'

'There is nobody to see it, not here,' said Elthyrior. 'You chose your path well, keeping high up the mountains. Where do you intend to go from here?'

'I thought to head south for another two days until I come to the Naganath. Then follow the river west before turning south towards Tor Anroc.'

'I would counsel against that,' said Elthyrior, shaking his head. 'Bel Shanaar has his army stationed on the Naganath, watching the border. There is little chance your journey to Tor Anroc will be unobserved. Should you be found crossing from Nagarythe you will be taken into custody and brought before Bel Shanaar in full view.'

Alith swore gently.

'I do not know Tiranoc,' he said. 'Now that we speak of it, it seems foolish that I could reach the Phoenix King without suspicion. Even if I make it to the city, how do I contact Bel Shanaar?'

'I have no answers for your second question, but for the first I would say to keep on the southern path until you come to the Pass of the Eagle. Turn westwards and head to Tor Anroc from there. Only a few days to the south the weather is more welcoming and some travellers still pass between Ellyrion and Tiranoc at this time of the year. I am not saying you will go without being noticed, but coming from the east will attract less attention than the north.'

'Thank you,' said Alith. 'I do not know how I would ever survive without you to guide me.'

'Then you must learn, for I cannot be relied upon,' Elthyrior replied. His voice was quiet but stern. 'You are not my only concern, and you are an adult. I am your ally but I cannot be your guardian and guide forever. You know the right paths to take, but you argue with yourself constantly. Trust your instincts, Alith. Morai-heg speaks to all of us in our dreams and feelings. If you do not trust her, and many are wise not to, then find another in whose light you are happy to follow.'

Alith considered this for a moment, warming his hands at the fire.

'You did not answer my first point,' said Alith. 'Are you lonely?'

As if in reply, the crow cawed and flapped down to land upon Elthyrior's shoulder, nestling into the raven feathers that made up his cloak.

'Loneliness is an indulgence for those with the time to spare for it,' said Elthyrior. 'Some fill the emptiness with the meaningless chatter of those around them. Some of us fill it with a greater purpose, more comforting than any mortal company.'

'Then tell me one other thing,' said Alith, seizing the moment of companionship he felt with the raven herald. 'Have you ever loved?'

Elthyrior's face was a mask as he replied.

'Love was taken from my family in the time of Aenarion. Perhaps it may return before I die, but I think it unlikely. There will be little love for any of us in the years ahead.'

'Why? What have you seen?'

'I dream of black flames,' said Elthyrior, gazing deep into the fire. When he turned his attention to Alith, the Anar prince flinched from the icy stare of those emerald eyes. 'It is not a good omen.'

ELTHYRIOR TRAVELLED SOUTH with Alith for the best part of the next day, leaving him just before dusk.

'I cannot be found within the borders of Tiranoc,' the raven herald told Alith. 'They will think me a cultist, and my pledge is to the protection of Nagarythe and it is here that my powers are strongest. From here you can easily find your way to Eagle Pass.'

The snow stopped at about the same time and Alith pressed southwards into the night while the going was fair. His path took him across several streams and a broad river – the headwaters of the Naganath that marked the border between Tiranoc and Nagarythe. Crossing the water, he moved from the realm of Prince Malekith into the kingdom of Bel Shanaar. He truly was on foreign soil.

Looking westwards the sky was clearing and out on the plains many miles away he saw the dim flickers of camp fires. There the armies of the Phoenix King watched their neighbour. It seemed that Bel Shanaar was not yet convinced by the twenty years of peace that had followed Malekith's return. Alith was beginning to share his doubts.

EIGHT

A Dark Plan Revealed

TIRANOC WAS CERTAINLY warmer than Elanardris. The wind kept steady from the west, bringing air from the hot climes of Lustria across the seas and holding the wintry chill at bay. The sky was overcast though and the square that adjoined the great palace of the Phoenix King was all but empty. A few elves hurried from one place or another, eager to spend little time out of the warmth of the city's thousands of fireplaces.

Alith sat on a marble bench close to the wall surrounding the plaza, looking at the ceremonial gateway that led into the palace. Two white, circular towers soared above, each with a pointed gilded roof and capped with braziers that burnt with magical blue fire – a sign that the Phoenix King was in residence.

The city was utterly different to Anlec. Tor Anroc had been built and rebuilt in times of peace, of winding roads and open spaces, while the Naggarothi capital clung to its warlike past with its forbidding walls and garrison houses. Built around and into a solitary mountain that speared up from the plain of Tiranoc, Tor Anroc was partly opened to the sky and partly a maze of winding tunnels lit with silver lanterns. There was colour and light everywhere Alith looked, utterly unlike the grim greys and black of Anlec's naked stone.

He didn't like it at all. The city was for show and little else, like the enormous gatehouse to the palace. The city was dominated by the manses of princes and other nobles and vast embassies containing lords and ladies from the other kingdoms of Ulthuan. Most of the folk of Tiranoc dwelt in towns that surrounded the capital, riding in by wain and horse each day and returning home at nightfall. Only those close to the Phoenix King could afford to stay in the city.

Alith had been in Tor Anroc for three days. He had followed Elthyrior's instructions and travelled along the roads from Eagle Pass. He had been relieved if not also a little disturbed that his entrance into the city amongst a group of merchants went unremarked. It was fortunate for his personal circumstance, but it was clear that after so many travails across the isle the vigilance against the cults and their agents was weak, even here where the ruler of the elves lived. There were guards at the gates and on the walls, but they watched the masses passing with only vague interest.

For three days Alith had come to the plaza and thought on how he might enter the palace and contact the Phoenix King in secret. He had listened to the market stall traders gossiping and the exchange of rumours between the visiting nobles picking at the merchants' wares. Fashions in clothing and literature, talk of the colonies and the romances of the princes and princesses of Ulthuan dominated, and there was little spoken about Nagarythe, or Prince Malekith. It occurred to Alith that the Naggarothi were treated like distant cousins, occasionally wayward and attracting attention but otherwise left to their own means. If one did not pry too hard, one would not see things that might be unpleasant.

The hosts of Tiranoc camped close to the banks of the Naganath told Alith a different story, and he was astounded that having such a garrison in place caused so little remark amongst the Tiranocii. Even Morathi's imprisonment was old news and Alith had not heard her name spoken once in the time he had been in the city.

Alith admitted that he was at a loss concerning what to do next. His paranoia was such that he was loath to announce himself to any but Bel Shanaar, though as a prince of Nagarythe he could have simply walked up to the gates and demanded an audience with the Phoenix King. He had caught word that Bel Shanaar regularly held open sessions during which any elf could petition him, but also had detected an undercurrent that such audiences were not truly open and all petitioners were questioned and vetted prior to being allowed to come before the Phoenix Throne. A public audience would do Alith little good even if he could gain entry – the hall would surely be full of others to see Bel Shanaar and he would have no privacy to express his concerns to the Phoenix King.

As midday came, the market began to fill with elves as they made their way in from the towns and farms around the city. Alith wandered amongst the growing crowds, his grey and brown wilderness clothes at odds with the swirling robes and gaily coloured dresses of the urbane elite of Tiranoc. Fortunately most took him for a servant of some kind and paid him no attention as individuals in power often do when close to those of lesser station.

It was this invisibility that gave Alith an idea.

That night he stayed in the city, though the boarding house cost him a good proportion of the silver coins his father had furnished him with. After dark, when the gates were closed, the city took on a different life. Lanterns of red and blue sprang into life and those more modest elves who still lived in Tor Anroc finished their labours and came out. The wine houses threw open their doors and cellars and the merchants packed up their stalls to patronise these establishments.

Alith entered one of these drinking halls close to the palace and was pleased to see a variety of customers in the livery of the Phoenix King. Some were ageing retainers, most were young pages, maids, ostlers, cleaners, cooks and other mundane chore-workers looking for a way to establish themselves in court life. Alith picked a likely group – three male elves and four female – and bought a generous pitcher of hot spiced wine. This cost most of his remaining money and he hoped the expense was not in vain. He filled a tray with eight red-enamelled clay goblets, and the jug, and sat down with the palace servants.

'Hello,' he said, handing out the cups. 'I'm Atenithor. I'm new to the city and I'm wondering if you could help.'

'Is that an Ellyrian accent?' asked one of the maidens as Alith began to pour the wine. She was petite, for an elf, and her smile was warm and genuine. Alith took her to be a little younger than him, but only by a decade or so.

'Chracian,' he said, feeling that if someone knew the difference they would already have known he was Naggarothi. He guessed that few folk of Nagarythe would be found in the city.

'I'm Milandith,' said the girl, extending a hand. Alith shook it and there were peals of laughter from those around the table.

'One kisses the hand in greeting,' said one of the male youths. He took Alith's hand and quickly pursed his lips to the middle knuckle. 'Like so. I am Liaserin. Pleased to make your acquaintance, Atenithor.'

Alith returned the gesture, trying not to look self-conscious. In Naggaroth, a simple handshake was considered sufficient greeting, and perhaps an embrace for those who were family or well-regarded.

'It seems I have already displayed my ignorance.' Alith laughed off his embarrassment. 'It is a good job that I have some friends to steer me straight. I was a hunter, you see, and one does not get much time to learn the niceties of city life on a mountainside.'

He then went around the table kissing the hands of the others, nodding his head in deference as they told him their names.

'What brings a hunter to Tor Anroc?' asked Lamendas, a female elf that Alith judged to be a little older than the others, perhaps in her eightieth or ninetieth year.

'Ambition!' Alith declared with a grin and raised eyebrows. 'My father is a famous hunter in the south of Chrace, but it seems that the princes don't value his work as much as when he was young. I realised that if I am to make a name for myself it was either Tor Anroc or the colonies, and I've never been one for ships!'

There was more laughter, friendlier. Alith could feel his new companions warming to his presence and continued.

'Naturally, I am looking for a position at the palace. Might I enquire how one goes about securing such employment?'

'Well, that depends on what you can do,' said Lamendas. 'Not much need for a hunter in a palace.'

'Butchery,' Alith replied quickly. 'A hunter learns to use a knife as well as a bow, and so I thought perhaps I might make myself useful in the kitchens.'

'You might be in luck,' said Achitherir, a boy of perhaps no more than thirty years. 'The cooks are always looking for more help. Every banquet the Phoenix King holds is attended to by more guests than the last. You should speak to Malithrandin, the Steward of the Fires.'

'Malithrandin?'

Milandith, who was sat on Alith's right, leaned close to him and pointed towards a table close to the fireplace. There were six elves of more senior years arguing intently over a piece of paper. Her other hand brushed Alith's thigh gently but deliberately as she sat back.

'My father, he sits with the other stewards,' she said, placing a hand on Alith's knee beneath the table. 'I could introduce you if you like.'

'That would be most helpful,' said Alith, making to stand. Milandith's grip on his knee tightened and forced him to stay seated.

'Not now, the stewards would be most perturbed to have their leisure interrupted by us,' she said. 'I will take you to him in the morning.'

'Where might I find you in the morning?'

'Well, if you pour me another glass of wine,' Milandith purred, 'you'll find me lying next to you...'

Magical light flickered from the lantern in the corner of Milandith's small room, dappling everything in a muted yellow and green. Alith lay staring at the ceiling, feeling the warmth from Milandith beside him. He wondered if he had made a terrible mistake. It would have been unforgivable for him to sleep with Ashniel before they were wed and Caenthras would have been right to demand serious reparations for such an act, not to mention the dishonour Alith would have brought to the Anar name. Perhaps things were different for the lower orders? There had certainly been no hint of reproach or suspicion from the other servants when Milandith had brought him back to her quarters in one of the palace's long wings.

A thought occurred to Alith that brought a smile to his face. What would be Milandith's reaction if she learnt that she had bedded a prince of Ulthuan, heir to one of the most powerful families in Nagarythe, no less? As he dwelt on this, his mood darkened again. The encounter, passionate and honest, had been nothing like his dealings with Ashniel. There had been none of the coquettish flirtation and implied physicality, simply the mutual desire of two people. Maybe Ashniel had deliberately held back her attentions, to lead him on and tease rather than fulfil?

He felt Milandith stir next to him and looked to his left, letting his gaze linger on the smooth curve of her naked back and her thick curls of brown hair spilling onto the golden pillow. She rolled towards Alith, eyes half-opened.

'I would have thought your exertions would have left you ready for sleep,' she murmured, stroking a hand across his bare chest.

Alith leant across and kissed her on the cheek.

'I have a lot to think about,' he said. 'The city seems to offer many charms that a simple hunter is not used to.'

Milandith smiled and stretched, allowing herself to fall onto him, her head on his chest. She curled her fingers into his hair.

'The city has many delights to be enjoyed, but I would have thought that this one was not new to you,' she said sleepily.

Alith did not reply and she looked up at his face. Her eyes widened in shock and she covered her mouth, suppressing a light laugh.

'I did not know Chracian hunters were so chaste!' she giggled. 'Had I known, I would have been more… gentle.'

Alith laughed with her, feeling no embarrassment at his inexperience.

'If you could not tell that this was my first time, then I must have some natural talent!'

Milandith kissed him on the lips, cupping his face in her hands.

'Beginner's luck, perhaps?' she said. 'Of course, there is a simple way to find out.'

Any other thoughts fled Alith's mind as he held Milandith close; Nagarythe, Caenthras, Ashniel, the cults, all banished in a moment of peace and contentment.

ALITH WORKED HARD in the kitchens and, when time allowed, learnt as much as he could about the Phoenix King's palace. When not preparing boar or venison or rabbit or wildfowl for the cooks, his attention was divided between exploring the layout of the palace and socialising with the other staff, particularly Milandith. In this last case, Alith learnt a great deal of gossip over goblets of wine and in whispered, dreamy conversations lying in bed late at night. Milandith was naturally inquisitive and outgoing, and seemed to know much about the routines and rituals of palace life, as well as a good number of the hundreds of servants and guards that populated the citadel. Alith felt a little guilt about exploiting their relationship in such an underhand way, but Milandith seemed always ready to teach her new lover about Tor Anroc and its ways, and was honest about her own desire for companionship and intimacy without deep commitments required from either of them.

What Alith had learnt did not fill him with confidence. Bel Shanaar was only rarely alone, his days filled with audiences and meetings with persons of importance. His family – his son Elodhir principal amongst them – were also a constant presence during less formal occasions. When matters of state or family did not require his attention, the Phoenix King was shadowed by his chamberlain, Palthrain. Much as Gerithon managed many of the affairs of Elanardris for Eoloran, Palthrain was Bel Shanaar's chief advisor and agent. He oversaw the running of the palace, and every member of the staff from the maids to the captains of the guard ultimately owed responsibility to him. His dealings were not confined purely to the domestic, and he was pivotal in many negotiations between Tiranoc and the other kingdoms.

One other figure attracted Alith's attention, mentioned in passing by Milandith one evening. His name was Carathril, a slightly melancholy elf who served as the Phoenix King's chief herald. He was from Lothern and as Alith inquired more he learnt that Carathril had once been a captain in the Lothern Guard and had acted as Bel Shanaar's emissary when Malekith had first tried to retake Anlec and been thwarted at Ealith. That Carathril knew a little about Nagarythe and the prince intrigued Alith and he decided that he would attempt to make the acquaintance of the herald at the earliest opportunity.

Alith had been in the palace for nearly twenty days before such a circumstance arrived. Most of his labours in the kitchen, which he found surprisingly pleasant to perform for they were not taxing and gave him time to cogitate on other matters, were usually finished by mid-afternoon. This gave him until the evening to conduct his shadowy investigations before the expectations of social interaction required him to spend time with his fellow servants after dark. On this particular day, Alith was presented with the chance to enter the Phoenix King's great hall.

It was an open audience, as Alith had heard about, and such members of society as were able to beg, bribe or sneak their way into the hall were allowed to observe the proceedings. Dressed in his nondescript white robes, Alith was easily able to join a group of elves as they made their way into the central chamber, and then split from them to take a seat on the benches at the top of the tiers of seats surrounding the auditorium.

As he made his way up the steps, Alith spied a lonely-looking figure sat somewhat apart from the others, far from the crowds who jostled for places on the lowest benches nearest Bel Shanaar. From his appearance, livery and disposition Alith guessed this to be Carathril, and he walked around the top tier of the seats and sat down beside the elf.

'Are you Carathril?' he asked, deciding it was better to speak plainly than try to elicit what he needed by subterfuge.

The elf turned in surprise, and then nodded.

'I am the Phoenix King's herald,' he said, extending his hand towards Alith.

'You can call me Atenithor,' said Alith, kissing Carathril's hand. The herald took it away a little too quickly and Alith judged that he was as uncomfortable with this Tiranoc convention as Alith. 'I find it strange also.'

'What's that?' said Carathril, who had turned his attention back to the procession of elves making their way through the open doors.

'The hand-kissing,' said Alith. 'I'm not from Tiranoc either, and I find it most peculiar.'

Carathril did not reply and instead raised a finger to his lips for quiet and nodded towards the doorway. Alith looked down and saw Palthrain enter, dressed in a coat of deep purple with a wide blue belt studded with sapphires. He stood to one side and bowed.

Alith laid eyes upon Bel Shanaar for the first time. The Phoenix King was stood erect and proud, dressed in a flowing robe of white decorated with golden thread in the design of phoenixes rising from flames. Upon his shoulders he wore a cloak made of white and black feathers that trailed behind him. His austere face looked straight ahead, and atop his head he wore a magnificent crown of gold that sparkled in the sunlight that came from the windows surrounding the dome of the hall. Bel Shanaar paced evenly along the chamber and came to his throne. Pulling his lustrous cloak to one side, he sat down and gazed around. Even from this distance Alith could see the Phoenix King's sharp eyes passing over those in the hall, missing nothing. He resisted the urge to flinch when that steely stare fell upon him.

'Bring forth the first of the petitioners,' Bel Shanaar declared, his voice deep and carrying easily to every part of the hall.

'It's really not that exciting after twenty years,' Carathril said quietly. 'It's not as if anyone asks anything of import at these events. Usually the petitions are nothing more than an excuse to highlight some new trade opportunity, or announce a marriage or death. It's just for show, all of the real business happens when the doors are closed.'

'I would dearly like to see that some time,' said Alith, also keeping his voice low. The benches around them were not quite full but there were plenty of other elves close at hand who would have little difficulty hearing the conversation. 'I hear that you have been to Nagarythe.'

'I once had the honour of marching with Prince Malekith, it is true,' said Carathril. 'That is also old news, though once my exploits were remarked upon by the greatest of princes.'

'I too have fought with Malekith,' said Alith, his voice the barest whisper.

Carathril directed a sharp look at Alith and leaned closer.

'You come clothed as a servant, yet you claim to have fought with the prince of Nagarythe,' said the herald. 'One or the other, or perhaps both, are a deceit.'

'Both are true,' Alith replied. 'I serve in the palace kitchens, and I have met Prince Malekith. I would like to speak to you, but this is not the place.'

Carathril darted a suspicious glance at Alith but then nodded.

'There is more to you than a simple kitchen serf,' Carathril said quietly, his eyes fixed upon Alith. 'You are clearly not exactly what you say you are, even if what you have told me already is true. I do not know what your interest is in me, but you should know that I am but a messenger, I bear no power in the palace.'

'It is simply your attention that I desire,' said Alith. He sat back and breathed a sigh. 'I know that you have no reason to trust me, and I can make no argument here that would convince you. If you would agree to meet me soon, name the place and time of your choosing and take whatever precautions you see fit – though we must be able to speak alone.'

'I do not like intrigue,' said Carathril. 'It is one of the things that mark me out from everyone else in the palace. I will speak with you, but if I do not like what I hear I will call for guards and you will be turned over to Palthrain. My agreement to see you is no promise.'

'And I ask for none,' said Alith. 'When and where shall we meet?'

'There will be an interval soon enough, you can come with me to my chamber,' Carathril said. 'I see no point in waiting any longer than that.'

Alith smiled in thanks and turned his attention back to the proceedings below. Carathril had been right, it was a dull affair as petitioner after petitioner came to give praise to the Phoenix King and ask for his blessing for some venture or other. Others came to complain about the taxes levied by Lothern for passing the Sea Gate, while one thought it most important that Bel Shanaar knew of his intention to sail to Lustria to secure timber for his village in Yvresse.

AFTER THE TENTH such meeting, Palthrain announced that this session was ended. Servants came into the hall bearing platters of sliced meats and trays laden with small cups and decanters of fragranced waters and the juices of exotic fruits. These were then passed into the audience so that they might refresh themselves.

'Time to go,' said Carathril, standing.

Alith followed the herald down the steps onto the main floor, where Carathril turned and bowed to Bel Shanaar. The Phoenix King nodded in greeting and darted an inquisitive look at his herald's companion. Alith bowed also, avoiding Bel Shanaar's gaze lest he react in some way that aroused suspicion. When Alith straightened he saw that the Phoenix King had turned his attention to his son.

CARATHRIL LED ALITH towards the northern towers of the palace and up several winding flights of stairs. This area had been out of bounds for Alith, for only those servants that possessed the seal of the Phoenix King could enter, something far above a lowly kitchen worker. Carathril passed between the guards at the doorway of the fourth storey without incident, Alith following meekly behind. A few steps along the corridor, Carathril shot a warning glance at Alith: a reminder that the Phoenix King's soldiers were close at hand should Carathril need them.

They walked down a long carpeted corridor – the passageways of the servants' quarters were bare stone – and Carathril turned to the right into another passage. He opened a broad door on the left of the corridor and waved Alith inside.

The herald's quarters consisted of two rooms. The first was a square reception area with low couches and tables and a small fireplace. Through an open archway beyond, Alith saw the bedchamber, which was sparsely furnished.

'I spend very little time here,' Carathril explained, noticing the direction of Alith's gaze. 'I have found it best not to make my chambers here too home-like, otherwise I would be doubly homesick.'

'Doubly?'

'I already miss Lothern greatly, though my service to the Phoenix King is an honour and a duty I would not relinquish on a whim,' said Carathril, closing the door and motioning for Alith to sit himself down. 'I return there often enough to remind me of what I love about the city, but not frequently enough to satisfy my desire to be there.'

'Yes, it is a hard thing to leave behind our homes,' Alith said with true sympathy. He had been away from Elanardris for only a short time but had frequently found himself wishing to return swiftly. Leaving aside the painful memories of Ashniel, he still found he loved the mountains as much as anything else in the world.

'Yes, and there is a curious thing,' said Carathril, sitting down opposite Alith. 'I have travelled across all of Ulthuan, and I have learnt many things that other, less cosmopolitan observers might miss. You call yourself Atenithor, which I believe is Chracian in origin, yet your voice betrays that you are not from there. If I am not mistaken I would say you were Ellyrion, perhaps.'

Alith smiled and shook his head.

'Close, but not correct,' he said, leaning against the back of the couch with one arm. 'I am Naggarothi. You would not recognise my accent as such though, as I come from the east, close to the mountains.'

'I have never been there,' said Carathril.

'That is a shame, for not only have you missed the breathtaking beauty of Elanardris, but also the counsel and friendship of House Anar,' said Alith.

'I am bid to go where the Phoenix King pleases, not to choose my destinations,' replied Carathril with a sigh. 'If my duties have not taken me there, it is because Bel Shanaar has no cause for me to visit.'

'That may well change,' said Alith. 'I think that the Phoenix King's interest in Nagarythe is going to increase greatly in the near future.'

'How so?' asked Carathril, frowning as he leaned forwards.

'I shall speak the open truth now, for I trust you, though I do not know why, and I wish you to trust me,' said Alith.

'Bel Shanaar says that I have an honest face,' Carathril said, and a smile played on his lips, the first sign of humour Alith had seen from the herald. 'I am his most trusted subject after his family and chamberlain. Anything you tell me will be taken in full confidence provided that it does not threaten the Phoenix King. My position here is entirely founded on my reputation for absolute discretion.'

'Yes, I have heard the same from others,' said Alith. He stood up to address Carathril. 'I am Alith, son of Eothlir, grandson of Eoloran Anar. I am a prince of Nagarythe, come to Tor Anroc in secret to seek the aid of the Phoenix King.'

Carathril said nothing. He sat and looked at Alith for a long while, the smile gone from his face. Then it returned, broader than before.

'You have a tendency for the dramatic, Alith,' he said. 'You have my attention.'

Alith crossed the room and sat beside Carathril.

'I must speak with the Phoenix King in private,' said Alith. 'Can you help me?'

Carathril leaned away from Alith's earnest plea and again sat in silence for some time, scrutinising his guest. Eventually he stood and moved to a cabinet against the wall. From this he drew out two crystal goblets and a bottle of silvery wine. He poured two measures, precise in his actions, and placed the bottle back in the cabinet. He offered one of the glasses to Alith as he sat down again. Alith took the drink but did not sample it. Instead he studied Carathril's face for some sign of his intent.

'You put me in a very difficult position,' said the herald. 'I cannot take your claims at face value, not yet. However, if what you say is true and your coming here is a secret, then I am severely limited in what inquiries I can make without revealing your presence.'

'I have a letter of assurance from my grandfather, in my room,' offered Alith, but Carathril waved away the suggestion.

'I am in no position to judge the veracity of such a document,' he said.

Again the herald pondered his decision, staring at Alith with the tenacity and vigilance of a hawk trying to guess the next movement of its prey. Alith remained silent, knowing that there was nothing he could say that would sway Carathril's choice.

Eventually Carathril nodded to himself, having reached a decision.

'Bring me this letter and I will deliver it – unopened! – to Bel Shanaar,' he said. 'If the Phoenix King assents to see you, then I have performed my duty. If not, then I fear that things may go ill for you. Though from outside you might think that we are complacent of the cults and other wrongdoers, in truth our watch has not faltered nor have our suspicions waned.'

Alith put down his goblet on the floor and grasped Carathril's hand.

'I cannot thank you enough for this kindness,' said Alith. 'I will bring you the letter at once, and hope that the Phoenix King judges it to be true.'

'I will wait for you outside the south-east dining hall,' Carathril said, standing up. He opened the door to indicate the conversation had ended.

Alith strode to the door, eager. Remembering his manners he stopped before leaving and turned to bow to Carathril. The herald returned the bow with a nod and waved Alith away.

NEARLY A WHOLE day of fretting followed Alith's encounter with Carathril. The heir of the Anars was distracted during his evening revelry with Milandith and the other servants that formed the clique of the kitchens, and he decided to retire early – and alone – to his room. The next morning he set to his work in the kitchens, glad of the distraction yet unable to clear his thoughts of his concerns. Had he been right in trusting Carathril? Would Eoloran's letter convince the Phoenix King? Even if Bel Shanaar consented to a meeting, how could it be arranged without being observed?

Every time the kitchen doors opened, Alith looked up sharply, not sure whether to expect a messenger or soldiers. His diverted state drew scowls from the chief cook, a domineering elf called Iathdir who ran the kitchen as a captain of the guard commands his company.

At mid-afternoon word came down that Bel Shanaar had requested a light meal in his chambers. Much to the concern of Malithrandin, no kitchen servants were free as all were in attendance for a feast being held by Princess Lirian, Eothlir's wife. Malithrandin commanded Alith to carry the tray of herb-crusted meats and spiced bread the Phoenix King had requested, and led the way towards the heights of the palace where the royal quarters were found.

Here the corridors were wide and stately, lined with mosaics of cut gems and sculptures both classical and modern. Alith had no time to admire the art, not that he had much inclination to do so, as Malithrandin strode purposefully along the passageway casting impatient glances over his shoulder. They also passed guards dressed in light mail and breastplates of gold, with pairs of swords – one short, the other long – hanging at their hips. They ignored Malithrandin but gave Alith disdainful glares as he hurried past. At the end of the long corridor was an unassuming door of white-stained wood. Malithrandin knocked lightly and then opened it, waving in Alith.

The rooms within surprised Alith. Beyond the unadorned door lay the opposite of the flamboyant decoration and dress of court. Here was the simple beauty of the dove compared to the strutting grandeur of a peacock.

The Phoenix King's personal chambers were minimally but exquisitely furnished, and even Alith's awkward eye could recognise the elegance of design and craftsmanship in the fluted legs of the high tables, the delicate juxtaposition of geometry and natural shapes in the carvings around the fireplace. All was white, including the carpeted floor. The only colour was the Phoenix King himself, who sat close to the fire in a robe of shimmering scarlet, a weighty book open on his lap. Out of his robes of office and crown, he had a more approachable air, and reminded Alith of his grandfather, though Eoloran's expression was usually more severe.

'Put it down there,' Bel Shanaar said, pointing to a low table to one side of the Phoenix King.

Alith did so, with a bow. Bel Shanaar leaned forwards, examining the contents of the platter. He carefully picked up a slice of cooked meat between thumb and finger and as he straightened the Phoenix King glanced at Alith, unobserved by Malithrandin who was still stood by the door.

'Is this Yvressian loin?' asked Bel Shanaar, waving the sliced meat in front of Alith.

'That is Sapherian loin, your majesty,' replied Alith.

'Really?' exclaimed the Phoenix King. 'And what is the difference?'

Alith hesitated and glanced towards Malithrandin.

'Oh, you might as well leave us, steward,' said Bel Shanaar with a dismissive wave of the meat cut. 'My guards can escort your companion back to the kitchens when I'm done.'

'Yes, your majesty,' Malithrandin said stiffly, bowing as he left, though Bel Shanaar had already returned his attention to Alith.

'Well?' said the Phoenix King. 'What is so special about Sapherian loin?'

'It is smoked for three years, your majesty, over chips of mage-oak and whitegrass,' replied Alith, who was glad that Iathdir had taken it upon himself not only to improve Alith's butchery skills but also his general knowledge of meat preparation. 'After that, it is soaked in–'

'You can dispense with the pretence, Alith,' said Bel Shanaar. He delicately folded the thin meat into a small packet and popped it into his mouth. Alith waited patiently while the Phoenix King chewed deliberately. Swallowing, the Phoenix King smiled. 'Your acting is as good as your carving. Tell me, why should I not call my guards and have you arrested as an assassin?'

Alith opened his mouth and then shut it, taken aback by the accusation. He quickly rallied his thoughts.

'Have you not read the letter from my grandfather?'

'I am addressed as "your majesty",' Bel Shanaar said calmly. 'Even if you are a prince, I am still your king.'

'Of course, your majesty, my profound apologies,' Alith replied hastily.

'This letter indeed comes from Eoloran Anar, of that I am certain,' said the Phoenix King, pulling out the parchment from inside his robe. 'It makes assurances of the bearer and requests that I offer you every assistance that I am able. Other than that, it tells me nothing. It tells me not of your intent, nor of the loyalties of your grandfather. I know Eoloran Anar of old, and respect him very much, but it appears he does not extend me the same courtesy. It has been more than seven hundred years since I have seen Eoloran in my court. How do you explain this?'

Again Alith was unsure what to say.

'I cannot speak for my grandfather, your majesty, or his actions, or lack of them, your majesty,' he replied. 'I know only that he has also shunned the court at Anlec and has withdrawn from a public life to enjoy introspection and the comforts of Elanardris.'

'Yes, that sounds like the Eoloran I fought with at Briechan Tor,' said the Phoenix King. He thrust the letter back into his robe and waved Alith to sit down on the chair opposite. 'Nagarythe is an enigma to me, Alith, and I cannot say that I wholly trust you. You come in secret to my palace and masquerade as a servant. You waylay my chief herald and arrange a meeting in which only you and I should be present. My only comfort is that enchantments are woven about this chamber and any blade that passes the door would be revealed to me. So, I feel safe enough, I suppose. What is it that you want me to do?'

'I am not sure,' confessed Alith. 'All I know is that the Anars, a loyal family of Nagarythe and Ulthuan, are victims of some political game or vendetta, and we cannot withstand this on our own.'

'Tell me more,' said Bel Shanaar.

Alith then related the recent history of the Anars, from before the return of Malekith and the travails with Morathi, to their recent indictment and arrest as suspected cultists. Alith was not much of a storyteller and frequently he related events in the wrong order, forcing the Phoenix King to ask questions or press Alith to highlight some pertinent point that he had skipped earlier. Throughout, though, Alith kept secret the existence of Elthyrior and was vague when Bel Shanaar quizzed him on how he had come by a certain piece of information or other.

'You know that there is little I can do to act directly in the lands outside Tiranoc,' Bel Shanaar said when Alith was finished. 'The people of the kingdoms answer to their princes and the princes answer to me. Perhaps if it were some other realm than Nagarythe I might be able to intervene, but there has never been anything less than cool relations between the Phoenix Throne and Anlec.'

The Phoenix King stood and paced to the high, narrow window, the afternoon sun bathing his face. He did not turn around as he spoke, perhaps unwilling to look at Alith as he delivered his decision.

'I cannot act unless your grandfather petitions me directly,' he said. 'Or perhaps your prince, Malekith, though that would seem unlikely. Your opponents have woven their tapestry of lies with considerable skill it would seem, and nothing has occurred that would threaten the authority of my position.'

Bel Shanaar turned and there was sympathy written across his face.

'All I can offer you at the moment is the sanctuary of Tor Anroc and my palace,' he said. 'I will keep safe your secret, and in fact I will do what I can to make your life here as pleasant as possible without revealing who you are or drawing attention to your presence. You are, of course, free to return to Nagarythe whenever you wish, and I will provide papers and escort to the border to ensure your safety if you do so. I will also make discreet inquiries with Malekith as to his current plans and thoughts, though I will leave out any direct mention of the Anars. If you wish, I can arrange for a message to be delivered to your grandfather, and perhaps he will come to Tiranoc and speak openly of these problems with me. Whatever pressures I can bring to bear on the matter will be brought, but I can offer no promises.'

THE WINTER PASSED slowly for Alith, though it was not without event. Bel Shanaar was careful not to reveal Alith's true identity, but by subtle means was able to extend his patronage to the young prince. It was made known that the Phoenix King deemed his new servant too old and too sophisticated to work as a kitchen boy, and so Alith was, through the stewards, elevated to a member of the court staff, attending to the ruler of Tiranoc and his family. In particular, Alith's duties were directed towards the comfort of Yrianath, Bel Shanaar's eldest nephew. This new position required that Alith had the seal of the Phoenix King and he found his freedom to explore the palace greatly increased.

Alith's ascent was something remarked upon by the other servants for a short while, but it was not the first time Bel Shanaar had shown favouritism to a particular elf in the household and most of the staff speculated that Alith's star would soon wane. Though graceful and diligent, he was considered somewhat uncouth for a future career at court, and those jealous of his sudden rise in esteem put down Alith's promotion to an eccentric fondness of the Phoenix King for the rural, oafish mannerisms Alith occasionally exhibited.

With his rise in position Alith felt a change in his relationship with Milandith. A bearer of Bel Shanaar's seal, Alith was privy to parts of the palace his lover was not, and so frequently she interrogated him on the latest gossip from the royal family. Alith became acutely aware that the passion that had brought them together was diminishing, and where once Milandith had viewed him as a source of pleasure she now regarded him as a bottomless well of information. The irony that their expectations of the relationship had been exchanged was not lost on Alith. Milandith's constant delving disturbed him, through a combination of his natural reticence and discretion, and growing feelings that any gossip might be a disloyalty to the family of Bel Shanaar.

Alith was keen not to draw attention to himself nor make an enemy of Milandith and her friends, so over the course of the winter Alith saw less and less of her and began to feign disinterest in her advances. Sure enough, as midwinter passed, he heard rumour that Milandith had abandoned her pursuit of Alith and turned her amorous attentions upon one of the guards. Over a pitcher of Yvressian wine, Alith and Milandith agreed that what they had enjoyed had now passed and they were to go their separate ways with no ill-feeling.

Though his secret was now safer, Alith's loneliness increased. He felt trapped in the palace and missed his home. The mountains of Tiranoc were several days away, and even though the winter was far less harsh here than in Nagarythe, he could not spare the time to go hunting there.

His isolation was not helped by the absence of any news from the north. Bel Shanaar assured Alith that he had despatched a messenger to Elanardris, but Alith feared that the herald had been waylaid, or that his family found it impossible to reply. Information from Nagarythe was sparse, and during the winter months the icy waters of the Naganath seemed to separate the kingdom from Tiranoc as much as any ocean.

So it was a frustrated, lonely Alith who wandered the corridors of the royal palace, or could be found upon the walls of Tor Anroc at dawn, gazing to the north. A few of his new friends expressed concern for this behaviour but Alith was quick to assure them that he was simply feeling a little weary and homesick and promised that he would be more entertaining when spring returned.

Yet when spring came, there was no surcease to Alith's worries. Merchants who had tried entering Nagarythe had been turned away at the border without explanation. What little news that came south was startling. There was fighting between the army of Anlec and pleasure cultists, and even in Anlec it seemed as if Prince Malekith struggled to maintain his rule. Some of his princes had turned against him and supported the cults, while others remained neutral, waiting to see where this latest power struggle would leave Nagarythe. Alith became quite agitated and enquired as to the names of those families involved, but not once were the Anars mentioned, for good or ill.

* * *

As these disturbing tidings found their way to the capital, Alith resolved to head back to Elanardris. By means of Carathril, he sent word to Bel Shanaar of his intent and in reply was brought again to the Phoenix King's chambers.

Bel Shanaar's expression was drawn as he stood beside the high arched window that looked out over the south of Tor Anroc. He turned as Alith closed the door.

'I cannot allow you to leave Tor Anroc,' said the Phoenix King.

'What?' snapped Alith, forgetting his manners entirely. 'What do you mean?'

'I mean that it would be unwise of me to allow you to leave my protection at this time,' said Bel Shanaar. 'And I do not think it would be to your benefit either.'

'But my family will need m–'

'Will they?' said Bel Shanaar, his expression stern. 'Are you so great a warrior that if they are involved in the fighting you will swing the tide in their favour?'

'That is not what I meant, your majesty,' said Alith, regaining some of his composure.

'Then perhaps they think you are unsafe here, away from this violent dispute, and would be better protected in Nagarythe?'

Alith shook his head, confused. He *knew* he should return to Elanardris to help, but Bel Shanaar was distracting his thoughts with these questions.

'I am sure they think me safe, your majesty,' said Alith. 'It is my duty to aid my house if they are in peril.'

'Is it not also your duty to keep alive the future of that house?' said Bel Shanaar, his expression as unrelenting as his words. 'Though it pains me to say this, you may already be the last of the Anars. Would you see that name die to satiate curiosity? Would you risk every future generation of the Anars because you are afraid of your uncertainty?'

Alith did not answer but his expression made it plain that he would indeed do such things. Bel Shanaar frowned deeply.

'Let me make myself as clear as a mountain lake, Alith,' said the Phoenix King. 'I am not allowing you to leave these palaces until there is more clarity in this matter. I have given you the benefit of my patronage but these new developments in Nagarythe are disturbing – open fighting between Malekith's soldiers and the sects – and I wish to know where you are at all times.'

Alith guessed the intent behind the words.

'You are keeping me hostage, in case the Anars are traitors.'

Bel Shanaar shrugged.

'I must consider all eventualities, Alith,' he said. 'While at this time I believe that you and your family are loyal, that loyalty is to Anlec and Nagarythe. Where the loyalty of the kingdom resides is as yet uncertain. It would be foolish of me to allow a potential spy, one who knows much about Tor Anroc, to return to Nagarythe. It would be foolhardy not to keep what means I have for negotiation with your house. Your house decided to bring me in as a player of this game and so my fate is woven into yours. I will use all of the pieces at my disposal.'

Alith stared dumbfounded at this statement, quite unable to believe what he was hearing.

'I demand your word of parole that you will not attempt to leave my palace. If you refuse, I shall have you imprisoned,' said Bel Shanaar. His expression softened as he crossed the room to stand in front of Alith. 'I bear you no ill-will, Alith, and I give my prayers to the gods that your family is safe and that Nagarythe swiftly overcomes this current turmoil.'

It was plain to Alith that he had little choice in the matter. If he refused to give his oath, he would be thrown into the cells beneath the palace. Not only would he lose his freedom, even amongst such momentous times this scandal would not go unseen and questions would be raised over his identity. That risked his life and his family's fortunes. He took a deep breath, collecting his thoughts.

'By such gods as might bear witness, I swear as a prince of Nagarythe and Ulthuan to remain under the protection of Bel Shanaar, and to make no attempt to leave Tor Anroc until such time as he gives me leave or circumstances change.'

Bel Shanaar nodded.

'I wish it were otherwise, and when you become lord of the Anars you will understand that with power come hard decisions. If I learn of anything, I will pass this on to you, and you must promise to do the same for me.'

'I will, your majesty,' said Alith with a formal bow. 'Is there anything else that I might attend to whilst I am here?'

Bel Shanaar shook his head.

'No, that is all.'

THE LAST FINGERS of summer were struggling to keep their grip on Tor Anroc when Alith began to overhear reports from Bel Shanaar's commanders at the northern border, telling of how the skies above Nagarythe were filled with smoke. They sent scouts over the river and found villages in ruins, burnt to their foundations, corpses littering their streets. Seers proclaimed a great darkness was sweeping down from the north, and these rumours soon rooted themselves in the populace of the city.

Word came via the heralds of other princes that the cults were on the rise once more. For twenty years they had stayed hidden, plotting and growing. At some unheard command they attacked the soldiers of Ulthuan's rulers, desecrated shrines and temples to other gods, and kidnapped the unwary.

Even in Tor Anroc there were small sects found practising rites to Atharti and Ereth Khial, and their members fought to the death rather than be taken prisoner. Paranoia gripped the palace at the resurgence of the cults, and hundreds of soldiers were brought back from the border to police the citadel and the surrounding city.

Fifteen days after the violence began, Alith received a message telling him that his presence was required by the Phoenix King. Alith hurried to the south hall as he had been instructed, and entered to find a great many of the princes of Tiranoc and their households gathered there, along with a small army of attendants and councillors. Alith could not see what was happening and surreptitiously made his way to the front of the crowd.

Bel Shanaar and his son Elodhir were stood beside the throne at the end of the hall, and Alith could see that Carathril was also in attendance. But it was the figure standing with them that drew Alith's eye. He wore a suit of golden armour, decorated with the design of a coiling dragon, and a long purple cloak that hung to the floor. The warrior wore a long sword at his waist – unusual in that most elves were not allowed to bear arms in the presence of Bel Shanaar – and under one arm he held an ornate warhelm decorated with a silvery-grey crown. His features were severe, his hair black and his eyes glittered with a dark light.

It was Prince Malekith.

'I have three thousand soldiers and knights that need billets,' the prince was saying. 'Once again I find myself putting practicality before pride, and must ask for sanctuary and the hospitality of Tor Anroc.'

Bel Shanaar regarded Malekith calmly, no hint of his thoughts betrayed.

'This is a grave situation indeed, Malekith,' said the Phoenix King. 'Doubtless the woes of Tiranoc are not of the magnitude of Nagarythe, but here also the cultists seek to usurp just rule. I am afraid that such aid as I may have been able to provide in times past is now impossible.'

'I need nothing from the Phoenix King, save his patience and understanding,' said Malekith with a slight dip of the head. 'Those that seek to oust me from power have revealed their hand, and this time when I strike back my blow will find every mark. There are many in Nagarythe that fight to protect my rule. Anlec is currently denied me by these wretches. I need a place to rally those forces loyal to me. Soon enough I will commence a new campaign to free Nagarythe of this vileness, for good this time.'

Malekith's expression was severe, his manner exuding anger, a deep rage that set his jaw twitching, his eyes fierce. Alith had seen that expression once before, when Malekith had spoken of seeing his mother after taking the gate of Anlec.

'Though surprise has garnered some victories for my enemies, they haven't the means or the courage for a true war,' the prince continued. 'I offered clemency before. Now I offer only swift retribution.'

'It is in the interest of all of Ulthuan that Nagarythe returns to stability as soon as possible,' said Bel Shanaar. 'I cannot deny you the right to shelter, but I must warn you that no other Naggarothi may cross the border without invitation. Is that understood?'

'I agree,' said Malekith. 'At a time when it is difficult to know friend from foe, I commend your caution. Now, with your pardon, I must see my mother.'

At this Bel Shanaar paused. Alith knew that Malekith had visited Morathi on several occasions since her incarceration two decades earlier, and it seemed an expected request considering Nagarythe was in such disarray. Even so, the mere mention of the former sorceress-queen sent a shiver of fear through Alith, mixed with a deep-rooted hate. The hall was silent as the elves waited in expectation of the Phoenix King's reply.

'Of course,' Bel Shanaar said eventually. 'Though I have no love for Morathi, I would not deny you.'

Malekith again bowed in thanks and, accompanied by Elodhir, strode from the hall. Bel Shanaar and Carathril left by another archway, and as soon as the Phoenix King had gone chattering broke out amongst the crowd.

'What has happened?' Alith demanded, grabbing the arm of the nearest elf. The page looked at him with astonishment.

'Cultists have retaken Anlec and Prince Malekith has been deposed,' said the elf, with a haughtiness held by those who consider themselves important for having heard news moments before any other. 'It seems those Naggarothi fiends are fighting amongst themselves again.'

Alith stayed his tongue at this remark and instead walked quickly from the hall. He made his way back to his room in the servants' quarters and there sat on his bed, staring at the stone floor. He could make no sense of it. How could the cults have gathered such power unseen? How had they survived Malekith's diligent purging? Unable to comprehend what had occurred, Alith's mind was blank, numbed by the dire news.

FOR THREE DAYS the palace was chaotic. Rumours and claims spread through the residents and servants alike. Lodgings were found for the small army Malekith had brought south with him, and Alith was busy attending to the errands of his masters and mistresses. Yrianath was preoccupied with matters pertaining to Tiranoc's trade and how it might be affected by the situation in Nagarythe, which held considerable power in the Elthin Arvan colonies. Distracted, Yrianath often overlooked Alith's presence, allowing the heir of the Anars to overhear things that in normal times would have remained secret.

Malekith called upon the Phoenix King to assemble the princes of Ulthuan in council. They were to meet at the Shrine of Asuryan upon the Isle of Flame: the most sacrosanct of places where Aenarion and Bel Shanaar had been elevated to Phoenix King. Alith watched Carathril leave along with many other messengers, the chief herald's expression grim and distant.

Alith had his own distractions. His ignorance of how affairs in Nagarythe were unfolding was driving him to the point of madness and he spent each night unsleeping, toying with the idea of breaking his oath to the Phoenix King and fleeing Tor Anroc. Yet each morning he realised that the means by which his house might be saved lay here at the capital, not in the north, and so he remained.

Preparations were made for the Phoenix King's expedition to depart for the Isle of Flame. Elodhir had already departed and when Bel Shanaar left, control of the palace would fall to Yrianath, as the next prince of mature age. This made for much work for Yrianath's councillors and servants, who were kept busy at all hours to apprise themselves of every development. Despite his exhaustion, Alith still found no solace in sleep and became so irritable that others avoided him when they had the chance.

Frustration almost spilled into violence when Alith overheard a group of nobles speaking foully of the Naggarothi, blaming them for every ill that had befallen Ulthuan in recent centuries. It was only the accidental intervention of one of the stewards, calling upon Alith to attend to Yrianath, which prevented the young Anar from striking the nobles.

All of this frenetic activity reached a calm equilibrium the day before the Phoenix King was due to leave. In a rare moment of peace, Alith was in the gardens, staring wistfully at a marble sculpture of a waterfall. It was refined and finely detailed, but lacked all of the majesty of the real thing. Rivers cascaded down the mountains of

Elanardris with thunderous power, sending spray and fog across the surrounding slopes. The gentle tinkling of this fountain seemed ludicrous and trite in comparison.

'There you are.'

Alith turned and found Milandith sitting beside him on the white bench. She wore a green silken dress, her braids woven into showers of hair that spilled across her shoulders. In the autumn sun she was as pretty as Alith had ever seen her and for a moment he was lost in admiring her beauty.

'Why such worries?' asked Milandith, running a hand across Alith's brow as if to smooth away the creases of his frown.

'Do you not think these are dark times?'

'They are,' she said, grasping Alith's right hand in both of hers. 'Yet what is there that we can do? The princes will meet to decide, and we will be ready to help them.'

She laughed, a peculiar sound to Alith's ear given the grimness of his mood.

'I would not like to have such responsibility,' she said. 'Can you imagine? Trying to decide what to do about all of this? Raising armies and waging wars are not in my nature.'

But they are in mine, Alith thought. He was a son of House Anar and if battle was to be waged, he would be there to wage it. He looked at Milandith, soaking in her innocence and beauty. How simple it would be, he thought, to make the masquerade real. He could live in peace as Atenithor of Chrace, a servant to Prince Yrianath and nothing more. He could renew his relationship with Milandith, and perhaps they would wed and have children. Bloodshed and murder, darkness and despair would be the realm of princes and he would live out his life as a simple soul.

But that could not be. Not only did guilt gnaw at his heart, duty ingrained in him since he had been born stiffened his resolve. He could no more hide from this than a rabbit could hide from one of his arrows. He was Alith Anar, heir to a princedom of Nagarythe, and he could not pretend otherwise.

'You are distracted,' said Milandith, unhappy. 'Perhaps I am boring you?'

'I am sorry,' said Alith, forcing a smile. He ran his fingers lightly over Milandith's hair and cheek, his fingertips coming to rest on her chin. 'I am distracted, but not by the sort of distraction I would like.'

Milandith returned his smile and stood, pulling him up by the hand.

'I think I can find just the sort of distraction you need,' she said.

ALITH DOZED, FEELING the heat from Milandith beside him. In his half-asleep state he could hear doors banging elsewhere in the servants' quarters and feet running outside but he chose to ignore them. The moment had passed though, and the real world was beginning to intrude again upon the blissful ignorance brought about by Milandith's attentions. Hoping to set aside his pain for a while longer, Alith leaned across the bed and nestled his face in her unkempt hair, kissing her lightly on the neck. She murmured wordlessly and, eyes still closed, laid a hand upon his back, gently stroking his skin, tracing the whip-scar with a finger.

Suddenly there was a furious knocking at the door. A moment later it crashed open. Both of them shot upright as Hithrin, Steward of Halls, burst into the room. There was a wild look in the elf's eyes, bordering on terrified hysteria. His wide gaze settled on Alith.

'There you are!' he cried, running across the room and grabbing Alith by the arm. 'Your master calls for all his servants to attend!'

Alith snatched his arm away and shoved Hithrin backwards, though the steward was supposedly his superior.

'What?' snapped Alith. 'Can I not have a moment's peace? What could be so urgent?'

Hithrin stared dumbly at Alith for a moment, his mouth opening and closing without sound. He swallowed hard and then blurted out his news.

'The Phoenix King is dead!'

NINE

Darkness Descends

THE GREAT HALL was in pandemonium. Elves of all ages and stations had come from across the palace to hear what had happened. Yrianath stood beside the Phoenix Throne, Palthrain and many other nobles and councillors with him. As Alith pushed his way through the throng, there was an air of panic and desperation. Some elves were shouting, others weeping, many stood in shocked silence, waiting to hear the words of Yrianath.

'Be calm,' he cried out, raising his hands, but the cacophony continued until Yrianath raised his voice to a roar. 'Silence!'

In the stillness that followed only the rustle of robes and quiet sobbing could be heard.

'The Phoenix King is dead,' Yrianath said solemnly. 'Prince Malekith found him in his chambers early this morning. It would seem that the Phoenix King took his own life.'

At this there was another outburst of anger and woe, until Yrianath signalled again for the elves' attention.

'Why would Bel Shanaar do such a thing?' demanded one of the nobles. It was Palthrain who stepped forwards to answer the question.

'We cannot know for sure,' said the chamberlain. 'Accusations had come to Prince Malekith that the Phoenix King was embroiled with the cults of pleasure. Though Malekith disbelieved such claims, he has sworn in this very hall to prosecute all members of the cults, regardless of station. His own mother is still imprisoned in this palace. When the prince went to Bel Shanaar's chambers to confront him with the evidence, he found the Phoenix King's body, with the marks of black lotus on his lips. It seems that the charges were true and Bel Shanaar took his own life rather than face the shame of discovery.'

The hall shook with a rising clamour as the elves surged forwards, making demands of Palthrain and Yrianath.

'What charges?'

'What evidence was presented?'

'How can this have happened?'

'Are the traitors still here?'

'Where is Malekith?'

This last question was asked several times, and the call grew louder and louder.

'The prince of Nagarythe has departed for the Isle of Flame,' said Yrianath when some measure of order had been restored. 'He seeks to inform Elodhir of his father's demise, and to take guidance from the council of princes. Until Elodhir returns from the council, we must remain calm. The full facts of what has occurred here will be brought to light, rest assured.'

Though still much distressed, the elves were somewhat quietened by this statement and instead of angry shouts, a conspiratorial murmuring filled the hall. Alith ignored the buzz of gossip and the tearful lamentations and turned to Milandith. Her cheeks were wet with tears and he clasped an arm around her and pulled her close.

'Do not be afraid,' he said, though he knew his words to be a lie.

A STRANGE ATMOSPHERE enveloped the palace over the following days. There was little activity and Alith could sense that his fellow elves were each trying to come to terms with what had transpired. Few were willing to talk about their shock and grief, which was unusual in itself, and fewer still would mention the circumstances surrounding Bel Shanaar's death. There was an undercurrent of suspicion, formless and unspoken but palpable.

Alith's first thought was to leave the city, now that he was no longer bound by his oath to Bel Shanaar, but he decided against this course of action. Though events could threaten to expose him, he heard no hint or rumour concerning his arrival not long before Bel Shanaar's demise. To leave hastily would perhaps invite more attention than staying.

Instead, Alith stayed close to Yrianath, as required by his position and as his curiosity desired. The prince was as shocked as any by the tragic turn of events and seemed content to await Elodhir's return rather than take any lead himself.

Bel Shanaar's body was made ready for interment in the great mausoleum of his family in the depths of the mount beneath Tor Anroc. The funeral proceedings could not start without Elodhir, and so the elves found themselves in a spiritual limbo, unable to publicly express their grief. For once, Alith missed the idle chatter that used to distract him so much. In the echoing quiet of the palace his dark thoughts resounded all the more.

SIXTEEN DAYS HAD passed when new arrivals caused a great stir in the palace. Alith had been attending to Yrianath, who was in discussions with Palthrain concerning the funeral arrangements of Bel Shanaar. A herald entered hastily, announcing that he had come from the Isle of Flame.

'What news of Elodhir?' asked Yrianath. 'When can we expect his return?'

At this, the herald began to weep.

'Elodhir is dead, among many other princes of Ulthuan,' he wailed.

'Speak now, tell us what has happened!' demanded Palthrain, grabbing the messenger by the arms.

'It is a disaster! We do not know what happened. A mighty earthquake shook the Shrine of Asuryan, and there were signs of violence. When we entered, only a few princes had survived.'

'Who?' insisted Palthrain. 'Who survived?'

'A handful only came out of the temple,' said the herald, almost buckling at the knees. 'So many nobles dead...'

The herald swallowed hard and straightened, wiping a hand across his eyes.

'Come,' he said, turning towards the door.

Alith followed a little way behind Palthrain and Yrianath, and they seemed content to allow him, if they even noticed his presence. The herald took the group across the courtyard and out of the great gate of the palace where a large crowd had gathered. There were many carriages, each draped in white awnings. Tiranoc soldiers held back the throng, casting their own shocked glances back towards the coaches. Palthrain forced his way through the crowd and Alith followed in his wake.

The chamberlain pulled back one of the white curtains and Alith caught a sight of Elodhir, lying upon a bier inside the carriage. His face was as white as snow and he was laid upon his back, arms folded across his chest. Yrianath gasped and looked away. Just before Palthrain allowed the curtain drop back, Alith thought he saw the red mark of a wound across the dead prince's throat, but so brief was the glimpse that he could not be sure.

Another elf came striding through the carriages. She was clad in silver armour and a black cloak. Alith immediately recognised her as Naggarothi and shrank back towards the other elves, though he did not know her. She spoke briefly to Palthrain and pointed at one of the other carriages. An expression of dread passed over Palthrain's face before he composed himself. Without a word, he turned and hurried back into the palace.

Yrianath sent the captains of the guard to bring more soldiers from the city. With a stone-faced expression the prince gave instructions for the staff of the palace to begin moving the dead Tiranocii nobles inside. Alith was pleased not to be counted amongst the number tasked with this unpleasant chore, and stayed out of sight as best he could.

THE GRISLY LABOUR was interrupted by shouts of dismay from the crowd around the gates. Alith turned to see Palthrain ordering elves out of his path. He was followed by a contingent of the Naggarothi warriors who had come with Malekith. They created a line through the thronging elves and behind them strode another.

She was tall and stunningly beautiful. Her long black hair fell in lustrous curls about her shoulders and back, and her alabaster skin was as white as the stone of the gate towers. Her dark eyes were fierce and Alith flinched from their gaze as the elf stared scornfully at the assembled watchers. Alith knew her immediately and felt fear grip his heart.

Morathi.

The crowd fell back in fear as she swept through the gate, the train of her purple dress streaming behind her, boots ringing on the flags of the road. Her full lips were twisted in a sneer as she surveyed the frightened mass. As soon as she came within sight of the carriages, her entire attention was fixed upon them and so swift was her stride that Palthrain had to run to keep pace.

He led her to one of the coaches and Morathi threw back the coverings with a beringed hand. She fell to her knees and uttered a shriek, an awful wail that pierced Alith's mind and echoed from the walls of the palace. Looking beyond Morathi, Alith saw what lay upon the board of the wagon.

It was a blackened mess and at first Alith did not recognise what it was. As he forced himself to look closer, Alith saw streaks of gold that had melted into rivulets and then solidified, and links of chainmail burned into charred flesh. It was the figure of an elf, obscene in its desecration. Two unblinking, unmoving eyes stared out and half of the elf's body was seared down through flesh and muscle, revealing burned bone. Dark flakes fluttered from the corpse, drifting on the wind. Alith stepped a little closer and could make out something of the design on the figure's breastplate, though it was much disfigured. It was the remnants of a coiling dragon.

At that moment Morathi rose to her feet and wheeled towards the watching elves. Her eyes were orbs of blue fire and her hair danced wildly in an unseen gale while sparks erupted from her fingertips. With cries of fear, the crowd turned and ran from the sorceress.

'Cowards!' she shrieked. 'Look at this ruin! Face what your meddling has brought about. This is my son, your rightful king. Look upon this and remember it for the rest of your wretched lives!'

Elves were shouting and screaming as the stampede continued, pushing and pulling at each other as they tried to press back through the gatehouse. Alith ignored them, transfixed by the apparition of Malekith's corpse. He felt sick, not just from the sight, but also from a foreboding that welled up in his stomach and froze his spine.

The tramp of many booted feet echoed around the plaza, joined by the clattering of hooves. Such elves as remained scattered ahead of a column of black-clad spearmen and knights: the rest of Malekith's warriors. Like a black snake they advanced from around the palace and for a moment Alith feared that they would attack. They did not.

Instead they formed a guard of honour three thousand strong around the carriage as Morathi climbed aboard. Alith looked to the Tiranocii warriors to intervene, but those that had remained were afraid to confront the grim-faced soldiers in front of them. He did not blame them, and was rooted to the spot by the stern lines of spears and the immobile knights. Morathi signalled to the driver and the carriage moved away with a rattle of wheels and the crunch of the marching Naggarothi.

One of the captains of the Tiranoc guard stepped forwards, somewhat cautiously, hand on sword hilt at his waist. Palthrain intercepted the warrior and put a hand to his chest.

'Let them go, Tiranoc is well rid of them,' said the chamberlain. Without incident the Naggarothi left the plaza down the tunnel-road to the east, and then were out of sight.

With that, Prince Malekith passed out of Tor Anroc for the final time.

THERE WAS A deathly hush in the grand hall and an air of reverence surrounded the two bodies laid in state upon marble slabs either side of the Phoenix Throne. Though Bel Shanaar's death remained contentious, he had ruled over Ulthuan for one thousand, six hundred and sixty-eight years and was accorded due respect from all present. Thousands of elves had filed past the Phoenix King's remains, preserved by the attentions of priests dedicated to Ereth Khial, the blemishes of his poisoning removed by priestesses of Isha. Alith noted that Elodhir's body wore a collared robe that concealed his neck and so was unable to confirm the wound he had thought he had seen in the carriage.

The doors had been closed after five days and only the household of the princes remained. Alith was in attendance to Yrianath, as were other servants to their masters and mistresses. The hall was almost empty, for many nobles from Tiranoc had travelled with the Phoenix King to the council of princes and not returned alive. The bodies of some had been brought back from the Isle of Flame and were with their families in the manses around the huge palace. Some had not returned at all and their fate remained unknown.

'A grievous wound has been done to Tiranoc,' declared Yrianath. He seemed just as stunned as when he had first looked upon Elodhir's corpse. Beside him were Lirian, Elodhir's widow, and the dead prince's son, Anataris. She was draped head-to-foot in white robes of mourning, her face concealed behind a long veil, the babe in her arms swathed in white cloth. Of her expression, Alith could see nothing.

'Tiranoc will not stand idle in these times,' Yrianath continued. Though his words were meant to be defiant and stirring, his voice was hollow. 'We shall prosecute by whatever means those who have heaped this hurt upon us, and taken from Ulthuan its rightful ruler.'

There was a discontented rustle of voices and Yrianath frowned. He cast his weary eyes over the nobles.

'Now is not the time for whispers and secrets,' the prince said, gaining some vigour. 'If there are any present who wish to speak their mind, they are free to do so.'

Tirnandir stepped forwards with glances to the rest of the court. He was the eldest member of the court after

Palthrain, born just twenty years after Bel Shanaar's ascension to the throne and respected as one of the Phoenix King's wisest advisors.

'With what authority do you make such promises?' the noble asked.

'As a prince of Tiranoc,' replied Yrianath.

'Then you claim succession to the rule of Tiranoc?' asked Tirnandir. 'By tradition, the line does not pass to you.'

Yrianath looked confused for a moment and then turned his eyes upon Lirian and Anataris.

'Bel Shanaar's heir was Elodhir, and Elodhir's heir is no more than three years old,' said Yrianath. 'Who else would you propose?'

'A regent, to claim rule until Anataris comes of age,' said Tirnandir. It was clear from the nods of other council members that this had already been discussed in private.

Yrianath shrugged.

'Then as regent I will make these promises,' he said, uncomprehending of any cause for objection.

'If a regent is to be appointed, then he or she need not be of the descent of Bel Shanaar,' said Illiethrin, the wife of Tirnandir. 'You are no more than six hundred years old, there are many in this hall better suited to the role of regent.'

Palthrain intervened before Yrianath could reply.

'These are uncertain times, and our people will look to us for leadership,' said the chamberlain. 'It is not proper that the stewardship of Tiranoc passes far from the royal line. Other realms are facing the same woes as we, and surely our enemies will exploit any dispute to their own purposes. Yrianath has a claim by blood that is strong, and with such advisors as are gathered here, his policies can yet be wise. To do otherwise invites claim and counter-claim by those who seek to undermine the true rule of Ulthuan.'

'And where is that true rule to be found?' snapped Tirnandir. 'There is no Phoenix King, and we have had no word from the council of princes regarding a successor. Morathi has been let free once more, and her ambition will not have been dimmed by twenty years of imprisonment. No doubt she will put forth some claimant of her own. Does the elf we choose here also take on the Phoenix Crown and cloak of feathers?'

'I do not seek the Phoenix Throne,' Yrianath said hastily, holding up his hands as if to ward away the suggestion. 'It is for Tiranoc that I will act. Other kingdoms shall surely look to themselves at this time.'

There was angry muttering and Palthrain raised his hand for silence.

'Such a matter cannot be decided in a moment,' he said. 'All concerns can be raised and deliberations made in due course. It is unseemly to squabble in this fashion, here beside the body of our Phoenix King. No, this will not do at all.'

'We will talk on this matter again when respect has been paid to the deceased and the memory of our lord properly regarded,' said Tirnandir with an apologetic bow. 'It is not division we seek, but unity. Ten days hence we will convene again and make such petitions as are required.'

The nobles bowed to the bodies of the dead, and a few nodded their heads to Yrianath as they left, but several darted suspicious glances at the prince. Alith believed Yrianath beyond reproach, for he had been in the prince's entourage for several seasons and seen or heard nothing to raise his suspicions. However, the sudden removal of both Bel Shanaar and Elodhir had left the subject of succession wide open for debate, as Alith suspected those who had perpetrated the deaths had intended.

Though these lofty concerns occupied a little of Alith's thoughts while the final arrangements were made for the twin funerals, he was mostly concerned for events in Nagarythe. He decided that as soon as the ceremony was concluded, he would head north and rejoin his family. Who could say what chaos reigned with Prince Malekith dead?

THE BURIAL RITES of the Phoenix King and his son would be long, even by elven standards, and were due to last ten days. On the first day, Alith joined a long line of mourners who passed by the dead to celebrate the lives of those who passed. Poetry was recited praising the achievements of Bel Shanaar as both a fighter in the time of Aenarion and a king in times of peace. Under his auspices, the elven realm had grown every year, so that the colonies of Ulthuan stretched across the world to the east and west. The alliance with the dwarfs in Elthin Arvan was lauded by a choir of three hundred singers, and this irritated Alith more than he had thought it would. In those conversations he had shared with Yeasir at Elanardris, the commander had made it clear that it was Prince Malekith who had forged the friendship with the dwarfs and Alith was inclined to agree.

The second day was spent in silence, the whole of Tor Anroc eerily quiet as the populace meditated upon the memories of Bel Shanaar and Elodhir. Some would write down their thoughts in verse, others kept their recollections to themselves. This period of solitude gave Alith time to sit in his room and think deeply on what had happened. His thoughts were never focussed on one thing, and he reached no conclusion as to what had passed or what he needed to do next. He longed more than ever to return to the mountains and the support of his family.

Thinking of Elanardris took Alith onto a dark path, and he horrified himself with all kinds of fearful imaginings of what might await his return. He had received no word from family or friend for almost a year and he did not know whether any were still alive. The frustration he had felt over that period welled up inside him in one wave and he vented his anger and fear with violence, smashing lamps, tearing at the sheets on his bed and driving his fists into the walls until his knuckles were bleeding heavily. Panting, he collapsed onto the floor, weeping uncontrollably. He tried without success to fight back the images of torment that assailed him, until long after midnight he fell into an exhausted sleep.

WHEN HE AWOKE, Alith found himself refreshed, though no more optimistic than he had been the night before. Though shared by no other, his personal outpouring had cleared his mind and he knew what he needed to do. His decision to remain at Tiranoc for the ceremony of burial was simply an excuse to delay his inevitable return. While ignorance tortured Alith for the most part, it also gave him hope, a hope that might be crushed as soon as he returned north. He realised he was being immature, seeking reasons to keep himself in this vacillating state, and set about packing up such possessions as he would need on the journey.

There was a knock on the door and Alith pushed the half-filled pack beneath his bed before opening it. It was Hithrin, who glanced at the destruction Alith had wrought the night before but made no comment.

'We are to attend our master, Alith,' said the steward, not unkindly. 'He is to receive an important guest at midday. Tidy yourself up and come to his chambers as soon as you can.'

Hithrin gave Alith a look of sympathy and then walked away. The look was like a barb to Alith's pride and he busied himself clearing up the ruin he had made of the room and dressed himself carefully. This menial activity allowed him to gather his thoughts after the interruption and he weighed up whether to attend to Yrianath or depart straightaway. Alith decided to remain a little while longer, intrigued to find out what manner of guest would call upon Yrianath at this time of mourning.

THE RECEPTION FOR Yrianath's visitor was a sombre, stately affair. Alith, amongst the other servants, had prepared a simple cold luncheon in the lower east chamber, a small hall overlooked by two galleries. Just before the prince's guest was due to arrive, the servants were asked to leave and Alith filed out with the rest of them.

He was perturbed by this secrecy and slipped away from the other staff as they made their way back to the servants' quarters, doubling back to the hall. Using the serving stairs normally employed to bring trays of food and drink to parties gathered on the galleries, Alith slipped unseen into the main chamber. High windows lined the south and north walls of the hall, but shed little light on the galleries, which were usually lit by lanterns when in use. From the hazy gloom, Alith peered down into the hall.

Yrianath was sat at one end of the long table, the platters of food arrayed before him. He picked nervously at their contents until there was a resounding knock at the door.

'Enter!' Yrianath called out, standing.

The door opened and a functionary bowed low before ushering in the prince's visitor.

Alith suppressed a gasp and shrank back towards the wall as Caenthras strode into the chamber, resplendent in armour and cloak. Yrianath hurried forwards and greeted the Naggarothi prince at the near end of the table.

Alith began to panic. Why was Caenthras here? Did he know of Alith's presence, and if so what was his purpose in coming to Tor Anroc? The urge to flee before discovery gripped Alith and it took all of his nerve to remain where he was. He told himself that he was over-reacting, and that if he were to remain a while longer he would soon have the answers to these questions. He slipped forwards to the balustrade and nervously looked down on the elves below.

'Prince Caenthras, it is a pleasure to welcome you,' said Yrianath. 'Long have we yearned for news from beyond the Naganath. Please, sit down and enjoy what hospitality one can in these dark times.'

Caenthras returned the bow and placed his helm upon the table. He followed Yrianath to the food and sat down at Yrianath's right as the prince seated himself.

'These are indeed dark and dangerous times,' said Caenthras. 'Uncertainty holds sway over Ulthuan and it is imperative that authority and order are restored.'

'I could not agree more, and may I offer my condolences to all in Nagarythe, who have also suffered the loss of a great leader,' said Yrianath, pouring wine for himself and his guest.

'I am here as official embassy for Nagarythe,' said Caenthras, picking up the goblet and swirling its contents. 'In order that any turmoil is dealt with, it is vital that the rulers of Ulthuan work together. It is a woe to us, then, that so many realms are as yet without leaders, and we know not with whom to discuss these matters. I hear that Tiranoc is embroiled in such a debate at the moment.'

'I think embroiled is perhaps too strong a word...'

'Is it not true then that there is disagreement over who will succeed as ruling prince?'

Yrianath hesitated and sipped his wine as a distraction. Caenthras's forceful stare did not waver and Yrianath put down his glass with a sigh.

'Issues have been raised over the succession,' he said. 'As the oldest blood descendant I have offered to act as regent for the time being, but there is opposition from some of the other court members.'

'Then I should tell you that Nagarythe supports your claim to Tiranoc,' said Caenthras with a broad smile. 'We are strong believers in tradition, and it is fitting that the relatives of Bel Shanaar succeed him.'

'If you could but convince my peers of my case, then the matter would be settled,' said Yrianath, leaning towards Caenthras with earnest intent. 'I do not seek division, and a swift end to this matter is the best outcome for all concerned, so that we might turn our attention to graver issues.'

'Most certainly,' said Caenthras, patting Yrianath's hand. 'Stability is the key.'

Caenthras helped himself to a little food, arranging it carefully on his plate. When done, he cocked his head to one side and directed a thoughtful gaze at Yrianath.

'I would say that the word of one prince, an outsider at that, would do little to sway the opinion of the Tor Anroc nobles,' said the Naggarothi. 'As a sign of support I am willing to petition certain other princes and officers of Nagarythe to travel to Tor Anroc and speak on your behalf. I am sure that having such allies will increase your standing and strengthen your claim beyond reproach. It is, after all, unity that we seek at this time.'

Yrianath considered this for a moment, but Alith could already see the trap being laid. If Yrianath wanted to be leader of Tiranoc he needed to do so from his own strength. Had not the Anars suffered greatly of late for relying too much on the support of others? Alith wanted to warn the prince not to agree, to tell him that it was a false bargain, but he dared not reveal his presence to Caenthras. Instead, he remained mute and watched the terrible plot unfold.

'Yes, that would seem a good course of action,' said Yrianath. 'I see no problem with that.'

'Then might I impose a certain request upon you?' said Caenthras.

Here it comes, thought Alith as he watched Yrianath drawn towards the lure like a fish.

'Your northern border is closed to the Naggarothi,' continued Caenthras with a disarming shrug. 'It is only by chance that I met one of your officers who would vouch for me, and thus allowed me to pass into Tiranoc. I fear such embassies as would come south on your behalf will not be so fortunate. I wonder if perhaps you could write me several letters of passage, which I might send to my fellow princes to act as permission to cross the Naganath with their bodyguards?'

'Well, yes, of course,' said Yrianath. 'I will give you the seal of my princedom as a guarantee of safe passage. How many would you need?'

'Let us say a dozen,' said Caenthras, smiling. 'You have many allies in the north.'

'A dozen?' replied Yrianath, flattered. 'Yes, I see no reason why that cannot be arranged.'

The prince's expression of happiness then faded and his shoulders slumped.

'What is the matter?' asked Caenthras, the picture of concern. 'Is there some problem?'

'Time,' muttered Yrianath. 'Deliberations are due to recommence at the ending of the funerals, only seven days hence. I fear my supporters will not arrive in time to swing the debate, and my rivals already arrange their arguments against me.'

'I have riders ready to go north at once,' said Caenthras. 'I cannot guarantee that our friends will be able to reach Tor Anroc in seven days, but perhaps you could delay proceedings in some fashion.'

Yrianath brightened at this suggestion.

'Well, the discourse of court never runs swiftly,' he said, as much to himself as his companion. He gave Caenthras a determined look. 'It can be done. I shall provide you with my seal before night comes. I am sure that a final decision can be averted until I can make my strongest case.'

Caenthras stood and Yrianath rose with him. The Naggarothi extended a hand, which the prince shook enthusiastically.

'Thank you for your understanding,' said Caenthras. 'A new alliance between Nagarythe and Tiranoc will no doubt set our people on the path to greatness again.'

'Yes, it is time that history took its place behind us and we looked to the future once more.'

'A most progressive and commendable attitude,' said Caenthras. He turned for the door but then looked back at Yrianath after a few paces. 'Of course, we will keep this arrangement between us for the moment, yes? It would be counter-productive if your opponents were to hear of what has passed between us.'

'Oh, that is for sure,' said Yrianath. 'You can rely on my secrecy, as I can on yours.'

Caenthras gave another nod and a smile and then left. Yrianath stood for a moment tapping his fingers upon the tabletop, obviously happy. With a self-assured stride, he walked out of the room, leaving Alith alone in the silence.

As he had listened to the exchange between the princes, Alith's fear had disappeared, to be replaced by anger. It was clear that Caenthras had long been manipulating events in Nagarythe to increase his own standing, and had worked against the Anars even as he had pretended to be an ally. Alith did not know how long this treacherous, selfish goal had driven Caenthras, but he looked on everything the prince had done with suspicion. Caenthras had once been a true friend of the Anars, of that there was no doubt, but somewhere, at some time, he had chosen to take a different path. The betrayal burned inside Alith, igniting the jealousy, fear and frustration that had been swirling inside him since Ashniel had been taken away.

Now that Caenthras's plots were involving the rule of Tiranoc, there was a clear danger to all of Ulthuan.

Caenthras had to pay for his duplicitous crimes.

THE RITES OF passing for Bel Shanaar and Elodhir continued for the next seven days. There were ceremonies of mourning led by the greatest poets of Tiranoc, who recited anguished requiems to the Phoenix King accompanied by dirgeful wailings and choruses of weeping maidens. Alith found these recitations utterly lacking in originality or special significance, bland oratories of loss and woe that spoke nothing of those who had died. In Nagarythe, such verses would be filled with true lamentation for those who had been taken away, composed by the families who had lost a loved one. In all, Alith found these professional mourners to be overblown and impersonal.

The next day heralded the first of several rituals of sanctity during which the rightful priests and priestesses of Ereth Khial prepared the bodies and spirits of the deceased for the afterlife. These spiritualists were unlike the cults of the dead that had risen in Nagarythe. They sought not to converse with the supreme goddess of the underworld, but to protect the souls of the departed from the attentions of the ghost-like rephallim that served the Queen of the Cytharai. As with the mourners, Alith was left a little confused. In Elanardris it was well understood that the spirits of the dead would go through the gate to Mirai, there to dwell forever under the watchful eye of Ereth Khial. There was no fear, only acceptance that death is the natural conclusion to life.

Unlike the wild chanting and sacrifices Alith had witnessed in Anlec, these true priests bathed the bodies in blessed water and used silver ink to paint runes of warding on the dead flesh. He watched from the back of the attending crowds as they made whispered intonations to placate the rephallim, and wove chains of beaded gold around the limbs of the departed so that they would be too heavy for the vengeful ghosts to carry away.

During the funeral, Caenthras was housed as a guest of Yrianath and Alith had to move warily, to avoid discovery by the Naggarothi prince. He spied on the pair whenever the opportunity presented itself, which was rare, but was nearly always clever enough to pass on some duty that required his presence to another of Yrianath's household. On occasion Alith was forced to take extreme measures to avoid being seen by Caenthras, ducking into doorways or running down halls on hearing his approaching voice. At one time he even resorted to hiding behind a curtain, something Alith had thought only occurred in children's tales.

Simply killing Caenthras would not be as easy as Alith had first thought. Certainly slaying him without being caught was quickly looking impossible, as the prince never seemed to be out of company, either of Yrianath, Palthrain or some functionary of the palace.

While the keen edge of his hatred for Caenthras remained undiminished, as Alith observed the prince from afar, his vow to slay him was mollified by a desire to visit upon him the same ruin as he had perpetrated against the Anars. A simple knife in the back in the darkness would only cause more suspicion and grief, while an open challenge would reveal his presence and raise all number of unpleasant questions regarding his presence in the palace at the death of Bel Shanaar. On top of that, Alith was pretty certain that in a straight fight with Caenthras, the veteran of the wars against the daemons would surely win.

If Alith could understand more the nature of Caenthras's scheming he would be able to bring about a more just downfall than simple death. Alith wanted Caenthras exposed and shamed before his life was ended. To do that he needed to know everything about Caenthras's plans, his allies and his minions. That would mean awaiting the arrival of the other nobles who would vouch for Yrianath's accession. For the time being, Alith was patient enough to stay his hand and see what was unveiled.

THE DAY CAME for the final interment of the dead rulers of Tiranoc, and tens of thousands of elves travelled to the capital to pay their respects and witness this last journey. There were, some commented, few princes and nobles from other realms. Speculation was rife on why this might be so. The more pragmatic observers simply mentioned the travails that had beset Ulthuan's rulers of late and suggested that most would be busy keeping order in their own lands. The more conspiracy-minded locals believed that there was a deliberate snub implicit in the absence of so many worthwhile citizens of Ulthuan. A few elves, after encouragement from friends who should probably have known better, even went as far as to say that the Phoenix King's death was held in such suspicion by the other kingdoms that they feared to come to Tiranoc.

Alith's own conclusion was that those princes who had survived the tragedy at the Shrine of Asuryan, of which there were very few by many accounts, had far more important things to do than doff their crowns to a dead body. Though some in Tor Anroc had forgotten, the uprising from the cults that had preceded the council of princes was still ongoing. It was the nature of folk to concentrate on their own perils and woes, and none in Tiranoc could consider the grief of other people to be anything like as great as theirs. For the sake of peace, Alith kept these opinions to himself when asked to venture his thoughts on such matters.

THE BODIES OF Elodhir and Bel Shanaar were set in state upon the backs of two gilded chariots, each pulled by four white steeds. Three hundred more chariots rode in escort with the departed, followed by five hundred spearmen and five hundred knights of Tiranoc. Yrianath, Lirian, Palthrain and the other court members were also driven in chariots, decorated with chains of silver and flying the pennants of their houses, following behind the body of the Phoenix King.

Alith and the other servants were gathered in the plaza outside the gatehouse, which had been cleared of all other elves, so that they might witness the passing away of their former lords. Alith watched the thousands-strong cortege wind its way out of the palace grounds and take up station in the square. The golden chariots then emerged and all present gave up a great shout, declaring their farewells to the fallen king and prince. Sonorous pipes sounded from the towers of the palace to warn the city below, and the blue flames of the gatehouse flickered and died.

Alith had not known Bel Shanaar well, and had cause to resent some of his actions. Yet he could not stop tears forming in his eyes as he watched the procession clatter out of the plaza. Thus had passed the first Phoenix King since Aenarion, and the world ahead lay uncertain. No matter what came next, Alith knew that an age had ended and felt in his core that his generation would not know peace. Blood had been shed, the kingdoms of Ulthuan were divided and there were those who seemed determined to drag the elves down into darkness.

WITH THE PHOENIX King and his son interred within the sepulchres at the heart of the mountain, the business of the palace was soon abuzz with the succession. The servants were full of opinion as to who would be the more suitable prince to rule. However, all of their heightened speculation was to be for nothing. Yrianath claimed a sickness had befallen him, brought about by the grief of the funerals, and would not be able to participate in any debate whilst he was under the influence of this affliction.

'It must be a tremendous burden,' said Sinathlor, guard captain of the towers where Yrianath's chambers were located. He and several others of the prince's household were in the common room of their quarters, drinking autumn honeywine. Alith sat a little way apart, attentive to the discussion but far enough away that he need not participate directly.

'I am not surprised that he has been set low by this malady, not surprised at all,' added Elendarin, Stewardess of the Halls. She swept back her white hair and gazed at her companions. 'He has always been of a delicately sensitive disposition, ever since he was a child. His empathy for the people's grief is a tribute.'

Alith suppressed a disparaging remark at this saccharine observation, but Londaris, Steward of Tables, was not so polite.

'Ha! I have never seen anything so obviously false in my life,' he declared. 'This very morning, I found the prince on his balcony taking in the dawn sun and he seemed as fit as a hunter's hound.'

'Why feign such weakness?' argued Sinathlor. 'Surely that gives argument to Tirnandir and his cronies?'

Alith was fascinated by the professional loyalty of the household of each noble, who would argue the cause of their master and mistress in the fiercest of debates, yet as soon as their role and duties changed would switch their defences to their new lord or lady. It was not so with Gerithon, whose family had served the Anars since Eoloran had founded Elanardris, or the other subjects of the house who owed their loyalty alone to their prince and their kingdom.

'Yes, it does,' Londaris was saying. 'That is why I think it a risky move. I am sure the prince knows best, but I cannot see at the moment what advantage he gains.'

Another thing that occurred to Alith during the debate was that all of the elves present had a personal stake in the unfolding events. If Yrianath's bid succeeded, they would be members of the ruling household of Tiranoc, with all of the privilege that entailed. It was in their own interests to see the court's decision favour their master.

'He gains time,' said Alith, sensing an opportunity. 'Have you not noticed that of all the visitors who have requested to see him, only the Naggarothi, Caenthras, has been admitted? Not even Lirian, who is the ward of our lord since the death of her husband, can see Prince Yrianath. I fear that this illness may not be the fault of the prince at all, but some ploy by the Naggarothi envoy.'

There were frowns from some of the elves, but nods from others.

'What have you heard?' demanded the Fire Master, Gilthorian.

Alith held up his hands as if in surrender.

'I know nothing more than I am saying, I assure you,' he replied. 'Perhaps it is simply idle speculation on my part, for I am still a novice in the ways of politics. Yet it occurs to me that this envoy has Yrianath's ear by some means, and their meetings are always held in secret. Not even Palthrain attends them, and he supports Yrianath's claim. I do not know what this means, but it makes me wary.'

The others attempted to question Alith further and then took up his line of reasoning when he declined. It was, they agreed, somewhat suspicious for a Naggarothi prince to arrive in Tor Anroc during the funeral, and Caenthras certainly had unprecedented access to Yrianath. Though no conclusions were drawn, Alith went to his bed that night content that he had stirred up an unwitting force of spies on his behalf. He hoped the rumour would spread to other households and perhaps the nobles themselves, so that they might pay closer attention to Caenthras's activities.

On the seventh night after the conclusion of the burial ceremonies, at a time when the demands for Yrianath to come to the court were becoming louder and louder, Alith was woken by the thud of booted feet in the corridors above his room.

He dressed quickly and slipped quietly out of his chamber. The palace was in a new tumult and Alith followed the other servants as they made their way towards the main halls. He froze when they came out into the courtyard at the centre of the palace grounds, for stood there were rank upon rank of spearmen and bowmen, several thousand of them. They were not dressed in the white and blue of Tiranoc, but in the black and purple of Nagarythe. Alith immediately ducked back inside, his heart beating.

The Naggarothi princes had arrived, and they had not come alone.

TEN

A Loyal Traitor

ALITH ARRIVED IN the corridors outside Yrianath's chambers just in time to see Caenthras and an escort of Naggarothi entering the prince's rooms. Alith ducked down a servants' stairwell as the group emerged, Yrianath in the midst of the imposing warriors, looking much distressed. There was nothing Alith could do, even if he had been armed. He slipped away down the stairs to the floor below, where Lirian lived.

As he emerged from the stairway, a group of Naggarothi, four of them, rounded the corner. Alith turned to run but the closest leapt forwards and grabbed his arm, hauling him back into the passageway.

'Please,' Alith begged, falling to his knees. 'I'm just a poor servant!'

The warrior sneered as he hauled Alith to his feet.

'Then you can serve us, wretch,' he snarled.

Alith smashed the heel of his hand into the soldier's chin and as the warrior fell, snatched free the sword at his waist. The blade cut the throat of the next before the Naggarothi could react. The remaining pair split, coming at Alith from both sides.

Alith parried the first blow and leapt backwards as the point of a sword stabbed towards his chest. His return attack crashed against the shield of the warrior to his left and his arm jarred from the impact. Alith's heart was in his throat as he dived beneath another swinging blade, rolling on his shoulder to come up to a guard position a moment before the other warrior launched a furious assault. Blow after blow rang from Alith's sword as he backed down the corridor, heading towards Lirian's chambers.

In a momentary respite from his assailant, Alith used his free hand to tear down a tapestry upon the wall, hurling it at the warrior. He followed up with a jumping kick, the ball of his foot smashing into the swathed figure, sending him toppling to the carpeted floor.

The other leapt over his fallen comrade, but Alith had expected this and lunged, chopping at his foe's leg. Blade bit into armour and rings of mail scattered across the corridor in a spurt of blood. The Naggarothi fell to the ground, a cry of pain torn from his lips. Alith drove the point of his sword into the warrior's exposed neck.

The remaining soldier disentangled himself from the tapestry but lost his sword and shield in the process. As he bent to retrieve his weapon, Alith brought his blade down hard on the back of his head, splitting the warrior's helm and biting into his skull.

Panting, Alith straightened and assured himself that his foes were dead. He leant the sword against the wall and hurriedly unfastened the belt of one of the soldiers, wrapping it around his own waist. Sheathing his stolen blade, he ran down the passageway to the royal chambers.

THE TWIN DOORS were open and there was no sign of anyone within. Alith stepped cautiously inside, ears alert for any sound, but there was none. A quick glance through the doors and archways leading from the antechamber confirmed that the Naggarothi had already taken Lirian and her son.

Alith could spare no further thought for the missing heir to the Tiranoc throne. The Naggarothi would be searching the whole palace and sooner or later he would run across opposition he could not avoid or overcome. It was inevitable that he would be recognised by someone. He needed to get out of Tor Anroc.

Alith assumed that the Naggarothi had entered by the main gateway, and so headed through the palace towards the north towers, hopefully ahead of any search parties. He kept to the side corridors and hidden stairwells used by the servants to move about the palace unseen by their masters. As he came closer to the servants' quarters he could hear yells and cries from ahead.

He changed route, cutting eastwards across the lawn of a night garden, skimming from column to column, through moonlight and shadow, along the edge of the cloister. Beyond were the outer parts of the eastern wing, and from there he would be able to reach the formal gardens at the back of the palaces.

Several of the ground-floor windows were unshuttered and open, and Alith jumped through the closest. He heard tramping feet echoing from bare stone to his right and so turned left at a run. His headlong sprint brought him out into one of the smaller gateyards that led out of the palace into the grounds. He was about to haul open one of the solid wooden gates when he heard footsteps behind him.

Turning, Alith saw more than a dozen spearmen entering the paved square. He saw a flash of white amongst them: Lirian carrying Anataris. The nearest warriors levelled their weapons and advanced slowly. Alith drew his sword and put his back to the closed gate.

'Wait!' the officer at the back of the group called out. Alith recognised the voice.

The small troop parted and the captain strode forwards. Though much of his face was concealed by his helmet, Alith could see that it was Yeasir.

The commander of Nagarythe stopped suddenly on seeing Alith. For his part, Alith was unsure what to do. If he turned his back to open the gate they would be upon him, and if he tried to fight, he would have no chance of victory.

'Put down your weapon, Alith,' Yeasir ordered.

Alith hesitated, flexing his fingers on the grip of his sword. He glanced at Lirian, who seemed oddly calm. She nodded reassuringly. Alith reluctantly let go of the sword, the clatter of its fall like a mournful knell as it echoed around the gateyard. Alith slumped back against the gate, raising his hands in a gesture of surrender.

Yeasir handed his spear to one of his soldiers and approached, his gauntleted hands held up in front of him, palms upwards.

'Do not be afraid, Alith,' said the captain. 'I do not know how you come to be here, but I am not your enemy. I mean you no harm.'

Yeasir's words did not relax Alith in the slightest and the young Anar's eyes darted around the yard seeking some other avenue of escape. There was none. He was trapped.

'Come, quickly,' said Yeasir, waving a hand over his shoulder.

Lirian, her baby in her arms, trotted forwards. As she did so, Yeasir gestured to one of his warriors.

'You, give me your bow and arrows,' snapped the commander. The soldier complied, slinging his quiver from his shoulder and passing it to Yeasir. To Alith's surprise, the Naggarothi captain handed them on to him and then stooped to pick up the discarded sword.

'There is little time to explain,' said Yeasir as he slipped the weapon into the sheath at Alith's waist. 'This is a most fortunate encounter for both of us. Now you can take the heir of Tiranoc to safety.'

A handful of the soldiers stepped forwards and opened the gate, letting in the moonlight from the gardens beyond. Lirian hurried through.

Alith could say nothing and stood shaking his head.

'Morathi has returned to Anlec and not all are pleased,' Yeasir said hurriedly. 'She wishes to punish Tiranoc for what happened to Malekith – it is not safe to be here. There is a haven to the east; I have told Princess Lirian its location. I will do whatever I can to delay pursuit, and will join you there in a few days' time. My wife and daughter are hidden there also, and together we will head east to sanctuary in Ellyrion.'

'What?' was all that Alith could muster.

'Just go,' snarled Yeasir. 'I must report the escape of the princess to the others and a search will soon follow. I will come to you and explain all.'

With that Yeasir shoved Alith unceremoniously through the gate, which closed soundlessly behind him. Lirian was already hurrying along a paved path ahead and Alith ran to catch up. Sounds of fighting echoed from the towers of the palace as the three of them headed into the night.

YEASIR LED HIS troops into the great hall, where other parties of Naggarothi had brought the various members of the court, as directed by Palthrain. The chamberlain stood beside the Phoenix Throne with Prince Yrianath and Caenthras. The last of these frowned when he saw Yeasir.

'You are unaccompanied,' said the Naggarothi prince.

'It seems our prey has eluded us for the moment,' replied Yeasir lightly. 'She will not get far, not with a child to care for.'

'That is unfortunate,' growled Caenthras.

'You believe she is still in the palace?' asked Palthrain.

'It is unlikely that she will quit Tor Anroc,' said Yeasir. 'Where else would she go? We are upon the brink of winter and the princess is no expert of the wilds. Tomorrow we will begin a search of the city.'

'I expected more of you,' Caenthras hissed quietly as Yeasir took his place beside the others.

'Though I may not be a prince, I am still Commander of Nagarythe,' Yeasir replied, keeping his tone level. 'Do not forget that.'

Caenthras remained sullenly silent as Palthrain called for the attention of the fearful Tiranocii nobles.

'There is no cause to be afraid!' the chamberlain announced. 'These warriors are present at the request of Prince Yrianath. In these uncertain times, it is important that we all remain vigilant for the corrupt amongst us, and our Naggarothi allies are here to help.'

'You invited them here?' said Tirnandir, his voice dripping with scorn.

'Well, I...' began Yrianath, but Palthrain cut across him.

'It is imperative that we choose a new prince to succeed Bel Shanaar, who might treat with our allies with authority,' said the chamberlain. 'Prince Yrianath has declared himself fit to be regent. Are there any present that oppose his claim?'

Tirnandir opened his mouth and then shut it again. Like all the other assembled courtiers, his eyes strayed to the Naggarothi warriors lining the hall, their swords bared and spears in hand. Palthrain waited for a moment and then nodded.

'As there is no objection raised, I declare that Prince Yrianath shall be our new regent, until such time as Prince Anataris comes of age to assume his rightful position. Hail Yrianath!'

The Naggarothi shout was far louder than that of the Tiranocii, who mumbled their praise and exchanged fearful looks.

'These are unprecedented times,' continued Palthrain. 'When faced with usurpers and traitors, we must act swiftly to ensure the safety of all loyal elves and prosecute those that would undermine the true rulers of Ulthuan. To that end, Prince Yrianath will enact the following laws.'

Palthrain then produced a rolled-up parchment from the sleeve of his robe and handed it to Yrianath. The prince took the scroll uncertainly and, prompted by a stare from Palthrain, unrolled it. His eyes scanned the runes upon it, widening with shock. A fierce glance from Caenthras quelled any protest and Yrianath began to read aloud, his voice wavering and quiet.

'As ruling prince of Tiranoc I decree that all soldiers, citizens and other subjects give their utmost cooperation to our Naggarothi allies. They are to be extended every courtesy and freedom whilst they aid in the protection of our realm. You are to obey the commands of such officers and princes of the Naggarothi as if they were mine. Failure to comply will be considered an act against my power and punished by death.'

Yrianath's voice broke at this point and he swayed as if about to faint. Eyes closed, he steadied himself and then continued reading.

'Due to the uncertain loyalties exhibited by some within the army of Tiranoc, I also decree that every soldier, captain or commander is to surrender his weapons to our Naggarothi allies. Those who secure our faith will be allowed to return to their positions as soon as practical. Failure to comply will be considered an act against my power and punished by death.'

A profound silence had fallen upon the hall as Yrianath's words settled in the minds of the Tiranocii. The prince's eyes glimmered wet as he continued, casting plaintive glances at those he had unwittingly betrayed.

'My last decree of this accession is to temporarily disband the court of Tiranoc until such investigations surrounding the demise of Bel Shanaar clear those present of involvement in this unspeakably vile act. I hereby take all authority to rule as regent and my word is law. Such commands as issued by former members of the court have no validity and should be disregarded until confirmed by myself or our Naggarothi allies. Failure to comply will be considered an act against my power and punished by death...'

There was open discontent, a ripple of whispers, short-lived as Caenthras stepped forwards and took the scroll from Yrianath. The Naggarothi's expression was stern.

'In order to comply with the wishes of your new prince, you will all be escorted back to your homes and placed under house arrest. You will be called for in the following days to account for your actions.'

With a gesture from Yeasir, the Naggarothi soldiers ushered the assembled nobles towards the open doors. When the Tiranocii had been escorted out, Palthrain turned to Caenthras.

'That went better than I expected,' said the chamberlain. 'Now our work can begin.'

DAWN HAD YET to creep above the mountains when Lirian led Alith to a stretch of wooded hills north and east of Tor Anroc. The pair had spoken little on the journey, much to Alith's relief. He had no words of comfort and though he had known about the conspiracy between Caenthras and Yrianath, he had suspected nothing of what was to unfold from that partnership. As they silently followed road and path, and finally cut across the meadows of outlying farms, Alith had tried to make sense of what had happened.

They walked steadily uphill through the darkness of the trees, Lirian clutching Anataris to her chest. Alith studied the princess out of the corner of his eye, seeing strain on her face. She was dressed in a light robe, utterly unsuitable to cross-country travel and very much stained and ragged. Her usually perfectly arranged hair fell in blonde disarray and her eyes were red from suppressed tears. There was bleakness about her expression that echoed the emptiness in his heart.

Alith tried to think of words of comfort that he might say but he could find none. Every turn of phrase seemed trite or nonsensical. He could offer no reassurance for he felt none himself. Everything had fallen apart, and as far as Alith could work out, it all pointed back towards Nagarythe. He found that he had far more questions than answers and wished that he had been able to find out more from Yeasir.

Lirian stopped and wordlessly pointed to the left. In the gloom Alith could just about make out the darker shape of a cave opening. Drawing his sword, he signalled for the princess to hide behind a tree. Stalking ahead, Alith heard whispered voices. Both were female.

Coming to the cave he found a small group huddled around a shuttered lantern, the dim light barely reaching the cave walls. There were three elves, two female and a child wrapped in a bundle of blue cloth. Both of the adults were clad in heavy robes of deep blue and embroidered shawls of the same colour. The older of the two, perhaps seven or eight hundred years of age, jumped to her feet, a dagger in her hand. She stepped protectively in front of her younger companion and the baby.

'Friend,' said Alith, swinging his sword to one side. The terrified elves remained unconvinced and he tossed the blade out of the cave. 'I am here to help, Yeasir sent me.'

His protestation was met with fearful looks and Alith returned outside, calling for Lirian. The princess walked warily through the trees and would not enter the cave until Alith stepped inside. The two groups of elves looked suspiciously at each other for a moment.

'Who are you?' asked the younger elf. 'What do you want?'

'I am Alith Anar, friend of Yeasir,' Alith replied. 'I am escorting Princess Lirian and her son.'

'What is happening, where is my husband?' demanded the elder of the pair. 'Where is Yeasir?'

'He is in Tor Anroc, misdirecting the pursuit,' replied Alith. 'What is your name?'

'Saphistia,' she told him, placing the knife back in her belt. 'This is my sister, Heileth, and my son, Durinithill. When will Yeasir come?'

'I do not know,' said Alith, leading Lirian by the arm. He gestured for her to sit beside Heileth. 'He instructed me to wait here but promised he will join us soon. Have you any food or drink?'

'Of course,' said Heileth.

She stood and carefully handed the child to his mother and then turned to a row of packs laid against the rock wall. She brought out a waterskin and several small cups and passed them to Alith. Wrapped packets of cured meats followed.

'Anar is not a trusted name in Nagarythe these days,' said Saphistia as Alith poured water for each of them.

'Lies,' snarled Alith. 'We have been victims of a campaign to discredit our house. Yeasir trusts me, and so should you.'

Alith did not wait for any further comment and left the cave to retrieve his sword from the fallen leaves outside. He stayed there a while, scanning the woods for any sign of pursuit. There was none. Ducking back inside, he grabbed a cup and some food.

'I'll keep watch,' he told the others before swiftly retreating again.

He had no desire for company and sat with his back against a tree. He barely tasted the spiced meat, his thoughts far away in Nagarythe. When Yeasir returned Alith would leave and go north. Yeasir could run to Ellyrion if he wished – he had his family with him. Alith would return to Elanardris to discover what had befallen his kin.

Dawn brought no sign of any other elf, friend or foe. Alith looked into the cave and found all within were asleep. Taking his bow in hand, he set off to find some fresh food.

'So it seems that your assumptions were wrong,' said Palthrain. 'The princess has escaped the city.'

Yeasir did not reply, but simply hung his head, feigning shame. He was alone in the great hall with the chamberlain and he longed to strangle the traitorous noble, but knew that he needed to keep his own loyalties concealed if he was to rejoin his family.

'Two days have been wasted,' continued Palthrain. 'Two days ahead of your forces.'

'I believe they are on foot. Our riders will swiftly catch them,' said Yeasir.

'They?'

'Yes, it is also my belief that the princess has help,' Yeasir said quickly, keeping his expression bland whilst inwardly he cursed his slip of the tongue. 'A soldier perhaps, or a servant. I cannot imagine that Lirian has the wit to contrive such an escape on her own. She is a spoilt Tiranocii bitch.'

'And when were you going to appraise me and Caenthras of this conclusion?'

Now Yeasir allowed his anger to show.

'While you may take some credit in creating this situation, remember that I am commander here! You are not even Naggarothi, so be mindful of your accusations.

Morathi might be mildly distressed should anything happen to you, but we are a long way from Anlec. Bad things, unseen events, happen in war. If you were a Naggarothi, you would know that.'

Palthrain seemed unconcerned by Yeasir's threats.

'So what is your plan to continue the search?' asked the chamberlain.

'She will not go north, that takes her closer to the Naganath,' said Yeasir.

'But much of Tiranoc's army is camped in that direction. The princess might seek sanctuary with them.'

'Possible but unlikely,' said Yeasir. 'I very much doubt that she trusts anybody in Tiranoc at the moment. I think she will go west, heading for the coast. There she will be able to take ship to any other realm in Ulthuan.'

'Why would she trust other kingdoms when she does not trust her own?'

'She might not, but the sea is the greatest obstacle to recapturing her. If she has headed south or east, we will be able to catch her before she reaches Caledor or Ellyrion. If Lirian reaches a ship, we have no means of pursuing her.'

'I can see there is reason in your argument,' Palthrain said, leaning upon the arm of the Phoenix Throne.

'I was not asking your permission,' said Yeasir.

'Of course not,' Palthrain replied smoothly. 'Still, it might be better that you inform Caenthras of your plan so that you can... coordinate your forces.'

'What of Yrianath?' said Yeasir, keen to steer the topic of conversation away from the question of who had authority amongst the occupying soldiers. Morathi had charged the commander to lead the warriors, but many of those troops were direct subjects of Caenthras and owed their loyalty to the prince. 'He is little use as a regent until we have the heir in our possession.'

'Yrianath gives us a veil of legitimacy for the time being,' said Palthrain. 'He understands his position very well, as do the other members of the court. Once we have Lirian and her brat, Yrianath will be able to conduct affairs with the other kingdoms as we desire.'

Yeasir nodded and turned towards the door. Palthrain's words reached him at the end of the hall.

'That is, of course, assuming you actually *find* Lirian.'

Yeasir stopped but did not turn.

'When this is done, there will be a reckoning,' he whispered to himself before striding away.

FOUR DAYS HAD passed since the flight from Tor Anroc and there had been no sign of Yeasir. Saphistia was becoming distraught and repeatedly urged Alith to head back to the city to find out any news concerning her husband. Alith flatly refused to do so, saying that he would not leave the group unprotected.

'How long must we stay here?' asked Lirian as the fourth day turned to the fourth night. The princess had regained little life, and spent most of her time listlessly wandering around the cave, whispering to her son.

'We wait until Yeasir arrives,' replied Saphistia.

'What if he doesn't come?' the princess said with a long sigh. 'He could be dead already.'

'Don't say such a thing!' snapped Heileth.

Saphistia merely directed a venomous gaze at Lirian and retired to the back of the cave where the two children were laid upon beds Alith had made from leaves and a cloak. There was another opening beyond, which led into a network of water-carved tunnels that ran through the hills. This was to be their escape route if they were discovered, and Alith had spent some time exploring them at night while Heileth had kept watch. If the worst occurred, there was a small tunnel they could use to head north, and Alith had assembled a small trap made of branches and rocks that could be used to block the route to delay any pursuit.

'It was a grand procession,' Lirian said idly. 'All of those banners and chariots.'

'What was grand?' asked Heileth.

'Elodhir's funeral,' the princess replied, her voice distant, her gaze directed at nothing in particular.

'Stop talking about funerals,' hissed Saphistia. 'Yeasir is alive. I would feel it if he were dead.'

'Elodhir died so very far away,' said Lirian. She turned her empty eyes to Saphistia. 'I didn't feel a thing.'

Alith quit the cave with a shake of his head. He offered praise to any gods listening, asking if they would deliver Yeasir soon so that he could leave the bickering group behind. Even as he formed these thoughts, a movement amongst the trees caught his attention. In a moment Alith had his bow in hand and an arrow to the string.

Listening, Alith could hear the muffled hoof-beats of several steeds and soon he saw a figure leading half a dozen horses across the leaf mould. Alith slipped behind a nearby tree, arrow aimed at the new arrival. A few heart-beats later and Yeasir came into view. Alith stepped out and lowered his bow.

'You do not know how pleased I am to see you,' Alith called as he walked down the hill.

'Your celebration may be short-lived,' replied the commander. 'I cannot stay long.'

'How so?' Alith asked as Yeasir joined him. The pair walked towards the cave, the horses trailing obediently after them.

'Caenthras's forces are close by,' said Yeasir. 'It is not yet safe to leave and I must return before my absence is noted.'

When they came to the cave, Saphistia ran to the cavern entrance and embraced her husband tightly.

'Thank the gods that you are safe,' she gasped. 'I feared the worst with every passing moment.'

Yeasir calmed his wife, kissing her on the cheeks, before turning his attention to his son. He picked up the babe from where he lay swaddled in a blue blanket, and held him close to his chest, his eyes lingering lovingly on Durinithill's small face.

'He has been so brave,' said Saphistia, clasping her arm around Yeasir's. 'Not a whimper or a tear the whole time.'

As if emerging from a sleep, Yeasir then straightened and handed the child to Heileth.

'I have brought steeds and more supplies,' he said. 'I must divert the pursuit further south today, and tonight I will return. Then we can leave before the search begins afresh in the morning.'

Lirian stirred at the back of the cave.

'What of Yrianath?' she asked. 'Perhaps you could rescue him also?'

Yeasir shook his head sadly.

'Yrianath is caught in his own folly,' said the commander. 'Palthrain and Caenthras watch him every moment. It is you and your son that must be kept safe. Without the true heir their claim to any legitimate rule is weak.'

Yeasir then shared another long embrace with his wife, and as they parted his face betrayed his pain. For a brief moment, Alith thought that Yeasir would not go, and he wondered what it was like to share such love.

His expression full of stern resignation, Yeasir tore his eyes away from his loved ones and left the cave. Alith followed him out.

'There is something I wish to speak to you about,' said Alith.

'Be quick,' said Yeasir.

'I am returning to Nagarythe,' Alith told him. 'I cannot go with you to Ellyrion. I must go to my family.'

'Of course,' said Yeasir, his eyes straying for a heartbeat towards the cave. 'Keep them safe until tonight, and then you may follow whichever path you need.'

Alith nodded. He watched Yeasir head off through the woods, heading to the west, until the commander had disappeared from sight. He sat down on a rock and began his melancholy watch.

NOT FAR FROM the cave a figure swathed in magical shadow watched Yeasir leaving. He swung into the saddle of his black horse, his raven-feathered cloak swirling behind him. Silently, he steered his steed south, riding swiftly.

A SENSE OF foreboding filled Yeasir as he crossed the plaza towards the palace. As he came to the gatehouse, he saw Palthrain standing with a small company of warriors. Yeasir's heart began to pound. Something was wrong.

'How fares the search?' the chamberlain asked, his manner off-hand.

'No success today,' said Yeasir as he stepped past.

'Perhaps you would have more luck if you did not waste your time visiting secret caves,' said Palthrain.

Yeasir whirled around to confront the chamberlain. A sly smile crossed Palthrain's lips.

'Did you think you could betray us?' he said.

Yeasir ripped his sword free and lunged before the guards could react. The blade punched through Palthrain's robes, sliding effortlessly into his gut.

'I'll see you in Mirai,' hissed Yeasir, dragging his sword from the blood-bubbling wound.

He cut the arm from the first warrior that approached and drove its point through the throat of the second. Yeasir dodged aside from the spear of a third and broke into a run, sprinting through the gateway.

Running to the corral that had been made where the market had once stood, Yeasir jumped onto the back of a horse and urged it into a gallop. Three Naggarothi attempted to bar his path but he rode straight through them, snatching the spear from the grasp of one of them as he passed. With the echo of thundering hooves resounding from the walls, he passed into the tunnel-street that wound down through the mount of Tor Anroc.

There were shouts of alarm from behind Yeasir but he paid them no heed, growling at his mount to run as fast as possible. Elves threw themselves from his path as he raced through the city. His heart was pounding with the hooves of his steed and he was gripped by a breathless panic. Everything in the world seemed to disappear around him. All that existed was the thought of his wife and son.

DUSK WAS SETTLING on the fields of Tiranoc as Yeasir's headlong rush across the countryside continued. He spared no thought for his steed falling foul, his every intent upon the wooded hills ahead. In the ruddy light Yeasir could see armed figures marching into the woodland.

Steering left, he sought to overtake the warriors. He ducked as he came to the edge of the trees, branches whipping at his face and shoulders. A glance to his right confirmed that several hundred Naggarothi were converging on the cave.

His horse stumbled on a root and Yeasir almost fell. With a ragged gasp, he righted himself and urged the horse onwards. The glint of armour and weapons could be seen in the gloom ahead.

With a last effort, Yeasir forced his mount up the hillside that led to the cave, cries from the warriors around him sounding through the trees.

'Alith!' he shouted as the cave came into view. The young Anar leapt up from where he was sat, his bow suddenly in hand.

Yeasir reined his mount to a skidding stop, sending a cloud of leaves swirling in the air. He swung himself down to the ground and ran for the cave.

'We are undone!' said the commander.

Saphistia and Heileth dashed from the cave. Yeasir waved away the attentions of his wife.

'Take the children and flee!' he rasped. 'The enemy are at hand.'

Even as he spoke these words, the first of the Naggarothi could be seen advancing through the woods. They pointed up the hill towards the cave and hastened their attack.

'Flee!' cried Yeasir, grabbing Saphistia and shoving her towards the cave. She fought back, slapping away his arm.

'You are coming with us!' she said, tears streaming down her face.

Yeasir relented for a moment, pulling her close, his arms tight around her. He caught the scent of her hair and felt the warmth of her against his cheek. Then hollowness gripped him, welling up from the pit of his stomach, and he pushed Saphistia away.

'Take Durinithill and go,' he said hoarsely. 'Protect our son, and tell him that his father loved him more than anything else in the world.'

Saphistia looked as if she would stay, but Heileth grabbed her arm and dragged her towards the cave. With a wordless cry, Yeasir bounded after them and threw his arms around Saphistia for a last time.

'I love you,' he whispered and then pulled away.

Yeasir looked at the Naggarothi stalking through the woods and his sorrow was burned away by a bright anger. His body was aflame with rage, his hands trembling with the emotion. He had known little peace in his long life.

He thought he had found it, but there were those who would rob him even of this small contentment.

'I will fight beside you,' said Alith.

'No!' Yeasir told him. 'You must keep them safe.'

The Naggarothi were barely a hundred paces away. Yeasir could hear the echoes of his wife and companions' shrill voices from the cave.

'Get them away from here,' he hissed. 'There is a darkness claiming Ulthuan. You must fight it.'

Alith hesitated, his eyes flicking between the cave and the closing Naggarothi. With a resigned sigh, he nodded.

'It has been my honour,' said Alith, grasping Yeasir's shoulder. 'I have met no truer son of Nagarythe and I swear that if need be I will give my life to protect your family.'

ALITH WAS NOT sure if his words had been heard, for all of Yeasir's focus was on the approaching warriors. Alith ran to the cave mouth and turned back. The black-clad Naggarothi were advancing more cautiously, in a line a dozen wide, shields raised and spears lowered.

Yeasir faced the dark mass coming through the trees; sword in his right hand, spear in his left. He appeared relaxed, already accepting of his fate. One might have thought the commander was simply taking in the fresh evening air. Yeasir spared not one glance back, his stare fixed upon those that would slay or enslave his family. Alith had never seen such courage, and though he knew what he must do, he felt a great shame that he was being forced to run.

Yeasir raised the spear defiantly above his head and his voice rang out, the cry of a commander who had bellowed orders over the din of a hundred battles.

'Know who you face, cowards!' he shouted. 'I am Yeasir, son of Lanadriath. I am Commander of Nagarythe. I fought at Athel Toralien and the Battle of Silvermere. I marched with Prince Malekith into the north and faced the creatures and daemons of the dark gods. I was the first into Anlec when Morathi was overthrown. Ten times ten thousand foes have felt my wrath! Come and taste the vengeance of my spear and the ire of my sword. Come to me, brave soldiers, and face a true warrior!'

Yeasir lifted up his sword also and his next cry caused the advancing soldiers to halt, sharing fearful glances with each other.

'I am Naggarothi!'

Yeasir broke into a run, heading down the slope at full speed. As he came to the line of shields, he leapt into the air, his spear flashing downwards. With a crash of metal, he plunged into the soldiers. Screams of pain and dread resounded over the hillside as a swathe of warriors fell before the commander's assault. In moments a dozen bodies littered the ground and the dead leaves were spattered with blood. Yeasir's sword and spear tip were a silvered whirlwind, cutting down everything within reach.

Then Yeasir was lost from view as the soldiers swarmed forwards and surrounded him.

Alith was choked with despair but his heart burned with pride as he turned into the cave. He followed the others and plunged into the darkness.

ELEVEN

A Beacon of Hope

ONCE MORE ALITH found himself in the mountains, though this time he was not alone. The group had ridden north from the caves and then turned eastwards. Alith's craft had allowed them to avoid their pursuers in the foothills before turning north again. It was the morning of the sixth day of their flight when Lirian reined her horse in beside Alith's.

'Why are we heading north?' she asked. 'The Pass of the Eagle is south. There is no way north to Ellyrion.'

'We are not going to Ellyrion,' Alith told her. 'We head for Nagarythe.'

'Nagarythe?' Lirian gasped. She tugged her horse to a stop and Alith paused beside her. 'Nagarythe is the last place we need to go. It is the Naggarothi who want to take my son!'

Heileth came alongside.

'What is the delay?' she said.

'He is taking us to Nagarythe,' Lirian said shrilly, as if accusing Alith of wanting to kill them all in their sleep.

'Not all of Nagarythe is ruled by Morathi,' Alith said. 'We will be safe in the lands of my family. Safer than anywhere else. The cults are everywhere, even in Ellyrion. Do you trust me?'

'No,' said Lirian.

'How can we be sure you will not abandon us?' said Heileth.

'I gave my vow to Yeasir to protect you,' replied Alith. 'It is my duty to see you all safe.'

'And what is the word of a Naggarothi worth these days?' said Lirian. 'Perhaps we should return to Tor Anroc and ask them?'

'Not all Naggarothi are the same,' Alith replied hotly. 'Some of us still value honour and freedom. We are the true Naggarothi. We have a name for those who have occupied Tor Anroc – druchii.'

Lirian was still uncertain, though Heileth looked more convinced. She was also Naggarothi and understood better the divisions that had grown there. She turned to Lirian and spoke softly.

'What Alith says is true,' she said. 'Not all Naggarothi pray to dark gods nor seek to enslave others. If you do not trust Alith, do you trust me?'

Lirian did not reply. She urged her horse away and turned back down the trail they had been following. Alith leaned forwards and grabbed the reins to stop her.

'We are going to Nagarythe,' he said quietly.

Lirian looked into his eyes and saw no compromise there. She lowered her head and turned back to the north.

ALITH HAD NEVER loved Elanardris so much as he did the moment they crested the ridge at Cail Anris. He stopped his horse and looked at the hills and mountains. He had wondered at times whether he would see such a sight again. For a moment he was lost in the beauty of the white slopes and the wind-swept grass. The autumn clouds were low, but here and there the sun broke through to dazzle from the peaks. The air was crisp and cool, and Alith took a deep breath.

The others had stopped with him, gazing in wonder, both at their surrounds and the change in Alith.

'Is this your home?' asked Saphistia.

Alith pointed north and west.

'The manse of the Anars lies over those slopes,' he said. 'Past those woods upon the shoulders of Anul Hithrun and two more days of riding.'

A movement in the skies caught Alith's eye and he was not surprised to see a crow dipping down over the hillside. It landed on the branch of a short bush not far away and cawed once before setting off again, heading south.

'I shall fetch us some fresh food,' said Alith. 'Go on ahead. I'll not be far away nor gone long. It is safe here.'

He turned his horse after the crow and set off at a gentle trot, his eyes keen for any sign of Elthyrior.

Coming around a pile of moss-covered boulders, Alith saw the raven herald sat on a rock, his horse nearby nibbling at the grass. The crow was perched on Elthyrior's shoulder and gave Alith a beady look as he dismounted and walked his horse closer.

'I should have expected your welcome,' said Alith. He let the horse walk free and sat down beside Elthyrior.

'I would have said it was coincidence, but I know the ways of Morai-heg better than that,' replied the raven herald. 'I was heading north when I happened to see you. What news from Tiranoc? I have heard little, but that has been enough to worry me.'

'Caenthras and others have usurped power in Tor Anroc,' Alith told him. 'I am escorting the true heir of Bel Shanaar to keep him out of Morathi's clutches. I have had no word from Nagarythe for almost a year. What manner of welcome can I expect in Elanardris?'

'A good one,' said Elthyrior. 'Morathi has other concerns than the Anars at the moment. Her army is split between those who were loyal to Malekith and those who have sworn fealty to her. She thinks the Anars are a trouble of the past, no threat to her.'

Alith took this without comment and Elthyrior continued.

'All of Ulthuan is in upheaval,' he said. 'Only a handful of princes survived the massacre at the Shrine of Asuryan.'

'Massacre?'

'Surely. Though it is hard to piece together what occurred, some treachery unfolded there. The cults have been patient, growing their strength, and now they strike. Attacks and murders plague the other kingdoms, turning their eyes inwards whilst Morathi readies for war.'

'War?' said Alith. 'With whom? It is one thing to occupy leaderless Tiranoc, it is another to march to battle against the other princes.'

'And yet that is her intent, I fear,' said Elthyrior. 'Once she has full control of the army again she will set Nagarythe against all of Ulthuan.'

'Then perhaps we should allow her to indulge this folly,' said Alith.

'Folly?' Elthyrior laughed bitterly. 'No, it is not folly, though there are risks. Ulthuan is an isle divided. No single realm can stand against Nagarythe. Their armies are small and untested, and no doubt there are traitors loyal to the cults in their ranks. Of all the kingdoms, only Caledor perhaps has strength to hold if the others do not unite.'

'And surely they will unite when they see the threat,' said Alith.

'There is nobody to unite them, no banner that they can come together beneath. The Phoenix King is dead. Who else would the princes follow? Whether it was some part of a grander scheme or simple opportunism, the death of Bel Shanaar and so many princes has left Ulthuan vulnerable. If Morathi can strike quickly enough, in the spring I would say, then nobody is ready to hold against her.'

As he absorbed this, Alith absent-mindedly plucked a long stem of grass and began to tie it into intricate knots. Occupying his hands allowed his thoughts to clarify.

'It occurs to me that the longer Nagarythe is unstable, the more time the others have to recover from this disaster.'

'I would agree,' said Elthyrior. 'What do you have in mind?'

'A banner, you said,' replied Alith. 'There must be a rallying call to all of those Naggarothi who would see the druchii menace opposed. The Anars can issue such a call.'

'The Anars did not fare so well last time they attempted to defy the will of Anlec,' said Elthyrior.

'Last time we had a traitor in our midst – Caenthras,' snarled Alith. 'We were unprepared for the foe we faced, isolated and outnumbered. This time there can be no doubting our cause. There can be no divided loyalty, and those families that perhaps once feared Morathi's anger and did nothing will know that they cannot simply stay silent any longer.'

Elthyrior directed a doubtful look towards Alith.

'How I wish that were true,' said the raven herald.

He started walking towards his horse when Alith called out.

'We are likely to need your eyes and ears in the days to come. Is there any way that I can contact you?'

Elthyrior mounted his steed, pulling his cloak over its flanks.

'No,' he said. 'I come and go at the whim of Morai-heg. If the All-seeing One thinks that you need me, I shall be close at hand. You know how to find me.'

The crow leapt from his shoulder and beat its wings thrice before soaring past Alith at head height. It gave a loud screech and climbed into the air. Alith watched it circle higher and higher until it was just a speck.

'I…' he began, turning to where Elthyrior had been. The raven herald was gone, without the slightest beat of hoof or jangle of tack. Alith shook his head in disbelief. 'Just for once, I wish you'd say goodbye properly.'

ALITH HAD QUITE an entourage by the time he was on the road to the manse. Loyal subjects of the family came out of their houses and stores to rejoice at his homecoming. Their cheers and smiles were just a little too desperate though, and the strain of the split within Nagarythe showed on their faces. Alith did his best to remain confident, playing the part of the lord of the Anars, but in his heart he knew that their woes were far from over.

The commotion brought a small crowd from the manse. Soldiers and servants came out of the gates and gazed in astonishment at the return of their master. Alith spied Gerithon amongst them, who sent several of his staff running back to the house. When Alith had reached the gate, his father and mother were striding across the courtyard, trying to hurry yet remain dignified at the same time.

Alith had no such pretension. He jumped from his horse and pushed his way through the knot of elves, receiving claps on the back and heartfelt welcomes. He broke into a run and met his mother halfway to the manse.

The two of them shared a deep embrace, Maieth's tears wetting Alith's cloak as she buried her face in his chest. Eothlir joined them, wrapping his arms around both of them. His expression was austere but there was a gleam in his eye that betrayed his joy at seeing his son alive. Alith was grinning widely. Then he remembered his charges.

Turning to the gate, Alith saw Lirian, Saphistia and Heileth sitting on their horses and gazing around in shock. Servants helped them down, taking the children for a moment before returning them. Alith performed the introductions quickly, mentioning only the names of his companions. Though he knew they were safe here, he did not want idle chatter to spread concerning Lirian and her son.

'We need to talk,' he said to Eothlir and his father nodded, waving them towards the house.

'Gerithon will ensure our guests are looked after,' he said.

'Where is Eoloran?' Alith asked as they walked along the paving.

'He'll be waiting inside,' said Maieth.

Indeed he was. Alith's grandfather was in the main hall, sat at the end of the table with his fingers steepled to his chin. He looked up as Alith entered, his face a blank mask. Alith felt a sudden nervousness at Eoloran's behaviour, and feared that he had done something wrong by returning. Or perhaps he should have returned earlier?

'You have been away a long while, Alith,' Eoloran said solemnly. His facade broke as a smile crept into the corner of his lips. 'I hope you have been busy with important matters to neglect your family for so long.'

'More than I can ever tell you,' laughed Alith, striding to his grandfather and embracing him. 'Yet, I will try to.'

Gerithon appeared at the doorway.

'Your guests will be quartered in the east wing, lord,' he said.

'Thank you, Gerithon,' Eoloran replied. 'And please ensure that we are not disturbed.'

'Of course,' Gerithon intoned with a shallow bow. He backed out of the hall and closed the doors soundlessly.

Alith gave as brief a summary as he could concerning the events in Tor Anroc and the circumstances of his departure. The others listened intently without interruption, but as soon as he was finished they had a barrage of questions.

'Do you think the Tiranocii will resist?' asked Eoloran.

'They will try, and they will fail,' said Alith. 'The court is held hostage and the army has no direction. If Morathi were to cross the Naganath, I doubt there is much that Tiranoc can do to stop her.'

'Tell me more of Caenthras,' demanded Eothlir. 'What was his part in all of this? Is he knowingly complicit?'

'It was Caenthras who entrapped Prince Yrianath, Father,' Alith replied. 'Though I doubt he is the sole architect of this usurpation he is certainly one of its chief agents. I saw banners of his house amongst the warriors that arrived.'

'You are sure that Yeasir fell?' Alith's father continued. 'Perhaps his troops will not be so happy to fight under Caenthras.'

'Some were loyal to Yeasir, but I do not know how many,' said Alith. 'And amongst those there were none that he trusted with the location of his wife and child. I do not think the druchii will turn on each other, if that is your hope. And Yeasir definitely fell. No warrior save perhaps Aenarion himself or Prince Malekith could have fought such numbers alone and survived. His family is now my responsibility.'

'And we will help you bear that,' said Maieth. 'Now, tell me more about Milandith...'

'There will be time enough later to hear about Alith's romances,' Eothlir said. 'First we must decide what we will do next.'

Alith nodded, knowing that it would be well into the night before such a decision was reached. Maieth fluttered a hand at her male relatives and stood up. She stood behind Alith and laid her hands on his shoulders.

'You can't hide from me forever,' she said, kissing him on the top of the head. She walked away and then looked back as she opened the door. 'I'll find out what you've been up to!'

'Give me Morathi's torturers before an inquisitive mother,' said Eothlir when Maieth had left the room.

Alith nodded in fervent agreement.

TWELVE

Dark Fen

As Elthyrior had predicted, the druchii were intent on subjugating all of Ulthuan. Over the course of the following winter Anlec strengthened its grip on Nagarythe, pushing back those factions opposed to Morathi's return. Elanardris again became a safe haven for these dissidents, including princes and captains. Thousands of Naggarothi warriors made camp in the foothills of the mountains. Durinne, lord of the port of Galthyr, resisted for the whole of the winter, but fresh forces besieged the city when the snows began to thaw and the druchii were victorious. They took many ships that had sought winter harbour, and with this fleet nowhere on Ulthuan was beyond their reach.

By mid-spring, the armies of the druchii marched. With Tiranoc divided, they were able to control the passes eastwards and advanced into Ellyrion. Their navy prowled the coast to the north and west, only kept from the shores of Caledor and Eataine by their fear of the powerful fleet at Lothern. All the while, the Anars expected the fury of the druchii to fall upon Elanardris, yet the blow never came. Morathi, perhaps out of arrogance, saw no threat from the mountains and was determined to subjugate the other kingdoms as swiftly as possible. The questioning of commanders captured by Anar raids confirmed as much: when Ulthuan was under Morathi's control, she would have time enough to deal with the Anars.

The Anars led sorties into the rest of Nagarythe, but were unable to mount any kind of meaningful offensive. Wary of being surrounded or leaving Elanardris unguarded, Eoloran and Eothlir could not bring their full strength against the druchii. Thousands of refugees had fled into the mountains around the Anars' lands. Food and other resources were scarce, and so the Anars fought a guerrilla war, hitting the druchii columns as they marched to Tiranoc, then withdrawing before their foes gathered their strength.

In this time, the Shadows were reformed, with Alith as their leader. Their numbers swelled to several hundred of the most deadly warriors in Elanardris, and Eoloran tasked them with disrupting the druchii as much as possible.

Under Alith's leadership, the Shadows terrorised their foes. Driven on by his memories of the Khainite camp and the occupation of Tor Anroc, Alith was merciless. The Shadows did not fight battles. Instead, they crept into camps and killed warriors in their sleep. They raided villages supplying the druchii armies and destroyed food stores and burnt down the homes of those that supported Morathi. Nobles loyal to Anlec soon began to fear for their lives as Alith and his Shadows hunted them down, slaying them upon the dark roads or breaking into their castles to kill them and slaughter their families.

IT WAS WHILE returning from an attack on Galthyr, during which the Shadows burnt half a dozen ships in the harbour with their crews still aboard, that Alith next met Elthyrior. A year had passed since the massacre at the shrine, and for all the psychological damage the Anars had inflicted, Alith knew that they had achieved little real gain. Yet what Elthyrior told him gave him some hope.

'There is a new Phoenix King,' said the raven herald.

The pair had met in a copse of trees not far from the Shadows' camp on the northern edge of Elanardris. It was night-time and neither moon had yet risen. In the darkness the raven herald was invisible, a disembodied voice amongst the trees.

'Prince Imrik has been chosen by the other princes and, thank the gods, he has accepted the Phoenix Throne,' Elthyrior continued.

'Imrik is a good choice,' said Alith. 'He is a warrior, and the realm of Caledor is second only to Nagarythe in strength. The dragon princes will be a firmer test for Morathi's warriors.'

'He has taken the name of King Caledor, in memory of his grandfather,' Elthyrior added.

'That is curious,' replied Alith. 'It is not without merit. It is well that the other princes are reminded that the blood of the Dragontamer runs in the king's veins. Do you know anything of his intent?'

'He intends to fight, but more than that I cannot say,' said Elthyrior.

'Perhaps there is some means by which we can send a message to Caledor,' said Alith. 'If we could join forces in some way…'

IT WAS WITH this thought that Alith returned to the manse to consult with his father and grandfather. Several messengers were sent south, but the Naganath was well patrolled. The bodies of three heralds were found upon stakes on the road to Elanardris, dismembered and flayed.

The winter passed without reply, and the fate of the last messenger remained unknown. What little news that reached the Anars was not encouraging. Despite King Caledor's appointment, the other realms still appeared much divided, especially those to the east that had yet to suffer the full wrath of the druchii. Far from joining forces behind Caledor, the princes were more concerned with protecting their own lands, so that Tiranoc, Ellyrion, Chrace and Eataine suffered greatly at the hands of the advancing armies.

IT WAS LATE spring when a bloodied herald rode up to the manse and demanded an audience with Eoloran. The lord of the Anars summoned Eothlir and Alith to the great hall.

'I am Ilriadan, and I bear tidings from the Phoenix King,' said the messenger. He had been given fresh clothes and a wound on his arm had been bandaged. He sat at the long table with the others, food and fortified wine laid before him.

'Tell us what you know,' said Eothlir. 'What news of the war?'

Ilriadan drank a little wine before answering.

'There is little to comfort those who resist Morathi's expansion,' he said. 'King Caledor does what he can to stem the attacks but the druchii, as you call them, have gathered their strength and no force the Phoenix King can yet muster matches them. He is forced to retreat from their advance, slowing it for a time and little more.'

Eoloran was disconcerted at these tidings. He sighed and bowed his head.

'There is no hope that the Phoenix King can mount an offensive?' he asked quietly.

'None at all,' said Ilriadan. 'His princes do what they can to rouse the dragons of Caledor to fight with them, but few of them remain willing to aid the elves. Without the dragon princes, the army of Anlec is too strong.'

'Is there any effort that we might make that will aid the Phoenix King in his cause?' asked Eothlir.

Ilriadan shook his head.

'The druchii hold several castles and towns in Ellyrion and Tiranoc,' said the messenger. 'The Phoenix King thought to raze the lands ahead of their advance, but the other princes have refused, and say that they will not starve their own people. Morathi consolidates her hold on what she has already gained and we fear a fresh offensive next year.'

'I cannot believe that in all of Ulthuan there is not the force that can match our foes,' snapped Alith. 'Nagarythe is strong, but surely the other kingdoms can muster an army to match!'

'You are Naggarothi, you do not understand,' said Ilriadan. 'You are raised as warriors. We of the other kingdoms are not. Our armies are small compared to the legions of Nagarythe. What warriors we did have, most left our shores to forge the colonies, and those that remain have never seen battle before. The druchii have beasts from the mountains that they unleash upon us, and deranged cultists that lust for blood and do not fear death! Many Naggarothi have returned from Elthin Arvan to swell the numbers of Anlec's host. Each of them is a veteran of war and a match for every five of ours! How can we fight against such an army, a monster driven on by a hate of its foes and a terrible fear of its commanders?'

The Anars all remained silent, absorbing the realisation that there would be no help from outside Nagarythe.

'We train such soldiers as we can, but King Caledor cannot throw his untried forces into reckless battle against such a superior foe,' said Ilriadan.

'How long before your army can fight?' said Eoloran.

'Two years, at least,' came the reply, and this was answered by a chorus of sighs.

'Not all is despair,' Ilriadan added quickly. 'The druchii do not have the ships to breach the Lothern gate and so cannot dare to cross the Inner Sea. Caledor to the south still holds strong, and the enemy face fierce opposition to fight their way through Chrace. The Phoenix King's cousin rules there and was not at the shrine, so Chrace is united under his rule. The mountains will not be as forgiving as the plains of Tiranoc. Should they pass Chrace, the druchii face Avelorn. Isha will not suffer such dark creatures in her forests and the spirits of the woods will fight beside the warriors of the Everqueen. Not all of those whose lands the druchii have occupied have capitulated, and maintaining their grip will sap their strength. In speed and surprise they have gained the advantage, but time is a weapon on our side. The victories of this past year will not be so easy to achieve in the next, and in the year after... Well, let us not get ahead of ourselves.'

THE ANARS WERE forced to conclude that they could do no more than they were already. They fortified the hills of Elanardris as best they could, expecting attack at any time. From this haven, the Shadows sallied forth on their raids and the warriors of Eoloran menaced troops moving along the eastern roads.

The situation in the mountains worsened as those fleeing Chrace crossed from the east, daring the treacherous peaks to get away from the druchii scourge. There had been little enough food to begin with and thousands more mouths needed feeding. Alith was forced to redirect the attentions of his Shadows. They ambushed the druchii caravans to steal supplies and raided grain houses. They attacked isolated patrols and stole their baggage – tents, clothes and weapons that the Anars needed.

Alith feared that the Shadows had been turned from feared warriors into quartermasters, but Eoloran was adamant that the refugees needed to be provided for.

Another bleak year passed, and another. Chrace was almost overrun. Groups of hunters held out in their mountain lodges, but the roads to Avelorn were open to the druchii. In this way, Ellyrion was surrounded, though Prince Finudel still held his capital at Tor Elyr.

Scattered word came from further east. In the lands of Saphery, some of the mage-princes of that realm had been lured to Morathi's cause by the promise of sorcerous power. Though outnumbered by the loyal mages, these sorcerers waged war with their kin. The meadows were blasted by magical fire, the skies rained down comets and the air itself seethed with mystical energy.

The druchii had dared an attack on Lothern, seeking to gain control of the formidable sea gate. The assault had been repulsed with heavy losses on both sides, the loyalists only claiming victory after King Caledor arrived with the army of his kingdom. That realm remained secure against the druchii advance and, like Elanardris, became a sanctuary for those from Ellyrion and Tiranoc pushed out by the warriors of Anlec.

Still the Anars waited for the time to strike.

It was not until the fourth year of the war that the druchii advance stalled. Hawks carrying messages from the Phoenix King arrived at the manse with the coming of the spring. Eoloran read these with some satisfaction.

'The dragon princes have ridden forth at last,' he told Alith and Eoloran. 'King Caledor has used the Eataine fleet to gather together his new army on the border of Ellyrion and is advancing north.'

'That is good news indeed,' said Alith. 'When he reaches Tiranoc, we should strike out to join him.'

'I fear that we may extend ourselves too soon,' replied Eoloran. 'We must judge the right time to strike for the greatest effect.'

'We cannot afford to be too cautious,' argued Eothlir. 'Though our army is not so large as Caledor's, it is in the right place to threaten the druchii. We cannot hold much longer, and certainly not another winter. Would you wait until Caledor is upon the borders of Elanardris before acting?'

'You go too far!' snapped Eoloran. 'I am still lord of this house!'

'Then act as a lord!' replied Eothlir. 'Lead out the army now! This is our best chance for victory. As we helped Malekith at Ealith, we can do the same for the Phoenix King. Bite into the heart of our foes and force them to bring back warriors from Ellyrion and Tiranoc. Our raids accomplish little, they have become nothing more than an annoyance to Morathi. Let us gather what warriors we can and act boldly.'

'It is folly,' said Eoloran with a wave of his hand. 'Who will protect Elanardris?'

'The Chracians and Tiranocii have enough warriors to hold the hills until our return.'

'Leave my lands in the hands of outsiders?' Eoloran laughed scornfully. 'What manner of prince would I be?'

'One who can swallow his pride to do the right thing,' said Eothlir.

Alith watched the argument with horror. His father and grandfather had quarrelled on occasion before, but he had never seen them both as angry. Always they had debated on principles but now they attacked each other.

'You think it is pride that steers me?' Eoloran roared. 'You think those helpless thousands camped in the mountains are of no concern?'

'They have no future unless we act,' Eothlir replied, chillingly calm in the face of his father's ire. 'They will starve or freeze to death by the end of the year, for we cannot continue to feed and clothe them. The only way to end their suffering is to end the war. Now!'

Eoloran strode towards the door and snarled over his shoulder.

'It will be your lands that you are throwing away, not mine!'

As the hall reverberated from the slamming door, Eothlir sat down and stared out of the high windows.

'What should we do?' asked Alith.

Eothlir looked up at his son, his eyes bleak.

'I will fight, no matter what the wishes of your grandfather,' he said. 'You are not a child, what you do is your decision.'

'I will fight as well,' said Alith, needing no time to think it over. 'I would rather try for victory and fail than suffer this wasting death that grips us. We can only get weaker the longer we wait.'

Eothlir nodded and reached up a hand to pat Alith on the arm.

'Then we will fight together,' he said.

EOTHLIR MUSTERED SOME fourteen thousand warriors in all. Each was Nagarythe-born and knew that he fought not only for his life but for the lives of future generations. This force marched westwards, to the edge of the foothills of Elanardris. To the east the rear of the host was protected by the mountains, while to the west and south stretched the marshes of Enniun Moreir – Dark Fen. To the north lay the broken ground of Urithelth Orir.

One thousand cavalry were sent north, all the riders that Eothlir could gather. Their target was the druchii camp at Tor Miransiath. With them had ridden a herald, Liasdir, who bore the banner of the Anars. He would announce that Elanardris was defiant of Anlec and would never bow down before the Witch Queen. They were the bait for the trap, for such an affront to Morathi would never be tolerated by the druchii commanders.

The remaining thirteen thousand soldiers, of whom more than half were archers, took up a horseshoe-like position at the crests of the hills, the open segment facing westwards. Each warrior had brought as many shafts as could be found in Elanardris and was ready to unleash a storm upon the enemy. The spearmen arrayed themselves into phalanxes in front of the bowmen, their shields overlapping to form a wall against the missiles of the enemy. The army was not hidden, for this was designed to be a gesture of defiance to goad the druchii into a hasty attack.

The cavalry would lure the druchii into the treacherous marshland, where Alith and his Shadows had spent two days, marking out the surest routes for the riders to follow. The riders would remove these markers as they retreated, leaving their pursuers mired and easy targets for the archers. Eothlir was determined that he would draw the ire of Anlec; if the Anars could inflict a sufficient defeat upon their foes, Morathi would have no choice but to bring troops back from Ellyrion, easing the pressure upon King Caledor.

Eothlir sent out the riders just before midday. Timing was everything. As the skies darkened the journey across the marsh would get ever more dangerous and the druchii casualties would be all the greater for it.

ALITH STOOD BESIDE his father, sword in hand. His Shadows were hidden amongst the mounds and reeds of Enniun Moreir to snipe the enemy as best they could, but Eothlir had insisted his son stayed close to him during the battle.

The enemy arrived at about the time Eothlir had hoped. Shrill whistles from the Shadows announced the coming of the cavalry and it was not long before Alith could see the riders picking their way along the trails, the last in each column tossing aside the rods the Shadows had used as markers. Upon reaching the hills, the knights cut to the north, ready to counter-attack against any foes that attempted to flank on the right. Liasdir split from the other riders and dismounted next to Eothlir, driving the banner pole into the turf of the hillside. Drawing his sword, he looked at his lords.

'There are quite a lot of them,' he said with an uncertain smile. 'I hope we are doing the right thing.'

Eothlir did not reply, his gaze was fixed on a dark mass moving through the marshlands. Like a spreading blot, the druchii army advanced slowly. It was as if a black mist followed them, and Alith could sense sorcery in the air. His skin crawled at the touch of the dark magic and could feel it seeping down from the mountains behind him, drawn by the enchantments of the druchii.

Larger shapes could be seen amongst the lines of infantry. Hydras splashed through the marsh, their bellows and roars sounding out like a challenge.

'Musicians!' called Eothlir.

Trumpeters raised their instruments to their lips and let out a long blast that echoed across the hills. The note filled Alith with pride, a pealing signal of refusal. Somewhere behind Alith voices rose in song and Eothlir turned in surprise. From one company to another the sound spread, the battle anthem of the Anars ringing from fourteen thousand throats. The rousing song rose in pitch and volume, sweeping away the noises of the druchii beasts.

Alith's heart thundered along to the rhythm as the verses recounted the feats of Eoloran during the time of Aenarion and recalled the battles to claim Elanardris from the daemons. When the tenth and final verse was finished, a deafening shout engulfed the hills.

'Anar! Anar! Anar!'

Alith joined in and saw also that his father cried out the family name, his sword held aloft.

'Anar! Anar! Anar!'

The druchii were close enough to judge their numbers. Alith guessed there to be at least thirty thousand foes. He was thankful that there were no knights, but less pleased that the army presented a wall of silver and black. All were Naggarothi soldiers, not a single cultist amongst them. They were battle-hardened and disciplined and would be deadly enemies.

The first arrows from the Shadows began to find their mark when the druchii were no closer than five hundred paces to the Anar line. The casualties inflicted were few, but the effect was considerable. Already hard-pressed to find a footing in the marsh, the druchii tumbled into the mud when their comrades' corpses tripped them. Standard bearers fell and the banners dragged up from the fen sagged wetly against their poles. Captains looked around fearfully as the Shadows picked their targets with deadly accuracy.

Alith knew from the battle at Anlec that the greatest weakness of the hydras was the handlers that goaded them. Unfortunately, it seemed that the druchii had also learnt that lesson, and the whip-armed elves tried as best they could to keep the bulk of their beasts between them and the Anar scouts. As they advanced, they steered their monsters between the regiments of spearmen, so that the Shadows could not draw aim upon them.

Here and there the druchii returned the shots of the Shadows. Archers tried to find their mark, but the scouts were well hidden. Companies carrying mechanical bows that fired several shots in quick succession poured bolts at their elusive enemies and the Shadows fell back, flitting from cover to cover.

Pace-by-pace the druchii continued their advance, harried by the Shadows and slowed by the sucking mud of Dark Fen. All the while the sun lowered towards the west and gloom descended.

Anar archers started their volleys as soon as the druchii were within range, the elevation of the hills allowing them to loose their arrows farther than their foes. Each company let free with a cloud of arrows in turn. The rate was not remarkable, but it was sustained. Storm after storm of black-feathered shafts fell into the druchii and they died in their hundreds. The dead sank into the mire and piled up on the firm ground; the warriors following behind were forced to shove aside these grisly mounds to keep to the meandering paths.

As more and more of the Anlec warriors fell, Alith felt the first glimmer of hope. Though he had readily agreed to his father's decision to sally forth from Elanardris, he had doubted whether it would achieve anything – little more than a diversion to provide small relief for Caledor's army to the south. Watching the druchii suffer in their thousands gave him a grim satisfaction.

Eventually the druchii archers and crossbowmen came within two hundred paces and began to loose their missiles against the Anars. The spearmen raised their shields while the archers above knelt behind them and continued to shoot, though with less venom than before.

When the druchii were almost at the edge of the marsh, the final part of Eothlir's plan was put into action. As well as marking out trails, the Shadows had laid a slick of oil on the water of the fens. At Alith's signal, the Shadows sent flaming arrows into the mire. The flames caught quickly, dancing across the marsh to engulf the leading ranks of the druchii spear companies. Burning warriors flailed at the fire and dashed to and fro in panic, spreading it further.

Alith began to laugh at the predicament of his enemies, but stopped himself when he caught a stern look from his father.

'You should not take joy in death,' said Eothlir. 'To revel in destruction is to desire it, and it is on that path that these unfortunate souls have trodden.'

'You are right, Father,' Alith said, bowing his head in apology. 'It is my happiness at success that gives me good humour, but I should not forget the price being paid for our victory.'

Victory certainly seemed likely. The first of the druchii that had survived the torrent of arrows and the conflagration were struggling from the marsh and pushing up the rise towards the Anar army. Spearmen came first, raising their shields above their heads to protect them from the archers. They remained resolute in the face of the volleys, forming their ranks again, allowing their numbers to grow rather than advance piecemeal towards the waiting phalanxes.

When several hundred warriors had assembled on the slope, two hydras flanking them, the druchii continued their advance. A drum boomed out the marching beat and the spearmen lowered their weapons to the attack and strode forwards. The hydras hissed and screeched, flames licking from their many mouths, a pall of smoke surrounding their scaled bodies.

'We must deal with those monsters swiftly,' said Eothlir. He turned to Nithimnis, one of his captains. 'Go to the companies of Alethriel, Finannith and Helirian and tell them to engage the hydra on our right. Signal for the cavalry to attack on the flank.'

The captain nodded and dashed off, heading for the warriors on the right flank. Eothlir moved his attention to Alith. 'Send word to your Shadows to lure away the hydra on the left.'

Alith gave a low, keening whistle and moments later a hawk skimmed across the hillside, bobbing over the heads of the archers and spearmen. Alith extended his arm and the bird landed on his wrist. He bent close and whispered in the language of the hawks, relaying Eothlir's message. The hawk twisted its head left and right and then leapt into the air with beating wings. It swooped down towards the fen, disappearing amongst the tangle of rushes and bushes.

It was not long before arrows with flaming heads began converging on the hydra. Though each did little damage, the weight of fire was enough to scorch its flesh, while some arrows found their mark in its eyes, mouths and softer underbelly. Its hide was slicked in places with oil from the marsh and the flames took hold, setting alight its flank and back. Enraged, it swung towards the source of its irritation, fire roaring from its mouths. Turning aside from the spearmen the hydra stomped down into the fens, sinking to its shoulders in the thick mud, more flames streaming from its screeching maws.

At fifty paces, the advancing druchii broke into a charge. This was not the wild attack of cultists, but a determined and cohesive thrust towards the Anar spearmen. The two walls of warriors met with a resounding crash and the true battle began.

Though they had suffered heavy casualties, the druchii numbers were still their greatest advantage. More and more of them emerged from the fen, to widen the line of attack or lend their presence to the companies already engaged. Archers and crossbowmen began to shoot into the troops stationed at the crest of the hill and a vicious exchange of missiles raged above Alith's head.

Alith watched the fighting with a careful eye. The Anar line was holding strong, the advantage of higher ground allowing them to plunge their spears over the shields of their foes whilst their attackers tried to gain some momentum as they pushed uphill. Faced with several hundred spearmen, the hydra on the right was causing a good deal of carnage, tossing aside warriors with its jaws and smashing more to the ground with its immense claws. The elves were not wholly outmatched. Thick blood streamed from dozens of wounds in the hydra's scaled skin and three of its seven heads swung limply against its chest.

The ground began to shudder under Alith's feet and he looked past the hydra to see the riders of Elanardris charge. Spears lowered, they crashed into the hydra, running down its handlers and driving their weapons into the creature's flesh. Horses whinnied and riders cried out as the monster's tail lashed viciously through their ranks, crushing elves and breaking the legs of their steeds. The spearmen redoubled their efforts and Alith watched as two of the hydra's legs gave way, its tendons severed by spearpoint and sword. The infantry clambered over its body, jabbing and stabbing relentlessly while the cavalry swept on, galloping into the flank of the druchii regiments.

The attack sent the druchii scattering down the hillside, some of them tripping over hummocks and dips or the bodies of the fallen. The knights did not push too far and at a signal from their captain wheeled their mounts around and retired back to the north to ready for another charge.

Again and again the druchii surged up the hill, only to be met by a wall of spears. Their commanders tried to turn the left flank of the Anars, furthest from the cavalry. Eothlir despatched his thousand-strong reserve to counter the threat, forcing the druchii regiments back towards the centre.

Alith could not count how many were dead and wounded. Certainly the druchii were at less than half the strength they had brought to the battle. His own side's casualties were far less, though there were gaps appearing in the line where the druchii had met some success. He was confident nonetheless, of both his father's ability and the resolution of the warriors. He had not yet needed to draw his sword and the battle was being won.

Shouts of alarm drew Alith's attention and he turned to see many of the archers looking skywards and pointing to the north-east – back towards Elanardris. Alith saw immediately their cause for concern: an immense black shape moving swiftly through the clouds.

'Dragon!' bellowed Alith, ripping free his sword.

THE DRAKE PLUNGED down towards the rear of the army, an oily cloud trailing from its mouth. It was the largest beast Alith had ever seen, at least as long as a ship from smoking snout to barbed tip of tail. Its serpentine body was as straight as an arrow, huge wings held stiff as it glided soundlessly downwards, four legs ending in massively clawed feet extended towards the ground. Upon its back rode a figure clad in shining silver armour. He was sat upon a throne-like chair, twin pennants trailing from its back. On his left arm he carried a shield taller than an elf etched with a rune of death. In the right hand he wielded a lance longer than two horses, its tip a dark crystal that streamed black flames.

Arrows rose up from the archers, but they might just as well have been throwing sticks at a city wall for the injury they caused. With a gargantuan beat of its wings, the dragon stopped in the air above the archers, the buffet of wind hurling dozens of elves from their feet. A huge cloud of thick vapour issued from its mouth, engulfing hundreds. Alith watched as skin flaked and flesh melted in the noxious mist. Choked screams sounded across the hill as the archers fell to the ground, grabbing madly at their faces, screaming in terrifying agony.

The dragon climbed upwards again, and Alith was filled with the urge to run. Its yellow eyes seemed to look directly at him. Its teeth were like long swords and its red claws glistened like fresh blood. The dragon's black scales glimmered in the setting sun, so that it seemed to be made of glowing embers.

Dozens of dreadful thoughts clamoured for Alith's attention, but one was louder than all of the rest: how had the druchii come by such a creature? The dragons of Ulthuan dwelt beneath the mountains of Caledor. Not since the time of Caledor Dragontamer had all but the youngest been coaxed from their centuries-long slumber. Yet the truth was right before him, in all of its horrific glory.

The monster was circling higher, getting ready to swoop again. It let forth a piercing shriek that set Alith's ears ringing. So dire was that noise that hundreds of warriors broke into flight, dropping their spears, shields and bows so that they might run all the faster. Alith had never witnessed such panic before.

'Alith!' he heard his father shouting and realised Eothlir had been calling his name since the dragon had first appeared. Looking over his shoulder, Alith saw that the druchii were surging up the hill towards them. All along the line the spearmen were being pushed backwards.

Alith turned his full attention on these attackers, bringing up his sword. The druchii came at a gentle run, still shoulder-to-shoulder. With a shout, Alith plunged forwards moments before the two lines of warriors met.

His first blow chopped the head from a jabbing spear, while he rammed his shoulder into the warrior's shield. Snatching a dagger from his belt, Alith plunged the blade back-handed into the druchii soldier's neck. His next sword thrust took another druchii in the chest. Something caught his shoulder and he felt a stab of pain. Twisting, he smashed the back of his fist into the jaw of a third warrior before bringing his sword down across the druchii's face.

Everything devolved into a chaotic melee: Alith, Eothlir and the others shouting and fighting, the druchii snarling and stabbing.

'Hold the line!' bellowed Eothlir. 'Push them back into the fens!'

Hundreds of spearmen gathered around their commander, with bitter war cries on their lips and blood upon their armour. Alith heard a gasp of pain and glanced to his right. Liasdir fell to the ground, blood gushing from a wound in his back. He grabbed hold of the banner to pull himself to his feet but another druchii spearman lunged, thrusting his weapon through Liasdir's chest. Falling, Liasdir dragged the banner down into the bloody grass.

Eothlir batted away a spear and stooped to pick up the fallen standard. Cutting the arm from yet another attacker, he raised the flag above his head.

'Fight on, Anars, fight on!' he cried.

A SHADOW SWAMPED Alith, blotting out the twilight. A rushing of air filled his ears and he looked up a moment before the dragon landed, crushing dozens of druchii and Anars alike beneath its bulk. Eothlir swung towards the monster, sword raised. His eyes widened in rage as he recognised the rider.

'Kheranion!' he spat. Alith knew the name only from rumour, and that told of how the renegade prince had been spared at Anlec by Malekith. He had been a scourge of those Naggarothi opposed to Morathi's rule, one of the most brutal slaughterers in Nagarythe. It was claimed that his back had been broken by Prince Malekith but he had been healed by dark sorcery, kept alive by potions made from the blood of his victims.

The prince's face was twisted into a cruel sneer framed by white and silver hair. He said nothing as he thrust his flaming lance. Alith gave a hoarse shout as the black-flamed iron burst through Eothlir's body, sending boiling blood steaming into the air. As quick as he had struck, Kheranion wrenched the lance free.

Eothlir staggered backwards a step and righted himself. He turned slowly towards Alith and then fell to his knees, his sword falling out of view into the trampled grass, the standard of the Anars fluttering from his grasp. Blood bubbled up from Eothlir's throat, foaming from his mouth. Alith's greatest horror came not from this, but from the look in his father's eyes. They were wide and wild, filled with utter terror.

'Flee!' Eothlir croaked before pitching into the mud.

Kheranion's mocking laughter drifted to Alith's ears. Alith gave a wordless scream of despair and rage, and hurled himself towards Kheranion and his monstrous steed. He had taken barely two steps when someone grabbed his arm and yanked him aside. Stumbling, Alith tried to wrest his arm free, but found himself grabbed roughly by many hands and bodily lifted away.

'Let me go!' screamed Alith, struggling as best he could as more spearmen surged forwards to put themselves between the dragon and their lord. 'Let me go!'

The army was broken by the death of their commander. Thousands of Alith's followers turned and ran, while a brave few hundred formed up to sell their lives dearly and stall the pursuit. Alith felt himself dragged up the hill. Desolation swept through him and he went limp, tears coursing down his face.

Sobbing, he let his warriors carry him to safety.

THIRTEEN

The Fall of House Anar

UNDER THE COVER of night, the remnants of the Anar army retreated eastwards towards the mountains only to find that more druchii barred their way. Forced to turn southwards, Alith stumbled numbly alongside his warriors, too scared to think of what had happened and too tired to wonder what might yet come to pass. It was if he sleepwalked, placing one foot in front of the other out of habit.

With the druchii close on their heels, Alith's lieutenants turned the army westwards again, seeking sanctuary in the marshes of Dark Fen. For twenty-three days they hid amongst the waterways, scattering for cover as the beat of dragon wings sounded overhead, travelling by night alone. The army splintered as companies and individuals sought to avoid the pursuit, each going their own way. Some were lost in the marshes, some made it far south only to be picked up by druchii patrols along the Naganath.

Those that stayed with Alith survived, though not through any action or decision of the prince. He was happy to follow instructions from the likes of Khillrallion and Tharion. The warriors began to whisper that Alith's mind had been broken, and they were not far from the truth. Alith was possessed by a waking nightmare, unable to rid himself of the vision of his father's death. Over and over he saw Eothlir fall beneath the lance of Kheranion, smelt the noxious stench of the dragon's breath in the air and heard his father's last, desperate command.

Eventually the druchii relented in their hunt and the survivors drifted eastwards again, heading for Elanardris. For two more days they trudged through the mists of the fen, exhausted, hungry and dispirited. That night they made camp just south of where they had fought the army of Anlec, though no warrior dared investigate the battlefield, fearful of what they might find there.

At dawn, smoke could be seen to the east, rising from the mountains. These were not wisps of campfires: towering columns of thick black smoke hung over the foothills like a shroud. Filled with foreboding, Alith and the army hurried towards the rising sun.

They came to the first burnt-out village just before midday. The white walls of the buildings were stained with soot and contorted, charred corpses could be seen within. They had been shut inside when the buildings had been set on fire. Along the road they found more bodies, mutilated in all manner of hideous ways. Scraps of flayed skin were hung upon the walls that bounded the fields, and garlands of bones and flesh were strung from the bare branches of trees.

More horrors followed as Alith hurried on. Naked bodies were nailed upon the blackened stones of towers and barns. The heads of children had been woven into the thorny stems of rose bushes like obscene replacements for their missing blooms. Symbols of the cytharai were daubed in blood everywhere Alith looked.

The survivors of the battle wept, some throwing down their weapons to cradle the remains of loved ones discovered, others breaking from the army to go to their homes. Alith's warriors deserted in their hundreds and he let them go. He could no more insist that they stay than he could stop them breathing.

By mid-afternoon, Alith had no more revulsion left. If he had been numb before, now he was utterly empty, devoid of any thought or emotion. The slaughter was simply too vast to comprehend, the atrocities too outlandish to remember. The refugee camps had been attacked and the dead were scattered about the fields in huge piles of cadavers. Some had died swiftly, cut down where they had been caught, but many showed signs of barbaric abuse, having perished of raw agony from the wounds inflicted upon them. Carrion-eating birds had come down from the mountains in great flocks and they lurched away heavily as the elves approached, gorged on the macabre banquet laid out for them.

ALITH FELT NOTHING as he saw the clouds of smoke billowing from within the walls of the manse. From his first sight of the smoke at dawn the previous day he had expected to see this and had already experienced such cold dread that he no longer registered the fact that the nightmare was real.

Coming through the gates, Alith thought at first that the walls of the manse had been changed into something else, or that the lengthening evening shadows were deceiving him. As he stumbled closer he saw that the ruined house was festooned with the bodies of elves, pinioned to the walls with metal spikes. All but a few hung limply, but a handful stirred at his approach.

He recognised the bloody remains of Gerithon nailed to the door and dashed to him. Spikes pierced his elbows and knees, driven into the hard wood of the door, and his blood dripped into a ruddy pool at his feet. The Anars' retainer raised his head a little and opened one bloodshot eye; the other was closed shut with a clot of blood dripping from a gash across his forehead.

'Alith?' he croaked.

'Yes,' Alith replied, taking a canteen of water from his pack. He tried to give some to Gerithon but the other elf turned his head away.

'Water will not save me,' he whispered. His eye wandered for a moment and then settled again on Alith. 'They took Lord Eoloran alive…'

This news was like a bolt of lightning. For a moment Alith felt elation that one of his family had survived. The next moment came the crushing realisation that his grandfather would suffer a far worse fate than death. With thoughts of family Alith raised Gerithon's head with a hand under his chin.

'What of my mother?' he demanded.

Gerithon closed his eye slowly in reply.

'Do not let me die in torment,' the chamberlain whispered.

Alith stepped away for a moment, unsure what to do. Others had come into the grounds of the manse and were wandering around, gazing with horror at the despicable cruelty on display.

'Bring them down!' snarled Alith, filled with a sudden energy. He pulled his knife from his belt and drew it quickly across Gerithon's throat. Blood trickled over his fingers and Alith flicked it away. 'Give peace to those that have not yet succumbed, and bring all of the bodies to the manse.'

Under Alith's instructions, the elves gathered the remains of those loyal to the Anars and arranged them inside the house. There were also druchii bodies amongst the dead, for the Chracians and Tiranocii had been true to their oaths and had fought to defend Elanardris. These Alith ordered to be left for the crows and vultures.

Undertaking this sombre task, Alith was blind to those whose bodies he carried. In his eye they were just a blur, not the faces of friends, servants and loved ones. He may have carried Maieth's body, he did not know. That she was amongst the dead was certain, he did not need to know by what manner she had been slain.

As dusk shrouded all in darkness once more, Alith and his followers brought wood and oil from their stores and with this turned the manse into a great pyre. Alith set a torch to the fuel and then turned away. He did not look back as the flames grew quickly, pushing back the night with their glow. His ears were deaf to the roaring and crackling, and his nose caught no stench of flesh and smoke.

All that he had was gone, and all that was left was a shadow, and as a shadow he walked towards the mountains.

ALITH BARELY REGISTERED the others around him as he made his way up the slope. He was aware of nothing; not the grass beneath his feet, not the cold air nor the stars glittering above. Soon he passed along the secret trails into the forest and was alone. He carried on a little further, each step harder than the last, until finally he fell to his knees with an anguished cry torn from his lips. He raised his head and howled like a wolf, giving vent to the rage and despair that was all he had left. Long and piercing was that cry and it echoed from the trees and slopes, mocking him.

When he could screech no more, he tore at the grass, ripping out great clods of earth and tossing them in all directions. He pulled free his sword and swung at the naked branches, hacking and slashing without thought. His stumbling assault brought him to a winding beck and he tripped, splashing into the freezing water. Even the shock of the icy brook did not shake the madness that gripped him. He pulled himself to his feet and waded upstream, cutting the water with his blade and hurling insults at the sky.

He came upon a still pool, shining in the white moon. Casting his sword aside, he threw himself down onto the rocks, his head in his hands. The coldness seeping up from the water filled him, but it was as nothing to the bitter chill in his heart. An icy void was all that remained, and its touch numbed every part of his body.

For a moment or an age he sat there, staring at his reflection. He did not recognise the elf trapped in the still water. There were scratches on a face marked by streaks of soot and filth cut through by the traces of tears. The eyes that stared back at him were dark and wild. This creature was not the son of the Anars, it was some dishevelled, abandoned thing swathed in pity and disgust.

Gripped by another fit of self-hatred, Alith took out a knife and hacked at his hair, and for a moment the blade hovered close to his throat. The temptation struck him to pull the dagger across, to end his misery as he had ended the misery of all those the druchii had tortured.

Yet for all his grief, he hesitated. It would be weakness to avoid his punishment. Hubris had destroyed his family – they had dared to believe themselves strong enough to resist Anlec – and they now lived on only in memory. When he died, the Anars would be no more, and that was a shame he couldn't bring upon them.

Alith let the knife fall from his fingers into the pool.

As he sat gazing into the water, Alith began to feel and hear and smell again: the tinkling of the stream, the resin of the pine trees. His keen ears could hear burrowing creatures rummaging amongst the fallen needles and the flutter of bats' wings. Owls screeched and hooted, fish splashed, branches creaked.

And then there came the cawing of a crow.

A shadow appeared beside Alith. He looked up into the face of Elthyrior. The raven herald's expression was as unmoving as a mask, showing neither sympathy nor scorn. His eyes were unblinking, staring at Alith.

'Begone,' said Alith, his voice a harsh and broken growl.

Elthyrior did not move, nor did his gaze.

The urge to strike the raven herald swelled within Alith. Unreasoning loathing filled him, and in his mind Alith blamed every ill that had beset him on Elthyrior. That calm gaze taunted him.

A snapping twig broke through Alith's thoughts and he stood, casting a glance over his shoulder. In the dim moonlight that penetrated the trees, he saw a small group of figures: three maidens and two children.

Alith walked towards them unsteadily, blinking. As he came closer he saw that this was no illusion. Before him stood the refugees he had brought out of Tiranoc.

'I took them from Elanardris before the druchii came,' Elthyrior said, answering Alith's unasked question. 'We must take them to safety in Ellyrion, as you should have done before.'

The words seeped slowly into Alith's mind, to be joined by the memory of the oath he had sworn to Yeasir. Alith looked at each of them in turn, feeling nothing. What did he owe to the shade of a dead commander? He turned his bleak look upon Elthyrior.

'You would be wise to leave,' said Alith. 'Without me. There is a cloud upon my life and you would do well not to stand beneath it.'

'No,' Elthyrior replied. 'There is nothing to keep you here, no reason to stay. This is not your destiny.'

Alith laughed bitterly.

'And what new tortures does Morai-heg have planned for me?'

Elthyrior shrugged.

'I cannot say, but it is not your place to dwindle into nothing here,' he said. 'It is not in you to let those who killed your family go unpunished, for all that you blame yourself and me. You deny it, but there will come a reckoning, and you will be the instrument of that vengeance. Remember your oath to slay Caenthras?'

The mention of the elven lord's name sparked in Alith's heart and for a moment he felt something. The smallest ember of a fire began to burn inside him.

'And what of the other druchii?' Elthyrior continued. 'Do they lay waste to Elanardris without retort? If you will not avenge them, then take up that knife and drive it into your chest, for though you still breathe, you are all but dead. I cannot offer you comfort, nor sympathy. I am also the last of my line, and perhaps you will be the last of yours. My deeds are the last testament to the memory of a father murdered and a mother killed and a sister taken by the daemons. Would you have the last act of the Anars be remembered shamefully, of their lands razed and their people slaughtered?'

'No,' snapped Alith, his vigour strengthening.

'Would you have the druchii claim to have wiped out the Anars?'

'No,' Alith replied, clenching his fists.

'Would you forgive those that have brought this doom upon you? Would you forget their misdeeds and seek sanctuary in your self-pity?'

'No!' Alith snarled. 'I will not!'

Alith plunged into the pool and retrieved his dagger and sword. Splashing onto the bank, he saw Heileth, Lirian and the others shrink back from him, their eyes fearful. Far from being ashamed of their reaction, Alith drew strength from their dread. As if in response to his mood the moon hid behind a cloud and the small clearing plunged into darkness. In that darkness Alith felt himself growing. The twilight poured into him, the shadows claiming him for their own.

There was fear in the darkness and he would become that fear. The druchii murderers would scream their guilt from bloodied lips and beg for a forgiveness that did not exist. They had claimed the darkness for themselves, but it was not theirs alone to rule. The night might belong to them, but the shadows would belong to Alith.

'Let's go,' he whispered.

PART THREE

The Wrath of the Ravens; War with Nagarythe; The Shadow King Awakes; The Witch King

FOURTEEN

Pursued by Darkness

THEY MADE CAMP just before dawn, in the lee of an overhang upon the western slope of Anul Arillin. Elthyrior warned them that it was unwise to move by day and then slipped away, back along the path they had followed.

The group shared a silent, cold breakfast. Alith sat apart, chewing a chunk of cured meat, staring at the peaks ahead as the first rays of sun broke over them. The sight that had once filled him with such joy did not move him in the slightest.

'Get some sleep,' he told the others, before climbing up the overhang to keep watch. Glancing down, he saw them gather together under their blankets, like birds seeking each other's warmth in a nest. He longed for the sight to stir something in him: a memory of his mother, the hint of the passion he had felt with Milandith. Instead, his thoughts turned to Caenthras and the other druchii. Only then did he feel anything, a deep anger that heated him far more than the rising sun.

* * *

Elthyrior returned not long after the sun had fully cleared the peaks. He arrived hurriedly, panting, and Alith saw that there was a slight cut upon his brow.

'We are being followed!' he said breathless, stooping to stir the sleeping elves.

'Who?' said Alith as he jumped down from the overhang.

'Renegades of my brethren,' snarled Elthyrior. 'Though perhaps it is I who has been named the renegade. They have thrown in their lot with Morathi, and I suspect they did some time ago. They tried to trap me but I escaped. We must hurry though, for they will not be far behind!'

The party readied themselves as swiftly as possible and followed Elthyrior east and south, climbing up the shoulder of Anul Arillin. Alith and Elthyrior carried the babes so that Lirian, Heileth and Saphistia could better keep pace. They followed no track, and instead hiked across bare stone and along the rocky banks of streams, so that they left little trail.

'It will not delay them for long,' Elthyrior told Alith as they helped the maidens scramble over a tumble of boulders damming a narrow stream. 'The raven heralds have means other than eyes and ears to follow their quarry.'

Onwards and upwards they marched, breaking only occasionally for rest and drink. Part of Alith hoped the raven heralds would catch them, longing to exact the first retribution against the druchii. For all his desire for a confrontation, he put aside his own wants, knowing that it would be a greater blow against the druchii cause to keep alive the sons of Yeasir and Elodhir.

By mid-afternoon they had crested a ridge on the southern side of the mountain. Alith turned to look down the slope, Elthyrior stepping back to stand beside him. Far below, faint black shapes could be seen moving amongst the rocks: the raven heralds.

Alith watched for a moment, and saw that there were five of them, perhaps more. Each led a horse as black as his raven-feathered cloak.

'Their steeds will be more of a hindrance than help in the mountains,' said Elthyrior. 'We should make as much gain as possible before we reach the plains of Ellyrion and their mounts become an advantage.'

'Then let us continue,' said Alith, turning his back on the pursuers.

ALITH HAD NEVER spent a night so high up in the Annulii. The magical vortex created by Caledor Dragontamer swept through the mountains, drawn by the waystones erected across Ulthuan. Magic flittered on the edge of visibility and a deeper sense inside Alith could feel its strength. Mystical winds vied with each other, twining and splitting, eddying and gusting across the slopes. Each successive draught brought a strange sensation, of lingering hope, or deepening despair, warmth or chill, wisdom or rashness. Though he had lived close to the mountains for all of his life, this was the first time he had truly felt their presence.

Not only the magical winds disturbed the travellers' rest. Howls and roars echoed from the peaks as warped animals defended their territories. Here in the wilderness, wyverns and manticores, hydras and basilisks prowled the darkness. The same creatures the druchii had enslaved for their armies wandered the peaks, enormous predators that were more than a match for Elthyrior and Alith's blades.

Though Alith was no stranger to mountaincraft, in these unfamiliar surrounds he was as dependent on Elthyrior's guidance as the rest of the group. The raven herald had a sense for the terrain and its inhabitants that went beyond familiarity and experience. He had taken them on circuitous tours to avoid the nests of monsters, and sometimes they had doubled back on a whispered warning from Elthyrior. As the others slept, Alith questioned Elthyrior on this.

'I have told you before that I follow a different path, one laid down by Morai-heg,' explained the raven herald. 'That path leads neither to good nor ill, save that I do not believe my mistress wishes me to end my existence in the gullet of some Annulii beast.'

'But how can you tell where to find this path?'

'One cannot think about it,' said Elthyrior. 'It is an instinct, a knowing within that guides me. It is something that cannot be seen or heard or smelt, only felt in your heart. Morai-heg tugs us this way and that as she is wont, and most pull back against her thread, refusing to accept her wisdom. I accept the fate she has woven for me and allow her hand to turn me left or right, to stop me or urge me on as she sees fit.'

Alith shook his head at this, uncomprehending.

'But if Morai-heg has chosen our fate already, then what of the decisions we make?' he asked. 'Surely we are more than puppets for the gods?'

'Are we?' said Elthyrior. 'Aenarion, for certain, dared the gods' wrath to save his people, yet did not Khaine claim him as his own? Did not Bel Shanaar offer himself to the mercy of Asuryan before he became Phoenix King? Even Morathi wields her power only from the pacts she has made with the darker gods.'

'And why should I care for such gods when they clearly do not care for me?'

'You should not,' said Elthyrior, eliciting a frown of confusion from Alith. The raven herald stoked their small fire as he continued. 'The gods are what they are, old and young, lower and higher. Only a fool attracts their attention or makes demands of them. The druchii do not realise this, thinking they are free to exhort the cytharai without consequence as long as the sacrifices are fresh.

But what happens if they are victorious? What if all elves become druchii and Morathi reigns in terror across the world? There can be no peace, no harmony, no balance in such a civilisation. Such dark gods thrive on strife and discord, so there can be no pleasing them.'

Elthyrior turned his earnest eyes upon Alith, fierce in their intensity.

'That is why we cannot allow the druchii to win,' he whispered savagely. 'They are the doom of our people, and their victory will condemn us to a bloody death at our own hands. A people cannot live in anger and hate for all time.'

'Is it not too late?' said Alith. 'The druchii have already divided our people and brought war, and only more bloodshed and war can follow.'

'Only if one lives without hope,' replied the raven herald. 'We can fight to achieve peace, knowing that no peace is preserved without further war. Once we lived in utter bliss, but that can never be regained. All we can hope for is balance, in ourselves and in our people.'

Alith pondered this for a while and Elthyrior left him to his thoughts. Talk of harmony and balance meant nothing to Alith except to reassure him that only the death of the last druchii would bring peace: to his people and to him.

For eleven more days they stumbled and clawed their way across the mountains, buffeted and chilled by the winds. Elthyrior and Alith pressed the others to keep moving, though Heileth, Saphistia and Lirian were soon wearied by the labour. At times it was if they walked without thought, following the lead of their escorts in silence. Though Elthyrior would occasionally relent and call for the group to stop, Alith spared only the slightest thought for his companions. He regarded their presence as a necessary annoyance, a duty to be fulfilled that kept him from pursuing his true goal. By sunlight and starlight he led them on until they could walk no further and only then would he allow them to sleep.

In all this time they saw nothing of their pursuers. Elthyrior would sometimes remain behind to keep watch, but whenever he reappeared he reported that they were alone. The news brought little cheer to Alith, for as Elthyrior warned the raven heralds would soon close the gap upon them once they were out of the mountains.

Having crossed the back of the peaks, the going became easier as the steepest peaks quickly gave way to the shallower mounts of Ellyrion. Within the encircling wall of the Annulii, the weather was warmer and the winds gentler, and they made swift progress. For three more days they descended, leaving behind the barren peaks, finding themselves once again amongst sparse forest and grassy valleys.

It was with a mixture of relief and trepidation that the party made camp in a dell nestled at the foot of the mountains. Alith stood atop a steep hill nearby and looked across Ellyrion. Dawn was rising and in the growing light he could see the grasslands of the Ellyrians stretching out to the south and east. As the sun rose it bathed the grass in its ruddy light, creating a glowing sea that undulated in the wind. Perhaps once Alith may have marvelled at the natural beauty of the plains, but his only thought was that there would be nowhere to hide in such open country.

'We should head south and find a river to follow,' said Elthyrior, striding up the slope.

Alith replied with a quizzical look.

'I do not know these lands, and neither do you,' Elthyrior explained. 'But the herds of the Ellyrians need water as much as elves, so a river will give us the greatest chance of reaching a settlement.'

Alith shook his head.

'We cannot be sure of the loyalties of any Ellyrians we meet,' he said. 'I have heard only that Prince Finudel has sworn to aid King Caledor. We need to make for Tor Elyr as directly as possible.'

'And you know the way to Finudel's city?' Elthyrior replied with a doubtful look.

'While you learnt to speak with crows and listen to Morai-heg, I was shut up in a study with my tutors who thrust maps of Ulthuan beneath my nose,' said Alith. 'Tor Elyr lies south of here, just east of the Eagle Pass from Tiranoc. It is situated on an inlet of the Inner Sea where the rivers Elyranath and Irlana meet the waves.'

Elthyrior nodded, impressed. Then a new doubt crossed his face.

'Eagle Pass is at least eight days' march to the south,' he said. 'And that is if we suffer no delay from our frail companions. The dark riders will surely catch us before then.'

'Not only that, but the druchii hold the pass,' Alith said with a grim smile. 'I would be surprised if we could reach Tor Elyr unhindered, but it is there we must deliver our charges. There is a forest between the Elyranath and the Annulii, Athelian Toryr, which should provide us with some cover.'

Alith pointed south to illustrate his point. In the dawn gloom a darker shadow could be seen on the eastern flanks on the mountains, starting just at the horizon.

'We can reach Athelian Toryr within two days,' he added.

Elthyrior thought about this for a moment, lips pursed.

'There is an alternative,' said the raven herald. 'The Ellyrian herds wander the meadows; we could find one and secure ourselves some steeds.'

'Steal horses?' Alith replied with disgust, though his disregard for the idea quickly passed as he considered the thought. He nodded appreciatively. 'If we see such a herd before we reach the forest, then perhaps you are right. For the moment, we head south, following the hills.'

Elthyrior signalled his assent and the pair returned to the camp.

THEY SET OFF as the sun climbed higher in the sky, trusting to swiftness rather than darkness for safety, following the hills to the south-west at the feet of the Annulii. Now that he had a plan, Alith's mood lifted slightly at the thought that soon he would be free of this burden, free to pursue his own war against the druchii.

He gave that matter some thought as they walked, daydreaming of the punishments he would exact upon Caenthras and the others once he had the opportunity. Gone was the shattered emptiness that had consumed him after the fall of Elanardris. He imagined returning to Nagarythe with more warriors, to challenge those who ruled from Anlec.

With these darkly entertaining thoughts, the time passed quickly, and soon it was midday. They came across a stream running swiftly down from the mountains and stopped a while to drink, fill their canteens and catch fresh fish to eat. Alith felt none of the pleasure of this simple activity, his mind fixed solely on thoughts of the future. He was only aware of the delay, which nagged silently at him as he stooped into the waters to snatch up fish with his bare hands while Elthyrior kept watch to the north.

Having refreshed themselves and eaten, the group moved on, following the path of the stream. It meandered to the south and Alith hoped that this would lead them to the Elyranath. Ahead the slopes of the mountains darkened with trees, still more than a day's travel away. Alith pushed them on, seeking the sanctuary of the woods.

THE NEXT DAY brought fresh hope, for the stream they followed came to a greater river, which Alith was convinced was the Elyranath. It swept powerfully from the north, heading almost directly south.

'If only there were boats,' said Saphistia. 'We could rest and travel swiftly at the same time.'

With this in mind, they searched the banks of the river but could find no sign of such craft. It seemed the Ellyrians preferred their steeds to water. The search was not entirely in vain, for just upriver the waters widened and slowed at a ford. Elthyrior and Alith both spied fresh hoofmarks on the banks to either side, many horses having stopped to drink before moving off to the east.

'I see no print of boots,' remarked Elthyrior. 'I would say the horses are not tended.'

'Or perhaps the riders simply did not dismount,' countered Alith. 'Either way, neither of us can say how far the herd has travelled since crossing. It could be many hours away by now.'

'There is a means by which we might find out,' said Elthyrior, turning away.

Alith and the others watched as the raven herald strode away from the river, up a small rise to the west. Here he sat upon its crest, almost hidden in the long grass, with his legs crossed and his arms held out to either side of him. He remained unmoving for some time and Alith chafed at staying in one place for so long. Continually his gaze strayed to the north, his eyes searching the hills for any sign of the dark riders.

Just as Alith was about to interrupt, irritated at this unnecessary delay, Elthyrior lifted his head back and let out a long whistling sound, which deepened into a low cawing. The noise swirled around Alith. The cry rose and fell in volume and pitch, creating harmonious echoes within itself, as if it came from many throats. Alith could feel the magic bound within the call lifting up, spreading higher and higher, and he turned his gaze to the clear skies.

He saw nothing at first. After a moment a black speck appeared to the north. Another came from the south, swiftly followed by several more. Other dark dots converged from every direction, revealing themselves as crows as they neared. Alith guessed there to be several dozen as they flocked together high above the hill, wheeling and swooping, the cacophony drowning out Elthyrior's ululation.

An eerie silence then followed. One-by-one the crows dipped to the hillside, settling in the grass on and beside the raven herald until he was obscured by a shuffling, ruffling crowd of feathers and beaks. The crows hopped and fluttered around Elthyrior, each cawing out in turn, as if in council. Alith watched with amazement as Elthyrior stood, the flock leaping into the air, circling around him.

With a sweep of his hand, Elthyrior bid the birds to leave and in a great mass they climbed into the air, shrieking their farewells. As suddenly as they had arrived they were gone, each flying back the way it had come.

The raven herald walked down the hillside, his expression grim.

'I have news, both good and ill,' he said. 'The herd that crossed the river has no guardians, and is but a short walk to the east, beyond that next line of hills.'

'That is the good news?' asked Heileth.

'It is,' replied Elthyrior. He turned to the north and pointed towards a towering white cliff they had passed early that morning. 'The dark riders are close on our heels, passing that bluff. If we cannot take steeds they shall be on us before nightfall.'

'Perhaps we can find a more defensible position further into the hills,' suggested Alith.

'It will be to no avail,' said Elthyrior, shaking his head. 'They will come at us in the darkness, clothed in shadow. I do not know if they mean to kill us or capture us, but we cannot fight them. There are eight of them, and we have no bows with which we might even the odds.'

'We must get horses!' said Lirian, clasping her son protectively to her chest as if the riders were bearing down on them at that moment. 'We can't allow them to catch us. Think what terrible things they will do to us!'

Elthyrior looked to Alith, seemingly happy to abide by his judgement. Alith considered his options and liked none of them, but for all that he wracked his mind he could not conceive of any better plan.

'We'll make for the herd,' he announced. 'If we cannot fight, then the swiftest flight is our best option.'

Though he sounded confident, Alith had no hope that they would outrun their pursuers. Perhaps for a day or two they would stay ahead, but it was still a long way to Tor Elyr and the dark riders would be relentless. If they came across a place that they could defend with any surety, he resolved they would stop and fight rather than be caught unawares.

As they headed east, Elthyrior walked beside Alith.

'There is something else that you should know,' he said quietly.

'What is it?'

'I did not want to alarm the others, but my summoning of the crows will have been felt by my former brethren. Just as they can spy for me, the crows will spy for them. Such birds have little loyalty. The dark riders will soon know that we are mounted and will ride all the harder to catch us.'

NIGHTFALL FOUND THE group riding into the eaves of Athelian Toryr. As Alith had feared, though their stolen mounts proved faster than travelling on foot, their progress had not been as swift as it could have been. He did not have much horse riding experience, having had little opportunity to learn in his youth, while all except

Elthyrior were unused to riding without saddle and harness. The Ellyrian steeds had been docile enough, and ran like the wind when urged, but Saphistia and Lirian, carrying their sons, had been afraid to give their steeds their full run. At times they had been forced to slow to a walk as the path wound round loops in the river or crossed other streams, and Alith knew such things would not delay the dark riders.

Picking their way slowly under the tree canopy, the fugitives continued south by the dim starlight that broke through the leaves. Alith constantly looked over his shoulder, expecting to see shadowy riders closing on them at any moment. Elthyrior seemed content, his gaze fixed ahead, or perhaps he simply accepted that there would be no warning of attack.

As the pale light of Sariour breached the roof of leaves, they came across a clearing, the stumps of felled trees stretching for several hundred paces. The smell of sawdust hung in the air.

'These have been freshly hewn,' said Elthyrior.

'There may be a lodge close at hand,' said Alith. 'Spread out and seek a path.'

The group did as he asked while Alith halted and turned back the way they came, keeping watch for pursuit. It was not long before he heard Heileth calling from the north-west. Alith guided his horse into a trot with a word, crossing the clearing swiftly. He found Heileth at the edge of the open area, Lirian and Elthyrior already with her. A wide trail in the fallen leaves and undergrowth struck out to the north, into the hills.

Saphistia soon joined them and, dismounting, they followed the path speedily, Alith at the fore, Elthyrior guarding the rear. Ahead something white shimmered in the moonlight. As he came through the trees Alith saw that it was a lodge, built of narrow planks, painted white. It had a steep tiled roof and a stone chimney, though the narrow, arched windows were dark and no smoke could be seen.

Elthyrior appeared and signalled for the group to halt before vanishing to the left. Alith drew his sword and turned about, seeking any sign of danger. A few roosting birds flapped from tree to tree and nocturnal hunters rummaged amongst the undergrowth. An owl called in the distance, but all else was still, even the wind. The starlight came fitfully through the branches, dappling the pathway and the clearing beyond.

Elthyrior emerged from the right, having circled the lodge.

'It is empty,' he told them. 'Whoever felled the trees has moved further south today.'

'Should we stay, or move on?' asked Lirian. 'Anataris is so tired, as am I. Can we not rest here for a while? Perhaps the riders will pass us by.'

'And then be between us and Tor Elyr,' said Elthyrior. 'No, we should not stop.'

Alith was about to agree when Elthyrior sharply raised his hand, warning for silence. The raven herald slowly drew his sword and waved Lirian towards the lodge.

'Get inside,' he whispered, his eyes fixed upon something out in the woods.

Alith followed his gaze, but could see nothing. He took Heileth by the arm and led her to the door, Lirian and Saphistia following close behind. When they were inside, Alith brought the horses around the back of the lodge, where a small stable was built against the back wall. Having hidden the mounts, he returned to the front of the building, where Elthyrior was crouched beside a tree close to the path.

Keeping low, Alith joined the raven herald. Peering around the tree trunk, he allowed his eyes to lose focus, looking for movement rather than detail. Things scratched in the dirt and shuffled in the leaves but he saw nothing else.

Then, no more than two hundred paces away, he spied a shadow. It moved slowly, seeming to seep from one tree to the next, momentarily blotting out the patches of starlight. Once he was aware of it, Alith watched more closely, following its course as it approached from the north, skirting around the edge of the clearing.

'There are three more to the south,' said Elthyrior, his voice nothing more than the barest sigh.

The raven herald tapped Alith on the arm and motioned slowly towards the lodge. Rising, the pair stepped backwards, inching away from the path. There was another hoot of an owl and Alith realised the call came from no bird. The shadow ahead stopped for a moment and then changed direction, heading directly across the clearing towards them.

Elthyrior sprang up, dragging Alith by the arm. The two bolted for the lodge, swerving left and right. An arrow whistled past, catching Alith's cloak before thudding into the wooden frame of the door. Another hit the door itself as Elthyrior wrenched it open.

'Get away from the windows!' the raven herald snarled. At his instruction Saphistia, Lirian and Heileth cowered behind the stone hearth, the two children huddled tight amongst them.

The inside of the lodge was a single open room, with windows to the north, south and east, the fireplace to the west. A long table with two benches dominated the centre of the lodge. Sheathing his blade, Alith crossed to the other side and looked out.

There was another shadow, a few dozen paces away, watching.

'Help me,' said Elthyrior, motioning towards the table. Between them, they managed to tilt it upon its side and scraped it across the leaf-patterned tiles to block the doorway.

Glass shattered as an arrow sped into the room, glancing off the mantel of the fireplace. Several more followed, snicking from the hearth. Alith crouched beneath the southern window and glanced out. He saw the flickering of a flame and then a flash of orange as a fire-tipped arrow sped towards the window, landing just short, smoke spiralling up from the sill.

'They'll burn us out!' hissed Alith as more flame-arrows came through the windows, thudding into the benches and skittering from the floor.

Heileth darted forwards, tamping down the burning arrows with her cloak, her demeanour calm. Another missile sped inwards and caught her in the leg just below the knee and she fell backwards with a suppressed squeal of pain. Alith grabbed her under the arms and hauled her to the others. A quick glance showed that the wound was not deep.

'Bind it,' he said, looking at Saphistia. He heard the sound of tearing cloth as he turned back to the windows.

The fire-arrows had not done much damage to the seasoned wood of the lodge, but smoked fitfully where they had hit. Alith glanced towards the back of the lodge and saw a raven-cloaked figure moving closer to the stable.

Alith leapt through the broken window with a crash, snatching his sword free. The raven herald straightened in surprise as Alith dashed across the ground between them. The druchii tossed aside a bow and a gloved hand pulled free a slender blade as Alith reached his foe.

Alith swung back-handed towards the raven herald's head. His enemy ducked and Alith almost lost his footing, stepping to his right to regain balance. The herald lunged, raven-feather hood falling back, revealing a cruelly beautiful face. Alith was almost caught by the thrust, momentarily stunned by the maiden's appearance.

He raised his sword to parry another blow, stepping backwards again until he sensed the stable wall at his back. Dodging to the left, he avoided the next attack, the herald's sword carving a furrow in the white planks.

Alith spun away from the next thrust, bringing his sword swinging up. The blade cut into his foe's arm, under the shoulder, and blood sprayed in the starlight. The raven herald gasped, lurching away, and Alith swiftly followed, driving the point of his sword into her back. She twisted as she fell, blood dribbling from her lips and running down her pale chin. Her eyes were filled with hate.

A shout from Elthyrior brought Alith back to the window to see flames flickering along the eastern wall, lapping at the window. The fire was taking hold and smoke was quickly filling the chamber despite the broken windows. Lirian was sobbing in the nook beside the fire, bent protectively over her son.

A flash of panic crossed Elthyrior's face as he realised the peril of their situation. If they stayed inside the smoke would choke them, if they left they would be easy prey for the raven heralds' bows.

'Out the back,' snapped Alith, gesturing to Saphistia. He took Durinithill as she clambered through the window and then handed back Yeasir's son, gesturing for Lirian to follow.

'Wait!' said Elthyrior. He pointed towards the southern windows. 'Listen!'

Alith froze, his breathing still. He could hear nothing for a moment, but then his keen ears detected something at odds with the sounds of the forest. It was a tremor, distant but powerful. Dashing to the side of the lodge he saw white shapes moving quickly through the woods.

Riders!

From the south and east the Ellyrian reavers came, upon pearl-white steeds, dashing amongst the trees with reckless speed. There were dozens of them, galloping between the boles, bows in hand. The raven heralds turned in shock as the Ellyrians thundered across the clearing and streamed up either side of the path. One of the heralds loosed arrows as they approached, felling three knights before the shafts of the other Ellyrians found him, hurling him into the bushes with four arrows in his chest. The surviving raven heralds fled, disappearing into the shadows between the shafts of starlight, skimming from trunk to trunk before vanishing completely.

The riders of Ellyrion quickly encircled the lodge and Alith was struck by the memory of his first encounter with these headstrong folk, so many years ago. He searched their stern faces but recognised none. Climbing back into the lodge, Alith helped Elthyrior pull the table from the door and the two of them stepped out, dropping their swords to the ground.

'Once again it seems I owe my life to the proud knights of Ellyrion,' said Alith, forcing a smile.

The knights' captain, his silver breastplate chased with sapphires in the form of a rearing horse, urged his steed forwards. He stowed his bow and brought forth a long spear whose tip flickered with magical energy.

'Do not be so glad to see me,' he said fiercely. 'In Ellyrion, spies and horse thieves are punished with death.'

FIFTEEN

The Clarion Sounds

THOUGH THEIR HANDS were not bound, Alith was in no doubt that he and the others were prisoners of the Ellyrians. They had ridden south with an escort of a hundred knights, who constantly darted suspicious glances at the Naggarothi. Anataris and Durinithill had been taken away, despite the wailed protestations of their mothers. Though it was a callous act, Alith knew he would have done the same.

Five days after their capture, the Ellyrians brought them to Tor Elyr. To the east the Inner Sea sparkled in the afternoon sun, waves crashing upon a steep pebble shore. Two glittering rivers wound towards the coast from the north and west, converging on the capital of Ellyrion.

The city was unlike anything Alith had ever seen. Built upon the confluence of the rivers and the sea, Tor Elyr was a series of immense islands. These isles were linked by bridges, graceful arches covered with turf so that it seemed as if the meadows rose up of their own accord and spanned the water.

The towers of the Ellyrians were like ivory stalagmites, open at the base, soaring high upon circles of carved columns above spiralling stairs. Not a paved path or road could be seen, all was grassland, even under the platforms of the towers.

White horses roamed freely within and without, gathering in herds to crop the lush grass, trotting over the bridges alongside their elven companions. White ships with figureheads of horses with golden harnesses bobbed on the water, their huge triangular sails reflecting the sun. It was as different from bleak Nagarythe as the summer is from winter. All was warmth and openness, even the skies were cloudless, their deep blue mirrored in the waters of the Inner Sea.

There were many looks at the group as their captors led them through the wide, winding avenues of Tor Elyr, crossing from island to island. There was a babble of talk as they passed and the Ellyrians were not restrained in voicing their disapproval as insults and curses followed Alith.

They came to the great palace, alone upon an isle at the mouth of the rivers, larger than the manse of Elanardris, though not nearly so grand as the citadel of Tor Anroc. The palace was shaped as an amphitheatre, a huge enclosed field surrounded by an arch-broken wall and six towers built upon hundreds of slender pillars. At the centre of the arena rose a stepped hill, runes of white carved into the turf, a circular stage of dark wood and silver at its summit.

About this circle stood tall banner poles, each hanging a standard from one of the great houses of Ellyrian. Blue and white and gold fluttered in the gentle breeze, topped with streaming tails of horsehair. At their centre were two thrones, their backs carved in the likeness of rearing horses that appeared to be dancing with each other. Ellyrian nobles were gathered upon the stage and hillside, some on foot, some upon the backs of haughtily stepping steeds. All turned to look at the new arrivals, their expressions unwelcoming.

The rightmost throne was empty save for a silver crown upon its seat. On the other sat Princess Athielle, and the sight of her stirred within Alith feelings he had thought gone forever. Her hair reached to her waist, spilling across her shoulders and chest in lustrous golden curls, braided in places with ruby-studded bands. She wore an elegant sleeveless gown of light blue, garlanded with dark red roses and embroidered with golden thread and more red gems. There was also a golden hue upon her skin, glowing in the sunlight.

The princess's eyes were a startlingly deep green flecked with brown, beneath a brow furrowed with anger. Lips pursed, Athielle regarded Alith and the others with a smouldering ire that did nothing to abolish Alith's admiration; if anything her intemperate expression only served to display a fiery disposition that attracted him more.

'Dismount,' commanded Anathirir, the captain who had taken them prisoner.

Alith duly slipped from the back of his horse and immediately stepped towards the thrones. Knights closed in swiftly, placing themselves between Alith and their co-ruler, their speartips directed towards him. There could be no danger, for Alith and Elthyrior had no weapons.

'Bring them,' said Athielle. 'Let me see them.'

The knights parted and, urged on by the presence of the riders, the group walked towards the princess. She stood as they stopped a few paces short, and strode from her throne. Taller than Alith, arms folded across her chest,

Athielle walked back and forth in front of them, her eyes taking in every detail.

Alith bowed briefly and opened his mouth to speak but Athielle recognised his intent.

'Say nothing!' she snapped, a finger raised to silence him. 'You will speak only to answer my questions.'

Alith nodded in assent.

'Who here is your leader?'

The captives exchanged glances, and the eyes of the others eventually fell upon Alith.

'I speak for all of us, Lady Athielle,' he said. 'My name is–'

'Have I asked your name?' Athielle interrupted. 'Is it true that you took from our herds by the ford of Thiria Elor?'

Alith darted a glance at the others before answering.

'We took horses, it is true,' he said. 'We were–'

'Did you have permission to take these horses?' Athielle continued.

'Well, no, we needed–'

'So you admit to being horse thieves?'

Alith stuttered for a moment, frustrated by the princess's interrogation.

'I'll take your silence as agreement,' said Athielle. 'In these times, save for the slaying of another elf there is no greater crime in Ellyrion. Even now my brother fights to free our lands from the Naggarothi menace, and we find you in our borders. You came across the mountains to spy for Morathi, did you not?'

'No!' said Heileth. 'We were fleeing Nagarythe.'

'But you are Naggarothi?' Athielle turned her full intent upon Heileth, who shrank back from her wrath.

'I am not,' said Lirian. She cast a plaintive glance back towards the knights. 'Please, princess, they have taken my son.'

'And how many sons and daughters of Ellyrion have been taken by this Naggarothi war?' Athielle retorted. 'What is one child amongst so much destruction?'

'He is the heir of Bel Shanaar,' said Alith, drawing gasps from the Ellyrian nobles. Athielle turned her glare back upon him, her expression doubtful. Then she laughed, without humour.

'The heir of Tiranoc? Out of the wilderness with a ragged party of Naggarothi? You expect me to believe that?'

'Highness, look at me,' said Lirian, her voice growing in insistence. 'I am Lirian, widow of Elodhir. We have met before, at Bel Shanaar's court, when Malekith first returned. I was not so unkempt then as I am now, and my hair was almost as long as yours.'

Athielle cocked her head to one side as she studied the Tiranocii princess. Her eyes widened with recognition.

'Lirian?' she whispered, covering her mouth in horror. Athielle skipped forwards and threw her arms around Lirian, almost crushing her with the intensity of her embrace. 'Oh, my poor child, I am so sorry! What has become of you?'

The princess of Ellyrion stepped back.

'Bring the children here,' she snapped, her sudden anger focussed upon Anathirir. Shame-faced, the captain hurriedly gestured to his knights and within moments two rode forwards and handed the babes back to their mothers.

'And who are you to have delivered this gift to us?' Athielle said, looking at Alith.

'I am Alith,' he said solemnly. 'Last lord of House Anar.'

'Alith Anar? Son of Eothlir?'

Alith merely nodded. To his surprise, Athielle then hugged him tight as well, squeezing the breath from his body.

'You fought beside Aneltain,' Athielle whispered. 'I have so longed to meet a lord of the Anars to thank them for their aid.'

Alith's hands hovered close to Athielle's back, unsure whether he should return the embrace. Before he had decided, she broke away, a tear in her eye.

'I am so sorry,' she said, addressing all of them. 'Such wickedness as Morathi has unleashed has spawned a darkness in all of us! Please forgive my suspicions.'

Alith almost laughed at the transformation in the princess. Faced with such earnest contrition, there was little else he could do.

THE HOSTILITY WITH which the group had been greeted was matched by the Ellyrians' hospitality once Athielle had given her blessing. Spacious chambers were given over to them in the palace, and Alith found himself attended by several servants. He found their constant presence a distraction and despatched them on pointless errands so that he could be by himself. His quest for solitude was waylaid by an invitation from the princess to attend a feast that night.

Alith was conflicted as his servants led him out into the great arena. Deep within, he longed to leave Tor Elyr having discharged his duty to Lirian and the others. The memories of razed Elanardris haunted his thoughts and he nurtured this bleak remembrance, drawing resolution from his bitterness. Yet the thought of spending more time with Athielle, of forgetting the woes that had burdened him, teased him. This desire made him feel weak and selfish, so it was in a sour mood that he stalked from the palace to join his hosts.

The meadow-hall had been filled with long tables and hundreds of lanterns glowed with a rainbow of colours, dappling the ground with green and yellow and blue. Ellyrian knights and nobles strolled along the tables, sampling the many drinks and delicacies on offer. Their chatter was light and drifted out into the evening sky, and there was much laughter. Alith cast his gaze across the crowd, seeking a familiar face, but saw nothing of Elthyrior, Saphistia or the others. Athielle had not yet arrived.

A few of the Ellyrians tried to engage him in conversation, wandering over in small groups to meet their strange guest. His civil yet curt replies soon rebuffed their attempts at friendship, and the sympathetic looks of the departing nobles did nothing to ease the residual anger he felt. To Alith, it seemed impossible that such a banquet could be held while elves fought and died not so very far away, the future of Ulthuan hanging in the balance. It was such a far cry from what he had left in Nagarythe that he was taken by the urge to leave immediately. He wanted no part of this false display of gaiety and wellbeing.

As he resolved to depart, Athielle made her entrance. Flanked by a bodyguard of knights, she rode into the arena upon a high-stepping white stallion, her long tresses flowing behind her like a cloak. Diamonds glittered in the harness of her steed and flashed like stars from the threads of her blue gown.

The crowd parted before the princess and she rode quickly up to her throne while her knights wheeled away, picking their way easily through the mingling elves. Athielle dismounted with a flourish and sent her horse running with a whispered word. Servants were on hand with platters of food and goblets of wine, but she ignored them, casting her gaze across her assembled subjects. Her eyes stopped when they fell upon Alith, who was stood away to her left, far from the rest of the elves.

Athielle beckoned him to approach. Taking a deep breath, Alith strode up the throne hill, ignoring the looks directed at him from the other Ellyrians. His eyes were fixed upon Athielle, as hers were upon him. The princess smiled as Alith reached the stage and extended a hand in greeting. Alith took her hand in his, bowed and kissed her slender fingers.

'It is my pleasure to see you again, princess,' said Alith. To his surprise he realised that he meant these words, all his misgivings having been dispelled by her warm smile.

'And it is an honour for me, prince,' Athielle replied. She turned and whispered something to one of her retainers who slipped away.

'I hope that you are finding your stay in Tor Elyr more comfortable than your journey here,' she said, gracefully withdrawing her hand before sitting upon her throne.

Alith hesitated before replying, not wishing to be dishonest but cautious not to voice his misgivings.

'The hospitality of your city and people are a great credit to Ellyrion,' he said.

Servants returned carrying high-backed chairs, which they arranged around the throne. As Athielle waved for Alith to be seated, she looked away with a broad smile.

'You need not suffer my company alone, Alith,' she said.

Before Alith could dispute that such an encounter was anything but pleasant, Athielle pointed past him. Alith turned to see Lirian, Heileth and Saphistia walking up the hill, clad in flamboyant dresses of silk and jewels. There was no sign of the children, or Elthyrior. Alith's companions seated themselves around him, looking comfortable in their finery, pleased with the attention being heaped upon them.

'Our vagabond maidens have been restored to their glory,' said Athielle. 'Like fine steeds that need to be well-groomed after a long ride through briar and wood.'

Alith murmured his agreement, for his companions looked every part the nobles that they truly were. Still, there was something stiff about the beauty of Lirian, like a finely rendered statue, which reminded Alith too much of Ashniel. Heileth and Saphistia were more familiar, being Naggarothi, but even they had taken on an other-worldly air with the pampering of their attendants. Alith returned his gaze to Athielle, admiring all the more her natural beauty. Though her appearance was as meticulously designed and styled as the others, Alith saw a light within her, a glow of life that couldn't be swathed by all the gems and cloth in Ulthuan.

Alith tried to dismiss these thoughts but Athielle leaned forwards towards him, her scent enveloping him. It was the perfume of Ellyrion itself: of fresh sea air and grass, of open skies and rolling meadows.

'You seem uncomfortable, Alith,' said the princess. 'You are not at ease.'

'I am perplexed,' said Alith. 'If you will pardon the question, I must ask how it is possible that so many Ellyrians can be brought here, while the Naggarothi wage war upon all of Ulthuan?'

A scowl marred Athielle's perfect features and Alith felt a stab of regret at his words.

'You come to us in a brief moment of respite. Even now my brother fights in the north, defending these lands.' Her tone and expression relented as she continued. 'Is it wrong to enjoy these fleeting moments of peace? If we do not treasure our lives as they can be without war, what is it that we fight for? Perhaps it is a failing of the Naggarothi that they could find no contentment within themselves, that only in action and not quiet do they measure the success of their lives.'

Athielle's words stung Alith and he looked down, shamed. He had no right to bring his own darkness here, to taint the light of the festivities of others, but for all his misgivings, a part of his soul protested against acquiescence. This was an illusion, a fake revelry that tried to defy the blights of Ulthuan, hollow and meaningless.

Alith curbed his tongue, wishing to cause no further offence. Athielle was speaking to the others, but her questions and their replies were faint in Alith's ears. Only after some time did he look up, stirred by movement. Lirian, Saphistia and Heileth were leaving the throne-stage. Alith stood and mumbled a few parting words, and then he was alone with Athielle and her court.

'I see that my attempts to lighten your mood have been for naught,' said Athielle. 'Please, sit, and we will talk of matters that are perhaps of more concern to you.'

'Forgive my mood, princess, I am not ungrateful for your kindness,' Alith said, taking his seat again. 'I have suffered more than any from this war and it is not in me to put aside my woe. I would have it that every day could be spent as this one, but wishing it will not make it so.'

'I will not deceive you, Alith,' said the Ellyrian ruler, her mood serious. 'The war has not gone well of late. King Caledor's gains of the summer have been reversed and we expect the Naggarothi to march again for Tor Elyr before the end of the season. I do not know if we can hold them this time, for they seem reckless in their hatred and determination to crush all opposition.'

'There is no alternative but to fight,' Alith replied. 'I have seen the horror of Morathi's rule, the wickedness of her followers. It is better to fight and die than submit to such barbarous slavery.'

'And how will you continue to fight, Alith?' asked Athielle. 'You are a prince without a realm, a leader without an army.'

Alith said nothing, for he had no answer to the question. He knew not how he would fight, only that he must.

He refused to entertain the hopelessness that churned within him; refused to consider any thought of surrender. The blood in his veins burned, his heart set to racing at the merest contemplation of the druchii and the wrongs they had heaped upon him.

He looked up at Athielle and she shrank back from his piercing stare.

'I do not know how I will fight,' Alith said. 'I do not know if any will fight with me. While I still draw breath, I will not suffer a single druchii to live. This is all that is left of me.'

THE SEASONS PASSED differently in Ellyrion, the weather far milder than in Nagarythe, and Alith became unsure how long he had spent in Tor Elyr. The passing days melded into an interminable limbo, and Alith felt the same frustrations that had beset him in Tor Anroc. He had no plan, no course of action to follow, only the burning desire to do something.

He spent little time with the others he had arrived with; Elthyrior had disappeared soon after their coming, and the rest were quickly adjusting to court life in their new home. Alith found the Ellyrians intolerable company, even more garrulous and overly friendly than the serving folk of Tor Anroc. The wide meadows surrounding the city had none of the bleak charm of Elanardris, the sun-drenched fields only serving to throw his own cold feelings into stark contrast. The Inner Sea held no appeal for Alith either, nothing more than a means to travel further east, away from Nagarythe.

So it was that he spent much of his time alone, brooding on his fate. The Ellyrians soon came to shun his company, and he encouraged this. He even turned down requests from Athielle to join her, driven by a self-torturous need to deny himself any form of pleasure. Alith came to hate and love his own suffering, taking comfort from his bitter thoughts, confirming his own dark suspicions about his fellow elves.

When even the clement weather within the Annulii began to grow colder, Prince Finudel returned from his campaign. Alith joined the Ellyrian court to welcome the prince, and was introduced by Athielle that evening. The three of them met alone in the prince's chambers, high within one of the palace's towers. Alith again related the circumstances surrounding his exile from Nagarythe.

'All that I desire is to strike back at those who have destroyed my family and my lands,' Alith concluded.

'You wish to fight?' said Finudel. The likeness between him and his older sister was remarkable, though Finudel was even more animated and prone to changes of mood. The prince paced to and fro across the circular room, his hands in constant motion, seeking activity.

'I do,' said Alith.

'Then you will soon have the opportunity,' replied Finudel. 'You were not the only Naggarothi to have crossed the mountains. They joined with us as we pursued an army of cultists. Many spoke highly of you, Alith, and they will be heartened to hear that you are alive.'

'I am glad that others have evaded the clutches of Kheranion and his army,' said Alith. 'How many have made the crossing?'

'A few thousand in all,' said Finudel. 'They are camped to the west with my army. It would do me a great service if you would lead them into battle beside me.'

'Nothing would give me more satisfaction,' said Alith. 'Against whom are we to fight?'

'The druchii have retaken the Pass of the Eagle, its eastern reaches no more than three days from here,' Finudel said. 'I ride out again tomorrow.'

'And I ride out as well,' said Athielle. 'We cannot allow our foes to approach Tor Elyr. As you see, our city has no walls to defend, no keeps to hold the druchii at bay. We must meet them in open battle, and must do so with all of our strength.'

'We must deal with this threat,' added Finudel. 'In the north, there are still those who were once our subjects who have been swayed by Morathi. They are a blight within Ellyrion but they cannot be swept away whilst the threat from the west remains.'

'I will fight for Ellyrion as if they were my own lands,' said Alith. 'The druchii will pay a bloody price for their treachery.'

SIXTEEN

Blood on the Plains

CHEERS GREETED ALITH'S arrival at the Naggarothi camp, but the enthusiasm of his followers was soon quelled by his dour expression. Amongst those that thronged towards him from the tents, Alith recognised many faces. The former Shadows Anraneir and Khillrallion were there, with Tharion, Anadriel and several others who had fought at Dark Fen. All seemed pleased to see him, but there was a drawn, haunted look about their faces.

'We feared for you, lord, when you disappeared from Elanardris,' said Anraneir. 'We thought you dead, or worse.'

'You were not wrong,' replied Alith. 'Though I am not dead in body, I suffer all the more for it.'

Some of the captains exchanged worried glances at this, but remained silent.

'What are your orders, prince?' asked Tharion.

It struck Alith as strange that one of his father's closest friends, who had fought beside Eothlir in the colonies, would look to him for leadership. Alith considered the question for some time.

'Fight until your last breath, and with that last breath spit out your hatred of the druchii.'

THE ARMY MOVED westwards towards the Pass of the Eagle, a force of several hundred knights riding ahead of the host to spy the position of the enemy. The Naggarothi marched alongside the Ellyrian spearmen and archers, and Alith walked with them, choosing to accompany his warriors on foot rather than ride with Finudel and Athielle.

Two days from the pass, scouts returned with word of the druchii army. Messengers asked Alith to attend the Ellyrian prince and princess so that they might devise a strategy. They met just after midday, as the army took a break from its march along the southern bank of the Irlana River. Beneath a pavilion roof of blue and gold, the commanders sought the counsel of each other whilst they refreshed themselves with water from the river and fruits brought from orchards further south.

'We are outnumbered, that is for certain,' they were told by Prince Aneltain, who had met Alith whilst returning from the ill-fated expedition to Ealith more than twenty-five years earlier. It was Aneltain's warriors that formed the vanguard and the prince had troubling news. 'Forty thousand infantry at least, and some ten thousand knights. Few are cultists, most are soldiers trained in Anlec.'

'That is nearly ten thousand more warriors than we have mustered,' said Athielle. She paused to take a bite from a red apple, her expression pensive.

'It is, but we have the greater number of cavalry,' said Finudel. 'We have twice as many riders.'

'These are knights of Anlec, not reavers,' said Alith. 'You cannot count their strength by numbers alone.'

'And the reavers of Ellyrion carry bows,' countered Finudel. 'And ride swifter steeds. The druchii knights can chase us for a year and a day and they will never catch us.'

'They do not need to chase us, brother,' said Athielle, finishing the apple, tossing the core towards her horse, Silvermane. 'The enemy know that we must stand at some time, to protect Tor Elyr.'

'Why?' asked Alith. The other elves directed surprised looks towards him. 'Why do you need to protect Tor Elyr?'

'Fifty thousand of our subjects live in the city,' said Finudel, a touch of anger in his voice. 'We could not abandon them to the cruel intent of the druchii.'

'Evacuate them,' said Alith. 'By land and ship, have your people leave the city. It is only stone and wood, after all. Why hang such a weight about your necks when you have such a swift army?'

'It matters not,' said Athielle. 'Though many of us can ride away from the druchii, even in Ellyrion there are not enough horses for every elf. Half our force is on foot.'

'Have them hide in Athelian Toryr, where the enemy will not happily follow.'

'Hide?' spat Finudel. 'You would have us allow the druchii to ravage our lands at will, leaving us destitute and homeless.'

'Better that than make food for the crows,' Alith replied. 'While you live you can fight.'

'We will not run like cowards,' said Athielle. 'Too many have done so and paid the price later. The Naggarothi only grow stronger the longer we delay confrontation.'

Alith shrugged.

'Then we will fight them,' he said. 'It would be wise to attack while they are still in the pass, where their numbers will count against them. Ambush them from the slopes, lure them onto your blades and surround them.'

'A rock-strewn valley is no place for cavalry,' said Aneltain. 'We would surrender the advantages that we possess.'

'We will meet them upon the open field, and fight as Ellyrians,' said Finudel.

'It is clear you have already set your minds on one course,' growled Alith. 'No argument I can make will convince you of the error of your actions. If you do not wish to hear my counsel, why did you ask me here?'

'And who are you to tell us better?' said Finudel. 'A dispossessed prince; a wanderer with nothing but hate.'

'If you would suffer the same fate as I, then do as you say,' snarled Alith. 'Ride out in glory, with your banners streaming and your horns ringing. You think that because you have defeated the druchii before that you will have victory today? They do not fight on your terms, and they will win. Unless you crush them, kill every one of them, they will not relent. Morathi drives them on, and their commanders fear her far more than they fear your knights and spears. Have you mages to match their sorcery? If you win and they flee, have it in you to chase them down, slay them as they run? Is it in your noble hearts to butcher and kill, so that they will not return?'

'Darkness cannot be defeated by further darkness,' said Athielle. 'Did you not hear what I told you in Tor Elyr? It is because the druchii despise peace, loathe life, that they must be defeated. If we become the same, we have lost that which we fight for.'

'Fools!' said Alith. 'I will have no part of this folly. The true Naggarothi have already paid the price for thinking that they can stand face-to-face against the might of Anlec. The corpses of my mother and father are testament to that course of action.'

Alith stormed from the pavilion, scattering the Ellyrians in his path. He strode through the camp, heedless of the shouts that followed him. Despair vied with rage inside him: despair that the Ellyrians would die; rage that the druchii would gain an important victory.

HIS CAPTAINS MET Alith as he entered the Naggarothi camp. They immediately sensed his foul mood and followed in silence as he cut between the assembled regiments towards his tent. A glare from Alith halted them at the door as he ducked inside.

Alith sat listening to the musicians of the Ellyrians calling them to the march. The ground trembled beneath the tread of horses and elves as Finudel and Athielle mustered their army. Let them march to their pointless deaths, he told himself.

It was Khillrallion who dared his foul temper, standing calmly upon the threshold of the pavilion, hands behind his back.

'The Ellyrians have broken camp, prince,' he said quietly.

Alith did not reply.

'Should we make ready to march as well?'

Alith looked up at Khillrallion.

'We will follow behind,' he said. 'If they call for our aid, I will not deny them.'

Khillrallion nodded and withdrew, leaving Alith with his tumultuous thoughts.

FINUDEL AND ATHIELLE chose to make their stand upon the meadows of Nairain Elyr, less than a day's march from the mouth of Eagle Pass, where the Irlana flows from the mountains and loops widely to the north before continuing east towards the Inner Sea. The Ellyrians put their infantry upon the right, with their flank protected by the river, while their cavalry they kept to the left, giving them the freedom of the wide fields to the south. Alith encamped his small army, four thousand in all, even further to the south. Here he stayed within his tent, and dismissed all visits from his lieutenants.

The following dawn Alith was roused from his sleep by Tharion.

'One of the Ellyrians wishes to see you,' said the captain.

Alith nodded and signalled for the messenger to be brought to the pavilion. A few moments later Tharion entered with Aneltain in tow. Alith nodded in greeting but did not rise from his cot.

'The druchii have been spied by our scouts,' said the Ellyrian. 'They will be upon us before noon.'

'And you still intend to meet them in open battle?' asked Alith.

'There is no other choice,' replied Aneltain.

'Send your infantry across the river, and take your riders to the east,' said Alith, his tone off-hand. 'That is one alternative to throwing your lives away in this pointless gesture.'

'You know that we will not retreat,' said Aneltain. He took a step forwards, his expression imploring. 'Fight with us and we can win.'

'Four thousand spears and bows will not win this battle,' said Alith. 'Even Naggarothi spears and bows.'

'Then at least promise that you will hold this position,' said Aneltain. 'At least give Finudel and Athielle your assurance that you will defend the southern flank.'

Alith looked at Aneltain with a frown, sensing the accusation implicit in the request.

'I swore to defend Ellyrion as if these were my own lands,' Alith said sharply. 'I do not make such oaths lightly. Though I do not agree on this course of action, I will not abandon my allies.'

Aneltain's relief was palpable as he bowed in thanks.

'I remember a time when it was I that came to the aid of the Anars,' he said. 'I am glad that I was not wrong to do so.'

Alith pushed himself from his bed and strode up to Aneltain, staring him in the eye.

'Perhaps you think that I owe you this favour?' snarled Alith. 'You think that I feel some debt?'

Aneltain stepped back, aghast at Alith's aggression. His expression of gratitude became one of anger.

'If you do not feel the debt, then I will not claim it,' Aneltain said fiercely. 'If it does not matter to you that brave Ellyrians died restoring Malekith to his throne, and Chracians and Yvressians as well, then perhaps you should consider who it is that you wish to fight for.'

'I do not fight *for* anyone!' roared Alith, forcing Aneltain to retreat quickly to the tent's opening. 'I fight *against* the druchii!'

With a venomous glare, Aneltain left, shouting for his horse to be brought to him. Tharion directed a sharp glance at his prince.

'Would you have us left with no allies?' said the veteran captain.

'No allies would be better than poor allies,' Alith replied, slumping back onto his bed. 'They talk of honour and glory, as if that counted for anything. They do not understand the manner of foe they fight, even though they have looked it in the face a dozen times. Fear is all the druchii understand, and fear is a power we can wield as well if we choose. Morathi and her commanders do not fear the cavalry charge or the volley of arrows. No, it is the darkness they have unleashed, it causes them to pause for thought, wakes them in the cold hours before dawn. They look over their own shoulders, dreading to see who wields the knife for them. Fear binds them more than loyalty, and with fear we will break them apart.'

Tharion considered this for a moment, doubts scribed upon his brow.

'What is it that you fear, Alith?'

'Nothing,' he said. 'There is no pain that can be visited upon me that I have not already felt. There is no torment I can suffer that my memories do not inflict upon me every day. I have nothing left to be taken away, save this existence that hurts me with every breath. I do not seek death, but I have no fear of being sent to Mirai. There I will find my family again, and take vengeance upon those that killed them. Beyond even death my hatred will continue.'

Tharion shuddered and turned away, terrified by the look in Alith's eye.

ALITH STOOD AT the edge of the Naggarothi camp, looking out over the two armies as the druchii advanced. In long lines of silver, white and blue, the Ellyrians stood their ground against the encroaching black host. White steeds stamped and whinnied, sharing the excitement of their riders. A hundred banners streamed from silver poles, and golden horns were lifted to lips to let forth peals of defiance.

The reaver knights were split into two forces, one led by Finudel, the other by Athielle. The princess sat upon Silvermane at the head of the closest division, her long hair flying free in the wind, her slender form encased in silver armour studded with sapphires. In her hand she held aloft a white sword, the winterblade Amreir, and upon her left arm hung a shield in the shape of a horse's head, its mane a flowing mass of golden thread.

Finudel was no less impressive. He carried Cadrathi, the starblade lance forged by Caledor Dragontamer, whose head burned with a golden flame. In gold panoply sat the prince, a cloak of deep red flapping from his shoulders. His steed Snowhoof, sister to Athielle's mount, was enveloped by a long caparison of gilded ithilmar, every scale of armour inscribed with a rune of protection.

Studying the druchii, Alith saw that their standards also bore runes, of bloodthirsty gods and wicked goddesses. Many had painted or embossed symbols of cults upon their shields, twisted script that seethed with dark magic. In columns the Naggarothi advanced, black and silver snakes whose coming was heralded by the tramping of thousands of boots.

The knights of Anlec turned to the south, to face the reavers. Harsh battle cries and shrill horns announced their challenge to Finudel and Athielle while black and purple pennants snapped upon golden lances. Their steeds were black, with chamfrons of silvered armour decked with blades, flanks covered with shining links of mail.

Sorcerers and sorceresses there were too, prowling amongst the regiments, their magic coiling and weaving around them. Dark clouds swathed the sky at their commands, flickering with lightning, thunder matching the crash of the army's advance. The shadow of the storm swept over the plains, shrouding both armies in gloom.

Glancing at the heavy skies, Alith saw a dark shape, enormous and winged. Despite his earlier words, for a moment he was gripped with fear as the dragon circled menacingly. His father's bloodied face flashed in front of Alith, and his muscles twitched with the memory of the terror that had filled him.

'Kheranion,' Alith snarled, allowing his anger to flood away all dread.

Turning on his heel, Alith shouted for his captains. They came running from across the camp and waited breathlessly for their commander's decree.

'We attack,' said Alith. 'Sound the muster, gather your regiments. Today we will slay these druchii dogs and send a message back to Anlec. Bring me the head of Kheranion.'

There was no argument from the lieutenants, who hurried back to their companies, calling for musicians and banner bearers to signal the attack. Alith returned to his tent and took up bow and arrows, given to him by Khillrallion.

'Shadows, to me!' he called upon returning outside. Soon he stood at the centre of a circle of black-swathed archers, bitter survivors of Dark Fen. 'Today I lead the Shadows again. The enemy bring their own darkness, and that suits us well. Show no mercy. Every arrow brings death. Every sword thrust is vengeance. Every drop of blood is owed to us. We will be the nightmares once more, and the druchii will remember well why they fear the Shadows.'

In all, more than two hundred of the Shadows had survived the disaster at Dark Fen, and clad in their black cloaks they followed Alith westwards, circling around the right flank of the druchii host. The rest of Alith's army stood ready at the camp, with orders to engage the enemy if they came too close. Not until Alith returned from his foray were they to move forwards.

It was the druchii that started the battle. They had brought with them repeater bolt throwers: war engines that hurled half-a-dozen spear-sized shafts with each salvo. The opening volley from ten of these machines screamed into the air above the advancing druchii and plunged down into the Ellyrian infantry. To Alith it was clear that Kheranion thought the reaver knights unable to match his columns and sought to destroy the spearmen and archers first and then drive away the cavalry with weight of numbers.

Alith found it curious that the druchii prince remained in the skies, observing the unfolding battle from the back of his black dragon. At Dark Fen he had only become involved when it was obvious that the Naggarothi were losing. Perhaps he was a coward? Or perhaps there was some other reason Kheranion feared to commit to the fighting.

As he pondered this, Alith signalled for the Shadows to halt. The long grass of Ellyrion reached above waist height and provided ample concealment for the scouts. The storm overhead continued to growl and rumble, growing in intensity, shrouding the meadows with a yellowing gloom close to twilight. In the darkness, the Shadows readied their bows and waited for Alith's next command.

As he looked at the druchii army, Alith was surprised to see that they had brought no hydras with them. He had no idea why they had left their monstrous war-beasts behind, but was pleased that such was the case, though it was small comfort when he remembered the dragon climbing and swooping through the storm clouds.

The druchii halted their advance just out of the range of the Ellyrian bows as the repeater bolt throwers continued to unleash their deadly volleys. The closest of the war machines was about four hundred paces from the Shadows, its crew working quickly to replace an empty magazine.

'Split into fives, target the bolt throwers,' Alith told the others. 'I want the crews dead.'

In small groups, the Shadows broke away, flitting through the long grass towards their targets. Alith and his four companions headed directly for the closest while the other Shadows fanned out around the rest of the battery. Companies of spearmen stood close to the war machines, guarding against any attempt by the Ellyrians to circumvent the main line, but their attention was focussed to the east not the south and the Shadows approached unseen.

Alith stooped in a crouch about seventy paces from the repeater bolt thrower. He fitted an arrow to his bowstring, rising just enough to see his target. The bolt thrower was crewed by two druchii, protected by breastplates and helms but no heavier armour. Having removed the empty shaft box from the top of their engine, they were carrying a new magazine of bolts back to the war machine.

'Now,' Alith said calmly, sighting upon the leftmost of the two druchii.

With a gentle exhalation, Alith loosed his string and the black-fletched arrow whistled just above the tips of the grass, taking his target in the right shoulder. Another shaft hit him in the thigh, punching deep through the flesh and out the other side. The druchii dropped his burden, spinning to the ground while three arrows found their mark on his companion, one of them hitting him through the eyehole of his helmet's mask.

The only sound was the clatter of the magazine tumbling from their dead grip, easily lost in the wind. Alith dropped down and made his way to the war engine as quickly as possible, exchanging his bow for a long hunting knife. With occasional glances to check that he was unobserved, he reached the bolt thrower.

Alith sawed at the rope coils that provided the tension for the war engine's mechanism. His sharp blade quickly parted the cords twisted around one launching arm and the rope fell slack. It would take hours to restring the machine, but for good measure Alith used the tip of his knife to pry out the trigger mechanism from the main body of the machine. He levered out several springs from the delicate workings and tossed them into the grass.

Satisfied with his work, Alith began to head back southwards, keeping a close eye on the nearby druchii regiments.

As the other Shadows unleashed their attacks and more war machines were dismantled, the captains of the spear companies realised something was amiss. The rate of fire had fallen dramatically and officers turned back towards the bolt throwers to find out why. There were shouts of alarm as black shadows flitted between the engines. The captains' commands ringing in their ears, the druchii warriors brought up their weapons, their eyes searching the grass for the mysterious archers.

Alith made a long screech of a hawk, the signal for the Shadows to withdraw and rejoin him. He kept his eye on the closest regiment of druchii, who had begun to wheel in his direction, though they were several hundred paces away. Alith could not believe that the Shadows had been seen, but then amongst the front rank of armoured warriors he spied a slender, semi-naked figure.

It was a sorceress, her long white hair flickering like the lightning in the clouds above, her pale flesh painted with runes of mystical power. She lifted a slender arm and pointed in Alith's direction, turning to the captain marching beside her.

Even as Alith saw motes of magic dancing from the sorceress's fingertips he felt a strange pressure, a build-up of dark magic in the air around him. A moment later a crackling bolt of energy leapt from the druchii's hand, exploding just to Alith's left, hurling him sideways with the force of its detonation.

Picking himself up, Alith saw a charred circle of grass, at its centre the distorted, broken body of Nermyrrin, her skin blackened, her eyes nothing more than dark holes from which two wisps of vapour coiled. More magical blasts leapt across the meadow as the sorceress advanced with her bodyguard, setting the grass alight and hurling smoking bodies into the air.

'Fall back!' Alith called out, picking up the remains of Nermyrrin. She was strangely cold to the touch. 'Bring the dead!'

One hundred druchii spearmen locked their shields as the Shadows covered their retreat with arrows. The sorceress stepped back into the press of bodies, shielding herself from harm as black shafts felled the warriors around her.

Alith stowed his bow and hiked Nermyrrin's body over his shoulder. Turning away from the druchii, he hurried back through the grass, sensing the presence of the other Shadows around him moving swiftly but stealthily across the meadow. A glance back showed that the spearmen had been called to a halt, and mocking shouts followed the Shadows as they headed back to the Anar camp.

The druchii's contempt was ill-placed. Half of the druchii war machines could no longer fire and the crews of several more were dead. Without the weight of fire from their machines to pressurise the Ellyrians into an attack, the druchii were forced to continue their advance. Drums rolled once more and horns blared as the massive shape of Kheranion's dragon swooped down over his army. The monstrous creature landed in the midst of the host for a moment, the druchii general atop its scaled back bellowing orders to his lieutenants. Alith had barely taken three breaths before the dragon sought the skies again, lifting itself higher and higher with powerful sweeps of its clawed wings.

Alith noted this with interest, realising that Kheranion was taking great pains to spend as little time as possible on the ground. Clearly the strength of the dragon and its lance-wielding rider were on the attack, smashing into the foe at speed. For the moment, Alith could think of no way of grounding his enemy though, and so turned his attention to other matters.

NEITHER SIDE WANTED to commit themselves to the attack. The Naggarothi and Ellyrians closed within bow range of each other, exchanging clouds of arrows. The reavers led by Athielle darted forwards to loose volleys before wheeling away out of range of the repeater crossbows of their enemies. All the while the menacing knights of Anlec stayed in the reserve, waiting for the crucial moment to unleash their devastating charge.

The druchii wizards conjured up storms of blades that slashed through the Ellyrians, and cast spells that wracked their enemies with bone-deep agony, searing their flesh and stripping away skin. There was little the Ellyrians could do to counter these spells, and they were suffering badly from the disadvantage.

Alith called his Shadows to him again as they gathered on the edge of the camp.

'Hunt the sorcerers,' he said. 'Make every shot count. Attack and then fade north and we'll regroup on the right of the Ellyrian infantry.'

The Shadows nodded their understanding and melted away into the greyness, Alith following. For some it would appear foolhardy, sneaking between two armies about to engage each other. Alith knew better. Across Nagarythe the Shadows had tormented and terrorised the druchii using the same tactics. Approach close and unseen, kill the enemy and then vanish. It made soldiers think they faced more foes than they actually did, and made commanders fear for their safety. The disruption would serve the Ellyrians well and Alith hoped that Findel and Athielle were wise enough to take advantage when the time came.

Alith approached the closest druchii at a crouch, sliding effortlessly amongst the grass blades, barely another ripple amongst the swaying caused by the storm winds. He was close enough to hear the chatter of the spearmen as they stood in their ranks waiting for the order to advance.

'These horse fondlers are no match for Naggarothi blades,' one lieutenant said, drawing harsh laughter from her comrades.

That the druchii still dared to call themselves Naggarothi bit at Alith's temper. They had spurned all right to that claim when they had turned on Malekith, the heir of

Aenarion, and cast him from Anlec. They were traitors – dark elves – and nothing more. Alith forced himself to relax, aware that the enemy were little more than two dozen paces away. With deliberate slowness, he drew up the hood of his cloak, whispering a few words to draw his hunter's magic into its fibres.

Alith felt the vaguest shimmer of energy tingle on his head and shoulders. To him nothing changed. To another, Alith would have disappeared; one moment a black-swathed figure, the next nothing more than bending grass stems. Thus concealed, Alith rose gently until he was standing at his full height. The front rank of the spearmen was directly ahead of him, so close he could have thrown an arrow at them. Their captain was a female druchii with red-dyed hair bound into plaits with bloody sinew, and a scar cut across her face from chin to right ear. Her eyes were a piercing ice-blue and Alith resisted the urge to flinch as that cold gaze was directed straight at him. The captain did not see him at all, her eyes staring just past his shoulder at the Ellyrians some distance beyond.

Alith took his bow from the quiver on his shoulder and calmly set an arrow to the string. Pulling up his weapon, he sighted along the shaft, lining up the arrowhead with the captain's throat. Alith enjoyed the tension as he pulled back his right arm. He revelled in the moment, the captain ignorant of her imminent death, the power he held to bring about that fate. A satisfied smile danced briefly on Alith's lips as he watched the druchii turn at some comment from her standard bearer, grinning with teeth filed to sharp points.

Without ceremony, Alith let go of the bowstring. The arrow hit its mark perfectly, spearing through the captain's neck. Blood frothed from her mouth and sprayed from the wound as she collapsed, spattering the other druchii. Shouts of horror rippled through the dark elves and Alith savoured the uncertainty, the panic. Alith silently lowered himself back into the grass and slipped away.

As he crept northwards he spared glances for the work of the other Shadows. Alith watched as company banners fell, sorceresses were pinned by shafts and lieutenants toppled to the ground with grievous wounds. Alith could feel the disconcertion spreading through the druchii ranks, but not all of the Shadows went unobserved. Alith also saw repeater crossbows scything through the long grass with their missiles, and companies of warriors dashing forwards with their spears to hunt down their ambushers.

THOUGH THE ATTACKS of the Shadows caused scattered confusion, the druchii pressed on, sweeping Alith's warriors northwards before them. Thirty of his warriors did not join their leader, their bodies lost out on the field. The black host of Kheranion resolutely advanced into the teeth of the arrow-storm coming from the Ellyrians, forcing Finudel to order his infantry to withdraw towards the river. The reaver knights formed up to protect the retreat as Alith and his Shadows joined the move, stalking unseen alongside the Ellyrian regiments.

Kheranion's commanders split their force, sending a third of their infantry towards the retreating Ellyrians while the remaining spearmen and archers advanced on the reavers, the knights of Anlec ominously shadowing them. Finudel and Athielle ordered their riders south knowing that they could not contend with the enemy's numbers directly. Alith was horrified to see the Ellyrians thus split, the druchii pushing forwards between the two wings of the infantry and cavalry.

Hidden within the high grass on the bank of the Irlana, Alith realised he had made the same mistake. The rest of his army was still at the camp to the south, on the other side of the druchii host. Alith instinctively looked into the storm clouds, seeking Kheranion's presence. He saw the dragon to the west, beating its wings slowly to keep station in the strong wind, drifting southwards above the reavers as the Ellyrians pulled back from the attacking army.

Kheranion's full plan was then revealed. The druchii infantry lengthened their lines, creating a barrier that kept the Ellyrian infantry penned in at the edge of the river. The black-armoured Anlec cavalry came forwards at last, winding columns of grim riders snaking between the companies of spearmen and repeater crossbowmen, their lances lowered. In their hundreds the knights gathered, sinister squadrons of black and silver, their faces hidden behind ornate visors.

'There's nowhere else to run,' said Lierenduir, crouched close at hand to Alith's left. 'Those knights will sweep the Ellyrians into the water.'

'At least that means the Ellyrians are forced to fight,' replied Alith. 'Better that they battle to the last elf than try to flee.'

'What of us?'

Alith looked around, analysing the immediate vicinity. The river broadened to the west where the meadows were flat, opening out into a ford at least five hundred paces wide. On the far side the trees of Athelian Toryr stretched down almost to the northern bank, the depths of the forest hidden in shadow. Alith nodded towards the crossing.

'When the charge comes, head for the ford,' he said. 'We'll disappear into the woods if necessary.'

'What about the others at the camp?'

'There is nothing we can do for them at the moment,' said Alith. 'We can try to draw some of the druchii across the river and into the trees, to buy the others time to head south and join with Caledor.'

Lierenduir looked pained at Alith's fatalism but said nothing, turning his gaze back to the ranks of the Anlec knights. Ellyrians and Naggarothi waited in disturbing silence, each hoping for the other to show some indication of their intent. With several of the druchii magic wielders slain by the Shadows, the storm above was abating, though thunder broke the quiet occasionally and flickers of lightning crawled across the thinning clouds. To the east, shafts of sunlight pierced the gloom, shining from the armour of the reavers. At this distance Athielle was nothing more than a golden gleam amongst the silver and Alith was suddenly concerned for the princess. Against the dark swathe of Nagarythe the army of Ellyrion seemed pitifully few.

Alith thought back to the sweeping bridges and boulevards of Tor Elyr, the white towers that would be blackened and broken if the druchii were victorious. He cared nothing for the city itself, but the memory of his coming there, of meeting Athielle, lingered with him. Her refusal to allow the city to be sacked told Alith all he needed to know about Athielle, of her love for her people and her home. That thought brought more painful memories, of scorched Elanardris and Gerithon nailed upon the door to the manse.

In his mind's eye the two scenes overlapped, so that he saw the arena-hall of Tor Elyr, Finudel and Athielle dead upon their thrones, elves and steeds lying in bloodied heaps around them. Such was the fate they had dared by resisting the druchii, and Alith felt a stab of shame at his harsh words to them. They had chosen to risk all, not for glory or honour, but for survival. Athielle's warning repeated over and over in his mind:

'It is because the druchii despise peace, loathe life, that they must be defeated. If we become the same, we have lost that which we fight for.'

Looking across the meadows of Ellyrion it was as if she said the words again, so clear was her voice to Alith. He fixed his gaze upon that distant shimmer of gold, dismissing the nightmare visions of destruction that haunted him. Then Alith turned his eyes upon the ranks of the druchii, the unending lines of black and purple, the wicked signs upon standards proclaiming their bearers' unfettered depravity.

'Gods curse us all,' he snarled, standing up fully.

The other Shadows cast glances at their leader, brows creased with concern. With an almost lazy slowness, Alith nocked an arrow to his bow and sighted upon the Anlec knights. With a grim smile, he loosed the shaft. He followed its course as it looped over the meadow and struck a knight's horse in the neck. The steed reared and then fell, crushing its rider beneath its dark bulk.

As Alith fitted and loosed another shaft, the Shadows joined him, a ragged volley of arrows arcing towards the knights. Several more of the riders fell to the missiles, their black-armoured corpses tumbling from their saddles.

Alith turned to Khillrallion.

'Give me your hunting horn,' said Alith.

Khillrallion pulled out a curled ram's horn from his belt and ran through the grass to place it in Alith's outstretched hand. Alith looked at the gold bands that coiled around the horn, seeing flickers of lightning reflected in the metal.

Alith lifted the instrument to his lips and blew a note that rose in pitch and then swung into a long bass tone. Squadrons of knights were turning their horses towards the sound, their angry shouts heard even at this distance. Again and again Alith sounded the notes, the Anar call for attack. Tossing the horn back to Khillrallion, Alith knew not whether Tharion would hear the command, or how the captain would respond. All Alith was sure of was that today would not be the day he ran away to fight another day.

Today Alith would stand and fight, and fall if necessary.

* * *

Alith gave silent praise to Finudel, or perhaps Athielle, as he heard answering horn blows from the Ellyrian host. Spurred into action, the archers on the river bank lifted their weapons and unleashed a salvo against the druchii knights, a shower of white-feathered shafts glittering through the storm gloom. The Shadows added their own arrows to the attack. The spearmen raised their voices in a bold war cry and formed up for the advance.

Ahead of them, the knights of Anlec were thrown into disarray. Alith could see their officers arguing, and judged that they debated whether to confront the threat of the infantry or turn their attention to the hated lord of the Anars that had taunted them. Indecision reigned for a while and the Ellyrian infantry closed in under the cover of a hail of arrows.

Some semblance of order was finally restored and three squadrons of knights wheeled towards Alith, six hundred riders in all. The rest of the cavalry urged their mounts, breaking into a run towards the advancing Ellyrians.

Alith had no time to spare for the coming clash; the knights were bearing down fast upon the Shadows.

'Into the river!' Alith cried, knowing that they would not outpace the riders in a race to the ford.

Alith leaped from the high bank into the flowing waters as the knights broke into a charge. His breath was knocked from him by the cold river, and for a moment the current buffeted and wrestled him beneath the surface. Breaking back into the air, Alith unfastened his cloak, which hung like an anchor from his shoulders. Freed of its constrictions, Alith struck out towards the far shore with confident strokes, the other Shadows around him in a shoal of black and grey, discarded cloaks swirling downriver.

A glance over his shoulder showed Alith that the knights had reined in their mounts at the water's edge, unwilling to plunge into the swirling waters. Insults and curses followed the Shadows as they swam away, before the knights' officers signalled for them to continue west towards the ford.

Halfway across the river, Alith looked to his left, at the receding knights, and tried to judge whether they would complete their circuitous journey to the far side before the Shadows. He was confident that the riders would still be crossing the ford when he set foot on dry land. To the right, the battle between the Ellyrian infantry and the druchii was in full tumult. The other knights had smashed through several of the spear companies already, their path marked by a litter of bodies. From the river's surface, Alith could see nothing of the reavers or his own army and he hoped that they fared well. Knowing that he could do nothing else for the moment, Alith focussed on swimming, driving himself swiftly through the water.

PANTING, ALITH DRAGGED himself through the reeds and pulled himself up onto the northern bank of the Irlana. The other Shadows followed, slipping into the grass like dark otters, glistening with water. Alith shuddered from the wet, the warmth of the sun still kept at bay by the dark clouds, the wind stealing the heat from his body.

'What now, prince?' asked Khillrallion. Alith was taken aback for a moment by the use of his proper title. Bedraggled and cold, he certainly did not feel like a prince. 'Alith? What now?'

Westwards Alith could see the first of the knights surging from the ford amidst spumes of water. Northwards stood the dark forest of Athelian Toryr, sanctuary from the Anlec riders.

'Into the woods,' Alith said, wringing water from his sodden shirt. 'We'll try to lure them into the trees. Get up into the branches and shoot them from out of harm's way.'

The Shadows did not hurry; there was plenty of time to reach the forest before the knights would catch them. They restrung their bows with dry cord taken from waxed pouches, emptied water from their quivers and flicked droplets from the feathers of their arrows in preparation for the fight to come.

They were just over halfway to the trees, perhaps a hundred paces from safety, when the foremost Shadows stopped and signalled for the others to wait. Alith hurried forwards to where Khillrallion was staring beneath the thick canopy of leaves.

'I think I saw something moving,' said Khillrallion.

'*Think* you saw?' said Alith, peering into the darkness. 'Saw what?'

'I don't know,' Khillrallion replied with a shrug. 'A movement in the shadows. See, there it is again!'

Alith followed the direction of Khillrallion's finger under the eaves of the wood. Sure enough, there was something in the darkness, indistinct and motionless. Alith knew immediately what it was: a raven herald.

As he looked, he saw more riders sitting silently in the gloom upon unmoving steeds, little more than patches of deeper black amongst the shadows. Alith could not focus on them and could not accurately judge their number, but at a guess he thought it to be more than several dozen rather than less.

'Morai-heg has a cruel humour,' hissed Alith with another glance westwards. Most of the knights had crossed the river, and the first squadron had formed up and was advancing swiftly and purposefully towards the Shadows.

Khillrallion gave Alith a look of incomprehension.

'Raven heralds,' Alith explained. Khillrallion looked back at the woods with fresh fear, his hand reaching for an arrow. The other Shadows followed his lead as word of the danger spread in whispers, readying their weapons.

'They will have surely seen us,' said Alith. 'Why do they not attack?'

'Perhaps they would prefer to have us run down by the knights rather than risk themselves?'

Alith was not satisfied by this answer and continued to stare at the vague shapes between the trees as if he could discern their intent in some way. The noise of the approaching knights grew louder but Alith refused to take his eyes from the raven heralds. What were they waiting for?

As if in reply, something moved through the tops of the closest trees. A flitting black shape landed on a branch at the edge of the woods. A single crow lifted its head and let out a loud cawing.

Alith laughed for a moment, not quite sure he believed what he saw and heard. The other Shadows were looking at him quizzically as Alith stood up.

'Target the knights,' Alith said, pulling free his bow.

'The heralds will run us down in a heartbeat!' protested Galathrin.

Alith looked at the Shadows, seeing uncertainty in their expressions.

'Trust me,' he said before redirecting his attention to the approaching cavalry, nocking an arrow to his bowstring.

ALITH FELT NOT a moment of doubt as the knights of Anlec broke into a gallop. Everything dropped away: his worries, his fears, his anger. Alith stood in a moment of calm, his breath coming slow and steady, limbs light, movements precise and focussed. As he looked at the approaching riders, Alith saw every detail as if it were frozen in time. Droplets flew from the manes and tails of their horses, surrounding the squadrons in a fine mist. Water glistened on the black rings of the knights' armour. Golden lancetips and silvered helms sparkled with reflected lightning.

At three hundred paces Alith took aim at the knight bearing the banner of the closest squadron, closing fast. The arrow sped into the storm-wracked sky and then fell, striking the charging knight in the head. As he slumped sideways, the standard fell from his grasp but the following knight swayed to one side and snatched up the falling flag before it touched the ground. Alith let fly another arrow, but the wind gusted and carried the shot short to disappear into the grass in front of the knights. Adjusting his aim, Alith shot again, the shaft spinning away from the raised shield of another knight.

At two hundred and fifty paces, the rest of the Shadows were also shooting. Alith reached back and his fingers fell upon a lone flight, the last of his arrows. He took it out with measured slowness and examined its shaft and feathers for any damage. There was none and he fitted it to his bowstring, his hands working without conscious thought.

At two hundred paces, Alith released the string and his final shot soared towards the knights. It struck one of the lead riders in the shoulder of his lance arm, spinning him from his mount to be trampled by the hooves of the following knights. Alith placed his bow in its quiver and drew his sword.

At one hundred and fifty paces Alith saw blackness moving under the trees. The ground was shuddering under the impact of the charging horses, but it was the stillness of the woods that drew his attention. In a long line the raven heralds burst from the woods, eerily silent. Several hundred feather-cloaked riders streamed from between the trees, ghosted by a strange darkness, moving impossibly fast. Behind them came a great flock of beating black wings and raucous cries, hundreds of birds pouring from the woods in a billowing cloud of feathers and snapping beaks.

The raven heralds loosed a volley from their bows as they closed, the squadron of knights closest to the woods thrown into a confusion of falling knights and tumbling horses. Stowing their bows, the riders brought out narrow-bladed spears, tips lowered full-tilt.

At one hundred paces from Alith the raven heralds hit the knights, driving into their flank like a black dagger. Caught utterly unawares, dozens of the Anlec cavalry were cast down by the spears of their attackers. The shrill whinnies of horses and the panicked shouts of elves rebounded from the trees as the raven heralds continued on, cutting through the knights towards the river.

The lead riders turned to see what had happened, dragging their mounts to a standstill.

'Attack!' bellowed Alith, raising his sword and breaking into a run. He did not look to see if the other Shadows followed.

The closest knights twisted left and right, caught between the raven heralds and the Shadows. Alith covered the gap at a full sprint, his blood surging as he sped through the long grass.

One of the knights dragged his horse around and tried to charge but Alith was too close, nimbly leaping aside from the lance point directed towards his chest. With a shout, Alith grabbed the knight's arm and used it as a lever to jump up behind the rider.

Alith drove his sword into the knight's back, the point cleaving through cloak and mail. Tossing the elf's body aside, Alith slipped from the steed's haunch as it galloped on, the knight's dead grip tight on the reins, his body dragged through the grass.

Alith threw himself down as another lance flashed towards him, its point passing a hair's-breadth above his head. Diving between the legs of the knight's steed, Alith swept upwards with his blade, cutting through the cinch of the saddle. With a shout the knight toppled sideways, crashing heavily beside Alith. The Anar prince drove the point of his sword through the knight's visor and then looked for a new foe.

Ahead the fight between the knights and heralds had become a vicious melee. Swords rang against each other and curses were spat. Horses fought as well, flailing hooves and gnashing teeth at one another while their riders slashed and stabbed. It was no place for an elf on foot and Alith kept his distance with the Shadows, looking for stragglers to ambush.

A knight staggered from the fighting, clutching his arm. Blood flowed freely down his mail skirt as he fell to one knee. The Shadows pounced, driving their swords into him. As Alith wrenched his blade from the dead knight's chest, he cast his eye over the battle.

The Anlec cavalry had been beaten on the first charge, yet though they had lost more than half their number they fought on stubbornly. Those of Alith's followers that still had arrows occasionally loosed a shaft into the swirling press of bodies, picking off such targets as presented themselves. Naggarothi corpses of both sides were trampled beneath iron-shod hooves while the wounded tried crawling to safety. The Shadows tended to the injured raven heralds with bandages torn from their cloaks; and to the wounded knights with their swords.

The crows whirled and swooped around the fight, adding to the confusion. They fluttered into the faces of the knights, pecking at exposed lips, digging their beaks into visors seeking eyes. Some of the flock had settled on the corpses, tearing at cloaks and robes, clawing at any exposed skin, peeling strands of bloody flesh from the fallen.

Alith noted that the carrion birds feasted only on the slain knights, avoiding the dozens of raven herald corpses that were heaped in the long grass.

The knights fought to the last elf, a captain clad in ornately etched armour of silver and gold. He had discarded his lance and struck out at his enemies with a long sword whose blade flashed with magical fire, every blow he landed cutting through body or limb with ease. His identity was concealed by a full helm styled in a daemonic, snarling face, his eyes hidden in shadow. As his horse turned and wheeled, the raven heralds pulled back from the druchii officer, a dozen of their number already lying dead around him.

Without any spoken command, several of the riders stowed their spears and brought out their bows as the circle widened around the captain. The druchii realised what was about to happen and kicked his steed into a run, levelling his sword for a final charge. Eight arrows converged on him before he reached the raven heralds, taking him in the head and chest, flinging him ignominiously to the blood-wetted grass amongst those he had slain.

THE RAVEN HERALDS gave no cheers of victory, waved no weapons in celebration. They weaved their horses around the piles of the dead and injured, their speartips seeking any surviving foes. Alith watched without emotion as they plunged their spears into any knights still drawing breath, and then he turned away to look to the south.

Alith could not see much beyond the river, only a chaotic mass of white and black pitted against each other. He saw the banners of Ellyrion mingled with the standards of Nagarythe, and could make little sense of the confusion. Manoeuvre and strategy had played its part, but the battle would ultimately be decided by strength, skill and courage.

A shadow fell across Alith and he looked up into the face of a raven herald. He held a blood-stained spear in his right hand, his arms and gloves slick with crimson.

Emerald eyes shone from the depths of his hood and Alith smiled.

'Morai-heg must have some devious plan for me indeed, to save me once again,' said the lord of the Anars.

'It was not The Allseeing One that brought me here,' replied Elthyrior.

'Then by what guidance do you come to my rescue?'

'By the request of Princess Athielle,' said Elthyrior. 'On the first night after our arrival, she asked me to return north and bring back those heralds that still opposed the darkness of Anlec.'

'Your intervention is timely, nonetheless,' said Alith.

'The battle is not yet won,' Elthyrior said, nodding out across the river. 'Finudel and Athielle are attacking and Kheranion makes his final move.'

Alith spun quickly and searched the skies. To the south-east a black shape descended like a thunderbolt. Wings furled, thick vapour streaming from its mouth and nostrils, the black dragon plunged earthwards towards the reavers. For a moment it seemed as if the beast would slam into the ground, but at the last moment its wings flared open and the dragon levelled just above head height, its claws raking a massive furrow through the ranks of the Ellyrian riders, carving through elf and steed alike. As the monster climbed back into the sky it lifted up two more riders, flinging them to a bone-crushing death amongst their kin as it banked away.

Alith saw this destruction at a distance, unmoved until his eyes fell upon the small shape of a golden rider: Athielle. The dragon soared over her reavers, arrows pattering harmlessly from its thick hide.

Alith cast about for a spare steed, for there were many left riderless after the fighting. He ran to the closest, the unarmoured horse of a dead herald, and leaped onto its back.

'What do you think you can achieve, Alith?'

Alith did not reply, but simply urged the horse into a gallop, heading for the ford. He glanced over his shoulder constantly, keeping watch on the dragon as it circled and dived down, mauling yet more Ellyrians before spiralling back towards the clouds. At this distance Alith could hear nothing of the slaughter. The carnage being wrought was like a tableau picked out in a tapestry, a representation of something horrific yet almost beautiful.

Water splashed up Alith's legs as his steed forged across the ford but he did not notice, nor did he feel the bite of the wind on his skin or hear the splash of the river. His eyes were fixed on Athielle and her reavers; Finudel's companies of riders were already driving into the rear of the druchii fighting close to the river. The dragon continued to menace the Ellyrian cavalry; with fang and noxious breath it gouged holes in the reavers. Many of the riders were fleeing the beast, but around Athielle a knot of several hundred held their courage, sending showers of ineffectual arrows towards their monstrous tormentor.

The horse reached the opposite bank and surged up through the reeds, almost toppling Alith. He swayed wildly and as he righted himself his gaze passed to the south. For a moment all thoughts of Athielle and the black dragon were dispelled.

Alith saw his army marching northwards to the aid of the princess, but it was not this that stunned him so. Behind them came another host, many thousands strong, in lines of silver, green and red. Above the army four lithe shapes swept through the air, two red and two a deep blue in colour.

The dragon princes of Caledor!

ALITH CALLED HIS steed to halt with a word and sat in amazement as the four dragons glided effortlessly over the plains, flying so low that their wingtips almost brushed the grass. Fire snaked from their mouths, leaving a trail of grey haze whipped into vortices by their beating wings. Each dragon bore a rider upon a throne, long pennants of red and green streaming from poles and lance tips.

Alith gave a shout of wordless joy at the sight, and then fell silent, admiring the power and grace of the dragons as they swept onwards towards Kheranion's army. The druchii commander seemed unaware of his peril as he and his monstrous steed ravaged Athielle's bodyguard.

Two of the Caledorians broke to the left, heading towards the battle at the river. They flew past Alith barely fifty paces away, gusts of wind from the dragons' wings washing over Alith as they sped on towards their foes. The other two dragon riders peeled to the right, straight towards Kheranion.

THE DRUCHII PRINCE laughed as he plunged his lance through the gut of another Ellyrian. Beneath him, Bloodfang tore and ripped and shredded with teeth and claws, revelling in the slaughter. Kheranion fixed his eyes upon the gold-armoured princess, imagining the agonising delights he would visit upon her that night. He would take her alive, and her brother, and shame them both before handing their broken remains to the priests and priestesses of Khaine.

With this in mind, Kheranion wrenched back on the gilded chains that served as Bloodfang's reins, arms straining to pull in the beast's bloodthirsty enthusiasm. The dragon swept a rider from his horse with raking claws and looked back at its master, lips rippling with annoyance.

'Do not harm the princess!' Kheranion commanded. 'She is mine!'

Bloodfang gave a growl of disappointment but offered no argument, turning his bloody attentions back on the

Ellyrians. His jaws snapped shut around the head of a horse, decapitating it in one bite. A lash of Bloodfang's barbed tail speared three more riders, buckling breastplates, smashing ribs and pulverising vital organs.

The path was almost clear to Athielle; barely a dozen more reavers stood in Kheranion's way. He could see the princess clearly as she fixed him with a contemptuous stare from beneath the flowing waves of her long hair. Kheranion wondered how defiant she would be when that hair had been cut from her scalp and her beautiful features had felt the caress of a dozen blades. The prospect sent a thrill of excitement through the prince and he urged Bloodfang forwards again.

Bloodfang took a step, striking out with a clawed wing to send more knights tumbling, and then stopped. The dragon arched his neck, nostrils flaring, and then turned suddenly to the left.

'What are you doing?' demanded Kheranion, heaving back on the chains with all of his strength.

Bloodfang ignored his question and bunched his muscles, ready to spring into the air. Kheranion quickly cast about for the source of the dragon's distemper. Looking south the prince saw two immense shapes hurtling through the sky towards him.

'Khaine's bloody mercies,' Kheranion whispered as Bloodfang hurled himself into the air, the dragon's wings creating a downdraught that sent riders tumbling, toppling horses to their flanks. Kheranion could feel his mount's heart thundering, hammer-like vibrations pounding through the seat of the prince's saddle-throne and along his spine. Bloodfang's breaths came in stentorian blasts, clouds of oily vapour forming a fog around rider and beast as the dragon strove to gain more height.

The foremost dragon rolled right and then turned sharply left, the prince atop its back angling his long lance over the monster's neck. Bloodfang twisted away and the lance bit through the membrane of his right wing, ripping a large and ragged hole in the scaled skin. In a flash the dragon flew behind them, crashing its tail against Bloodfang's flanks as it passed.

The other Caledorian steered his mount higher and the great creature folded its wings into a stoop, coming at Bloodfang from above. Kheranion twisted in his saddle and set the butt of his magical lance against Bloodfang's flesh to absorb the impact, angling the point towards the approaching dragon prince. Bloodfang's wounded wing spasmed and faltered in its beat, sending the dragon lurching to the right, taking Kheranion's lance tip away from his foe.

Kheranion stared at his rival. The Caledorian's snarling face was framed with a shock of platinum blond hair that streamed back in the wind of the dragon's descent. There was nothing but anger in the prince's deep blue eyes as they met the druchii's gaze. Kheranion met that gaze with a curse upon his lips, a moment before the Caledorian's lance hit home.

Its tip sheared through Kheranion's breastplate in an explosion of magical fire, piercing a lung and shattering his spine. The prince was already dead as the impact lifted him from his throne, breaking his legs as he was torn free from the lacquered straps that had secured him there. His grip broke and the chains fell from his dead grasp. The Caledorian twisted his lance with a flick of his wrist, sending Kheranion's body spiralling to the ground far below.

The first dragon circled around and raked its claws across Bloodfang's snout, shredding skin in a spray of thick scales. Bloodfang gave a roar and spewed forth an immense cloud of poisonous gas. Pumping his wings, blood streaming from the injury, the black dragon turned and raced away, heading for the Inner Sea.

Rising into the clouds, freed of Kheranion's mastery, Bloodfang fled.

SEVENTEEN

A Bitter Fate

WITH ANELTAIN AS escort, Alith rode into the Caledorian camp. He had already met with Tharion and learned that over four hundred of his warriors had fallen in battle and more than twice that number were badly wounded. The arrival of the Caledorians had turned the balance, but the druchii had fought on fiercely, breaking only as the sun dipped towards dusk. The army of Anlec had fled back towards the pass, pursued by the vengeful reaver knights and the dragon princes.

There was an air of celebration in the encampment. Fires burned and songs and laughter drifted between the red and white tents. The pavilion of the dragon princes rose high above the rest of the camp, its roof held up by three mighty poles, flags of Caledor streaming from their tips.

Warriors came to take their horses as they dismounted outside the open flaps of the huge tent. Entering, Alith found himself in a swirl of elves; Caledorian and Ellyrian.

The conversation was animated, eyes were bright and faces flushed with victory and wine. The four dragon princes were holding court at the centre of the pavilion, still bedecked in their blood-spattered armour. With them stood Athielle and Finudel, smiles upon their faces.

All turned at Alith's approach, but it was Athielle's reaction that he noticed. Her expression grew sombre and she stepped away, placing her brother between her and Alith. Before Alith could speak one of the Caledorians interrupted, his voice deep, his tone unwelcoming.

'What do we have here?' said the prince, his deep blue eyes gauging Alith coolly.

'I am Alith Anar, prince of Nagarythe.'

'A Naggarothi?' replied the Caledorian with a dubious eyebrow raised, recoiling slightly from Alith's presence.

'He is our ally, Dorien,' said Finudel. 'Were it not for Alith's actions I fear your arrival would have found us already dead.'

The Caledorian prince regarded Alith with contempt, head cocked to one side. Alith returned the look with equal disgust.

'Alith, this is Prince Dorien,' said Finudel, breaking the awkward silence that had rippled out through the nearby elves. 'He is the younger brother of King Caledor.'

Alith did not react to this, meeting Dorien's stare.

'What of Elthyrior?' Athielle asked, stepping past her brother. Alith broke his gaze from Dorien to look at her. 'Where is he?'

'I do not know,' Alith replied with a shake of the head. 'He is where Morai-heg leads him. The raven heralds took their dead and vanished into Athelian Toryr. You may never see him again.'

'Anar?' said one of the other Caledorians. 'I have heard this name, from prisoners we took at Lothern.'

'And what did they say?' asked Alith.

'That the Anars marched beside Malekith and resisted Morathi,' replied the prince. He extended a hand. 'I am Thyrinor, and I welcome you to our camp, even if my intemperate cousin will not.'

Alith shook the proffered hand quickly. Dorien snorted and turned away, calling for more wine. As he marched off through the crowd, Alith saw that the prince walked with a limp.

'He is in a grumpy mood,' said Thyrinor. 'I think he has broken his leg, but he refuses to allow the healers to look at it. He's still full of fire and blood after the battle. Tomorrow he will be calmer.'

'We are grateful for your aid,' said Athielle. 'Your arrival is more than we could have hoped for.'

'We were brought word of the druchii marching along the pass four days ago and set out immediately,' said Thyrinor. 'I regret that we cannot stay here, for we are needed in Chrace. The enemy have all but overrun the mountains and the king sails with his army to thwart them at the border with Cothique. Tomorrow we continue north and then through Avelorn to strike at the druchii from the south. Today is an important victory, and Caledor recognises the sacrifices made by the people of Ellyrion.'

Alith suppressed a snort of derision, turning away to hide his expression of disgust. What did these folk know of sacrifice?

'Alith?' said Athielle, and he felt the princess at his shoulder. He turned back to her.

'I am sorry,' said Alith. 'I cannot share your enthusiasm for today's victory.'

'I would think you happy that Kheranion is dead,' said Finudel, joining his sister. 'Is that not some measure of payment for your father?'

'No,' Alith said quietly. 'Kheranion died swiftly.'

Athielle and Finudel fell silent, shocked by Alith's words. Thyrinor stepped up beside Finudel, proffering a goblet towards Alith. The Naggarothi prince took it reluctantly.

'Victories have been few for us,' said the Caledorian. He raised his own glass in toast to Alith. 'I give you my thanks for your efforts and those of your warriors. Were the king here, I am sure he would offer you the same.'

'I do not fight for your praise,' said Alith.

'Then what do you fight for?' asked Thyrinor.

Alith did not reply immediately, aware of the coldness that gripped his heart and the warmth of Athielle so close at hand. He looked at the princess, gaining a small amount of comfort from the sight.

'Forgive me,' Alith said, forcing a slight smile. 'I am weary. Wearier than you can possibly imagine. Ellyrion and Caledor battle for their freedom and I should not judge you for matters that are not your responsibility.'

Alith took a mouthful of the wine within. It was dry, almost tasteless, but he feigned a nod of appreciation. He raised the goblet beside Thyrinor's and fixed his gaze upon the Caledorian.

'May you win all of your battles and end this war!' Alith declared. His eyes flickered to Athielle to gauge her reaction, but her expression was unreadable, her brow slightly furrowed, lips pursed.

'We should not impose upon you any longer,' said Findel, guiding Athielle away with a touch on her arm. She gave a last glance at Alith before being steered into the crowd of Caledorian nobles.

Alith returned his stare to Thyrinor.

'Will you fight to the last, against all hope?' Alith asked. 'Will your king give his life to free Ulthuan?'

'He will,' replied Thyrinor. 'You think that you alone have reason enough to fight the druchii? You are wrong, so very wrong.'

The prince left Alith with his thoughts, calling his cousin's name. Alith stood motionless for a while, staring into his cup. The red wine reminded him of blood, its taste still bitter upon his tongue. He wanted to let the goblet drop from his fingers and leave, to put as much distance as he could between himself and these nobles of Ellyrion and Caledor. They fought the druchii, and they spoke fine words against them, but they did not understand. None of them truly knew what they fought against.

As he looked at the elves within the tent, hiding his disdain, Alith spied a familiar face: Carathril. The herald was stood somewhat apart from the crowd, his expression one of discomfort. Carathril met Alith's gaze and waved him over.

'You are the last person I expected to see here,' said Alith as Carathril gestured to a bench and sat down. Alith stayed on his feet.

'It seems I am destined to serve another king as herald,' Carathril replied heavily.

'And is he a king you serve gladly?'

Carathril considered this, his expression pensive.

'He is a leader of action and not words,' the herald said. 'As the commander of our armies, I would wish for no other.'

'And when the war is over?'

'That is not yet our concern,' said Carathril. 'It would be unwise to worry about a future so uncertain. You would do well, Alith, to align yourself with Caledor. He has strength, and determination in abundance. With his aid, your lands in Nagarythe can be restored.'

'I have learnt well the harsh lessons of the last few years,' said Alith. 'A ruler can no more reign through the power of others than a cloud can move against the wind. We looked to Malekith and he could do nothing to halt the doom of the Anars. We turned to Bel Shanaar and he failed us. I have no more time for kings.'

'Surely you would not fight against Caledor?' Carathril said with genuine horror.

'In truth? I cannot say,' Alith said with a shrug. 'The future of Nagarythe is my only concern; let your king and his princes do what they will. I am the last loyal prince of Nagarythe and I will restore the rule of the righteous to my realm. Caledor has no sway over the Naggarothi, only from their own can they be led.'

WHILE DORIEN LED his Caledorians northwards, Alith chose to stay in Ellyrion. His army had suffered much and even he could see that they were in no position to wage further war for the time being. With Finudel and Athielle's permission, the Naggarothi built a camp on the plains not far from Tor Elyr and spent the winter recovering their strength.

The conversation with Carathril had unsettled Alith and raised many questions he did not yet know how to answer. Where would he fight, and for what cause?

He certainly could not bow his knee to a Caledorian, for all that others spoke highly of the new Phoenix King. The rivalry between Nagarythe and Caledor was ingrained, an unconscious suspicion of the southerners. The debacle with Bel Shanaar had proven to Alith that the title of Phoenix King was worthless; he could no more fight for a foreigner's crown than he could give his life for a blade of grass or the leaf of a tree.

Alith cared little for the fate of the Tiranocii, when he even spared a thought for them. They had sown the seeds of their own doom; the weakness of their leaders had brought about the occupation. While Bel Shanaar had reigned, Tiranoc had revelled in its status, its princes and nobles growing powerful and rich from their positions. Bel Shanaar was dead and now they looked to the east and south, to a Phoenix King from Caledor to save them. Tiranoc's fall of fortune was not lost on Alith, but he had no sympathy for the kingdom.

Ellyrion was a different matter. The Ellyrians had fought the druchii, and suffered the consequences of their opposition with the death of thousands. Alith also had enough self-awareness to recognise that his regard for Ellyrion was also due in part to his feelings for Athielle. But Ellyrion was not his home. He felt uncomfortable on the wide plains, exposed beneath the blue sky.

While the wounded healed and Tharion set about the reorganisation of the Anar regiments, Alith brooded alone, often riding out to the Annulii to walk in the foothills and contemplate his fate. He hoped that he would meet Elthyrior, but the raven herald remained unseen.

Pathless and lost, Alith taunted himself with memories of Elanardris in flames, of his father's death and the torments his grandfather undoubtedly suffered in the dungeons beneath Anlec. No course of action he conceived brought comfort to Alith; no destiny he could lay out for himself brought the answers he sought.

As summer, hot and beautiful, fell upon Ellyrion, Alith's mood changed. The shining sun and the verdant grassland turned his thoughts to Athielle, and he felt a deep longing to see her again, to know how she fared. Just as he had doubted himself that moment in the gardens with Milandith, Alith wondered if it was weakness to indulge the feelings he had for the princess.

IT WAS WITH a mixture of reluctance and excitement that he rode to the capital alone, having sent word to Athielle and Finudel that he wished to discuss the progress of the war. In truth the wider war was irrelevant to Alith. Neither side had won any great victory nor suffered any terrible loss. Only two battles had been fought since the engagement on the Ellyrion plain, both on the borders of druchii-assaulted Chrace. For the moment it seemed that both sides were content to maintain their current positions, building their strength further.

Alith was greeted with little ceremony, as he had requested in his letter. Retainers of Finudel met him at the edge of Tor Elyr and rode with him in silence to the central palaces. A small delegation led by Aneltain waited for the Anar lord in the amphitheatre and took him to a circular hallway in the north of the palace.

Finudel sat alone to one side of the hall, which was lined with curving benches in readiness for audience. High windows allowed the sun to stream down in shafts, casting rainbows upon the white floor. Reaver pennants hung between the windows, tattered and stained, honouring those that had given their lives in the war. Alith could not count their number; there were hundreds of them, perhaps thousands even, each marking the death of a brave knight.

Finudel looked up with a smile as the small group approached. He wore a light robe of white decorated with intricately flowing lines of blue and gold thread that made Alith think of the rising sun shining on waves. Finudel stood and nodded in greeting.

'Welcome, Alith,' said the prince. 'I hope that you are in good health.'

'I am,' replied Alith. He looked around the room, confused. 'Where is Athielle?'

Finudel's smile faded and he gestured for Aneltain and the others to leave. When they had gone, he motioned for Alith to sit on the bench opposite him. Alith did so, a frown creasing his brow.

'The princess? I wished to speak with you both.'

'I do not think that is wise,' said Finudel.

'Oh?'

Finudel looked out of the nearest window for a moment, gaze distant, clearly uncomfortable with what he was about to say. When he looked back at Alith his jaw was sternly set but there was sympathy in his eyes.

'I know that it is my sister that you really come to see,' said the Ellyrian prince, measuring every word, eyes searching Alith's face for reaction. 'I have seen the way that you look at her, and I am surprised you have kept yourself from Tor Elyr for so long.'

'My duties as a–' began Alith but Finudel cut him off.

'You deny yourself on purpose,' said Finudel. 'You think of your feelings for Athielle as a weakness, a distraction. You have doubts, about yourself and about her. That is natural.'

'I'm sure th–'

'Let me finish!' Finudel's tone was abrupt but softly spoken. He lifted a finger to emphasise his point. 'Athielle is quite taken with you as well, Alith.'

Alith felt a flutter in his chest as he heard these words, the stirrings of a long-dead feeling: hope.

'She will not say what occupies her thoughts, even to me, but it is plain that she wishes to see you again,' Finudel continued. 'No doubt she has some foolish notion that the two of you might have some kind of future together.'

'Why are such thoughts foolish?' said Alith.

'Because you are not a good match for her,' said Finudel, his expression apologetic but certain.

'I am a prince of Ulthuan, let me remind you,' said Alith hotly. 'Though my lands have been taken away, one day I will restore Elanardris to its former glory. There is not a prince on the isle who has not suffered some misfortune and waning of circumstance in this war.'

Finudel shook his head, disappointed.

'I do not speak of title or lands or power, Alith,' he said. 'It is *you* that is not a match for my sister. What would you offer her? Would you take her to Nagarythe, a bleak and cold land, and ask her to leave her people and join yours? Would you be content to allow her to stay here in Tor Elyr while you pursue this vengeful course you have taken? Allow her to drift about this palace, pining for your return, uncertain whether you lived or died?'

Alith opened his mouth to rebut the accusations, but Finudel continued.

'I am not finished! There is another course that you could follow. Athielle obviously cares nothing for your loss of power, or your lack of lands and subjects. It is *you* that enamours her. I cannot fathom her thoughts sometimes. Perhaps it is because the two of you are as night and day that you feel drawn together. Who can understand the twisted paths our hearts follow? If you feel as I think you do, you must ask yourself what you are prepared to sacrifice for her.'

'I would give my life for your sister,' said Alith, surprising himself, though Finudel merely shook his head.

'No, you would give your death for her, and that is not the same thing,' said the prince. 'Would you renounce any claims to your title in Nagarythe, and live here in Ellyrion? You cling to your revenge like a child clings to its mother, seeking some meaning from its emptiness. Would you resolve to banish the dark memories that haunt you, which drive you to seek the deaths of your enemies? Could you do such things even if you desired it?'

'I cannot change who I am,' said Alith.

'Cannot or will not?'

Alith stood and paced away, frustrated by Finudel's words.

'What right have you to make such demands?' Alith demanded.

'I do not make these demands for myself, but for my sister,' Finudel replied calmly. 'Do not tell me that you have not asked these questions of yourself. Surely you are not so obsessed with this bloody quest of yours that you thought Athielle would merely fit her future around yours?'

Alith growled, but his anger was not for Finudel, it was for himself. The prince's words, his doubts, gave voice to a lingering dread that had existed within Alith since he had first seen Athielle.

'You present me with a choice I cannot make,' said Alith. 'At least not here, not now.'

'It is a choice you have already made,' said Finudel. 'You simply need to recognise which way your heart has cast its vote. I have a suite of rooms already prepared for you, you can stay here as long as you wish provided that you do not try to contact or see Athielle. It would be a cruelty to stir her hopes if you do not intend to live up to them.'

'Thank you for the hospitality, but I do not think I can remain so close to Athielle without seeing her,' said Alith. 'Should I wish to meet her, I have the means to do so despite your precautions and guards. I do not want to go against your wishes, but I do not trust myself to leave her alone, so I will not stay.'

Alith quit the hall and found Aneltain waiting outside. The Ellyrian, normally talkative and inquisitive, remained quiet as he saw Alith's troubled look. He called for Alith's horse to be brought from the stables and they waited in silence.

Mounting his steed, Alith turned back towards Aneltain and extended a hand in farewell. The Ellyrian gripped it firmly and patted Alith on the arm.

'I feel that I will not see you again for some time, Alith, if at all,' said Aneltain.

'You may be right,' said Alith. 'Take care of the prince and princess, and of yourself. Though I cannot claim to be your friend, I wish you every fortune in the dark times ahead. Stay strong, and as you enjoy the sun and the light, think of us that must dwell in the darkness. I must go. The shadows beckon me.'

Alith rode away without another glance back, at Aneltain or the palace where Athielle remained. Did she perhaps look out of a window high on a tower and see him leave? Did she stand at a doorway, watching him go, perhaps not realising that he had no intention of returning?

Probably not, Alith told himself with a bitter chuckle. It had been a fantasy, a sliver of a dream that had brought him here, but Finudel had been absolutely right. He could not leave the shadows while the druchii remained, and he would not drag Athielle down into the darkness. Love was simply not part of Alith's future.

Only emptiness remained.

EIGHTEEN

The Call of Kurnous

ALITH RODE NORTH for several days, unwilling to return to his Naggarothi and wanting to get far away from Tor Elyr: from Athielle. He made no haste as he rode. There had been a time when he would have enjoyed the sun above, the fresh air and the wild meadows. Now he did not even see them. His thoughts were ever inward as he tried to wrestle a spark of bright truth from the darkness that had enveloped his heart.

As soon as he had left Tor Elyr Alith had known that he would not return for Athielle. Finudel had been correct, there was no life for him here; no life that he could share with Athielle. Across the mountains, Elanardris was a burnt ruin, his family destroyed, his people slaughtered or scattered. There was nothing in the world that Alith could hold on to, draw strength from. Like a leaf bobbing upon a bubbling stream, Alith was adrift on a current of violence and strife, unable to choose his course or destination.

Northwards Alith rode for day after day, guided by nothing more than a whim. He hunted rabbit and deer on the plains and kept away from the mountains, which were so like Elanardris and yet not his ancestral home.

Sometimes he rode by night and did not sleep, other times he meandered for days on end, fishing and hunting, not moving north nor turning back south. He did not count the sunrises and sunsets and lost track of how much time had passed since he had left Tor Elyr. It did not matter.

One sun-drenched afternoon, Alith saw a huge forest to the north-east and he turned his mount towards it. Following the curve of the Annulii, Alith headed towards Avelorn, the realm of the Everqueen.

TALL AND ANCIENT were the trees of Avelorn, growing upon the far bank of the winding river Arduil that marked the boundary of Ellyrion. It was a remarkable change of scenery. On the south-west banks the land mounded upwards into the plains and meadows of the horse-folk; on the far side a dark mass of foliage obscured the whole horizon, the tips of the mountains only dimly seen far beyond the immense spread of leaves.

Alith called his horse to a halt on the near bank of the river and looked out over the clear waters to the gloomy forest. Brightly coloured birds fluttered from branch to branch, their screeches and shrill chirps unwelcoming. Furred things snuffled in the undergrowth searching for roots and berries. Honeybees the size of Alith's thumb hummed to and fro, moving across the last blossoms clinging to the branches.

Alith was filled with a melancholy air. It was not so sharp as the depression that had often gripped him since Black Fen. There was no bitterness in his mood, only an ennui brought upon him by the doleful scene played out across the river. Avelorn was neither bright nor dark; it simply was what it was. Though a brisk wind blew across the plains at Alith's back, the branches of Avelorn remained motionless, still and quiet, sombre for eternity.

Birthplace of the elves, some philosophers had called it. The spiritual heart of Ulthuan; blessed by Isha and ruled over by the Everqueen. Alith had no desire to meet Avelorn's mysterious lady. His life of late had been full enough of princes and kings and queens. Alith's whim had brought him this far, to the furthest extent of Ellyrion, but he felt no inclination to go any further. Likewise, he had no desire to turn away, for southwards lay only more strife and the distracting presence of Athielle.

He sat for the rest of the afternoon watching the forest, seeing it change as the sun set. The shadows lengthened and the gloom deepened. In the twilight, feral eyes glittered from the dark, watching Alith closely. The day birds roosted and fell quiet, their cries replaced by the haunting calls of owls and night falcons. The underbrush came alive with a multitude of small animals; mice and shrews and other creatures ventured out under the cover of darkness.

There came a sound that sent a shiver down Alith's spine, of excitement rather than fear. It was the howl of a wolf, soon raised in chorus with other lupine voices. It came from the right, to the east, and moved closer. Alith turned his gaze in the direction of the sound but could see nothing between the dark boles of the trees.

A crash of leaves and snap of branches drew his attention, and Alith glimpsed a flash of movement. Something white leapt over a bush and disappeared behind a tree. Alith followed its progress and a moment later saw it in full: a white stag.

It swiftly disappeared from sight and the growl of the wolves grew louder. Unthinking, drawn by some instinct within him, Alith dismounted and waded into the river, following the noise. Soon the water was too deep to wade and he struck out with powerful strokes. His bow and sword were still in his pack on the horse's back, but he gave them no thought. He was filled with the urge to follow the stag.

A warm breeze sighed against Alith as he pulled himself onto the far bank, using the root of a tree for purchase. The wolves were close now; Alith fancied he could hear their panting and the pad of feet on mulch. Without hesitation he plunged into the undergrowth and entered Avelorn.

ALITH HEADED IN the direction in which he had last seen the white stag. At an easy run, he cut along winding trails and leapt over sprawling roots. The howl of a wolf echoed close at hand, to his left, and was answered from his right. Ignoring the hunting pack, he ran on, swift and sure.

The last of the sun disappeared and plunged Alith into darkness. His eyes quickly adjusted and he did not slow his pace, feeling his way between the rearing trunks of the ancient trees as much as he guided himself by sight. Now and then he glimpsed white ahead of him and he quickened his pace, until he was short of breath from the exertion.

Snarls and growls surrounded Alith but he was heedless of their threat. He had been seeking a guide and the stag had come to him. He was determined that this time he would find out where it wanted him to go.

Alith broke into a small clearing and stumbled to a halt. The stag was stood just ten paces away, head tossing as it sensed the wolf pack closing in. Alith glanced to his left and right and saw silvery wisps encircling the clearing; the flash of yellow eyes and the heavy pant of the wolves were all around him.

As one the pack advanced to the edge of the clearing. He counted fifteen wolves, and there were others still moving around the periphery. The stag stood rigid, eyes wide with panic, muscles quivering with exhaustion. It lowered its head and scuffed the leaf-strewn ground with a hoof.

The wolves glared at Alith and the stag from the bushes, pacing back and forth, uncertain. A few sat on their haunches and watched patiently, tongues lolling from their mouths. They were the largest wolves Alith had seen, their fur a mix of dark grey and glittering silver. He felt the piercing gaze of their opal eyes upon him, gauging him, watching for any weakness.

'The two-legs is lost,' growled a voice behind Alith. He spun to see a massive wolf stalking into the clearing. It was almost as tall as the stag, its shoulders as high as Alith's chest. Its fur was thick, a deep ruff of black running down its back, its tail thick and bushy. As it spoke, Alith saw fangs as long as his fingers, each as sharp as a dagger point. All these things Alith noted in an instant, but the creature's eyes kept his attention. They were a bright yellow and seemed to flicker with orange flames.

'Smell fish,' said another wolf. The beasts spoke in the language of Kurnous, the same tongue Alith used with the hawks of the mountains. 'Crossed river.'

The pack leader, for such was the black-maned wolf, took another pace, ears flicking.

'Our hunt,' the wolf said. It took a moment for Alith to realise the wolf was addressing him.

Alith glanced over his shoulder at the stag, which was standing motionless a few paces behind him. It appeared calm, one eye fixed on Alith.

'My hunt,' said Alith. 'Stag is mine. Follow long time.'

The blackmane snarled, lips rippling away from its savage teeth.

'Your hunt? No fangs. No hunt.'

Alith drew his hunting knife from his belt and held it in front of him.

'One fang,' he said. 'Sharp fang.'

The wolves yapped and wagged their tails in amusement and the leader padded even closer, standing only a few paces from Alith, muscles taut, tail rigid.

'Sharp fang, yes,' said the leader. 'We many fangs. Our hunt. You prey.'

The rustle of leaves betrayed other wolves advancing into the clearing, growing in confidence. Alith could not defend himself against all of them. He looked again at the stag, mind racing. He recalled the words of Elthyrior – that he should not second-guess the gods but should follow the instincts they had placed within him. He remembered also the shrine to Kurnous where he had first seen the white stag. It was a place of sacrifice, where the slain were laid upon the altar of the Hunter God. The black flash of Kurnous's rune upon the stag's breast burned in Alith's mind.

Kurnous was the god of the hunter, not the hunted. The stag was his gift to Alith.

'My hunt!' snapped Alith.

He leapt towards the stag and threw his left arm over its neck even as he drove the point of his knife into the rune of Kurnous, plunging its blade deep into the deer's heart. The stag leapt away, breaking from Alith's grasp, blood spuming from the wound. Taking a faltering step the stag fell to its side, back arched, and within moments was dead.

A cacophony of growls and barks surrounded Alith as he turned on the wolf leader, bloodied blade in hand.

'One fang, sharp fang,' Alith said. He strode to the stag and grabbed an antler, pulling up the animal's head. 'Plenty food. Our kill.'

The blackmane stopped, muscles bunching to lunge. It eyed the dead deer and then Alith's knife.

'Our kill?' said the wolf.

Alith let go of the antler and knelt beside the carcass, cutting around the wound he had inflicted. He pulled free a hunk of raw flesh and tossed it towards the black-mane.

'Our kill,' Alith said again, cutting more meat for himself. He waited until the pack leader took the offered meet, gulping it down in one mouthful. Alith took a deep bite, the still-warm blood dribbling over his chin, coating his hands. He could feel the power of the stag passing into him, firing his senses.

Cautiously the wolves approached. Alith stood up and stepped away, blood smeared on his clothes. The spirit of Kurnous raged within him, setting his heart to pounding, relishing the taste of the deer in his mouth.

As the wolves set upon the body of the white stag, Alith raised his head and howled.

WAKING SHARPLY, ALITH felt hot breath on his cheek and warmth all around him. He opened his eyes and glanced around, finding himself in the dimness of a cave, the early sun creeping through the entrance. The wolf pack lay around him, their breaths and snores reverberating quietly around the cavern. He was laid between two of the beasts, close but not touching.

The iron taste of blood filled his mouth and Alith licked his dry lips. He became aware of his own nudity, his exposed flesh slicked with cracking patches of dried crimson. His hands were similarly stained, blood beneath his fingernails and worked into the creases between his fingers. Blood smeared the muzzles of the wolves around him and matted the fur of their chests.

Alith remembered nothing of the night before, save for flashes of red, the tear of skin and the crack of bones. He dimly recalled the exultation he had felt, the victory of the kill that eclipsed his pleasure of any other hunt. Though he found his surroundings strange, he sensed no threat, no discomfort. No guilt. Some part of him that had lain hidden had been awoken, given freedom to show itself for the first time. He felt its aftertouch lingering inside, a savagery and fierce joy that had taken control of him but was for the moment sated.

Sitting up slowly, Alith discovered he still wore his belt, bloodied knife sheathed at his waist. Beyond the cave entrance he saw a wall of trees and ferns, blocking all sight beyond a dozen paces. He heard the gushing of a waterfall close by and the sound stirred in him a deep thirst.

Delicately, Alith stood, careful not to wake the wolves around him. As he picked his way between the slumbering hunters, he spied the enormous form of the blackmane, sprawled languidly next to a large female at the centre of the cave. Seeing the pack leader brought back the memory of his confrontation and he shivered at the recollection, realising that he had been but a heartbeat away from sharing the fate of the white stag.

Stepping out into the dawn Alith was surprised he felt no chill, unclothed as he was. The sun barely peeked through the treetops but he was warmed with a heat from inside.

Alith turned to his right, following the sound of water. The ground outside the cave was scuffed and marked by the paw prints of much use and the reek of the wolves' spoor was heavy in the air. The cave was a split in a rearing grey cliff face hung with ivy and other creeping plants. Far above Alith's head, more trees grew at the top of the butte, their roots jutting over the edge. Walking along its base, he came to a shallow pool, fed by a beck that tumbled down a gully etched through the cliff face.

Alith squatted by the pool and dipped his hands into the clear water. It was cold and refreshing and he splashed his face and the back of his neck, the sensation sending a thrilling ripple across his skin. Though his thirst was sharp, Alith washed away the stains from his bloody feast before raising a cupped hand to his mouth. A waft of hot breath struck his back and Alith whirled, water flying from his fingers.

Blackmane stood barely two paces away, several other wolves not far behind their leader. Droplets of water glistened on the fur of Blackmane's face. He looked up at Alith with his head cocked to one side.

'Young sun, early to wake,' growled Blackmane. 'Two-legs leave?'

Blackmane's hackles were rising and he ran his thick tongue over bloodstained teeth. It was clear that Blackmane still wanted to kill him.

'Thirst,' replied Alith, glancing back at the pool. 'Not leaving.'

'You hunt, you kill with pack,' said Blackmane. 'One of pack?'

Alith paused and in the moment of hesitation, Blackmane took a step. Alith held his ground, knowing that to show the slightest sign of weakness would be to invite attack. The other wolves regarded Alith with curiosity, but he felt no animosity from them. It did not matter, Blackmane would be more than a match for Alith if he chose to fight.

'One of pack,' Alith said.

'Who pack leader?' demanded Blackmane, advancing another step.

'You pack leader,' said Alith.

Blackmane snapped his jaw a couple of times and settled back, haunches tensing, his tail curling over his back.

'Show me!' snarled the wolf.

Alith was at a loss for a moment, until he saw the other wolves behind Blackmane cringing from their leader, dropping their bellies to the ground, their ears flattened against their heads. Alith did as best he could, falling to all fours and resting his chest on the dirt, his eyes fixed on Blackmane.

The pack leader straightened, towering over Alith. His eyes narrowed with suspicion and Alith met his gaze, not daring to move in the slightest. After some considerable time, Blackmane relaxed, ears flicking, and stepped away.

'Drink,' said Blackmane, before turning his back on Alith and stalking back to the cave.

Alith breathed a sigh of relief and sat back, his heart hammering. One of the other wolves approached him, a female with a silver streak along the top of her muzzle, and Alith tensed again, expecting another confrontation. None came, and the wolf licked his chin and cheek, her heavy tongue rasping against Alith's skin.

Turning back to the pool, Alith dipped in his hand once again and finally took a mouthful of water. Fighting the urge to drink heavily, Alith drank a few more mouthfuls and then stood. He reached down and stroked the head of the nearest wolf, scratching it behind the ear.

'One of the pack,' the wolf said, tail wagging. Some of the other wolves gave reassuring whufs and gathered around Alith, rubbing their furred bodies against him. Guided by his four-legged companions, Alith returned to the cave.

NINETEEN

Child of the Wolf and the Moon

Alith slept with the wolves for most of the day and woke as the sun was setting. He felt calm; a peace had descended upon him that he had not felt for many years. Stretching, he returned to the pool for another drink while the rest of the pack roused themselves for the next hunt.

Blackmane was amongst the last to wake, the fierce pack leader prowling from the cave, still suspicious of Alith. Alith deferentially dropped to his hands and knees without thought as Blackmane stalked past towards the water.

Rays of dusk streamed through the treetops as the wolves gathered around Blackmane. The pack headed northwards at a steady pace and Alith kept up with them with ease. Not far from the cave, the pack split, some of the wolves heading off in pairs, others alone. In this way they could cover more ground searching for a potential kill.

Alith could only follow their lead, staying close to the older female that had befriended him that morning. Her fur was a speckled dark and light grey that reflected the light, and Alith named her Silver. He had also dubbed a few others from instantly recognisable features: Snowtail; Broken Fang; Old Grey; One Ear; Scar. The others of the pack were still indistinguishable from each other in Alith's eyes.

From what he knew of wolves, most of the pack would be the offspring of Blackmane and Old Grey; a few of the others were stragglers like himself adopted by the pair. More than half were male, and they were of all ages, Blackmane and Old Grey being the eldest, with several young that Alith judged to be little more than a year old. The youngest playfully danced and wrestled with each other, swiping their paws across the muzzles of their rivals in mock fights, nipping at each other's necks and hindquarters in practice for killing prey.

Alith faced another difficulty in communicating with his new companions. They rarely spoke in Kurnous's tongue, preferring to express themselves with stance and position, the subtleties of which were entirely lost on Alith. He had already learnt not to meet Blackmane's eye; doing so always drew bared fangs and the need for Alith to quickly fall to his stomach in appeasement. Alith was most perturbed by this, as none of the other wolves seemed to suffer Blackmane's wrath so vehemently. As he ran alongside Silver, he pondered why Blackmane had allowed Alith to join at all if the pack leader felt such antipathy towards the two-legged arrival. There was no means by which Alith could ask this question, the language of Kurnous being devoid of any means to express such emotional concepts.

A howl to the east signalled that prey had been located. Silver stopped and sat back, raising her head to respond in kind. After receiving a reply, she quickly broke eastwards. Other howls sounded around Alith while the pack located each other. Within a short time, Alith found himself surrounded by converging silvery-grey shadows slinking through the twilight that shimmered through the canopy of the forest.

It was Scar that had found something. The male was sat on the lip of a rise, looking northwards, occasionally letting loose a howl to bring the other wolves to the hunt. The pack picked up the scent of prey, their tails straightening with excitement. Blackmane trotted into view and Alith drew back behind Silver. The other wolves let out an excited mix of barks and wails until Blackmane snarled them into silence.

Blackmane's mate, the one Alith called Old Grey, took the lead, forging down a steep bank covered with fern fronds. The air was filled with rustling as the wolves closed in on their quarry, clouds of spores floating in the dusk light. Alith followed closely behind, keeping bent low to avoid being seen. The pack slowed as they neared their prey, their voices falling silent as they did so. Alith could not tell what it was they hunted; the press of trees prevented him from seeing what the wolves could smell. He kept behind Silver as the wolves gathered together, stalking through the underbrush with purpose.

It was then that the wind brought to him the scent of deer, sharper than he had ever smelt it in the mountains of Elanardris. The musk set his heart beating faster, awakening an urge to chase and kill. He took deep breaths to calm himself and kept his gaze far ahead, seeking some glimpse of the herd.

At the bottom of the dell, Old Grey turned to the left and followed a shallow rivulet upstream, the ground rising higher and higher into the outermost reaches of the Annulii foothills. Alith realised with a shock that he was already a considerable distance from the Ellyrion border, deep within the realm of Avelorn. It occurred to him that he had never been in such danger – armed only with a knife and devoid of all armour – yet he felt no nervousness. It was as natural to him to stalk naked through these woods as it had been for him to stand upon the mountainside with bow in hand.

Despite the excitement of the chase, there was a peace in Alith's heart. Although he had only been with the pack for a day, he already felt a bond with them from sharing their food and sleeping with them the night before. It was not since his early days with Milandith that he had felt such closeness, such welcome familiarity.

Old Grey stopped as another howl split the air, not far to the north. The wolves closed in on Blackmane making uncertain noises, one or two of them whimpering. The howl sounded again and was taken up by other lupine throats, rising in pitch and volume. Blackmane's hackles rose and he stood with quivering legs, alert and enraged. He let loose a howl of his own, long and deep. The rest of the pack took up the call, issuing a challenge to the unseen newcomers.

The answering wails seemed to come from many places and of different tones, but Alith had learnt enough about wolves to know that they changed position and their howls to give the impression of greater numbers. Blackmane's pack was large and it was unlikely the interlopers outnumbered them. For all that, it was only Blackmane that showed no signs of fear. The other wolves punctuated their howls with quiet whimpers, their ears pressed back in distress, their tails rigid with tension.

The howling contest continued for some time. Blackmane stood his ground as the other pack's cries came louder and closer. All then fell quiet, save for the sighing of the wind in the leaves and the trickle of the watercourse down the middle of the tree-filled dell. The pack spread out a little, more than half of them moving a little way downwind, the direction from which any attack would be most likely. Blackmane stood on a rock barking, like a general ordering his regiments into position before a battle. Silver edged her way to the north and Alith followed for a few strides until Blackmane's voice cut through the stillness.

'Two-legs, come close,' the grizzled wolf snapped at Alith.

Alith did as he was told without hesitation, crouching beside the boulder upon which the pack leader was standing.

'Fight likely,' said Blackmane, turning his golden eyes on Alith. There was no sign of the pack leader's earlier aggression; Alith fancied that he detected a kinder tone in the old wolf's voice. 'Stay close. Sharp fang kill stag quick. Sharp fang not kill wolf quick. Two-legs tall, neck safe. Protect legs. Bite throat. Bite neck.'

Alith nodded in understanding and then caught himself, realising that the gesture meant nothing to Blackmane.

'Bite throat, bite neck,' said Alith.

Blackmane turned his attention away and Alith settled back on his haunches, his eyes seeking any sign of movement in the rapidly darkening forest. A cool breeze eddied down the steep valley.

A howl that Alith now recognised as Old Grey's echoed from ahead. Alith drew his knife but stayed crouched behind the rock, his glance flicking between the trees and Blackmane. The pack leader was stood erect, tail trembling, lips drawn back as a deep growl reverberated from his throat. Alith quivered from the vibrations of Blackmane's warning and from the rush of blood surging through his body. Leaves rustled close at hand as the other pack members drew closer to Blackmane, taking up guard in a circle around their leader.

Some of the younger wolves began to whimper, sensing the agitation exuded by the adults. They laid down in the ferns, ears flattened, shoulders hunched tight, while the older pack members stood protectively over them.

THE FIRST OF the rival pack appeared a short distance away to the right, bounding lightly over a fallen tree trunk, hairs bristling along her back. She stopped as she saw Blackmane and the others and was quickly joined by five more wolves, all of them nearly as large as Blackmane, all considerably older.

Blackmane turned towards the newcomers and snarled, his teeth glinting in the setting sun.

'Go!' he snapped. 'Our hunt!'

Now that he was becoming more familiar with the wolves' behaviour, Alith thought he detected a hint of uncertainty in the interlopers. They all stood with fangs bared and eyes narrowed, but the occasional nervous flick of their ears betrayed a lack of confidence.

'No hunt,' said the female. Alith saw that her jaws were bloodstained and she held herself awkwardly, favouring her left hind leg.

'She is wounded,' Alith whispered to Blackmane.

'Our hunt,' Blackmane repeated, ignoring Alith. 'Go back!'

A shiver of fright rippled through the rival wolves, and they sank lower to their bellies, giving up their pretence of aggression. Only the female stood her ground, her gaze constantly moving between Blackmane and the other members of his pack. Her eyes finally settled on Alith and she gave a startled yelp and flinched.

'Two-legs!' she yowled. Edging backwards, she started a constant whining that was taken up by the others of her pack.

Their reaction spread to several of Blackmane's wolves, who began to make inquiring barks, seeking reassurance from their leader. A few looked with suspicion at Alith and bared their teeth.

Blackmane glanced at Alith and then returned his attention to the strangers.

'Two-legs hunt with us,' he said. 'One of pack.'

'Many two-legs come,' said the female. 'Hunt with long fangs. Kill many. Not eat.'

'Two-legs not hunt wolf,' said Blackmane. 'Go now!'

'Two-legs kill wolf,' the female insisted, stepping forwards again. 'Long fangs and sharp fangs. Mate dead. Many packs killed.'

'How close?' Alith asked, standing up. This earned him a growl from Blackmane and more whimpering from the strangers, but he ignored both and walked forwards, slipping his knife back into its sheath. 'How close two-legs?'

'We run for two suns,' said the female hesitantly. 'Try to fight. Many killed. Two-legs not chase. Two-legs come from high ground. Come this way.'

'Many two-legs?' asked Blackmane, leaping down from the rock and padding between Alith and the other pack. Old Grey, Scar and a few others moved forwards also, backing up their pack leader with growls and snarls.

'Many, many two-legs,' the female answered. 'Many long fangs. Many sharp fangs. Two-legs fight other two-legs.'

Alith was taken aback by this revelation. He had suspected that the Chracians had come south over the mountains, fleeing the druchii. Now it seemed the druchii had come to Avelorn as well.

'All two-legs kill wolves?' he asked.

'Black two-legs kill wolves,' the female replied. 'Black two-legs bring noise. Black two-legs bring fires. Black two-legs burn other two-legs.'

Revulsion lurched in Alith's stomach at the thought of the druchii coming here. It could only mean that Chrace had been overrun at last, and Avelorn was now under threat.

'Two-legs come here?' Blackmane asked. In reply, the other wolf merely whimpered and flattened her ears. 'Two-legs come, we fight.'

'Not fight,' whined the female. 'Two-legs come with long fangs. They kill, not fight.'

'Our hunt!' snarled Blackmane. 'Not run!'

'Our two-legs has sharp fang,' added Old Grey.

'Two-legs has no long fang,' said the other wolf. 'Sharp fang not fight long fang.'

It was now that Alith realised 'long fang' was the wolves' expression for a bow; most likely the dwarf-made repeater crossbows the druchii brought back from the colonies of Nagarythe in Elthin Arvan. The wolves would have no chance to fight against such hunters, and would be slaughtered by the vicious druchii out of a sheer pleasure for killing.

'We run,' Alith said, turning to Blackmane. The pack leader snarled and snapped his jaws but Alith did not back down. 'Cannot fight long fangs. Long fangs kill many wolves. Wolves kill no long fangs.'

For a moment Alith thought Blackmane would attack. The wolf bunched his muscles, preparing to pounce, his tail as straight as a rod behind him.

'We run,' said Old Grey. 'Long fangs kill cubs. We run. Find new hunt.'

'No!' Blackmane rounded on his mate. 'Two-legs come, two-legs keep coming. Pack runs, pack keeps running. Better fight not run. Make two-legs go away!'

'Not run, hide,' said Alith. 'Black two-legs hunting other two-legs. Not hunting wolves. Wolves hide, two-legs go away.'

Alith knew this to be a lie; given any opportunity the druchii would scour Avelorn with sword and flame. The only chance for survival for the pack would be to lie low until the forces of the Everqueen and her subjects could push back the druchii advance.

The other wolves continued to argue, but Alith did not listen. He was confused by his own reaction. Why did he care whether the wolves lived or died? If they killed even a single druchii, would that not be a victory? He wondered what had happened to the hatred that had burned within him only two days before. Why did he not feel like striking out against the druchii?

A glance back at the worried pack gave him his answer. He saw the cowering cubs, heard the whimpers of their guardians. This was a family, and though they were not elves, they no more deserved to be sacrificed to the druchii's bloodlust than the people of Ellyrion, or any other creature of Ulthuan. The druchii despised all that they could not control, and they would come to Avelorn with their whips and their chains to tame the wilds. Morathi craved domination over all creatures, not just her fellow elves. Alith realised that Morathi must hate the Everqueen even more than she hated Caledor; an incarnation of purity and nobility that Morathi could never defeat save through force.

'We hunt,' Alith said suddenly, cutting through the wolves' argument. 'Not fight, hunt! Kill in darkness. Hunt two-legs.'

'Hunt two-legs?' said Old Grey. 'Not good. We kill two-legs, more two-legs come to kill.'

'I am two-legs, I know two-legs,' Alith told the wolves as they padded back and forth uncertainly. 'Black two-legs bad. Black two-legs kill and kill and kill. Other two-legs fight black two-legs and wolves hunt black two-legs. Two-legs afraid.'

Blackmane was staring intently at Alith, his posture more relaxed.

'Two-legs hunt with long fang, sharper than fang, sharper than sharp fang,' said the pack leader.

'Yes,' said Alith. 'Not fight long fang. Hunt two-legs. Hunt at night. Hunt quiet. Kill two-legs and hide. Come back and hunt two-legs again. Not fight.'

'Two-legs need long fang to hunt,' said Blackmane. 'Long fang sharper than sharp fang.'

'I have no long fang,' Alith replied. Save for his knife, his possessions had been abandoned.

'Water has long fang,' said Blackmane. 'Two-legs take long fang and hunt.'

Alith was confused, unsure what Blackmane was telling him. Frustration welled up within the elf, unable to speak properly with the rest of the pack.

'Water has long fang?' Alith said.

'Old long fang,' said Scar, a grizzled-looking wolf with a greying muzzle and the jagged remains of a wound across his right shoulder. 'Long fang in water old as forest, older. Wolves not need long fang. Two-legs need long fang. Long fang hide from two-legs. Only bright face of night show long fang.'

Scar's words bordered on the meaningless, but his tone was low, almost reverential. Alith sifted through the jumbled phrases trying to discern any sense, but the wolf's references were entirely lost on him.

'Yes,' agreed Blackmane. 'Water hide long fang. Bright face of night come soon. Two-legs take long fang. Hunt black two-legs. Pack hunt.'

'Show me long fang,' said Alith, realising that the wolves were speaking of a real place.

'Bright face of night show long fang,' said Scar. 'Six more suns before bright face of night come.'

Slowly understanding dawned on Alith as he pieced together the strands of the wolves' story. 'Suns' were days, and in six days' time the moon Sariour would be full: the bright face of the night. Whatever it was the wolves were talking about, it could only be seen by the light of the full moon.

'Good,' said Alith and Scar wagged his tail appreciatively. 'Hide six suns. Bright face of night show long fang.'

'Hide six suns,' said Blackmane, his words punctuated with snarls. 'Watch black two-legs. Two-legs take long fang. Hunt black two-legs.'

THE STRAGGLERS THAT had been fleeing the druchii were welcomed into the pack by Blackmane, and the wolves headed east to seek a lair. As they travelled, the howls of other packs could be heard, all of them moving southwards and eastwards away from the mountains.

They encountered other animals retreating from the druchii invasion. Herds of deer threw aside their usual caution, risking the attention of the wolves rather than be caught by the invaders. The pack still needed to eat and the terrified deer proved to be easy prey. That dusk, Alith again gorged himself on fresh flesh, filled with the thrill of the hunt and the energy of the kill.

Over the following days the pack moved into the territories of rival wolves. Each sunrise was heralded by a cacophony of howls as the two packs strove to assert their dominance. Each time neither side was willing to retreat and the two packs came together. Clearly outnumbered, the rival wolves nevertheless stood their ground, daring Blackmane to attack. On the first occasion, Alith feared that there would be bloodshed, but Blackmane surprised him, and the rest of his pack. He told the other wolves of what was happening and warned them to head east. The other pack became fearful and begged Blackmane to help them. The old leader was reluctant, but Alith persuaded him to allow the pack to grow even larger.

Three more encounters ended the same way, and the pack grew to over fifty in number. Alith was reminded of the mustering of regiments at Elanardris. The growth of the pack came with the same problems the Anars had faced. There were more mouths to feed and the huge pack was forced to range far and wide to seek food, their prey having also been driven away by the presence of the druchii. This slowed down the pack and one night Alith could smell the fires of the druchii camp and hear their raucous celebrations on the wind.

That night Blackmane told the pack they could not hunt but had to run as swiftly as they could, to keep the druchii from catching them. Always the wolves headed east, but the druchii were never more than a day's travel behind as they drove into the heart of Avelorn.

As the pack continued to move, some of their number would break off, alone or in pairs, and head northwards to spy upon the druchii. They returned with news that the druchii were burning many trees and had slain hundreds of creatures from the forest. Alith tried to find out the druchii numbers, but the best the wolves could tell him was 'a flock' and 'many packs'. On the eighth night since coming to Avelorn, Alith convinced Blackmane to allow the elf to see for himself the strength of the enemy.

HAVING ACCLIMATISED QUICKLY to the sounds and rhythms of the forest, Alith was confident as he set out at dusk, following back along the path the wolves had taken. As the sun set and the forest was plunged into starlight, he turned northwards and kept a fast but steady pace. He ran for most of the night, stopping only to drink occasionally, the moons rising and falling before he first smelt the smoke of fires drifting through the trees.

Slowing to a walk, Alith saw distant flickers of orange and red. The stench of the charnel fires drifted to him on the gentle wind, a choking mix of woodsmoke and burning flesh. Swathed in almost total darkness, Alith stalked towards the camp with dagger in hand.

Amongst the long and wavering shadows cast by the pyres, Alith spied several sentries. He watched for a while, noting the routes of their patrols and the timing. For all of their depravity, these druchii were disciplined and organised and at first Alith could see no way past the cordon. It was only after further observation that Alith noticed the sentries kept their gaze groundwards; none of them looked up into the trees as they patrolled. And why would they? As far as the druchii knew, there was no threat from the leaves and branches above their heads.

Smiling grimly, Alith slipped forwards silently and climbed the bole of a tree overlooking one of the patrol paths. He waited patiently in the branches, not a muscle moving, his breathing slow and shallow, eyes scanning the path below for the approach of an enemy.

As Alith had predicted, one of the guards came marching between the trees with spear and shield ready. His eyes never once looked up as he passed below Alith.

Alith soundlessly dropped down behind the druchii and plunged his knife into the side of his neck, killing him instantly. Quickly stripping the body, Alith took the clothes and armour before dragging the corpse into a nearby bush so that it would remain unseen.

Clad in the uniform of the slain soldier, Alith headed towards the druchii camp.

WITH A SWAGGER Alith had often seen affected by the druchii, the lord of the Anars strolled into the enemy camp. He knew that his Naggarothi features would blend in with the druchii, and it was far easier to avoid detection in plain sight than to skulk in the shadows. As he expected, there were no challenges and the elves of the camp never gave him a second glance. To walk so boldly in front of his enemies sent a frisson through Alith's body. It pleased him immensely to masquerade as one of them; an invisible foe ready to strike at their heart.

The druchii force was not as large as Alith had first feared. He guessed by the size of the camp that there were three or four thousand in this army, almost half of them cultists of Khaine. He was surprised by this, noting that the worshippers of Khaine seemed to be gaining power over their rivals. He saw a few Salthite totems and heard chants to Ereth Khial, but it was the sacrificial pyres to the Lord of Murder that dominated the ceremonies.

As he walked between the black and red pavilions and weaved his way between stupefied cultists, Alith detected an atmosphere of desperation. It was intangible, but Alith could feel an edge in the words of the priests as they raised their voices to the cytharai, imploring for their favour. The braziers sputtered not with the organs of elves, but with the hearts and livers of deer and bear and wolf. Alith saw not a single elven prisoner.

As he walked, Alith noted the layout of the camp. The cultists were confined to the centre, surrounded by the tents that housed the soldiery. Morathi's commanders were taking no chances with their unreliable allies, keeping a close watch on the cultists. Combining this observation with the lack of cultists in the army on the Ellyrion plain, Alith wondered if Morathi was finally tiring of her sectarian lackeys. They had been useful to her in claiming power, but now their presence created more chaos and problems for the druchii.

Alith was also able to compare his experience in the camp with the time the Shadows had spent in Anlec. Many of the warriors were younger, less than three hundred years old. In times past, such youngsters would never have been allowed to march in a Naggarothi host. It gave Alith hope to see this, knowing that with every year that the druchii were held back, their numbers would dwindle. Morathi's gambit had been to seize Ulthuan before the princes could organise themselves in the wake of Bel Shanaar's death. It seemed that the actions of the Anars had perhaps helped in some way to prevent this. Alith doubted whether history would remember the brave deeds of his house, or the tragedy at Black Fen, but it gave him some momentary pride to recall them. For the first time since the massacre, he was able to look back on that day with a feeling other than hatred and misery.

He had seen enough to convince him that the druchii were vulnerable. If they stayed together, they would eventually be found and destroyed by the Chracians or the warriors of the Everqueen. If they split… Alith would be waiting for them with his newly met friends.

ALITH CUT SOUTH through the camp, moving at a nonchalant walk, his spear over one shoulder, shield slung on a belt across his back. He left the circle of pyres and strolled into the darkness, the only light the flicker of firelight from a spearpoint or link of mail. He saw a sentry a little apart from the others and approached, gently humming the battle anthem of the Anars. The warrior carried a bow and a long sword hung at his waist.

Alith deliberately snapped a twig beneath his foot and the guard turned at Alith's noisy approach, relaxed and unwary.

'You should see some of those Athartists,' Alith said with a leering look. 'You could stretch them any which way you want and they wouldn't make a whimper.'

'I wouldn't mind the odd scream or two…' the guard said with a lewd chuckle.

'I've had my fill already, why don't you go and enjoy the festivities,' suggested Alith, half-turning back towards the camp. 'I drank some moonleaf tea and I can't sleep a wink. I'll keep watch. You never know when we'll be attacked by a badger or something!'

'I'm not so sure,' replied the sentry, glancing between the beckoning fires and the looming shadow of the commanders' pavilion.

'Oh well, if you want to stay here in the dark...' said Alith, taking a step back towards the glow of the flames.

'Wait!' hissed the guard. Alith smiled to himself before turning around to face the soldier.

'I won't tell anybody, if you won't,' Alith said with a smirk. He enjoyed the dilemma playing out on the druchii's face. His indecision, his uncertainty, gave Alith a sense of power over him. He wasn't sure why he toyed with the elf in this way, when he could have easily surprised and overpowered him. There was something about making the druchii dance to the tune of the Anars that was immensely gratifying.

Alith stood next to the druchii and laid his arm across his shoulders.

'I don't think the commander is going to let them stay that long,' Alith added, imagining himself tying the hook onto the end of a fishing line. It was almost too easy to enjoy. Almost.

'I heard as such,' said the guard. 'He said it was "bad for discipline", or something like that.'

'It is a bit of a distraction,' said Alith.

As quick as a serpent, Alith slipped behind the warrior and tightened his arm around his victim's throat and neck. The sentry barely had time for a few choking gasps before he slumped into Alith's arms.

'A terrible distraction,' Alith whispered as he hefted the unconscious elf across his shoulders and headed into the woods.

* * *

Tarmelion woke with a thunderous headache and a biting soreness in his chest. He felt dizzy and did not risk opening his eyes immediately. As he recovered his senses, fear gripped him. He could feel nothing, except for a throbbing in his wrists and ankles and a sharper pain in his chest. He was cold. There was something sticky on his face.

Opening his eyes, Tarmelion found himself looking at the leaf-strewn ground, some distance away. It took a moment for him to realise that he was hung from a tree branch, naked, with blood dripping from a cut in his chest.

'How long before you bleed to death?' a voice asked him from above. Something shifted its weight on the branch and Tarmelion began swaying gently. He craned his neck to catch sight of his tormentor but he could not twist his head far enough to see. He caught a glimpse of a shadowy figure just above him, but it moved out of sight as soon as his eyes fell upon it.

'Who are you?' Tarmelion begged, the pain in his chest growing as his heart began to beat faster, forcing more blood from the wound.

'Why are you here?' the voice asked. 'What do you want with Avelorn? How many more of your kind are coming?'

'I don't know!' sobbed Tarmelion, already terrified out of his wits. He could remember nothing of how he came to be in this place. His last memory was talking to one of the other sentries outside the camp. 'What are you?'

He repeated this question again and again, tears streaming from his eyes, the blood rushing to his head and spilling across his face from the gash above his heart. All became silent save for the distant patter of blood drops hitting the leaves far below.

The branch creaked and a moment later Tarmelion was confronted by a horrifying apparition. A face appeared right in front of him, upside-down and covered in blood.

It was smiling. Tarmelion shrieked and tried to get away, straining every muscle, sending himself swinging dizzyingly from side to side. The face followed him, close enough he could smell blood on its breath. The smile faded and the creature bared bloodstained teeth at him.

'You are going to tell me everything you know,' the thing snarled.

HAVING LEARNED WHAT he wanted, Alith knocked the druchii unconscious and cut him from the tree. He carried him back towards the camp and left him close to one of the paths. Avelorn was the subject of many strange tales and dark legends, and it served Alith well that the sentry be found and spoke to his comrades of his terrifying encounter with a bloodthirsty denizen from the forest. It would sow more doubt in the hearts of the druchii and add to their fear of this unnatural place.

Alith stripped off the druchii clothes, glad to be rid of them for they had been ripe with the stench of fire and death. He did this not only for his personal comfort, but because he was afraid the smell of the druchii would mask his own scent and confuse the wolves. If he came upon the pack in such a fashion, they would attack without question and perhaps only later realise their mistake. Better to walk as nature intended. He kept the bow, arrows and sword.

Dawn came as Alith was making his way back through the woods at a swift run. The chorus of howls that greeted the sun allowed him to steer towards the pack's location. They would be on the hunt at this time, padding sleekly through the early morning twilight in search of prey. He felt the same urge and slipped an arrow to the bow. Slowing, he searched for tracks and soon came across a run used by rabbits. A surge of excitement welled up inside Alith at the thought of catching his prey and it took all of his willpower to remain calm. The bow trembled in his hand; he wanted to cast it aside and hunt with knife and teeth.

What was it that he had awoken with the slaying of Kurnous's stag?

It was dusk once again before Alith caught up with the rest of the pack, which had made its lair in a thin grove of trees beside a wide lake. Silver was the first to greet him with barks and licks and Alith ruffled her fur and stroked her chest in return. They were interrupted by Scar.

'Two-legs come,' said the wolf, turning away without waiting for acknowledgement.

Alith gave Silver a parting pat and followed Scar down to the water's edge. The lake was quite large, easily more than a bowshot wide and twice as long, aligned roughly north to south. The water was crystal-clear, a perfect mirror of the ruddy skies fringed with the silhouettes of the trees. Scar turned northwards and followed the edge of the lake, which was marked by a ribbon of shore upon which only grass grew, sloping gently down to the bare earth at the lake's bank.

In the twilight Alith saw Blackmane at the northern end of the lake, sitting attentively at the water's edge. The pack leader stared out towards the middle of the lake. Alith followed his gaze but could see nothing. There was no wind and not even a ripple disturbed the lake's surface.

'Water holds long fang,' said Scar as they approached Blackmane. 'Two-legs take long fang, hunt other two-legs.'

Scar sat down to the right of his leader and Alith crouched down on the other side. Blackmane had not moved a muscle for the entire time, but now turned his head and looked at Alith.

'Long time, many lives, since two-legs came to forest,' said Blackmane, his voice quiet, respectful. 'Long fang in lake before two-legs came. Long fang old as forest.'

Blackmane returned to his vigil, his immobility a reflection of the utter stillness that surrounded the lake. Alith sat cross-legged and waited also, comfortable in the silence. His mind drifted, memories and feelings swirling together, pictures forming in his mind's eye on the tranquil water.

He had always craved space and peace. Having grown up with no brothers or sisters, there had always been somewhere he could find away from other elves, to listen to his thoughts alone. He remembered gala banquets in the great hall and on the lawns. He recalled long days spent with tutors in the library, trying to absorb the knowledge they were imparting, their voices becoming a drone while his mind wandered to the mountains. He had enjoyed the company of his friends, but their presence was something that could be chosen. When he wanted companionship he had been able to find it, and when he wanted solitude, the wilds had always beckoned.

As he allowed himself to drift into a trance-like state, Alith's senses sharpened. He could hear the playful yaps and yelps of the pack across the lake and the chirruping of birds in the trees. Blackmane's breathing was slow and regular, while Scar panted with excitement. The evening air was cool on Alith's skin, but not unpleasant. He felt the weight of the quiver across his back and realised he still held the bow he had taken from the druchii sentry. These objects felt out of place, and he stood and strode across to the line of trees encircling the lake clearing. He took off the accoutrements of war and placed them beside a tree, noting its position so he could return for them later. Completely naked once again, he returned to Blackmane's side.

Alith quickly fell back into his contemplative state. All turmoil gone, Alith sensed something else. It was magic. Since the time of Aenarion and Caledor, the winds of magic had been drawn into the Vortex of Ulthuan and Alith had grown up knowing but not really noticing the immaterial winds that swept through the mountains of his home. He had felt their coil and eddy as he gave thanks to Kurnous, and had enjoyed their suffusing energy when he had called upon them to shield him from view or guide his aim.

Here, in Avelorn, the magic was different, of an entirely older order. It was rooted in the trees, lingered in the grounds and was contained in the waters of the lake. Having focussed on this realisation, Alith noted that the lake was particularly strong in mystical energy. It reminded him of silver-yellow rain, of calm dew on an autumn morning or the scent of a spring flower. There was potential here, life that was ancient and eternal. This was the magic of the Everqueen, the source of her power. It was this that the druchii – Morathi – wanted to desecrate. The druchii could never enslave such a power and so they sought to deny it to their foes. It was their way, to destroy that which they could not claim, to taint that which could create.

A sharpness, a sudden spike in the magic of the pool, brought Alith out of his waking dream. He opened his eyes slowly, as if from a long and refreshing sleep. The twilight had gone, replaced by a clear sky full of stars and the full moon. Alith turned to Blackmane, but realised with a shock that both the pack leader and Scar had left him. He sat alone on the edge of the lake.

Even as he wondered why the wolves had brought him here, Alith saw something shimmering in the middle of the lake. He took it to be the reflection of the moon above and stood for a better look. The glimmer of light was not the moon, which strangely did not reflect on the water at all. The source of the light was within the water, at the bottom of the lake.

Alith looked around him, suddenly disconcerted. In the night the trees seemed different, the lake more menacing. It was a sheen of black; even the stars did not show on its surface. Only that light in the depths illuminated the scene, dappling the shore and the surrounding trunks and branches with a silvery hue.

Alith fought back his fear with reason, pushing aside the animalistic instincts that had suffused him during his time amongst the pack. It was not dread that filled the clearing, but there was something that tugged at Alith's heart. It was a deep sorrow, a longful mourning. He sensed that a great tragedy had occurred at some time in the distant past. It was neither a memory nor a sensation he could define, but there was something about the bleakness of the scene that told him of an emptiness and loss of hope that only he could understand; something as alone as he was called out to him from the waters.

Alith waded into the lake, warm against his skin. He felt as if he strode into a pool of quicksilver, meeting slick resistance. Pushing forwards, he began to swim, striking out towards the strange light with slow, measured strokes. His passage made not a single ripple and no splash spoiled the silence. He kicked his legs and swam faster, but still the lake was as calm as it had been when he first laid eyes upon it.

Though he swam, Alith could feel no sense of motion or time and he could not tell for how long he forged towards that light. It grew neither stronger nor weaker but remained constant, bathing him in its glow. Had the lake been normal, he could have crossed it a dozen times over without too much effort, but Alith found his breath coming in short gasps, his limbs tired. It felt like he had been swimming for an eternity but he pressed on, ignoring the burning of his muscles and the pressure in his chest. The light surrounded him, dragging him forwards.

When he knew he was above the light source – and he did not know how but he just knew – Alith stopped and treaded water for a moment. He looked down but all he could see was the white and silver that engulfed him.

Taking a deep breath, he plunged downwards, towards the sunken moonlight.

Down and down he swam until his lungs were fit to burst. Down even further he went, his world now a bubble of silver that embraced him. Part of him wanted to stop, wanted to turn and break for the surface, fearful of drowning. Another part of Alith welcomed the oblivion the light offered. Yet still another part of him heard a voice.

It was a female voice, which Alith recognised as if in distant remembrance, but he did not know whether the voice came from the water or inside his own head. The voice reminded him of safety and boredom but he could not place it. It told him a story as he swam, the words coming to mind as if recalled, yet Alith did not know from where the memory might come.

In the age before the elves the gods were as one with the world and the heavens. They played and schemed and fought with one another. And loved. Greatest of the godly lovers were Kurnous the Hunter and Lileath of the Moon. For eternity Kurnous wooed Lileath but the two of them could never meet, for Kurnous dwelt in the endless forests of the world and the Moon Goddess haunted the skies. To show Kurnous that his love was not unrequited, Lileath petitioned Vaul the Smith to create a gift for the Hunter. She poured her love and her soul into that gift and bade Vaul to take it to Kurnous as a token of her affection. Khaine the Warrior, ever jealous of Kurnous and Lileath's love, intercepted Vaul as he returned from the moon. He demanded that Vaul give him the gift that Lileath had commissioned. Vaul refused, telling Khaine that it was not for him. At this Khaine grew very angry and threatened to torture the crippled Smith if he did not give him Lileath's gift. Vaul refused again and instead passed the gift to Isha to hide it from Khaine. Isha, Mother of the World, proclaimed that none save for Kurnous would ever find the token of Lileath's love. Shedding a tear, she cast the gift down from the heavens to the world. Vaul suffered greatly at the hands of Khaine for his defiance, but the Smith-God did not know where the gift was hidden. When Khaine released him, Vaul told Kurnous of what had happened. Kurnous was the God of the Hunt and there was nothing he could not find, but the gift of Lileath eluded him. Every month she looked down upon the world and stared at her gift, so that Kurnous might follow her gaze. Yet the Hunter never found it before the elves came and the gods were forced to dwell evermore in the heavens. So it was that Kurnous and Lileath would remain apart for eternity and Kurnous's children would howl their love for Lileath every full moon.

Alith felt something in his grasp, solid yet flexible. He tightened his grip on it and turned, heading for the surface. The glow diminished around him while fatigue and lack of breath played tricks on his mind, confusing him with glimpses from his past and a cacophony of noise. His heart thundered and his body screamed in pain along every vein and fibre of muscle. His prize tight in his hand, Alith pushed upwards, feeling the strength leaking from him, the last bubbles of air streaming from between his gritted teeth.

With an explosive gasp and a spume of water, Alith broke the surface of the lake. The starlit sky spun and the moon swirled. His whole body was numb, save for his right hand, which was pained by the tightness of his grip. Alith took in great lungfuls of air and after a while the pain and dizziness receded, though he still felt as weak as a newborn cub. Only when the rushing in his ears had stopped and he could feel the water against his skin once more did he look at what he held.

It was the most beautiful bow he had ever set eyes upon. Crafted from a silvery metal that glittered in the moonlight, its tips were each decorated with a crescent moon. No droplet of water clung to its length and its string was all but invisible, finer than a hair. It felt as light as air in his grasp and perfectly balanced for his hand. It was warm to the touch, reassuring, almost loving with its presence.

Alith heard noises from the edge of the lake. Looking around he saw that the moon was just above the treetops, almost gone from view. In the dim light he could discern the shadowy shapes of the wolf pack, spread around the shore of the lake. Dozens of pairs of eyes glittered in the shadows, watching him. Keeping himself afloat with gentle kicks and sweeps with his free arm, Alith kissed the bow and held it triumphantly above his head.

All around him the wolves howled as the Children of Kurnous cried their love for Lileath.

TWENTY

The Taming of the Wolf

ALITH WAS BREATHLESS as he ran through the woods. Glancing over his shoulder, he could see the knights chasing him, ducking beneath branches as they steered their heavy mounts between the trees. More than a dozen of them had given chase when Alith had shot their captain as they patrolled southwards from their camp. The thud of the horses' hooves reverberated from the steep sides of the wooded dell as Alith led them towards the pack.

Alith put in a fresh spurt of speed and cut to his left, disappearing from the knights' view. He leapt onto a rock and from there jumped into the branches of a tree with the swiftness of a squirrel. He ran lightly along the branch and crouched next to the trunk, peering between the leaves at the approaching riders.

The foremost rider signalled for the pursuers to slow as he passed Alith's hiding spot. Alith felt a tremor of fear as the small column came to a walk and paced by below him, their eyes scanning the trees for any sign of their prey.

'Halt!' called the lead knight, holding up his hand. 'It has stopped running.'

Alith caught his breath and his heart began to race. He glanced at the ground beneath the horses but knew he had left no tracks as he had run. He also knew that he could not be seen easily. His pale skin was obscured by mud and blood he had painted across himself, and immobile he was all but indistinguishable from the bark of the tree.

Slowly shifting position, Alith turned his attention to the knights' leader, wondering what sense it was that had alerted the rider. He was armoured as the others in heavy silver plate, his dark grey steed protected by a caparison of light mail and a black enamelled chamfron gilded with the rune of Anlec. A high war helm protected the rider's head, decorated with a plume of long black feathers that swayed as the knight looked to his left and right. There was something else on the knight's helmet, a band of gold that held in place a mask that Alith could not see until the rider turned fully around and stared directly at him. Alith gasped at what he saw.

The golden mask depicted a thin, snarling face sculpted with angular cheeks and diamond eyeholes. It was not the fierce expression of the war mask that so alarmed Alith, but what was set into it. A pair of blue eyes were bound to the mask above the eyeholes, a net of fine golden thread passing through the glistening orbs and the metal of the helm; real eyes that moved with a life of their own. A fine trickle of blood ran down the sides of the mask from these as they tracked back and forth, seeking something. They swivelled in unison towards Alith and the rider straightened as if startled.

For a moment Alith was locked in the unearthly stare of those magical eyes. He was transfixed with horror, not only of his discovery but by the means with which he had been found.

'There, in the tree!' the rider cried out, pulling free his sword and pointing towards Alith.

The knights' exclamations broke Alith's trance and he pulled himself higher into the branches with one hand, unslinging the moonbow from his back with the other. He felt the gift of Lileath pulse in his hand, mirroring his heartbeat. Angry shouts rose towards him as he lifted an arrow to the impossibly thin string. He pulled back on the shaft, with no more resistance than he would have from passing his hand through the air. Sighting on the knight with the abomination of a mask, Alith could hear the bow whispering to him, offering soothing encouragement. He could not discern the words, and doubted he would understand their language even if he could clearly hear them. Their tone was reassuring, relaxing him, quelling the trembling in his hands.

Alith loosed the arrow and it sprang from the moonbow as a flash of white, cutting straight through the breastplate of the knight and out of his back to bury itself up to the fletching in the leaf-strewn ground. A gaping hole in his body, the knight toppled sideways and crashed lifelessly into the dirt. As he had done since finding the moonbow, Alith marvelled at its power; it was strong enough to send a shaft through a tree bole yet so light that he could balance it on a fingertip.

Alith shot another of the knights, the angle of the arrow passing down through the rider's shoulder and splitting the spine of his steed. Both collapsed in a heap. With no means to shoot back, the knights turned and fled, one more of their number falling with an arrow through his back as they galloped back up the dell.

With moonbow still in hand, Alith dropped back to the ground. He felt a wave of revulsion wash through him as he stepped towards the knight with the grotesque helmet. Turning him over with his foot, Alith stared at the horrid contraption of gold and flesh wound into the helm. He knelt down for a closer inspection and saw that the wires holding the eyes in place passed through the helmet and into the face of the wearer. Though the knight was dead, the eyes continued to follow Alith, staring at him wherever he moved.

Forcing himself to look at those eyes, he regarded them with distaste, but also a feeling of recognition. There was something about their lidless stare that seemed familiar. Then it came to him: these were the eyes of the sentry he had interrogated. A sorcerer in the druchii camp had laid an enchantment upon them to seek out Alith, and gifted them with the ability to see him wherever he hid.

Disgusted, Alith drew his sword and sliced through the golden bindings, spilling the eyes to the ground. They swivelled amongst the leaves, still staring accusingly at Alith. With a lurch in his stomach, Alith brought his sword down onto them and hacked them into viscous pieces. As he straightened, Alith wondered if the unfortunate sentry had survived the donation of his eyes. It would be like the druchii to blind him for his error, rather than grant him the ignominy of death.

Stowing the moonbow and his sword, Alith retrieved his precious arrows and turned down the dell to head back to where the pack was waiting in ambush. He would have to tell them there would be no hunt today.

For a dozen days after finding the moonbow, Alith and the wolves assailed the druchii, but the opportunities to strike back at his hated foes were few. The enemy advanced relentlessly, driving the pack before them. The wolves tried to head north and circle back to the west but after a day they ran into another druchii host; this one coming directly south and heading for the Ellyrion border. Eastwards the black regiments marched, unwittingly herding Alith and the wolves before them as they pressed on towards the Aein Ishain, shrine to the goddess Isha and home to the court of the Everqueen.

Save for the phases of the moon, Alith had not counted the passing of the days, but he started to worry about time once more. How far was it to the Everqueen, and how fast were the druchii moving? Was the spiritual ruler of Avelorn aware of the danger that pressed so hastily into the forests?

This last question Alith dismissed as soon as it came to him. These were the lands of the Everqueen and she was bound to them in ways far beyond a prince's connection to his lands. The death of the beasts and the burning of the trees would be known to her, as Alith felt the cuts on his bare feet and the grazes on his skin. No, the Everqueen would not need warning of the threat that loomed over Avelorn.

Unable to hinder the druchii advance, Alith was at a loss regarding what course of action to take. Having seen the strength of his enemy, Blackmane wished to flee eastwards even further, down through the isthmus of Avelorn and into the Gaen Vale. Here the old wolf believed his pack would be safe from the druchii, though he would not tell Alith why he felt such surety.

In the following days Alith noticed a change in the forests. The nature of the trees altered, becoming even larger and older than those of the outer woods. Bramble and bracken barred their way and often Alith was forced to crawl after the wolves through natural culverts and along tunnels of sharp briar. Walls of thorns turned them northwards or southwards, and Alith was convinced the forest itself was trying to keep them from moving eastwards.

Sixteen days after drawing the moonbow, Blackmane's pack came to the borders of the Gaen Vale. No elves save for Malekith's half-brother and half-sister – and the

Everqueen herself – had ever travelled to the Gaen Vale, but the legends surrounding it were many. Some claimed it was the spiritual heart of Avelorn, of all of Ulthuan, where Isha had cried out her last tears before she left the world for the heavens. Other tales told that the Gaen Vale was the birthplace of the first Everqueen, the mortal incarnation of the goddess.

That strange spirits lived in the Gaen Vale was beyond dispute. The forest had a consciousness of its own in those dark depths. The trees could walk and talk, infused with the life of Isha. Legend claimed that these spirits protected Morelion and Yvraine, the first children of Aenarion, from the attacks of the daemons. The Everqueen sought counsel from the forest's immortal guardians and Alith believed that they would be no friends of the druchii.

Alith cared not for the legends of Isha, but he could recognise sanctuary. Separated from the mainland of Ulthuan by the narrowest strip of land, the Gaen Vale could be easily defended against the druchii. So he followed Blackmane as the pack forced their way towards safety, the druchii ever close on their heels.

As NIGHT FELL on Alith's thirtieth day in Avelorn, they came to the northern end of the isthmus. The skies were swathed with thick cloud, the forest bathed intermittently by the white light of waxing Sariour and the sickly green of the Chaos moon. A mood of unease spread amongst the pack, a feeling of foreboding that Alith shared. The air tasted strange and Alith wondered if the druchii conjured a foul sorcery to stain Avelorn with their dark magic. The wolves gathered close together, the pack rubbing against each other for reassurance, their mewls and whimpers sounding in the darkness. Blackmane strode confidently through his charges, his bark bringing comfort to the scared pack.

Alith was filled with the sensation of being watched, but though he scanned the trees for any sign of an interloper, he saw nothing. Then he became aware of movement and the whimpering of the wolves increased. Alith sensed it now. The breeze brought with it a different scent, that of autumnal rot and mouldering leaves. Shadows shifted at the edge of Alith's vision, but when he turned to look he saw nothing but bushes and trees. Eerie creaks and the swish of leaves filled the air. Things whispered in the undergrowth, a susurrus that came from every direction and none. Though he could see nothing, Alith was in no doubt that the forest was moving.

The trees were getting closer.

THE PACK GATHERED around Blackmane, Alith at his side. A near-impenetrable wall of trees surrounded the elf and wolves, branches reaching high overhead to blot out what little light crept through the clouds. A thicket of brambles had grown up around the trees, creating a thorny fence.

Alith drew the moonbow and nocked an arrow, glancing nervously all around. Even Blackmane's fierce confidence had disappeared and the pack leader hunched at Alith's side, ears flat against his head, eyes wide with fright.

Something shifted to Alith's right and he turned, bow raised.

'Not welcome,' said a voice on the wind, reminding Alith of the rustle of leaves in the wind. One tree stood a little further forwards from the others, a huge bowed oak heavy with leaf. It shuddered and acorns fell to the ground in a loud patter. 'Leave us.'

'Black two-legs come,' said Blackmane, standing up and taking a pace towards the arboreal apparition. 'Kill. Burn. We run.'

The tree might have twisted slightly towards Blackmane, though it could well have been a trick of the moonlight.

'Wolves may come,' the voice said. 'Two-legs must not.'

'Why would you deny your ally sanctuary?' demanded Alith, speaking in elvish. 'I would fight to protect these lands from the druchii.'

'Come here,' the treeman said, bending a branch in Alith's direction like a beckoning arm.

The elf approached cautiously, moonbow still in hand. He stopped a few paces from the treeman and saw a gnarled face in the bark, far above his head. Knots made for eyes and a split in the bark formed a mockery of a mouth, though neither moved as the treeman spoke.

'What manner of elf runs wild with the wolves?' the treeman asked.

'I am Alith, last of the Anars,' the elf replied, stiffening with pride as he spoke. The treeman said nothing and Alith continued. 'I am the son of the wolf and the moon.'

At this the trees around the trees began quivering violently, branches clashing, leaves fluttering. Alith did not know if this signalled anger or amusement, but he kept calm.

'I request passage to the Gaen Vale, to seek sanctuary from those that would hunt me down and slay me,' Alith said, taking the arrow from the string of the moonbow and placing both in his quiver. 'Or worse,' he added.

A branch reached out and laid leafy fingers upon Alith's brow, their touch as light as a feather. A moment after it had settled, the branch whipped away with a crack.

'No,' said the treeman, its voice deepening to a rumble. 'There is no place for you in Gaen Vale. You bring darkness with you. Death is in you. Only life is welcome in this place. You must go.'

'The darkness follows me, but it is not of my making,' said Alith, thinking of the pursuing druchii. 'I will help you fight!'

'The darkness is drawn to you, and you are drawn to it,' the treeman said, slowly straightening. 'You cannot pass into the Gaen Vale.'

Alith was aware of the eyes of the wolves upon him, Blackmane's stare the most intent. The wolves could not follow the words, but Alith's narrowed eyes and tense posture told them what they needed to know about the exchange.

'We go?' asked Blackmane. 'Hide?'

'Yes,' said Alith. 'You go. You hide.'

'Two-legs come,' said Blackmane.

'No,' said Alith, turning away from the treeman to focus on the wolves. 'Two-legs not come. Two-legs will hunt. Wolves will hide.'

'No!' snarled Scar, trotting from the pack. 'Two-legs hunt, wolves hunt.'

'Wolves hunt,' echoed Blackmane.

'Cubs not safe,' said Alith. 'Cubs not hunt. Black two-legs come soon. Wolves hide.'

'Cubs hide, wolves hunt,' said Blackmane. 'Pack hunts with two-legs.'

Alith wanted to argue, but there were no words to express what he knew. The druchii would come this way, in ever-increasing numbers. The wolves had to flee, to head to safety in the Gaen Vale. Yet there was no way he could convince them of their peril. Alith would have to leave them.

'Two-legs not run,' said Silver, joining Scar. It was as if the wily female had read Alith's mind. 'Two-legs stay with pack. Pack protects.'

'Black two-legs kill pack!' snapped Alith, causing Silver to shrink back as if he had taken a swipe at her. Alith felt a pang of guilt, but continued, knowing that he had to make the wolves understand the danger. 'Many, many black two-legs. Kill many, many wolves. Wolves run!'

Alith turned his back on the pack to a chorus of yelps and howls. He ignored them and strode westwards, away from the Gaen Vale. He'd taken only a few paces when he heard the padding of feet. Glancing over his shoulder he saw Scar, Silver, Blackmane and nearly two dozen other wolves following him.

'No!' Alith yelled, stooping to snatch up a handful of dirt. He flung it at the wolves with a wordless shout. Turning away, Alith stormed through a gap that had opened in the thorny barricade.

'Don't let them follow me!' Alith called out in elvish, his voice catching in his throat.

'We will protect them,' the treeman's haunting voice called back. The thorns writhed and within moments the gap was sealed once more.

Howls and snarls echoed through the trees, following Alith as he stalked into the darkness with tears in his eyes.

ALITH WEPT FOR the rest of the night, sitting on the root of an enormous tree. He wondered why the gods could be so cruel. They tempted him with love and peace and then took away that which he desired most: Ashniel; Milandith; his family; Athielle; the wolf pack. In his grief he was reminded of Elthyrior. *Loneliness is an indulgence for those with the time to spare for it. Some fill the emptiness with the meaningless chatter of those around them. Some of us fill it with a greater purpose, more comforting than any mortal company.*

Alith had entered Avelorn thinking he had found a purpose, but it had not been so. Had he been wrong to slay the stag? He thought not. Had Kurnous intended him to run with the pack? It seemed likely. If so, then what had it brought Alith save for more woe?

Alith heard a gentle whisper and without thought reached to the quiver on his back and brought forth the moonbow. He stroked a finger along the silvery metal, relishing the warmth. He held it to his cheek, his tears running along its length, soothed by its touch.

Here was the reason he had been brought to Avelorn.

Cradling the moonbow to his chest, Alith stood and took a deep breath. It was up to him to find his own purpose. Others could blame fate, or the gods, or luck. Alith was empty of blame, save for his hatred of those that had brought this woe upon Ulthuan. His fate had not been made by Kurnous, nor his father and grandfather, not even by Bel Shanaar. All that had happened to Alith had one source and one source alone: the druchii.

He had been a leaf on a river, pulled by currents beyond his control. Forced to fight. Forced to run. Forced to hide. That would change. The stag would run and be hunted down. The wolf chose its prey. Now was the time to act, not react. For too long the druchii had been allowed to choose the tune. That feral love of the hunt that Kurnous had awoken stirred in Alith's breast.

He looked to the north, where the druchii made their camps and despoiled the forest. With the moonbow Alith could slay many of them. They would come for him and he would elude them, just as the Shadows had done. But it was not enough. Even with the moonbow, he could not slay enough druchii to halt them, to turn the war against them. The lone wolf was no threat to them.

Moonbow in hand, Alith turned to the south-west, towards Ellyrion. He could not hunt alone, but he knew where he would find his pack.

TWENTY-ONE

An Oath Fulfilled

ALITH RAN FOR many days, heading south across Ellyrion, filled with the spirit of the hunt. Clad in naught but his weapons, he avoided the herds of the Ellyrians, travelling by day and night. He did not pause to kill and drank sparingly, possessed by the vision of his new war against the druchii. As packs his warriors would hunt, like the Shadows of old.

By the dark of night he crested a hill and looked south. To the east the lights of Tor Elyr glittered on the waters of the Inner Sea. He hesitated for just a moment, a last pang of regret upon seeing the city where Athielle lived. It was gone in an instant. To the south he saw the shrouded lanterns of the Naggarothi camp.

Approaching the camp, Alith was called upon by a picket to identify himself. It was only when he saw the astounded look upon the sentry's face that Alith became aware of his outlandish appearance. The Naggarothi eyed Alith for a long time, struggling between joy and incredulity as the prince made himself known.

'Send word to Khillrallion and Tharion that I wish to see them immediately,' said Alith as he strode unashamedly into the camp.

'My prince, where have you been?' asked the warrior, following a little way behind his lord. 'We feared that you were dead or taken prisoner.'

'Such a thing will never happen,' Alith replied with a grim smile. 'The druchii will never catch me.'

Alith sent the soldier ahead to fetch his lieutenants and made directly for the rough lodge that served as his quarters. More Naggarothi came from their huts and tents to stare at their returning prince. Alith ignored their inquisitive gazes, though he noted that while many were astounded by his appearance an almost equal number seemed to focus upon the moonbow in his hand.

Tharion came running through the camp as Alith reached the door to the lodge.

'Prince Alith!' the commander cried out with a mixture of relief and surprise. 'At first I did not believe it!'

There followed much inquiry as to the prince's whereabouts and actions, all of which Alith refused to answer. His experiences in Avelorn were his alone, to share with no other. All that his people needed to know was their prince had returned, and with fresh purpose.

When Khillrallion arrived, he brought with him another elf: Carathril. Alith was as surprised by the herald's presence as Carathril was by Alith's appearance. They greeted each other coolly, both unsure of each other's agenda.

'What brings the herald of the Phoenix King to my camp?' Alith asked as they walked into the main room of the lodge. He carefully placed the moonbow on the long table, before removing his belt and quiver and laying them to one side. Alert and dignified, Alith sat at the head of the table and gestured for the others to sit.

'Carathril is here at my request,' said Tharion, exchanging a glance with Khillrallion. 'When you disappeared we were at a loss. We sought the advice of King Caledor as to how we might best aid his cause. We have been discussing joining Caledor in his next campaign.'

'That will not be required,' said Alith. He turned to Carathril. 'However, your journey has not been entirely in vain. Return to your master with the news that the druchii have invaded Avelorn in strength. Even now they are probably at the border of the Gaen Vale.'

Carathril took this news with a frown.

'And how are you aware of this?' asked the herald.

'I have returned from Avelorn, and saw the druchii for myself,' Alith told the group. 'I fear Chrace is now entirely overrun, and the eastern kingdoms would do well to prepare their defences for a fresh onslaught by Morathi.'

Alith fancied he could see the questions burning in the minds of the others but none were voiced.

'That is grim news,' said Carathril. 'I will convey this to King Caledor. However, my reason for being here has not changed. I wish to discuss how best you might aid the Phoenix King in his war against the druchii.'

'Please leave me alone for a moment with the Phoenix King's herald,' said Alith, keeping his tone neutral.

'Perhaps we could, hmm, fetch you some clothes, prince?' suggested Tharion.

'Yes, do that,' Alith replied absently, his gaze fixed on Carathril. He continued when the others had left the room, finally allowing his anger to show. 'I am not some hound to be called to heel! I fight for my lands and my heritage, not for the Phoenix Throne. I will wage my war against the druchii in whatever way I see fit, and will suffer no interference or questions. Protect Ulthuan and its people, but know this: Nagarythe is mine.'

'You would set yourself up in opposition to the Phoenix Throne?' said Carathril, his face a picture of disbelief. 'You claim Nagarythe as yours? What makes you any different from Morathi? By what right can you claim such rule?'

'I am Naggarothi. The cold of winter runs in my veins. The legacy of Aenarion beats in my heart. My father and grandfather have given their lives to Nagarythe, not for glory or renown, but out of duty and love. I do not seek Nagarythe for myself, but to keep the land safe from the ambitions of others. The Phoenix King's grandfather chose to leave Anlec and found his own realm in the south, and by that action relinquished any claim to rulership over Nagarythe.'

'You owe loyalty to nothing,' said Carathril, bowing his head with sadness. 'You would make yourself a king, yet you would rule over barren waste and have no subjects. You will become a king of shadows.'

Alith smiled at Carathril's choice of title and remembered Elthyrior's words from so many years ago. *'In the mountains she sent me to find you, the child of the moon and the wolf, the heir of Kurnous. The one that would be king in the shadows and hold the future of Nagarythe in balance'.*

Since that first conversation, the raven herald had insisted that Alith should plot his own course, should follow his destiny without complaint. Alith found truth in that message. He had become the prime hunter, the leader of the pack. The druchii were his prey and he would never give up his pursuit of them.

Alith looked at Carathril, still smiling. The herald did not share Alith's amusement. The prince nodded.

'Yes, that is *exactly* what I will become.'

WHEN CARATHRIL HAD been abruptly dismissed, Khillrallion and Tharion returned with boots, robe and cloak for Alith. They also brought a pail of water and soap but Alith waved these away.

'We cannot win against the druchii in open war,' Alith told them as he pulled on the robe and fastened the broad belt around his waist. 'Not by our own strength. There are simply too few of us left.'

'Then we should fight alongside the Ellyrians or Caledorians,' said Tharion.

'No!' snarled Alith. 'We will continue to fight where we have always done, where it pains the druchii most: in Nagarythe. It could be years before Caledor is ready to march north in strength, and what will we find as liberators? A spoiled wasteland, destroyed by darkness and battle, and Anlec tumbled into stones, humbled. If Caledor invades Nagarythe he will destroy everything to cast out the druchii; everything that we would give our lives to protect. We can wage a different war, one that will eat at the druchii from within. Weakened, they will lose their war in the other realms and we will stand ready to claim power.'

'You would see us all become Shadows?' said Tharion, guessing Alith's intent.

'I would,' replied the prince. He wished to gaze outside but the hall had no windows. Instead he looked deep into the flickering light of the fire. 'Elanardris is no more; every crack and shadow will be our new home. The dark woods, the fens, the hills will conceal us. Not a single druchii will walk in Nagarythe without looking over his shoulder. Not a single army will march on the roads without fearing every outcrop and vale. This is a test of will, and we cannot flinch. For every one of ours that dies, a dozen druchii must be sent screaming to Mirai. For every drop of blood we give, we take a river in return.'

'Retraining all of your warriors will not be swift,' warned Khillrallion, sat upon one of the benches. 'Many have spent a lifetime in the ranks, learning discipline and the craft of open battle. These are not the skills of the Shadow, and they have no experience.'

'We will divide the army between you and the other remaining Shadows, that's roughly fifty warriors each,'

Alith declared. 'In Athelian Toryr they can learn the ways of the woods, be tutored by the wisdom of Kurnous. In the mountains and the passes they will come to know the secrets of rock and snow.'

'And what of weapons?' asked Tharion. 'We have less than a thousand bows for more than three thousand warriors, and that many Shadows will need a forest of arrows.'

'I will see what the Ellyrians can provide for us for the time being,' said Alith. 'In the end, our warriors must learn to make such things for themselves, or take them from their slain foes, for it is only thus that we will be able to continue to fight in Nagarythe. Just as the shrines of Kurnous exist as stores for the hunters in the wilds, we shall set up caches across Nagarythe, hidden from the eyes of our foes and made secret by enchantments. Remember that we will be Shadows, homeless and untraceable. The army must learn to hunt what it needs, to pass without notice, to leave no sign of their presence.'

'You are asking a lot,' said Khillrallion.

'Those that cannot learn will be left behind,' snapped Alith. He glared at his two captains, daring them to speak out. For a moment he bared his teeth and narrowed his eyes, much as Blackmane had done to cow his pack. 'I am your prince and these are my commands!'

Khillrallion nodded in silent acquiescence while Tharion leaned away from Alith, shocked by his ferocity. Alith relented and held out a placating hand towards the pair.

'We must be strong, stronger than ever before,' said the prince.

'As you wish, lord,' said Tharion, standing and giving a formal bow. 'I swore an oath to your grandfather and father, yet I have not had opportunity to give it to you until now. I will serve House Anar and its prince until the end of my days. As my lord bids me, so shall I act. By Asuryan and Isha, by Khaine and Ereth Khial, I am bound by this oath to you.'

Alith watched Tharion as he marched from the hall, looking at Khillrallion only when the ageing elf had left.

'Two years,' Alith said. 'In the spring two years from now, we will return to Nagarythe and begin our shadow war. I look to you to make sure that we are ready. I would have no other captain to aid me.'

'And I would have no other prince to follow,' Khillrallion replied with a wink. His mood then became sombre. 'Twice I thought I had lost you, and yet you have returned. Yet, neither time do I think the prince I knew has come back.'

'I will be a prince for only a little while longer,' Alith said. 'When we return to Nagarythe, I shall be the Shadow King.'

For most of the year the Naggarothi trained in their new style of war. Alith sent petitions to Finudel asking for weapons, which the prince granted as best as he was able. No mention was made by either of them regarding Athielle. Finudel informed Alith in one letter that she had heard news of his disappearance but not his return. Alith assured Finudel it was better that she believed him gone, lest she leave the city and come to the camp. Such an encounter would not be to the benefit of either.

The following winter, as far as the Ellyrians could tell, Alith's army simply disappeared. Riders brought news to Finudel and Athielle that at dawn they had passed the Naggarothi settlement and found it deserted where the night before it had been filled with life. No tracks told of where they had gone, and nothing remained of their occupation; not a single arrowhead or cloak, link of mail or water bottle had been left behind. Nearly three and a half thousand elves had vanished.

Alith had led his warriors into Athelian Toryr, dispersing them through the forest and mountains. Each of these groups was led by a former Shadow, respectfully known as shadow-walkers by the other warriors for their ability to move without trace. Alith led no cadre himself, but moved between the groups, monitoring their progress and instilling them with his bitter ethos.

For another year they continued to train, living in the wilderness without supply or support. The shadow warriors honed their archery and their stalking, and learnt the words of Kurnous that would bring fire to dead wood or summon hawks to be their messengers. They slept in tree branches or beneath arching roots, made pillows of rocks and lairs of caves. By Alith's design, no group knew where the others dwelt, and they were ordered to avoid each other as the wolf packs avoid their rivals. If one was seen by a shadow warrior from another cadre, the shadow-walkers would punish them, setting them arduous tasks of survival. To some it may have seemed cruel, but to Alith it was essential that his army be self-sufficient, not only physically but mentally.

Alith hardened the minds of his warriors as much as their skills. Whenever he visited a cadre he would speak to them at length, reminding them of the ills done to them by the druchii, passing on his own thirst for revenge, stirring up the dark passions that seethed beneath the civilised faces of all Naggarothi. He wanted his warriors not only to be skilled but to be as savage as the wolves, merciless and determined.

'When you look at your foe, do not see another elf,' he would tell them. 'See them for what they are: creatures less than animals. Remember that your enemy is responsible for all of your woes. It is he that cast you from your homes, tortured your friends and slaughtered your families. You can have no compassion for those you will slay, for it will be rewarded by failure. Hesitation is death, doubt is weakness. The druchii tore your lives from you and threw them upon sacrificial pyres, and anointed their priests with the blood of your kin. The ghosts of the fallen wander Mirai, wailing in grief for the wrongs done to them, pleading with the living to avenge them.

'Do not long for peace, for there can be none while any druchii still draw breath. Embrace war as the crucible of your valediction, the means to purge this stain upon our people. Swear oaths of vengeance, not to me or your companions or to the uncaring gods, but to fallen mothers and fathers, dead sisters and brothers, slain sons and daughters. Take the darkness that the druchii have created and rob them of its power. You are the blade that will strike down the wicked. You are the shadow warrior, the faceless bringer of justice.'

As the last days of autumn gleamed upon the red and yellow leaves, Alith called the groups together, assembling them in the foothills at the eastern end of Eagle Pass. By night they made camp, gathering silently by the dying light of Sariour and the ruddy glow of the Chaos moon.

'We are ready,' said Alith, his quiet voice the only sound to break the stillness. 'The wait is over, the fighting begins anew. By dawn we will be heading towards Tiranoc and war. I will not ask you to follow me, for you have all proven your loyalty to our cause. I will not exhort you to acts of bravery, for you have all shown great courage to be here. I will only say that this is our moment of truth. Let the princes of the east fight their great battles and hurl the lives of their subjects away in futile resistance. It is here, in the west, that this war will be won. We fight for loved ones lost. We fight for futures blighted. We fight to reclaim a land that was once gloried above all others. We fight for Nagarythe.'

'For Nagarythe,' came the hushed answer from the army.

As the shadow warriors melted away into the darkness, heading westwards along the pass, Tharion approached Alith and fell in beside his prince.

'Is it wise to march on the brink of winter, lord?' asked Tharion.

'Armies do not march by winter, but we are not an army,' Alith replied. 'We are hunters, remember. In rain and wind and snow and baking sun we stalk our prey, across moor and mountain, river and fen. Let the druchii worry about moving armies in the grip of the ice, with their wagons and their baggage. Let them stand helpless as we burn their towns and kill their folk, as we were once helpless against the legions of Anlec.'

Tharion nodded in understanding, and Alith saw a dark fire in the veteran's eyes. It was the same look that Alith saw whenever he chanced upon his reflection in a pool or patch of ice.

THE ATTACKS OF the shadow warriors came as a shock to all of Ulthuan. News quickly spread amongst the druchii and their enemies. At first Alith kept his army together, overrunning the eastern watch towers of Eagle Pass, ambushing druchii patrols on the road and waylaying their messengers. Isolated by the growing snows of winter, druchii garrisons huddled in their camps, casting fearful gazes into the night. They whispered that the shadow army was made up of the spirits of those sacrificed to Ereth Khial, who had escaped her underworld domain to wreak their vengeance.

Alith learnt of this and laughed at the superstition of his prey. He used their fears as weapons, terrorising the druchii at every opportunity. Before their attacks, his warriors hid in the shadows and made wailing cries to unsettle their foes. They called out names they had overheard, accusing the druchii of being murderers. Howling like wolves the shadow warriors prowled just beyond the light of the fires, allowing the sentries vague glimpses of movement before disappearing. With whispered spells the shadow-walkers cast a gloom upon the fires, dimming their light and sending the druchii into a fearful panic.

Then the shadow warriors unleashed the fury of their bows. Storms of black shafts enveloped the camp, each one unerringly finding its mark. Never once seeing their attackers, the druchii died by the hundreds, screaming and panicked. And always the shadow warriors left a few survivors, allowing them to escape so that they would take their dread and horror to others. The shadow warriors retrieved their arrows from the dead and left the bodies for the crows and vultures. Each dawn heralded a new column of smoke as a camp or caravan burned, and the druchii would look to the mountains and wonder if the next night would be their last.

AT KORIL ATIR, at the height of the pass, the druchii had built a keep to watch to the east and west. For two days the greater part of the shadow warriors marched, bypassing the camps and wayforts along the pass. A few bands were sent by Alith to harass the druchii garrisons at the Ellyrion end of the pass, obscuring the shadow warriors' true location.

At midnight, the shadow warriors gathered on the slope below Koril Atir. The citadel's battlements rose in a jagged spire above the valley, silhouetted against the sliver of Sariour as the white moon descended in the west. Thin pennants fluttered from the flagpoles in the strong mountain winds, but that same wind brought no sound save for the screech of owls and the occasional roar of a hunting beast.

The keep was the most ambitious target yet and Alith could sense the trepidation of his followers. It was one matter to attack poorly defended camps, another to storm a fortress. Alith had confidence though. This would be no frontal assault, with screaming battle cries and siege engines. Surprise and stealth would bring the shadow warriors a greater victory than any army of Ellyrion could achieve. It was his intent not only to send a message to the druchii that none of their lands were safe, that no army or fortress offered them protection; Alith wanted the princes of the east, and the Phoenix King in particular, to understand just how dangerous the shadow army could be. The Anars would never be underestimated again.

When the moons had disappeared and all was dark, Alith led his followers towards the citadel. Lanterns burned from the narrow windows of the tower, but there was still much shade to conceal Alith and his army. By the light of these lamps, Alith could see warriors patrolling the battlement, ruddy light gleaming from spearpoints and helms.

Alith led the first wave of shadow warriors, circling around the keep and moving on the citadel from the north along the butte on which it stood, picking their way across the cliff face itself. The stones of the tower were closely set, with no sure purchase for toe or finger between them. However, the shadow warriors used knives and climbing spikes to scale the wall, quietly driving their points into the mortar that held together the giant blocks. Alith and fifty warriors slowly made their way up the tower wall, pausing whenever they heard the tread of boots above, cautiously advancing when the danger receded.

Alith was reminded of the time he had scaled the citadel of Aenarion in Anlec. He wondered if any sorcerous ward protected Koril Atir. He could feel the vortex churning through the Annulii and nothing else, but he was not a mage by any means and much dark magic was subtle and difficult to detect. If there were magical barriers, he would have to overcome them; there was simply no way he could prepare for every eventuality.

Reaching the battlement, Alith waited until a pair of patrolling sentries passed. He slipped through the embrasure behind the guards and padded forwards on soft feet, knife ready for the kill. He heard a soft grunt behind him and glanced behind to see Khillrallion hauling himself over the battlement. The two of them exchanged nods and darted forwards, slicing the throats of their prey and toppling their bodies to the rocks below with fluid movements.

Alith leaned over the wall and signalled for the shadow warriors to finish their ascent to the rampart. When all were upon the top of the wall, Alith cupped his hands to his mouth and mimicked the cry of a snow owl. Within moments he heard shouts from the far side of the tower, on the south approach, as the remaining shadow warriors made their presence known. Flaming arrows arced through the night sky and it was not long before feet were pounding up the wooden steps within the tower.

Dozens of the garrison poured from the doorways onto the rampart and Alith's contingent struck with bow and sword, cutting down the druchii as they emerged. Their dying cries mingled with the shouts of the Anar warriors on the other side of the tower, adding to the confusion. Their bodies were dragged aside and Alith led his warriors into the red-bathed interior of the keep. The distinctive rattle of repeater crossbows sounded from below as the defenders shot from arrow slits on floors within the tower. These needed to be dealt with quickly. Alith signalled for Khillrallion to take half of the shadow warriors and deal with the missile troops. Alith would head for the main gate with the rest.

Just like Anlec, Alith thought with a satisfied smile.

As DAWN'S ROSY gleam reached the citadel, Alith ordered his warriors to bring the bodies of the slain druchii to the main gate, and to raid the armoury for spears and other weapons. Several Ellyrians were found in the tower's dungeons, tortured and bloody. Alith gave them clothes and weapons and sent them east upon the mounts once used by the citadel's messengers.

'When asked who liberated you, say that your saviour was the Shadow King,' Alith told the Ellyrians as they departed.

The Anar prince stood at the gate, seven hundred slain druchii piled around him. With a meaningful look at his warriors, he snatched one of the corpses by the ankle and dragged it to the open gate. He grabbed the front of the corpse's shirt and leant it against the black-painted timbers.

'Spear,' he snapped to Khillrallion, holding out a hand. The shadow-walker brought a weapon to his leader and stepped back. 'It is not enough that we kill our enemies. They fear their mistress in Anlec far more than they fear death. We need to send the druchii a message even their depraved minds can understand: even in death they are not safe from our revenge.'

With that, Alith thrust the spear two-handed, its point passing through the throat of the druchii corpse and into the gate. Alith gave the shaft a twist to ensure it was stuck fast.

Taking his knife from his belt, Alith cut a rune into the forehead of the dead druchii: thalui, the symbol of hatred and vengeance. He tore open the elf's shirt and across his chest carved another: arhain, the rune of night and shadows. Examining his handiwork, Alith wiped the blade clean on the rags of the corpse's shirt and placed it back in his belt.

Alith looked at his warriors, seeking any sign of disgust or horror. A sea of faces watched him blankly, a few with deep intent. Alith nodded to himself and pointed to the mounds of the dead.

'Send a message,' he told his shadow warriors.

* * *

'IT IS GRIM reading, my prince,' said Leothian, bowing obsequiously as he handed the parchment scroll to the lord of Tor Anroc.

Caenthras ignored the subservient herald and turned to the messenger's companion, one of the lieutenants tasked with guarding Eagle Pass. The Naggarothi prince fidgeted on the throne of Bel Shanaar, uncomfortable with its design. The three elves were swallowed up by the massive emptiness of the great hall of the palace, their voices echoing coldly from the bare walls and high ceiling.

The audience benches had been removed, and all petitioners were forced to stand or kneel before their new master. It was one of the few changes in Tor Anroc that had pleased Caenthras; the mewling Tiranoc nobles were still allowed to live by the direct order of Morathi, but they now knew their proper place.

'Tell me, Kherlanrin, why I should let you live,' Caenthras said heavily.

The warrior stifled a glance towards Leothian and kept his eyes downcast.

'I would gladly fight a foe that faces us in battle, but I can no more defeat this enemy than I can nail shadows to the ground,' Kherlanrin said quietly. 'Our soldiers awake in the morning to find their commanders dead, their despoiled remains hanging from trees outside the camp, with not a guard or other soldier harmed. Horses with the corpses of our scouts tied upon the saddles are sent into our camps, the mouths and eyes of their dead riders stitched shut, their wrists bound with the thorny stems of mountain roses.' He shuddered and continued. 'I found a squadron of knights that had been moving between Arthrin Atur and Elanthras. Their throats were slit and the bridles of their steeds had been nailed into their faces.'

'The situation is unacceptable,' said Caenthras. 'Anlec demands results. I will give you another ten thousand warriors, as many as I can spare. As soon as the snows abate, you will lead them into the pass and bring me the heads of these rebels. I want to know who leads them and I want to find out by looking at his dead face. Is that understood?'

The pair nodded and retreated swiftly when Caenthras dismissed them with a wave of his hand. The whole situation was embarrassing. The assault on Avelorn was faltering because Caenthras's commanders were fearful to march along the pass. This left the Ellyrians free to support Avelorn from the south. Caenthras had no idea how much longer Morathi's patience with him would hold, but he was determined that his would not be the first head on the block when that patience finally failed.

On a fresh spring day Alith looked down at the sinuous columns of black from atop a steep cliff, Khillrallion beside him.

'They will spend all of the seasons of Rain and Sun looking for us,' said the shadow-walker. 'The druchii will divide their forces to sweep the pass, and then we will strike at each part in turn.'

'No, that is not my intent,' said Alith with a grim smile. 'These warriors come from the west. Morathi's commanders have emptied their camps to search for us, leaving Tiranoc all but unguarded. They think that we cannot slip past so many eyes. They are wrong.'

'We go to Tiranoc?'

'To Tor Anroc, no less,' said Alith.

Ten days after the druchii offensive began, Alith was far to the west, hiding in the caves where he had first sought sanctuary with Lirian and the other refugees. With him he had brought only the shadow-walkers, leaving the rest of the army to the east, to amuse themselves at the expense of the druchii as they saw fit. He had brought only former

Shadows because what he had planned was beyond the skill of those so recently trained. When Alith explained his intent to the others he was met by confusion and incredulity.

'It is a great risk that you take,' said Khillrallion, giving voice to the concerns of his comrades. 'And for little gain.'

'You are wrong if you think this is merely a personal vendetta,' said Alith. 'Consider the despair of our foes when they realise that nowhere is safe for them, not even the palace of an occupied city. It will sow division in the druchii ranks, and cast doubt in the minds of their leaders. Think of their dread when they learn that no number of soldiers can keep them safe, no wall or gate can keep out the shadows that hunt them. We must not only be merciless, we must be daring! We will terrorise our foes and infuriate them at the same time. No locks or bars will keep us out! We will steal the swords from their belts and the gold from their treasuries. Not only will they fear us, they will hate us for our audacity. We will drive them mad, send them thrashing at illusions while we laugh at them from the darkness.'

'I am not sure it can be done,' said Gildoran.

'It can and it will,' Alith replied calmly. 'Did we not open the gates of Anlec under the noses of the druchii? Did I not scale the palace of Aenarion, and spy upon Morathi as she performed her dark rituals? Tor Anroc is as nothing compared to the perils of Anlec.'

'And you ask us to risk our lives in this endeavour?' said Gildoran. 'Some would think it vanity.'

'I do not *ask* anything!' Alith growled, losing patience. 'I command and you obey. I am the Shadow King, and I have made my will known. If you cannot live with that, then leave, go east and live amongst the Ellyrians or the Saphérians or the Cothiquii. If you would be a Naggarothi, you will follow me!'

'Forgive me, prince,' said Gildoran. 'It shall be as you say.'

Mollified, Alith clapped an arm to Gildoran's shoulder and looked out at his shadow-walkers. The prince was genuinely excited by the prospect of what he was about to do, the first time in several years.

'Good!' said Alith. 'Death to the druchii!'

SITTING ON YRIANATH'S throne, Caenthras looked up as the doors of the great hall opened and a messenger entered quietly. She was dressed in a long robe of deep purple, silver medallions in the shape of elongated skulls hanging on slender chains from her belt. Caenthras recognised her immediately: Heikhir, one of the Anlec heralds. The Naggarothi prince glowered at the emissary as she strolled languidly along the hall. No doubt she carried more demands from Morathi.

'I bear tidings from your queen,' said Heikhir with a bow. Her actions were deferential, but Caenthras sensed mockery in their exaggerated precision. He knew that the court in Anlec considered him a failure. The treachery of Yeasir had ensured that. Far from being the power he had envisioned, he was little more than a puppet of Morathi, in turn manipulating her gutless mouthpiece, Yrianath. At least Palthrain had had the good grace to get himself killed to leave Caenthras in sole command of Tiranoc.

'What is it?' Caenthras asked wearily.

'The queen yet awaits your latest report on the hunt for the rebels in Eagle Pass,' said Heikhir.

Caenthras shrugged.

'Every soldier that can be spared scours the pass for these ghosts,' he said. 'If the queen were to command me to lead the army I would drive on into Ellyrion. These attacks are nothing more than a distraction.'

'These attacks are a direct affront to Queen Morathi,' Heikhir said pointedly. 'Can you find no more troops?'

'Not without weakening our defences on the border with Caledor,' said Caenthras. 'Perhaps she could spare me a sorcerer or two from her little coterie, to use their magic to track these... rebels?'

'The pretender king fights in Cothique, what threat is there from the south?' Heikhir asked, ignoring the question.

'Enough,' Caenthras replied. 'Or perhaps Morathi would prefer the dragon princes to simply fly over Tiranoc and attack Anlec directly?'

Heikhir laughed but there was no humour in her tone. 'I shall report that your efforts are... ongoing.'

Caenthras did not have the will to argue. It mattered not at all what he said, Heikhir would take back whatever message she thought most pleasing to her mistress. For a moment Caenthras considered writing a letter, to put his concerns into record. He dismissed the idea. For one thing, he was too tired. For another, he doubted it would ever get delivered.

'Is there anything else?' he sighed.

Heikhir shook her head with an impish smile and then bowed. Caenthras stared daggers into her back as he watched her leave.

Caenthras stood with some effort, weighed down by his worries. He turned to the door on his left, to make his way back to his chambers. He stopped in mid-stride. In front of the door there stood a shadowy figure, swathed in black.

'Who are you?' Caenthras demanded. 'Did Morathi send you?'

The stranger shook his head slowly, the movement barely visible in the depths of his hood.

'Did you come with Heikhir? What do you want?'

In reply, the figure drew back his hood. For a moment Caenthras did not recognise who it was, but then realisation dawned. The face had not changed much, but its expression had. Once it had looked at him with fawning desperation but the face he looked upon was filled with utter contempt.

'Anar!' snarled Caenthras as he realised several things at once: that Alith was the leader of the 'rebels' in Eagle pass; that his capture would bring Caenthras renewed favour from Anlec; and that he would take some personal pleasure from killing the last of the wretched House Anar. The ruler of Tor Anroc reached to his waist for his sword and then remembered that he had none – his blade was still in his bedchamber.

Alith had not moved; his eyes were fixed on Caenthras.

'I will call for the guards!' Caenthras declared, suddenly less certain of himself.

'And I will disappear,' Alith replied quietly. 'Your only chance of capturing me is to defeat me by your own hand.'

Caenthras looked around the hall for something he could use as a weapon, but there was nothing. Grimacing, he turned back to Alith.

'You would kill an unarmed enemy?'

'I have done so already, hundreds of times,' Alith said.

'You have no honour.'

'I have seen what happens in so-called fair fights,' Alith told him. 'The honourable usually lose.'

Alith reached over his shoulder and pulled forth a magnificent bow, made of a shimmering metal, decorated with twin symbols of the moon. Caenthras's stomach lurched as Alith fitted an arrow to the impossibly thin bowstring and raised the weapon.

Caenthras considered his options. It was doubtful he could cross the hall and grapple Alith before he loosed his shaft. There was nowhere to hide. If he called for aid, Alith would still shoot and then slip away, no doubt.

'You have been wronged, I admit that,' Caenthras said, taking a step forwards. 'By me, I know.'

'Wronged?' Alith spat. Caenthras flinched at the scorn in the young warrior's tone. 'Because of you my family is dead, my people slain or enslaved and my lands are a razed wilderness. By your hand, thousands of true Naggarothi have died. Your ambition has welcomed vile war and spread darkness across all of Ulthuan. And you say you have done wrong?'

'Please, Alith, show some mercy,' Caenthras pleaded, taking another step.

'No,' Alith replied, letting go of the bowstring.

ALITH STOWED HIS bow and pulled free his sword. Crossing swiftly to Caenthras's body, he pulled the arrow from his prey's left eye and chopped off Caenthras's head, placing the bloody trophy in a tightly woven sack. Alith headed back towards the door by which he had entered, but then stopped. He walked back to the corpse and gave it a hard kick in the ribs.

'I'll see you in Mirai, you bastard,' Alith whispered. 'I'm not finished with you.'

HORNS AND SHOUTS and other clamour roused Yrianath from his fitful slumber. He awoke to find an elf dressed in the livery of his servants shaking him. He did not recognise the face, but that was not unusual. The Naggarothi regularly changed his staff to ensure he had no one with whom he might conspire.

'What is it?' he asked groggily.

'Fire, my prince,' the servant gasped. 'The whole palace is on fire!'

Instantly awake, Yrianath leapt from his bed and grabbed the robe proffered by another attendant. He could smell smoke and as the two servants ushered him out of the chambers he could see the flicker of flames at the eastern end of the corridor.

'You will be safe in the gardens, lord,' the first servant told him, steering Yrianath towards a stairwell half-hidden behind a tapestry. 'We'll use the servants' way, it'll be quicker.'

Yrianath allowed himself to be led down the spiralling steps and along a narrow corridor. They passed rooms and passages he had never seen before, but he spared them not even a glance. Other servants were hurrying past in the opposite direction, on their way to fight the fire.

The group passed through one of the smaller kitchens and out into a wide herb garden. From here, Yrianath's escorts turned right and led him through an arch in a hedge. Yrianath found himself in a circular garden, bordered by the hedgerow and night-flowering hisathiun.

'Wait here a moment, prince,' the servant instructed him. Yrianath was not used to taking orders from his subjects, but he was confused and so stood where he had been left as the two attendants vanished into the darkness.

He waited there for a moment, turning his eyes up to the towers of the palace where flames flickered from the windows and a blot of smoke swathed the stars.

'Do you have any regrets?' a voice asked him from the darkness. Whirling around, Yrianath searched the night garden but saw nothing.

'Who's there?'

'Your conscience, perhaps,' the voice replied. 'How does it feel to have the deaths of so many on your hands? What do you think history will say of Prince Yrianath?'

'I was tricked! Trapped by Palthrain and Caenthras!'

'And so you did the honourable thing and took your own life… No, wait, that isn't what happened, is it?'

'Where are you?' Yrianath demanded, continuing to turn on the spot, seeking his interrogator. 'Show yourself.'

'Do you feel guilty?'

'Yes, yes I do!' Yrianath shrieked. 'Every night I am haunted by what I have done. I know I was foolish, short-sighted. I meant no harm!'

'And what act of contrition would you perform to make amends?'

'Anything, oh gods, I would do anything to put this right!'

Something shimmered in the darkness and a sheathed dagger fell at Yrianath's feet.

'What should I do with that?' he asked, staring at the knife as if it were a poisonous serpent.

'You know what to do. I suggest slitting your throat would be quickest.'

'What happens if I refuse?' Yrianath flicked the dagger away with the toes of his bare foot.

'This happens,' said the voice, directly behind Yrianath. There was a flutter of cloth and a black-gloved hand closed over his mouth, stifling his scream. Yrianath felt a hot pain in his back and then everything went numb. Blackness swallowed him and he fell.

ALITH REMOVED THE prince's head and placed it in the sack with Caenthras's. He would have spared Yrianath the indignity if he had been brave enough to take his own life. Instead, he would also be used as an example. A glance confirmed the fire raged in the palace, its ruddy light creeping across the gardens.

Keeping to the shadows, Alith headed for the boundary wall.

CLOUDS SWATHED THE mountains to the east, turning to a blood-red as the sun rose. A pall of smoke hung over Tor Anroc, the scorched towers of the palace rising as blackened spires over the city. Here and there embers glowed, flickering through glassless windows.

There had been panic on the streets, but the druchii commanders had stamped down ruthlessly on the citizens of Tor Anroc, accusing any that were found outside of being arsonists, slaying them on the spot. Fear shrouded the Tiranocii capital as much as the swathe of smoke.

'I'm glad I wasn't at the palace last night,' said Thindrin, slouching against the battlement of Tor Anroc's eastern gatehouse. The druchii's spear and shield were leant against the stonework next to him.

'For sure,' replied his companion, Illureth. 'I think that those that died in the fire were the lucky ones. The Khainite witches will have plenty of bodies for their pyres tonight when Caenthras is finished.'

'Or perhaps he'll send them into Eagle Pass, for the rebels to torture,' said Thindrin. His vicious grin turned to a frown. 'I'm not certain which is worse: witches or rebels.'

'For sure,' Illureth said again, suppressing a yawn. The sentry glanced absently over the rampart. Something caught his attention. 'What is that?'

Thindrin looked down to the roadway leading up to the gate and saw an indistinct shape, tall and thin in the dawn gloom. For a moment he took it to be a person, but then dismissed the notion. There was another shape, of the same size and height, on the other side of the road.

'I don't know,' he said. 'Stay here, I'll take a look.'

Thindrin snatched up his spear and shield and jogged casually down the steps inside the gate tower. He signalled to Coulthir at the gate to open the small access door. Ducking through, Thindrin walked a few paces along the road. Two spears had been driven into the turf either side of the paved slabs, and something round hung from each. As the light brightened and Thindrin walked closer, he saw what it was. His spear dropped from his grasp and clattered on the flagstones.

Thindrin gathered his wits for a moment and turned back to the gatehouse.

'You better send for the captain!' he called out.

Upon the spears were the heads of Princes Yrianath and Caenthras; the rune of shadow carved into the forehead of the first, the rune of vengeance cut into the cheek of the second.

TWENTY-TWO

Blades of Anlec

As the legions of Anlec had brought misery and dread to Ulthuan, so Alith's shadow warriors visited terror and woe upon the druchii. They ranged across Tiranoc and Nagarythe, sometimes even daring Anlec itself to kill members of the courts and mutilate their bodies with symbols of dread: shadow and vengeance. Rarely did they gather in any numbers, so that the Naggarothi armies could not know whether to march south or north, to patrol the mountains or sweep the marshes and plains.

Alith would sometimes call a halt to the attacks, for dozens of days at a time. The first time he did this, the druchii believed that perhaps the mysterious Shadow King had been caught or slain. They were wrong, and in one night Alith unleashed coordinated attacks across the druchii-held territories, assassinating commanders, burning camps and stealing supplies. The next time there was a lull, the druchii were more fearful than when they were being attacked. The dreaded anticipation of what the

Shadow King would inflict upon them next occupied their waking thoughts and tormented their dreams.

They were not disappointed. On midsummer's day, an army marching east towards the Eagle Pass vanished. It set out from Tor Anroc and never made it to the garrison at Koril Atir. No bodies were found and there was no sign of ambush; five thousand warriors were simply never seen again.

THE WAILING OF the elf maiden diminished quickly to a whimper and then fell silent as her blood spilled from her throat and spread into a pool upon the marble floor. Morathi contemplated her crimson reflection for a while, pleased with what she saw. Six years of constant war might have taken their toll on her underlings but she remained as fresh and beautiful as she had been on that momentous day so many centuries before.

She smiled at the recollection of her own naïveté of youth even as she recalled the thrill of power she had felt during that first sorcerous bargain. She had not known then quite how far that fateful encounter with the daemons would take her, but she regretted not a single step along the path. It was true that the swift victory she had once envisaged was now beyond her grasp, but nevertheless the war progressed well.

She dismissed the distracting thoughts with a shake of her head, her long curls of hair sending a thrill through her body as they tickled her shoulders. She fought back the urge to indulge in the sensation and lifted the blood-stained knife in her hand. Delicately, she pricked the tip of her thumb and allowed a single droplet of her own blood to fall into the pool made by the sacrifice. Where it touched the offering, her blood spread in a slow ripple, forming shadows of deeper red. The shadows became more defined, showing a scene of the mountains. Clouds scudded across the red sky and hung about crimson peaks. With a word she focussed the vision, zooming in to Eagle Pass. Her magical eye swept over a column of warriors and knights as they marched eastwards to confront the army of upstart Imrik. They would not be victorious but they would distract the usurper king long enough for other parts of her plan to be set in motion.

A discreet cough pulled her attention towards one of the archways leading into the chamber. A functionary dressed in silken robes bowed low and the sorceress beckoned him in with a beringed finger.

'Your guest awaits your pleasure, majesty,' said the servant.

'Bring him up immediately,' Morathi replied. She turned back to the scrying pool, instantly forgetting the servant's presence.

'Who is it?' someone asked from one of the adjoining rooms. His voice was hoarse, a whisper wracked with pain. 'Is it... Hotek?'

'No, it is not,' Morathi replied. 'He labours still, but his work will be complete soon enough. No, our guest is someone else, who brings very good news indeed.'

The scrape of a metal-shod foot on stone announced the arrival of Morathi's guest. He stood in the archway clad in armour that had been tested much, scratched and dented in many places. His black hair was swept back with a silver band and the right side of his face was livid with a long scar, his eye on that side a blank white orb.

'Prince Alandrian, how good of you to come,' Morathi said huskily.

'Milady,' replied Alandrian with a bow. 'It is my honour to finally come here and see you in person after all these years.'

'Yes it is,' said Morathi. 'But it is one that you deserve. What news of my reinforcements?'

'I have left a strong garrison at Athel Toralien and the siege is ongoing, majesty,' said Alandrian, unconsciously lifting a hand to his ruined face. 'The other colonies have been emptied of troops who now sail for Ulthuan. Five hundred thousand of your bravest and noblest warriors will be on these shores before winter.'

The prince's smile was mirrored by Morathi.

'That is good,' she said. 'While you await your troops, there is a small matter I want you to deal with.'

'I understand you wish to be rid of the so-called Shadow King,' replied Alandrian. 'With your support, I will have his head on a lance by the time the fleet arrives.'

'You will have all the support you need,' said Morathi. She looked through the archway from which the other voice had come, her expression suddenly pained. 'It vexes us that all is not well in Nagarythe. I expect you to restore stability as you did in Athel Toralien.'

'It will be done,' Alandrian replied with another bow. 'I will bring you the head of the Shadow King myself.'

'I trust that you will,' said Morathi.

'Yeasir was a traitor,' the husky voice said from the adjoining chamber, its wavering tone hinting at delirium. 'You would not betray us, Alandrian?'

'Yeasir was once strong, but when asked for true sacrifice he weakened,' said Morathi. 'Alandrian has already proven his loyalty in that matter, haven't you, Alandrian?'

'Khaine called to my daughters and they answered willingly,' said Alandrian. 'That their mother did not agree was unfortunate for her, majesty. I regret her lack of wisdom but I cannot regret her death.'

'I am told that your daughters' studies go well and that they have progressed far in the arts of Khaine,' said the sorceress-queen. 'I can barely recall their demure attendance to me in Athel Toralien those many years ago. Tell me, are they as devoted to their father now as they were when last we met?'

'Not as devoted as they are to the Lord of Murder,' said Alandrian, his scarred face creasing into a wry smile. 'I am very proud of them and I do not doubt that one day they will make all of Nagarythe similarly proud.'

Morathi took a few steps towards Alandrian and laid a gentle hand upon his ravaged cheek.

'I could fix that for you, my dear,' she said. 'You could be as handsome as you were when we first met.'

'Thank you, majesty, but I must decline,' said Alandrian. 'My scars remind me of the price of overconfidence. A mistake I will not repeat.'

'You always... had the most sense... of us all,' the whisper announced between hissing intakes of breath.

Alandrian said nothing for a moment, but dared a glance towards Morathi. The sorceress was distracted, still with a hand on his cheek, staring into the adjacent room. He turned slightly to follow her gaze but Morathi stepped in front of the prince, obscuring his view. She drew her hand back slowly and shook her head.

'Not yet,' she said quietly. A golden tear formed in her eye. 'Soon enough you can see him.'

THE CRIES OF gulls and crash of waves masked what little noise was made by the shadow army. The tang of salt on the air reminded Alith a little of Tor Elyr, a taste unfamiliar to one who had lived most of his life far from the sea. The Shadow King felt ill-at-ease. The headlands of Cerin Hiuath, less than a day's march south of Galthyr, were relatively exposed in comparison to the shadow warriors' usual hunting grounds. The moorlands to the east provided cover for the two hundred warriors to approach the coastal road, but the tops of the cliffs were all but devoid of features to offer concealment.

Despite his misgivings, Alith had brought a force here to strike at a worthy prize. Word had come to the Shadow King that several of Morathi's court, leaders of the various cults that vied for power within Nagarythe, were to take ship at Galthyr and sail north to join the druchii armies in Chrace. Knowing that the route direct from Anlec would be closely watched, the cult magisters were to take a more indirect route, travelling south-west before heading up the coast to the port. The possibility of killing or capturing these influential cultists was too tempting to pass up, and so Alith had hurriedly put out the command to several of the shadow warrior cadres to join him in the west.

For two days since they had gathered the shadow warriors watched the coast road for signs of the entourage. Alith expected them to be travelling with little protection: any large force moving out of Anlec would have attracted unwanted attention. If his two hundred warriors were not enough for the task, they would simply withdraw without being seen. Although the shadow warriors' daring had become part of the myth surrounding the Shadow King, the truth was that Alith thought himself a cautious commander, risking his warriors only when the odds were in his favour or, as now, the gains of victory warranted additional gambit. In this way the shadow warriors had suffered only a few dozen casualties since they had begun their campaign.

If the cultists were as careful as Alith thought they would be, they would travel fast and light, hoping to avoid detection. The fact that the course of the war in Avelorn and Cothique had lured these primates out of Anlec was in itself a victory of sorts, upon which Alith intended to capitalise as much as possible. The disappearance of the cult leaders would send their followers into disarray for some time, the power struggles and internal conflict ravaging Anlec and leaving the druchii vulnerable to further attacks. It was pleasing to Alith to turn the cults' weapons of disorder and fear against them, inflicting upon them the woes they had engineered for the princes of Ulthuan for several centuries. As they lived, so would they die.

Shortly after midday, one of the shadow warrior scouts came running hard from the south. He breathlessly reported his news to Alith and Khillrallion.

'Riders, lord, coming fast along the road,' the scout told them. 'I would say no more than thirty of them.'

'Are they the counsellors?' asked Khillrallion. 'Are they the ones we hunt?'

'I believe so,' said the shadow warrior. 'There are some twenty knights, the others are armed but dressed in fineries. One of them has long white hair braided with black roses, which matches what we know of Diriuth Hilandrerin, the magister of the cult of Atharti. He is responsible for the massacres at Enen Aisuin and Laureamaris. Another rides under a red banner marked with the dagger of Khaine, which was borne by the warriors of Khorlandir during the first siege of Lothern. I do not recognise the others but they wear many of the profane symbols of the cults.'

'They are our prey,' said Alith. He half-turned his head for a moment as he heard the faintest of whispers from the moonbow in the quiver upon his back. 'I can feel it in my bones. Their darkness comes before them like a wave.'

'Make ready for the ambush,' Khillrallion told the shadow warrior. 'Send a hawk to us when our quarry have passed your position. We will come at them from north, east and south and trap them.'

Alith nodded his assent; this was the plan he had outlined to the shadow-walkers a few days earlier.

'I want prisoners if possible,' the Shadow King reminded his companions. 'These creatures may be able to tell us much of what passes in Anlec, and of forces loyal to them in the other kingdoms. For the violence and suffering they have unleashed upon us, their deaths should be neither swift nor painless.'

The messenger set off at a run as Khillrallion departed to bring news of the imminent attack to the other shadow-walkers. Alith stayed where he was, in the shadow of an outcrop of rock directly overlooking the road. The coastal path was broad and paved with white stone, winding its way along the edge of the land less than a bow's shot from the crashing seas. He had picked a stretch of the road where the coast heaped into rough hills and dropped away sharply to jagged rocks at the water's edge. The ambushers had not only the advantage of surprise but also position. The shadow warriors had the ambush site well scouted, and despite the scarcity of cover most of them could be concealed within a few hundred paces of the road and would strike before being seen. The rest were to remain out of sight further east, to move in as a reserve should resistance be stronger than anticipated.

Alith drew forth the moonbow and gave it a loving stroke.

'More blood for you today,' he whispered as he fitted an arrow to the string.

ALITH HEARD THE riders before he could see them. Hooves pounded on the cobbles of the road as the druchii made a dash for the comparative safety of Galthyr. He waited, fighting back tension and excitement, and cast a glance behind him to ensure that none of his warriors could be seen. In this regard the Shadow King was very pleased. Even though he knew where each shadow warrior lay in wait, not a single one caught his eye.

A troop of ten knights were the first to come into view, their silver armour gleaming in the summer sun, their black uniforms and banners streaming in the sea breeze. Alith let them pass without hindrance. A short distance behind, perhaps only a few dozen paces, the rest of the party galloped: ten more knights formed up around a knot of lavishly dressed nobles and retainers.

When the magisters and their bodyguards were almost level with Alith, he rose from his hiding place, moonbow ready. He was a heartbeat from letting loose the string when a shout from behind him drew his attention. Furious that one of his warriors had betrayed their presence, Alith turned to see what had happened. His anger quickly became alarm when he saw what had caused the cry.

Along the hills to the east a line of warriors appeared, regiment upon regiment of warriors in black and purple advancing beneath long banners. Crossbowmen formed into lines on the flanks as spearmen and swordsmen advanced in the centre. On and on they came, thousands of druchii.

Alith spared no time trying to answer the question that hammered into his brain at the first sight of the army: how did so many warriors come to be here? Rather than ponder that which he could not answer, Alith leapt immediately to a more pressing issue: how to escape?

The twenty knights had come together in a single squadron on the road and faced eastwards, barring any route to the north; their charges continued along the road and were quickly disappearing from sight.

Running figures from the south – shadow warriors shouting warnings as they approached – told Alith they there was no sanctuary in that direction either.

'To me!' Alith called out. 'Rally to me!'

The Shadow King watched the wave of black-armoured warriors advancing from the east as the shadow warriors gathered around him. A glance at the sun told him that the druchii had timed their attack well; they would be at the road some time before the first evening shadows fell.

'We have been lured into a trap,' Alith said hurriedly as the shadow warriors clustered around him. They crouched in a circle, partially concealed by the grass of the hills. Some stared intently at Alith with desperation in their eyes, others cast nervous glances at the knights on the road or allowed their gaze to be drawn to the army in the east. The riders close at hand seemed content to stay out of bow's reach. Why would they not? Alith thought, there is no need to attack with so many reinforcements on the way.

'The sea is our only escape,' Alith said. 'We must reach the waters and then swim south and come ashore at Koril Thandris. From there, we separate and make our way east, to meet again at Cardain.'

'The knights will charge if we attempt to cross the road,' said Khillrallion. 'We cannot outrun warhorses.'

'Then we must kill the knights first,' said Alith with a shrug.

'Bows against fully armoured knights?' asked one of the shadow warriors, a young elf called Faenion.

'There are only twenty of them,' snapped Alith. 'Shoot at their horses; on foot they will be little match for us. When the road is clear, we head down to the shore a little way to the south, where there is a shingle beach.'

At this the shadow warrior who had come from the south before the ambush spoke again.

'There are more knights moving up the road from that direction,' he said with a shake of his head. 'At least fifty of them. I do not think we can reach the sea that way before they cut off the road.'

Alith growled in frustration. It was not just the fact that he had been caught out that upset him; he had enjoyed so many successes of late his luck had been bound to run out at some point. What worried him more was the precision with which the trap had been set. The bait had been irresistible and the enemy had guessed exactly where and when he would strike. The Shadow King wondered for a moment if he had become too predictable, but dismissed the notion as soon as it came. Whoever had masterminded this particular trap had simply got the better of him this time.

'We'll have to climb down the cliffs,' Alith said at last. 'Slay the knights at hand and get to the clifftops. From there we'll just have to take our chances amongst the rocks.'

The shadow warriors exchanged worried glances and there were a few murmurs of dismay.

'The enemy will not wait for you to regain your courage!' snarled Alith, pointing a finger towards the lines of black steadily closing from the east. 'Follow me, or stay here and die.'

Alith stood up and strode purposefully towards the Anlec knights on the road. He lifted up the moonbow and sighted along the shaft, his aim settling on a rider at the front of the formation. The arrow leapt from the string and took the knight full in the chest, punching through iron and tearing from his back to pass through the throat of the rider behind him.

Startled, the knights took a moment to collect themselves ready for a charge, in which time Alith felled three more with another shot. Lowering their lances, the knights urged their steeds into a full gallop and thundered towards the shadow warriors. Alith watched them coolly. On the Ellyrion plains and in the forests of Avelorn, he had learnt the reputation of these deadly riders was greater than their actual strength. When he might once have trembled at the armoured warriors bearing down on him, he felt only contempt.

Another shot from the moonbow sliced through the neck of the lead horse and buried itself in the chest of the following steed, sending both crashing to the ground. The other shadow warriors sent their own arrows arcing into the knights in a series of deadly volleys and before the knights had crossed half the distance from the road all were dead or lying wounded in the grass.

A look over his shoulder confirmed to Alith that the approaching army was now closing fast.

'To the cliffs, follow me,' he shouted, stowing the moonbow and breaking into a run directly towards the sea.

Alith led the retreat, casting glances over his shoulder towards the approaching druchii host as the shadow warriors reached the road. The enemy were advancing quickly but Alith and his warriors would be at the cliff edge before their repeater crossbows were in range. A look to the south revealed the knights coming along the road; they too would not reach the shadow warriors before they were safely moving down the cliff. Though the situation was not good, Alith was more confident than when he had first seen the banners rising over the hills. Despite this he did not allow himself to relax.

'Keep moving!' Alith ordered as several of his warriors took up positions to shoot at the oncoming druchii. 'No rearguard will hold them back.'

When he was a few dozen strides from the cliff edge Alith caught his first glimpse of the sea. He marvelled at the unending dark blue horizon but as he continued forwards he saw the wider expanse of the ocean. High waves rolled in towards Ulthuan, far stronger than the tides of the Inner Sea he had witnessed at Tor Elyr. Ignoring his own command, he stumbled to a halt, mesmerised by the spectacle. As far as he could see in every direction stretched the Great Ocean, dwarfing him with its size. Far beyond lay the jungles of Lustria, where the descendants of the Old Ones' servants clung to civilisation. Ruined cities and steaming mangroves, treacherous swamps and ancient treasures awaited bold adventurers and explorers.

Alith realised how little of the world he had seen. He had never been to Elthin Arvan to the east, or the colonies of Elithis, or the towers of the elves far to the south. Had it not been for the civil war, would he have ever visited Ellyrion or Avelorn?

Shouts from his shadow warriors broke Alith's reverie and he snapped back to the current situation. His companions were pointing down to the seas and there he saw something that sapped his confidence as quickly as it had returned: three black ships at anchor not far from the shore.

Reaching the cliff edge, Alith looked down to gauge the difficulty of the descent. The cliff was not quite vertical, the strata of rocks pronounced in light and dark bands, the surface pitted with many holes and ledges. It was not the most difficult climb Alith had attempted. The cliff was not the problem, the greatest dangers were at their feet where surf crashed against jagged rocks and swirled in strong currents through jutting piles of tumbled boulders.

Something black and heavy blurred through the air close by Alith, quickly followed by other projectiles. Several shadow warriors were thrown from their feet with long shafts jutting from their bodies as the ships loosed their deadly bolt throwers. The swish of spear-sized missiles filled the air as more shadow warriors were cut down by another volley.

Along the cliff face warriors threw down their weapons to lighten themselves, some of them tearing off their cloaks and boots as well. Many hesitated, staring in horror at the black ships lurking out to sea or transfixed by the bodies of the slain.

'Keep moving!' Alith yelled again, unfastening his cloak and tossing it to the ground. Looking left and right he saw his followers pulling themselves over the cliff to begin the long descent. He grabbed the quiver from his back, ready to cast it aside, but hesitated. The moonbow gleamed in the sunlight. He could not abandon such a hard-won prize. Pulling it free, he passed the moonbow over his shoulder, threw away the quiver and then swung himself over the clifftop.

The shadow warriors were nimble and well-versed in climbing, and soon most of them were halfway down the cliff. Bolts from the lurking vessels hammered into the grey stone, some of the shots finding their mark, sending shadow warriors tumbling down to the frothing surf below. Rock shrapnel splintered from the iron heads of the bolts as they crashed into the cliff face, shredding Alith's clothes and grazing skin. One bolt missed his foot by the smallest of margins, pulverising the rock on which he had been stood. Alith scrabbled to find a new grip as he swung dangerously from one hand.

Panicked shouts and cries of pain mixed with the sound of the waves as Alith dropped from one handhold to the next, swinging from ledge to outcrop, his fingers finding purchase in small cracks, his toes making solid footing out of striations no wider than a finger.

More and more of Alith's warriors were falling to the bolt throwers, their screams drowned in the thunder of the sea as they plummeted into the swirling waves. Perhaps a quarter of their number had already been lost.

'They'll kill us all!' Alith bellowed to his followers. 'Leap into the water!'

The shadow warriors were too fearful of jumping to their possible deaths, but to Alith it was more certain that their doom would come if they remained on the cliff face.

'With me!' he cried, letting go his handholds and pushing out with all of the strength in his legs.

Wind battered Alith's face and tore at his hair as he fell towards the seas. He saw the foaming spume hurled into the air by the sharp pinnacles of the reefs, but it was the rocks below the water that he feared more. He closed his eyes and angled into a dive with a silent prayer to the sea god Mannanin upon his lips.

Hitting the water was like being kicked by a horse, forcing all of the air from Alith's body. He banged his right arm against something and immediately lost all feeling in his hand. He was engulfed by a storm of bubbles, tossing him this way and that, threatening to dash him against the rocks. He was turned upside down, twisted back and forth by the fierce eddies, the water colouring red from his wounds. Light and dark whirled as he rolled between the surface and the forbidding depths. Coldness seeped into his flesh and gnawed at his bones.

Alith struck out, fighting against a surge that threatened to drag him deeper and deeper into the water. One-handed he clawed his way to the bubbling surface, buffeted and buoyed by the heaving waves. Twice more the current snapped at his legs, pulling him under, filling his mouth with salt water. He coughed and spluttered, and gave a howl of pain as he was thrown into the sharp edge of a spire-like reef, a long gash torn across his stomach. The current tugged at the moonbow, its string cutting deep into Alith's arm. It tangled with his legs and batted against his face, but Alith would not relinquish his prized weapon.

Stroke by painful stroke, the Shadow King forged through the waters. He managed to gain his bearings and turned south, away from the druchii ships. A look back to the cliffs confirmed that the druchii army had arrived. Crossbowmen unleashed a storm of quarrels from above, picking off those shadow warriors who did not possess the courage to make the leap into the sea.

Slicks of red stained the water, and Alith had no idea how many warriors had been lost. He saw several, Khillrallion among them, clinging to the rocks, gasping for breath. They were sheltered in the lee of a giant pinnacle that stood apart from the rest of the cliff like a huge grey needle. Alith swam over to them and grabbed a handhold in the cracked surface of the rock.

'We cannot stay here,' Alith panted. He pointed upwards, to the gathering druchii troops, too breathless to say anything further. Khillrallion nodded in understanding and signalled for the others to follow.

Exhausted, Alith pushed away, unable to spare any more thought for his followers. He needed all of his strength and focus just to stay alive.

TWENTY-THREE

The Night of Dark Knives

MORATHI'S DISPLEASURE WAS not usually a survivable experience, but Alandrian held his nerve as he strode up the steps of Anlec's palace. It was true that he had not captured or killed the enigmatic Shadow King, but he had come much closer than anyone else in the last six years. He was not foolish enough to believe that Morathi would simply forgive him his failure, but Alandrian had already devised a new plan to ensnare the elusive renegade; a plan that would not only bring success but also be an act of contrition on his part. He had even taken the bold step of requesting an audience rather than awaiting the queen's summons.

Upon entering the throne chamber, Alandrian was taken aback by the smile that Morathi wore. She sat upon a chair beside the great throne of Aenarion, swathed in a voluminous robe of white fur and black silk, her bared arms and legs pale in the lamplight. Her whole demeanour was welcoming, its openness more disconcerting than a scowl.

Alandrian suppressed a shudder as he felt dark magic crawling across his skin and fancied he saw flittering shapes in the shadows at the edge of vision. Half-heard voices whispered and twittered around him, and he struggled to ignore their taunts and promises, focussing on the sorceress-queen.

'Majesty,' said Alandrian, bowing long and low. 'I offer my deepest apologies for the lack of success in apprehending the deviant who has so vexed your thoughts of late.'

'Stand up,' said Morathi, her voice neither cruel nor kind. She continued in the same matter-of-fact tone. 'We could waste a great deal of time, with me reminding you of your failings, and you offering apologies and excuses. Let us assume that such a conversation took place in the manner we both anticipated.'

Alandrian felt a flutter of fear. Was he to be presented no opportunity to argue his case? Perhaps he had overestimated his position and influence.

'With that in mind, I am sure your arguments would conclude with an offer to make amends,' Morathi continued, her voice softening.

She stood and beckoned to a group of shadowy figures who had been lurking in the darker recesses of the hall. Three sorcerers – two female, one male – came out of the gloom, clad in robes of dark purple, their skin dyed with archaic symbols that set Alandrian's teeth on edge. He had never been comfortable with sorcery; it seemed a dangerous weapon to wield.

'These are three of my most promising protégés, Alandrian,' Morathi said, gliding effortlessly across the hall towards the prince, her sorcerers falling in behind her. Alandrian swallowed hard, eyes flicking from Morathi's alluring eyes to the harsh stares from her disciples.

The sorceress-queen stopped in front of Alandrian and placed a finger to his lips as he was about to speak.

Alandrian felt a thrill of energy surge through him from her touch, stirring his heart, awakening urges he had not felt since the sacrifice of his wife.

'Hush, prince, let me finish what I have to say,' she said, her voice as soft as a velvet caress. 'You have another plan to apprehend the Shadow King, if I am but merciful and generous enough to grant you another chance. Something like that, was it?'

Alandrian nodded dumbly, not trusting himself to speak. Between the dark magic clouding his senses and the sensuous presence of Morathi, he was quite unable to gather his thoughts. He quivered uncontrollably, caught between lust and abject terror, both emotions stemming from the same cause.

'Good,' said Morathi, stepping back and crossing her arms across her perfectly formed chest, her weight on one leg, her smooth thigh exposed through a slit in her robe. Alandrian forced himself to keep his gaze on her equally beautiful face, dismissing the temptation to reach out and stroke that delightful skin. 'I am not known for my mercy, nor my generosity, but I would offer nothing less to one who has known such favour from my son and has given so much in the service of Nagarythe. Your past actions and loyalty far surpass those of my other subjects, and you may rest easy for the moment, knowing that you also have my favour, despite the recent setback you have suffered.'

Released from Morathi's spell, Alandrian recovered his wits and was about to offer his profuse thanks, but was stifled by a slight shake of the head from the queen.

'Don't grovel,' she said, 'it's beneath you.'

She turned with a sweep of her arm, hair swirling in a dark cloud about her shoulders. Alandrian had to look away as Morathi prowled back to her chair, hips swaying. He looked at her again only when she was seated, regal and austere once more.

'Tell me how my faithful minions might help you in your efforts,' Morathi said.

'I fear that there is no bait that we can now dangle that will lure the Shadow King into a trap,' Alandrian said, speaking confidently, glad that his speech was well rehearsed, for his thoughts had been scattered by Morathi's actions. Just as she had intended, he realised. 'If we are to slay this scorpion, we must find his nest and drag him out by the tail.'

'I agree,' said Morathi. 'How do you plan to find him when so many thousands of others have failed?'

'I have been studying the attacks of his warriors, in great detail,' Alandrian explained. 'At first they appear capricious, striking east and west, north and south without pattern. But there is a pattern there, I have seen it before.'

'Really?' said Morathi, leaning forwards with interest, one hand stroking her delicate chin. 'What have you seen?'

'In Elthin Arvan I became a keen hunter; the forests there teem with game,' Alandrian said, cautiously taking a step forwards. 'Some chase boar, others prefer deer, but I was not interested in those things. I much preferred to hunt those that also hunt. If you can best the hunter at his own game, you have truly proven yourself.'

'A trait I find most appealing at the moment,' Morathi said with a smile, her eyes alight with a glimmer of silver fire. 'Please, carry on.'

'The Shadow King hunts like a wolf,' Alandrian announced with a grin. 'It is difficult to discern, but it is there. Nagarythe is his territory and he patrols it regularly, putting his mark on one area before moving on to the next. In any given year he could strike anywhere, but it has been six years now and his thoughts are known to me. The attack near Galthyr is an aberration created by us and I must discount that from my thinking. After his next attack we will know where he has been and, more importantly, I know where he will have moved to. We will strike swiftly, take him unawares.'

'All of this sounds very worthy, but what is it that you need from me?' Morathi asked.

'Nagarythe is too large an area for your sorcerers to cover with their scrying powers, especially when looking for something constantly moving,' Alandrian explained. 'I can only estimate the Shadow King's presence in a general area, too large to sweep by conventional means without alerting him to our presence. Between my theory and the abilities of one of your sorcerers we should be able to locate the Shadow King with precision.'

'And how will you deal with him once you know where he is?' Morathi inquired, sitting back and crossing her arms again.

'If you would indulge me for a moment, majesty?' Alandrian asked, receiving a nod of assent in return.

He left the hall briefly and returned with two other elves, females so alike as to be twins. They wore breastplates and vambraces of gold chased with rubies carved with runes of Khaine, which flickered with a bloody light. Their silver hair was drawn back into long tresses bound with sinew and circlets of bone; bright blue eyes stared out of masks of painted blood. Each carried numerous blades: several daggers at their belts and in their boots; pairs of long swords hanging from their waists; matched scimitars upon their backs; boots and fingerless gloves armoured with spikes and blades. Even their fingers were hung with rings armed with curving talons of gilded iron.

'Two of Khaine's most promising slayers,' Alandrian announced with a proud smile. 'I present my precious daughters, Lirieth and Hellebron.'

Morathi stood and walked forwards again, her expression appreciative. She nodded, gauging the two warrior-maidens closely.

'Yes,' Morathi purred. 'Yes, they would be very fine weapons indeed. You need someone to guide them to the target.'

Morathi turned and looked at her disciples, before gesturing to one of the females. She was short and slight in comparison to Alandrian's assassins, her dark hair cut at the shoulder. Her skin was even paler than the queen's and her hair was shot through with streaks of icy silver, giving her the appearance of a winter spirit. She regarded the Khainites coolly, lips pursed, eyes analysing every detail.

'This one is the best at scrying,' Morathi announced. 'Get her close and she will be able to find the Shadow King for you. Step forwards, dear, and introduce yourself to the prince.'

The sorceress did as she was bid, giving a perfunctory nod of the head.

'It will be my pleasure to serve you, Prince Alandrian,' she said, her voice as cold as her demeanour. 'My name is Ashniel.'

ALITH'S LAUGHTER WAS echoed by a few of the other shadow warriors, but many did not share his sanguine view on his close encounter upon the cliffs. Both Khillrallion and Tharion had voiced concerns that Alith was becoming reckless, though they had couched their misgivings in more polite terms.

Some of the survivors of the ambush Alith had sent further east, to recuperate from their wounds and spread the word of what had happened; Alith was aware that the druchii would try to claim some form of victory from the affair and wanted his continued survival to be widely known. The others he had brought to this haven and some of the shadow-walkers had been summoned for an impromptu conference, at one of several sanctuaries the shadow warriors had created across Nagarythe.

Alith held court in a farmhouse a short distance from the town of Toresse in the south of Nagarythe; a place that had once been populated by a mix of Naggarothi and Tiranocii and had suffered greatly as a result while Prince Kheranion had lived. Many of the inhabitants had been killed or enslaved as 'half-breed' and all discontent had been violently put down by the prince's soldiers. Like many other brutalised towns and villages, Toresse had become a centre of quiet dissent against druchii rule that had found new hope with the coming of the Shadow King. The owner of the farm moved around the table with loaves of bread and cuts of lamb, casting awestruck glances at his guest.

'I am the rat that nips the fingers of those who try to catch me,' joked Alith, searching through the wine bottles on the table seeking to refill his goblet. 'There is nothing more frustrating for our foes than success snatched away at the last moment.'

'Our foes might call the deaths of more than a hundred warriors a success,' Tharion said sombrely. He gave a maudlin shake of the head and stared into his half-empty cup. 'We have grown arrogant with our success, believing ourselves untouchable.'

Alith's humour dissipated and he directed a frown towards Tharion.

'Every cause demands sacrifice,' said the Shadow King.

Tharion looked up and met his lord's stare with a bleak gaze.

'No cause is furthered by pointless sacrifice,' he said. 'Just ask the thousands that have burned on the pyres of the cultists.'

'You compare me to the leeches that have sucked the life out of Nagarythe?' snarled Alith, hurling aside his goblet. 'I have asked no elf to risk any more than I risk myself. I do not send my followers out to die while I remain safe behind castle walls. I gave you all a choice, one that you freely accepted. I repeat that now, to you and every shadow warrior. If you no longer believe in our cause, if you feel you can no longer fight the war we must fight, you are free to leave Nagarythe. If you remain, I expect you to fight for me, to follow me as your rightful king. I demand much, I know, but it is nothing less than I demand of myself.'

'You misunderstan–' began Tharion but Alith cut him off.

'Now is the time to strike again!' he declared, turning his attention away from Tharion to address the others in the room. 'While the druchii pat each other on the back and tell each other how close they came to catching the Shadow King, we will visit upon them a fresh humiliation, a punishment for their hubris.'

'*Their* hubris?' muttered Tharion.

'Forgive him, lord,' cut in Khillrallion before Alith could reply. The shadow-walker took Tharion by the arm and pulled him up. 'He has been most distressed by the thought that you might be taken from us, and he is not used to strong wine.'

Tharion snatched free his arm and smoothed out the creases in his shirt sleeve. He looked at the assembled shadow warriors, somewhat unsteadily, and then focussed on Alith.

'We fight for you, Alith,' Tharion murmured. 'You are the Shadow King, and we are your shadow army. Without you, there is no us. Are no us? Whatever. Don't get yourself killed trying to prove something you've already proven.'

Tharion pushed his way across the room followed by glances from the others, some angry, others sympathetic. The slam of the door brought a disconcerted silence, many looking to Alith, some avoiding each other's gaze out of embarrassment.

'He's just a little drun–' began Khillrallion.

'He is in danger of becoming a mother hen, a smothering hen even,' said Alith. 'I am no helpless chick, and neither are my brave, my very brave shadow warriors. That is the nature of the hunt. Succeed and eat, fail and starve.'

Alith rounded on the others, anger written across his face.

'Do you think I want my followers to die?' he snapped. 'Did I ask for our families to be butchered and our homes destroyed? I did not choose this life, it chose me! The gods and the druchii have made me what I am, and I will be that thing because our people need it. I do the things I do, terrible things, we do the terrible things we do, so that those that come after us might not have to do the same.'

Alith ripped off his woollen shirt and turned his back on the shadow warriors, showing them the scar of the whip blow he had suffered in Anlec. He turned back to face them, pointing to more wounds upon his body and arms, those from the flight at the cliffs still livid.

'These injuries are as nothing to the suffering our people endure!' he raged, scattering the bottles with a sweep of his arm. He looked upwards but in his mind's eye did not see the beamed ceiling but rather the everlasting heavens where the gods were said to dwell. 'A cut, a bruise, what do they mean? True torment is in the spirit. The spirit of a whole generation crushed by the evil of the druchii. What more must I give to spare them what I have experienced?'

Alith stooped and picked up a bottle from the floor. He brought it down on the edge of the table, smashing it. Staring again at the gods only he could see, he raised the broken pottery to his chest.

'Do you want more blood, is that it?' he cried out. 'Perhaps you want me dead? Like my mother and father. No more Anars. Would that satisfy you?'

Khillrallion grabbed his lord's arm and wrenched the broken bottle from his fingers, tossing it aside. He said nothing and simply laid his arm across Alith's shoulders, pulling him close. The Shadow King pushed him away and half-turned before stumbling and falling to his knees.

'Why me?' Alith sobbed, burying his face in his hands, blood streaming as his fresh wounds reopened.

The other shadow warriors gathered close, patting Alith on the shoulder and laying comforting hands on his head.

'Because you are the Shadow King,' said Khillrallion, kneeling next to his leader. 'Because nobody else can do it.'

THE FOLLOWING MORNING no mention was made of Alith's outburst. The discussion amongst the shadow warriors after Alith had departed had been one of solidarity with their leader. They knew they could never share the burdens he had chosen to bear, and had reaffirmed their faith in each other and the Shadow King. Some had remarked that it was all too easy to think of the Shadow King and forget the Alith Anar that was obscured by the title: an elf barely into adulthood who had lost everything and taken it upon himself to become the spirit of vengeance for all of them.

After breakfasting, Alith called his band to him and took them south, coming upon the waters of the Naganath before midday. From the concealment of a boulder-strewn hillock, Alith pointed westwards, to a stone bridge that arced over the river, a fortified tower at each end. The river was narrow and fast, less than two hundred paces wide.

'The Ethruin crossing,' Alith told his warriors with an impish smile. 'It is the most direct route between Anlec and Tor Anroc. In the summer the closest crossings are two days west or a further day and a half east. In the winter the ford at Eathin Anror is impassable, adding another day to the journey if one wishes to go by the eastern route. Imagine Morathi's irritation when next an army marches south only to find the bridge gone?'

'Irritation, lord?' said Tharion. 'Two garrisoned towers seem a tough nut to crack only to cause some irritation.'

'You're missing the point, Tharion,' said Alith. 'I *want* the druchii to come after me. It was a close thing at Galthyr, but I have learnt the lesson. Our enemies will divert valuable resources to finding *me*. They are used to the attacks of the shadow warriors, but the Shadow King, well he is the source of all their frustrations. I want to mock them. I want them so mad that they'll do whatever they can to find me. When they do that, they will make a mistake and we will exploit it, whatever it turns out to be. Imagine having to double the garrison on every crossing in Nagarythe. Every storehouse and grain barn will need guarding. While they scrabble around for the Shadow King, the other shadow warriors will roam free and cause anarchy.'

'You think that being deliberately petty will rile them even more?' asked Tharion.

'I wanted them scared, but their near-success will allay some of that fear, for a while at least,' said Alith. 'That being the case, I must select a different shaft for my bow, one that will not strike deep but will strike many times. Like the persistent wasp, I shall sting them again and again, each wound not sufficient to kill, but enough to infuriate. If they think they can get the better of the Shadow King, I will prove them otherwise. Just when they think I'm done, I'll be back, again and again, stinging them until they cry. They can swat and flail until they are screaming and breathless, and still I'll come back!'

'I understand,' said Tharion. 'One other question, though.'

'What?' replied Alith.

'How do we make a bridge disappear?'

ALITH WAS HEARTILY sick of the stench of fish. It was in the fisherman's smock he wore, in his hair, under his fingernails. He sat in the shadow of the fishing boat's sail as it slid gently along the Naganath towards the Ethruin bridge. Druchii soldiers stood at either end of the span, checking the occasional carts and wagons that crossed the border. More warriors could be seen drilling close to the northern tower.

All was as it had been for the last fifteen days. The druchii were content to let the flotilla of boats pass up and down the river, as they had done so for hundreds of years. The white-painted vessels warranted barely a glance, so familiar were they. All of the boats were from Toresse. Their owners did not know what Alith had intended, but had been willing to aid the Shadow King if it meant discomfort for their overlords.

As the boat lowered its mast and passed under the bridge, Alith slipped over the bulwark into the water, along with the other three shadow warriors hiding amongst the crew. They swam swiftly to the brick bank beneath the bridge and pulled themselves out of the water. Removing several of the blocks to reveal a hiding place, Alith pulled out wool-wrapped bundles of tools: broad chisels and mallets with cushioned heads.

The four of them pulled themselves up by means of a web of narrow ropes that had been constructed under the bridge, hung from hooks that had been screwed into the mortar of the bridge itself. Taking up their places, backs to the water rushing below, they continued their work, carefully chipping away at the mortar, the soft taps of their muffled hammers hidden by the gurgle and swirl of the Naganath. When a stone had been sufficiently loosened, they brought out wooden wedges, knocking the supports into place to keep the bridge intact for the time being.

In this painstaking fashion Alith and his followers had taken apart the bridge block by block, using the wedges and the natural pressure of its arch to keep the structure in one piece. The ropes that held them out of the water were also passed through holes cut in the thick ends of the wedges, allowing them to be pulled free at a later time.

Nearly two-thirds of the bridge had been thus prepared for demolition, by small teams of shadow warriors working in shifts from dawn until dusk. It was muscle-aching and mind-numbing work, lying virtually immobile in their rope cradles, repetitively working away at a finger's length of mortar at a time.

Until midday Alith and his companions laboured, when the fishing fleet returned and they were picked up, another team of shadow warriors replacing them. The boats were moored at Toresse and Alith stepped onto the quay to find Khillrallion waiting for him. The shadowwalker was pensive.

'Bad tidings, friend?' Alith asked.

'Perhaps,' said Khillrallion. The two of them turned off the road that led into the town and made their way along the reed-strewn bank of the river. 'Tharion is missing.'

'I saw him only this morning, as I left on the boats,' said Alith. 'He cannot have gone far.'

Khillrallion's expression was part-grimace and part-smile.

'I sent some of the others to look for him, but though he was late to the lesson he has learned the arts of the shadows well. There is no sign of where he has gone.'

'Sometimes we all need some time alone,' Alith reasoned.

'Not Tharion,' Khillrallion argued. 'He has never been shy in speaking his mind amongst others, and has no problem confiding his woes to me. He feels his age and a misplaced guilt over the fall of Elanardris.'

'Misplaced?' said Alith. 'None of our guilt is misplaced, we all must accept that we played a part in the downfall of the Anars, even if our intentions were the opposite.'

'I would suggest you do not say such things to Tharion, if we find him,' said Khillrallion. 'Since Cerin Hiuath he has been preoccupied with the dynasty of the Anars. He is of a far older breed than you and I, one of your grandfather's generation. We all despise what has become of Ulthuan, but it is only those that were there when she was saved from the daemons who really feel what has been lost. They gave their blood once to save our people, and they thought they did so in order that we who came later would not have to.'

'But why has this affected him now?' asked Alith. He sat down at the river's edge and Khillrallion sat beside him. 'For six years we have fought the druchii.'

'You have become the Shadow King, but Tharion can only see you as Alith Anar, grandson and son to two of his closest friends, the last of their line. For you Elanardris is now a memory, the shadow war has become your new legacy. For Tharion, that lineage, that tradition, is still embodied in you. You are not the Shadow King, you are the last of the Anars. He does not trust the Caledorians or the Chracians or any of the others to restore that which has been lost in our lands. Only while you live can he still cling to the hope that the glory of Elanardris, all of Nagarythe, might be restored. He fears that if you die, all hope dies with you.'

Alith pondered this without comment. He had endured some of Tharion's stubbornness and old-fashioned thinking out of a sense of duty to the veteran. In truth he tried not to dwell on the ageing elf too much, for Alith could not think of Tharion without also thinking of Eoloran, possibly dead, more likely languishing in some cell in Anlec. In all he had found it better not to think too much about the past, only the promise of revenge held by the future.

Alith thought about Tharion's concerns, as voiced by Khillrallion. Perhaps he was too possessed of being the Shadow King that he had forgotten who he was beneath the title. But that person lived in constant pain, surrounded by dark memories and feelings of impotence. The heir of the Anars had been powerless; the Shadow King was powerful. It brought its own woes and pain, but they were as nothing compared to the agony that awaited him once he had fulfilled his oath. What then? Alith asked himself. Who would he be when the shadow war was over? Perhaps Tharion would know.

'Find him for me,' Alith said quietly, laying a hand on Khillrallion's arm. 'Tell him that I need him with me, and I have something very important for him to do.'

THARION HAD STILL not been found when the time came for Alith to enact the second part of his plan. It was dusk, thirty days since the peril of Cerin Hiuath, and the Shadow King was poised to prove that he was not dead. Alith and his warriors were concealed amongst the trees and rushes that bordered the river east of the bridge. The boats and their crews were at the Toresse quays, ready for the signal to come downriver.

As darkness fell, several lights could be seen to the north, in woods that bordered the Anlec road. Flickering red and thin columns of smoke betrayed the presence of several fires. Their presence did not go unnoticed by the watchers in the guard towers and soon the trumpets were calling the garrison to order. Spear and sword companies were mustered at the north end of the bridge, their commander shouting excited commands. With a tramp of feet, the force marched to investigate.

When they were out of sight, Alith and the shadow warriors slipped out of hiding, bows ready. The towers would not be completely abandoned, but Alith knew he had enough warriors to deal with those druchii that remained.

The Shadow King led his fighters to the north tower, approaching the bridge silently. A cluster of figures stood atop the battlement gazing to the north. As at Koril Atir, the shadow warriors soundlessly scaled the walls of the tower. The druchii had hung chains festooned with barbs and spikes beneath the battlements to prevent such a move. Alith and the others bound their hands with cloth and pulled them gently aside to allow each other to pass.

Once on the rampart, it was a matter of a single volley to fell the guards, though two let out piercing cries of pain as they died. Alith had considered this and ran to the south side of the tower.

'Come quickly!' he cried out across the river. 'We caught some of the Shadow King's scum! The others are getting away! Quick!'

Alith split his warriors, sending some into the tower to ensure every room was clear, keeping the rest atop the tower. It was not long before the gate of the other guard house swung open and a stream of several dozen warriors emerged onto the bridge.

'Wait until they're close,' Alith told the warriors crouched behind the embrasures even as he waved the druchii to hurry up.

When the enemy were halfway across the bridge, Alith gave his shadow warriors the nod. They rose up behind the battlement and unleashed a storm of arrows at the druchii, cutting down half of them. They turned tail, fleeing towards the far end of the bridge, only to be met by another contingent of shadow warriors that had swum across the river to cut off their retreat.

As the last of the sun's rays glimmered and then disappeared, Alith had control of both ends of the bridge. Looking to the east, he saw white shapes ghosting down the river: the sails of the fishing fleet. After mooring their ships, the crews swarmed over the bridge with more lengths of rope, which they tied to the net already hanging under the bridge. The elves crowded the banks of the river, a dozen to each rope. Alith took his place, gripping the rope tight.

'Heave!' he bellowed, pulling with all of his weight.

The wedges resisted at first, but after a moment there was a shift as the elves strained on the ropes. First one wedge fell free, and then another. Alith exhorted his company to a greater effort and with one pull the supports were dragged free. With a drawn-out grinding, the keystones fell into the river and the whole bridge collapsed after, sending up a splash that spattered Alith with water. Waves lapped over the banks, wetting Alith's feet.

Already the ship crews were jumping aboard their vessels, ropes still in hand, dragging the stone blocks out of the river's depths. As each block was hauled over the bulwark, a slipknot was loosened and the stone fell free onto the deck. The fisherman had assured Alith that the twelve boats would be sufficient to move the stones upriver, where they would be dropped back into the river, hidden but never forgotten.

The Shadow King turned to the warrior behind him, a youngster named Thirian.

'Time for some heavy lifting,' Alith said with a wink.

WITH A MIXTURE of disappointment and relief, Khelthrain led his warriors back down the road. Whoever had lit the campfires had decided to flee rather than face his soldiers. On the one hand it was a shame that the insurgents had eluded him; on the other, Khelthrain was glad he had not faced the terrifying apparitions that so many other captains had fallen prey to. Not wishing to be out in the wilds while there remained the potential of ambush, he had quickly turned the column around and headed back to the safety of the towers. It was in generally light spirits that he marched along the road to his guardhouses, mentally composing the report of the incident he would have to send to Anlec. The orders had been explicit: *any* sighting or possible sighting of the so-called shadow warriors was to be passed on, with specific details of time and place.

The reassuring presence of the two towers rose up in the starlight and Khelthrain's thoughts began to turn to his bed. It was a pity that he would be sleeping alone, unlike some of those lucky wretches who had garrisons in the towns and cities, but at least he was out of the way and rarely bothered by the rulers in the capital. Ambition had never been high on Khelthrain's priorities, and a certain degree of middle-rank obscurity suited his nature.

Something seemed wrong as they approached the northern tower. Khelthrain wasn't sure what was amiss. He could see several figures standing immobile atop the battlements and the gate was closed. Then it struck him. He could see the glitter of the river beyond the gatehouse where he should have seen dark stone.

Khelthrain stopped dead in his stride, the warrior behind him clattering into his back, almost knocking the commander from his feet. The warrior bent to help him and then straightened, eyes wide with surprise.

'Captain?' he said hesitantly. 'Where is our bridge?'

THERE WERE DOZENS of maps of Nagarythe arranged over three tables. Alandrian paced between them with a sheaf of parchments in one hand.

'Here,' he said, pointing to a village where grain intended for horse fodder had been stolen.

A functionary, barefoot and clad only in a black loin-cloth, stepped forwards with a quill and a pot of red ink. He delicately marked a cross on the map at the indicated place, adding it to the many such marks already made.

'And here,' Alandrian continued, indicating an attack on a patrol out of Ealith.

'Oh, wait...' the prince whispered. He stopped and read the next report again, letting the others shower to the floor. 'Oh, yes. You're a cunning bastard, aren't you?'

'Prince?' said the servant.

Alandrian ignored him, striding to the map of the Naganath area. He stared at the chart for some time, his mind firing fast. He traced a finger eastwards along the Naganath. No, there was nothing there. The Shadow King wouldn't be dull enough to take another bridge. But he would go eastwards. Always after his most daring escapades he went east, back towards the mountains. It was like a homing instinct.

Alandrian brought another map to the top of the pile, of the area north and east of Toresse. He scoured the landmarks and settlements, seeking something of significance. A yellow circle caught his eye.

'This?' he demanded, gesturing to the servant. 'What is this? At Athel Yranuir?'

The functionary peered at the map, brow creased in thought.

'It is a tax house, prince,' he announced. 'Tithes are gathered there before being brought by armed column to Anlec.'

'And when is the next collection due?'

'Give me a moment, prince, and I will find out,' said the servant.

While he was gone, Alandrian stared at the map. The servant's information would confirm it, but Alandrian already had a strong suspicion about the Shadow King's next move. Eastwards he would go, away from the torrid time he had suffered at Galthyr, away from his joke at Toresse. But he wouldn't go too far east before striking again, not while he was still riding high from his prank.

'The harvest taxes will be collected in four days' time, my prince,' the servant announced as he entered. 'A contingent of knights will be moving out of Ealith tomorrow.'

Alandrian closed his eyes, blocking out everything save his knowledge of the Shadow King. Four days was not a long time to prepare. Would the Shadow King be able to put together an ad-hoc plan at such notice? Did he even realise the opportunity that awaited him?

It didn't matter. If Alandrian was the Shadow King, that's where he would be. He knew it.

'Please send word to Lady Ashniel, and to my daughters,' Alandrian said, his eyes snapping open. 'Ask them to prepare for a ride. We have a wolf to catch.'

'Shall I also send warning to the troops at Ealith and the garrison of Athel Yranuir?' the servant inquired.

Alandrian looked at the servant as if he had suggested that the prince dance naked around the room singing children's songs.

'Don't be ridiculous,' he said. 'Why spoil the fun?'

THERE WAS AN aesthetic pleasure in the contrast between gold and red: gold of coin and red of blood. Alith wiped a thumb across the face of the coin, smearing the crimson across the rune of Nagarythe imprinted upon it. Blood money, he thought, smiling at the joke.

He tossed the coin to Khillrallion, who was sweeping piles of money from the tables into a heavy sack. Another five shadow warriors did likewise in other counting rooms while a further twenty-five kept watch, stationed on the tiled roof and at the narrow arrow slits that served as windows.

Alith strode to one such embrasure, checking the time. The sun had set and the Chaos moon was already easing above the mountains, its sickly glow heavy behind the gathering clouds. The tax collectors were on their way; he had learnt as much from the gasped confessions of the druchii who had guarded the money. He glanced towards their bodies, faces and mouths glistening from molten gold that had been poured down their throats as punishment for such greed. It was unlikely the knights would arrive during the night, giving the shadow warriors plenty of time to take everything and disappear.

Rain pattered on the stone road outside, and Alith peered again into the gloom, irked by some sense he could not quite define. He had been on edge since coming to Athel Yranuir. The town was unremarkable save for the counting house, neither a safe haven for the shadow warriors nor dominated by the druchii. Alith had noticed the elders' hall showed signs of perversion to Khaine – bronze braziers in the archways and bloodstains upon the steps – but he had seen no other signs of the cults' sway.

The attack had gone just as he had planned and not a single shadow warrior had been wounded. There was no reason for his disquiet, and Alith dismissed it as understandable paranoia following his experience at Cerin Hiuath. In some ways he welcomed the thrill of uncertainty. It added an edge of excitement that he had not felt in some time, a feeling of being alive.

Between the darkening skies and the growing downpour, Alith could barely see the other buildings around the tax house. He looked out across the market square and could dimly see the elders' chambers on the far side. To the left stood a row of craftsmen's stores, their fronts enclosed by blue-painted boards. To the right were winehouses and stables. The former were empty, having been closed at Alith's first appearance. The people of Athel

Yranuir would not hinder the shadows warriors, but they would not help, and had vanished as soon as the fighting had begun. Alith could not blame them; most folks feared reprisals from Anlec for aiding the shadow warriors.

'We're almost finished,' announced Khillrallion. Alith turned to see him hefting a laden sack onto a pile beside the main door.

'Good,' said the Shadow King. 'There should be wagons and horses at the stables. Send Thrinduir and Meneithon to fetch two.'

Khillrallion nodded and left the room. Alith heard him relaying the order and turned back to the square, ill-at-ease. He glared at the concealing rain, wondering what it was that his eyes could not see but his heart could feel. He cast his gaze higher, seeing the tops of the enormous evergreen forest that surrounded the town, which shared its name. Perfect cover for his forces to use if the knights arrived from Ealith. He was worrying about nothing.

'Are you sure?' Alandrian asked again.

Ashniel nodded once, her face showing a glimpse of irritation. Alandrian looked away, unable to meet the sorceress's gaze. Her eyes had become glistening orbs of black, which reflected an exaggerated version of Alandrian's face when he looked into them: a cyclopean mask of scar tissue.

'He is there,' she said calmly. 'He is touched by Kurnous and he leaves a trail upon the winds. It passes quickly but I can sense it. Your assumption was correct.'

'Do we get to kill him now?' asked Lirieth, baring teeth filed to points and capped with rubies.

'I want to taste his blood,' said Hellebron, panting with excitement. 'I've never tasted the blood of a king, shadow or not.'

'He'll taste like wolf meat,' laughed Lirieth. 'Isn't that right, magic-weaver?'

Ashniel turned away with a sneer while Alandrian smiled at his daughters' enthusiasm. Truly they had embraced the changes of these new times and he was certain they would both enjoy great success and power in the regime that was rising to rule Ulthuan.

He didn't understand much of it himself, being of a far older breed, but he knew opportunity when it came and had exploited this one to its full potential. Morathi had brought her priests and sorcerers to Athel Toralien and it had irked Malekith, but when the prince had left for his campaign in the northlands Alandrian had seen the wisdom of allowing them to flourish. He had been careful to curb too many excesses, wary of allowing the colony to devolve into the kind of barbarism Yeasir had warned was gripping Anlec.

That foresight had paid off. The Cult of Khaine was fast-growing, second in power only to Morathi's court. His daughters were well placed to ride the bloodthirsty stallion trampling upon the heads of the other sects of Ulthuan. In the shorter term, they had developed skills that were profoundly useful in this current matter.

'Yes, you can kill him soon,' the prince said. While there were advantages to bringing in the Shadow King alive, dead was safer for all involved. One did not bring Khainite assassins to take prisoners.

Rain began to fall, splashing through the needle canopy above. In the darkness, the lights of Athel Yranuir shone between the trees. A murmur from Ashniel caused him to turn.

'I sense he is getting ready to leave,' the seeress said, staring through Alandrian at some otherworldly sight. 'We must move now.'

ALITH WORKED WITH the others, carrying the bags of gold from the treasure house to the carts in the square. His hair was plastered across his face, his clothes sodden and chafing. It seemed an inglorious end to what should have been one of the great tales of the shadow warriors. He shrugged and exchanged a smile with Casadir as they passed in the doorway.

'It rains on the druchii as well,' remarked the shadow warrior.

'They have roofs to cover them tonight,' replied Alith. 'We'll be sleeping in the woods.'

'I wouldn't have it…' Casadir's voice trailed off and his eyes narrowed. Alith looked over his shoulder into the town square to see what had alerted him.

Four figures approached through the rain, walking calmly towards the shadow warriors. They were hard to make out, but there was something about their demeanour that fired Alith's instinct for danger.

'Everyone inside!' he hissed, waving the shadow warriors into the trove.

The shadow warriors barred the door and Alith called out the orders, positioning his warriors at the casements and sending them up the spiral stairs to the roof tower.

'Oh…' exclaimed Khillrallion, looking out of one of the windows. 'That's not good.'

'What is it?' Alith demanded, stepping to the window.

'Best not to look,' said Khillrallion with a haunted expression, standing between Alith and the embrasure. They jostled from side-to-side until Alith shoved Khillrallion out of his path and strode up to the narrow opening. He gazed out into the night to see what had caused Khillrallion's consternation.

He saw a druchii in the ornate silver armour of a prince, sword in his left hand, a shorter blade in his right. He was flanked by two outlandish maidens, Khainites by their dress and weapons. Water sparkled from bared metal, the edges of their blades glinting menacingly. For all of their fearsome appearance, Alith did not quite understand Khillrallion's discomfort.

His eye was drawn to a fourth figure, a little way behind the others. She wore a heavy purple robe tied with a belt studded with diamonds. In the light of the Chaos moon her skin took on a pale green tone, the white streaks in her hair standing out in the darkness like lightning strikes. Her face...

Her face was known to Alith. The eyes were whirling orbs of magic and the expression one of cold indifference. But her lips, thin, and her delicate nose and chin were all too familiar.

Alith fell back from the window with a groan of pain, the sight of Ashniel like a physical wound in his gut. Alith stumbled to his knees, moaning wordlessly.

'I told you not to look,' rasped Khillrallion, grabbing Alith by the shoulders and hauling him to his feet. There was panic in the Shadow King's eyes, the look of a child suddenly finding himself lost and alone.

Alith took a step towards the door, mindless, and Khillrallion hauled him back.

'You can't go out there,' said the shadow-walker. 'They'll cut you to pieces.'

'I want the Shadow King!' a deep voice called from outside. 'Nobody else has to die.'

Alith was regaining something of his composure but was still unsteady on his feet.

'It is her, isn't it?' he whispered.

Khillrallion nodded. There was nothing he could say. Alith closed his eyes, steeling himself, and then looked out of the window again. The prince and Ashniel were still there; the two Khainites were nowhere to be seen.

'Be on your guard,' snapped Alith, his instincts taking control. 'Watch the door and the roof!'

A tense silence descended, broken only by the rattle of rain on the rooftiles and the splash on the square outside.

Alith went from one arrow slit to the next, trying to find where the Khainites had gone. It was not long before Khillrallion called him back to the front of the building.

Outside, the Khainites flanked the prince once more. At their feet knelt two children: one a boy, the other a girl. They gripped their captives by the hair, pulling back their heads, curved daggers at their throats.

'I want the Shadow King,' the prince called again. 'These will only be the first two if you do not come out.'

Alith snatched the moonbow from its quiver and took a step towards the door before Khillrallion tackled him from behind, both of them tumbling to the floor.

'You cannot go out there!' the shadow-walker repeated as Alith kicked himself away and got to his feet. Several of the shadow warriors had closed in, standing between their lord and the doorway. Their expressions betrayed their agreement with Khillrallion.

'Have it your way!' came the pronouncement from the square.

Alith leapt to the window in time to see arcs of blood streaming from the two children, the Khainites' blades flashing in the rain. Spilled blood merged with the puddles as the small bodies were dropped like rag dolls.

'Shall I have them fetch two more?' the prince taunted. 'Perhaps some even younger this time?'

'No!' wailed Alith. He wheeled on the shadow warriors, lips curled back in a snarl. 'We cannot allow this!'

The shadow warriors by the door looked resolute.

'We'll deal with this,' said Casadir, pulling back the heavy bolt.

'If they want the Shadow King, they shall have him,' Alith said, fitting an arrow to the string of the moonbow. 'Kill the Khainites first. Leave the sorceress to me.'

Alith looked out of the window as the door was thrown open. Arrows sped through the darkness. In a whirl of shining metal, the Khainites swung their blades and cartwheeled away, the arrows ricocheting from their swords. At a nod from their master, they came forwards at a run.

More arrows sliced through the rain to meet them. With supernatural speed, the pair somersaulted and swirled, dodging every missile. They reached a full sprint and would have been at the door in moments. Several of the shadow warriors leapt out into the square to meet their charge while Casadir swung the door shut behind them. The clang of the bolt rang heavily in Alith's ears, like the locking of a condemned elf's cell.

Alith felt the bite of every cut with a gasp as the Khainites sliced through the four shadow warriors without breaking stride. Throats were slit, tendons severed, limbs lopped away. It was over in a heartbeat, the remains of Alith's followers lying at the Khainites' feet, blood running in rivulets across the flagstones. One of the Khainites lifted a dagger to her mouth and licked the blade clean. She turned to her companion with a feral grin.

'More dog than wolf,' she said.

The two took up defensive stances next to each other, one fixed on the doorway, the other looking to the warriors on the roof.

'Can we have some more playthings?' the Khainite with bloodied lips called out.

'This has to end!' said Alith, crossing quickly to the doorway.

'Yes it does,' agreed Khillrallion. Behind Alith, the shadow-walker glanced at the others and received nods of understanding.

'CAN I KEEP one as a pet?' asked Lirieth, darting a quick glance over her shoulder towards her father.

'Bring me the head of the Shadow King and you can have whatever you desire,' Alandrian replied.

He felt a chill and looked to his right. Ashniel was standing beside him. The rain around her was turning into snowflakes, freezing on her skin, tiny icicles hanging from her long eyelashes, her hair rimed with ice.

'It's true what they say in Anlec, isn't it?' said the prince. 'You really are a cold-hearted bitch.'

Ashniel turned a haunting smile towards him but said nothing.

The door to the tax house slammed open again and the shadow warriors poured out, some with bows in hands, others grasping swords. Lirieth and Hellebron spun around each other as they deflected the hail of arrows, cutting through the shafts in flight.

Ashniel stepped forwards and threw out a hand. Alandrian felt the warmth leeched from his body as the air around her churned with ice and blackness. A storm of snow-white shards flew from her fingertips, scything into the shadow warriors. Frozen droplets of blood tinkled to the ground where the chill wind slashed through flesh, skin turning blue from cold at their slightest graze. Bows dropped from numbed fingertips and arrows splintered in the air.

Under the cover of the arrow volley the other shadow warriors had charged forwards, meeting the Khainite sisters blade-to-blade. Iron chimed against iron, but the fight was over in moments, Lirieth crouching low to cut the legs from her foes while Hellebron struck high, decapitating everyone within reach. The scene more closely resembled a butcher's yard than a town square by the time they had finished. Lirieth stooped and with a flick of her wrist, cut free the heart from one of her victims. She sheathed her other weapon and flicked the still-warm organ to her free hand. With a pout, she raised it above her head, squeezing hard, blood streaming down her arm and splashing onto her face.

'Praise Khaine!' she shrieked.

There was a flicker of movement at the doorway. A cloaked elf appeared with a silvery bow in hand. Quicker than the eye could follow, he loosed an arrow. The shaft took Lirieth in the throat, ripping her from her feet, sending her sprawling onto the wet flagstones.

Hellebron screamed, a sound of pure rage, and leapt forwards. Another arrow sang through the air but she cut it aside. She dodged the next with a spinning leap, her long bound bringing her within striking distance of her foe. Her left hand lashed out, its blades barely missing the face of her enemy. The right hand found its mark, plunging a slender sword under the ribs of her prey, its point erupting in a fountain of blood from his right shoulder. Blood bubbled from his lips as Hellebron ripped the blade free and twirled, slashing head from neck.

Flicking droplets of blood from her blades, she sheathed her weapons and prised the magnificent bow from the elf's dead fingers. Hellebron turned and held her trophy towards Alandrian, who clapped appreciatively.

'I think we best make that a gift to Morathi,' said the prince and Hellebron's shoulders sagged with disappointment. Alandrian pointed to the shadow warriors who had been incapacitated by Ashniel's enchantment. 'You can do what you like with those.'

Alandrian's eye was drawn to a pair of shadowy shapes fleeing across the rooftop. Ashniel raised her hand to unleash another spell but the prince stopped her.

'Let them go,' he said. 'Let them take the news to the others. The Shadow King is dead!'

TWENTY-FOUR

Strength of Elanardris

THE MOOD AMONGST the shadow warriors was shock and dismay. Summoned by Tharion, they had come here, to the ruins of Elanardris, to hear what the future held for them. Many were at a loss without Alith's leadership and there were whispers of doubt that the shadow army could continue without him.

Tharion sensed a shift in the war. The news of the Shadow King's demise quickly spread. With one act, the balance of favour had moved, the druchii regaining their former aggression, sensing weakness in their foes. Their sweeps of the wilderness for the shadow bands became bolder, while the shadow warriors, who had long believed in the myths of their own invulnerability, became more timid. They had survived and prospered with their daring, but now they were too often surrendering the initiative to their foes. The momentum of the war was changing.

Tharion knew exactly what was happening: the hunters were fast becoming the hunted again.

With Alith's passing command had fallen to Tharion, who had gathered his followers in the ruins at Elanardris as a reminder of what they fought for. Hundreds of them were hunched around the fires, faces drawn, expressions bleak.

'We cannot allow these reverses to continue to sap morale,' Tharion told them, standing upon what had once been a wall separating the east gardens from the summer lawn. 'If the druchii do not fear us, we have failed.'

'We will continue the fight!' said Casadir, the only shadow warrior to have escaped Athel Yranuir. He looked around at the others, but their support was half-hearted.

'How do we fight without the Shadow King?' a voice called from the darkness. 'Our enemies grow stronger while we diminish.'

'It is true,' said another. 'I have come from Chrace, and the tidings are grim. A new force has arrived in Ulthuan, brought back from the colonies by Morathi. I do not know exact numbers, but tens of thousands of warriors, all of them hardened in many campaigns, have made landfall in Cothique. I fear the kingdom will be under Morathi's sway by the end of the year.'

'We must redouble our efforts here, to ensure that Caledor can concentrate all of his warriors on this new threat,' said Casadir.

Tharion sighed and then frowned.

'It will not be as simple as that,' he said. 'With fresh armies in the east, Morathi's commanders are likely to bring back much of their existing force to Nagarythe, to rest and resupply for a fresh offensive next year.'

'More targets for us,' growled Casadir, and there were words of assent from other shadow-walkers.

'That is true to a certain extent,' said Tharion. 'What will be more important will be the thousands of troops coming back to Nagarythe. No doubt they will not stand idle while we continue our attacks.'

The significance of this began to sink in and there was a disquieted whispering amongst the shadow-walkers.

'What do you propose that we do, lord?' asked Anraneir. 'The returning armies will use Dragon Pass and Phoenix Pass; perhaps we could gather in strength there and attack them on the move?'

'They will be expecting that,' Tharion said with a shake of his head. 'There are less than two thousand of us left, these six years of fighting having taken a steady toll. We could harass the druchii columns without committing our strength, but that will not serve our ends well. A few hundred dead here or there is of no meaning to them.'

'We can still hurt the druchii, of that I am convinced,' said Anraneir. He shrugged. 'I cannot see how, just yet. If we were to bring all of our forces together, we might be able to strike back powerfully once more, but to do so risks discovery and ultimate defeat.'

'We are growing fewer, that cannot be denied,' Tharion said quietly. 'In a war of attrition we have no hope of victory. What else can you tell us from the east, Tethion?'

'The wider campaign is at a stalemate, unless these new druchii forces turn the tide against us,' the shadow-walker announced. 'The enemy possess Nagarythe, Chrace and Tiranoc, and much of Ellyrion and Cothique. Lothern is frequently besieged. Cultist uprisings continue to plague those cities and realms not yet under the sway of Anlec. There is rumour that the mages of Saphery battle with some of their number who have been swayed to the path of dark sorcery.

'Even the realm of Caledor is not free from the taint of corruption. While the Phoenix King pursues the greater war, the cults have infiltrated his mountain realm to sow discord. Many Caledorians support the king but would look to the defence of their own realm before expending the lives of their kin for the protection of the other kingdoms. Earlier this year, several priests of Vaul were discovered to be in league with Anlec, making magical weapons and armour for the druchii and smuggling them north through Tiranoc. Their leader fled, having stolen the sacred hammer of his god. I am sure that he labours in Anlec now, forging new weapons for the princes of Nagarythe.'

'Is there no report that might give us hope?' asked Tharion.

There were shakes of heads and disconsolate sighs all around the fire.

'Then it is time that I revealed to you why I have brought you all here,' Tharion continued. 'I spoke with the Shadow King before he left for Athel Yranuir. I shared with him my doubts and he listened. He gave me instructions, which we will all follow.

'The shadow army will come together again,' he declared. There were happier murmurs from the shadow-walkers but Tharion cut them off with a gesture. 'Not for a battle. We have never been victorious by pure force of arms. Guile and deception are weapons as useful to us as bow and sword, and with guile and deception we must lure the druchii into a position more favourable for us.'

Some of the elves nodded; the faces of other betrayed incomprehension.

'The druchii are full of confidence. They have a right to be. If we stand face-to-face against this resurgence, we risk becoming overwhelmed. No, we will not fight that way. We will lie low, bide our time and wait for the right opportunity. The druchii will think they have crushed us. We will allow them this illusion of victory, it is only our pride that is wounded by it. Their eyes will turn elsewhere, to the fresh campaigns in the east, and they will believe Nagarythe safe under their control. Then, and only then, we will strike again, rising up from the shadows to deal a blow to our foes that will make them hate and fear us more than ever.'

'And where would you have us hide?' asked Casadir. 'If we scatter into the populace we risk discovery by the cults, if we continue to live in the wilds as we do now, then why not continue the fight?'

Tharion stood up and spread his arms, encompassing their surrounds. The tumbled stones of Elanardris glowed ruddily in the firelight, already overgrown by moss and creepers, the once-carefully maintained gardens reverting to wilderness.

'Here we were born, and here we will be reborn,' Tharion declared. 'For some time I have been thinking; thinking about the past and the future. Though Morathi may control the lands of Nagarythe, there are many that suffer under the yoke of her tyranny. There are those who are sympathetic to our cause, amongst the downtrodden folk who labour for Morathi and her minions. Those that can be wholly trusted we will bring here, adults and children alike, and found a new generation of shadow warriors. This war will not end soon and we must look to the future.'

Tharion began to pace around the fire, meeting the gazes of the shadow warriors.

'Have no doubts, no matter what happens we will never surrender. It is possible that none of us will see victory in our lifetimes, and so we must lay down the foundations for our army to continue the fight after we have passed on. While there remains any spirit of defiance to Anlec and resistance to the druchii, our enemies can claim no victory. Elanardris is no more, consigned to bitter history, bare stones and memories of better times the only testament to the dynasty that once thrived here. I will not rebuild the manse, nor replant the gardens. It is not in the bricks and the mortar that Elanardris found strength, but in the blood of its people and the power of the land. These are our lands still, and they need a people to live in them. While we draw breath and struggle, Elanardris will not wholly die.'

* * *

By secret means, word was brought to the disaffected and disloyal Naggarothi, those who served out of fear rather than loyalty. They were encouraged to desert, though few ever made it to Elanardris. In ones and twos they came, slipping away from their homes and garrisons under cover of darkness, to meet the shadow warriors in out-of-the-way places. Sometimes whole families came, making the journey on foot through the briars and across the moors, seeking sanctuary in the mountains.

Wary of infiltration by agents from Anlec, Tharion personally vetted every hopeful, killing out of hand any that caused him the slightest suspicion. There were some, he knew, that were innocent, but the lives of so many depended upon absolute security. It was essential that the druchii remained oblivious to the subtle stream of refugees fleeing their oppression. The slightest notion that all was not as they desired would bring down the wrath of Anlec.

The old refugee camps had long been swept away by the years and so the shadow warriors and their charges set to building new shelters. Hidden in caves and in the hearts of the mountain woods, they stored food and clothes, blankets and water.

Under roofs made of woven branches, in shelters made of rockpiles, in hollows behind waterfalls and in reed-covered huts in the marshlands, the new people of Elanardris eked out their existence. Tharion always felt an eerie calm when he visited these places, their inhabitants quiet, thankful for their salvation but extremely cautious. They spoke little of the lives they had left behind, and few cared to speculate on the future. Even the children were quiet; there were few sounds of innocent joy and laughter was a rarity. Survival became the goal; to avoid discovery and see another dawn was measured a success.

Despite Tharion's earlier belief, the druchii did not withdraw their exhausted, bloodied armies from the fighting in the east. The reinforcements from the colonies were simply added to their numbers and Morathi's commanders pushed them even harder. Nagarythe was made a little safer by this aggression, though the rest of Ulthuan suffered for it.

The shadow warriors patrolled the borders but did not attack unless necessary. Tharion wanted no attention to be paid to the shadow army, their lack of activity reinforcing the belief that the Shadow King's death had led to their dispersal. It gnawed at his pride to allow the druchii to gloat over this, but pride was an easy sacrifice when so much was at stake.

In the spring of the eighth year of the shadow war, a child was born in Elanardris, the first since the war had begun. There was little celebration, for everybody's mood was mixed. That new life had come to a land once desolate was a blessing, but there were many that wondered what sort of life, what manner of world the young girl would see when she grew older.

More newborns followed in the coming years. Tharion wondered what type of people they would grow into. He passed on Alith's edict that all youngsters were to be raised in the traditions of the Anars and when old enough would be trained in the craft of the shadow warrior. They would learn to hunt and fish, to wield sword and bow, and speak the secret words of Kurnous. Though there was no present end of the war in sight, Tharion hoped daily that such endeavour would prove unnecessary. He wanted nothing more than the children of Elanardris to grow up strong and full of pride, and in peace.

The new lord of Elanardris also worried what character of person would be made by this upbringing. Raising children with hate for the druchii clawed at his conscience, but he had made a promise that the Shadow King's teachings would be passed on. The symbols of vengeance and shadow became the sign of Elanardris. They were painted on cave walls and carved into the bark of trees. Amulets and brooches were fashioned in their shape. This concerned Tharion, reminding him of the cults they fought against, but he could not deny the people their right to express their fear and their hope, to cling to these symbols in the wake of Alith's passing.

The years passed slowly, each brief summer a time of worry when druchii armies were on the move; every winter a tortuous hardship when food was scarce and the winds blew cold from the north and the snows heaped upon the roofs of the bivouacs. Some of the shadow warriors took families, others vowed to remain alone. They kept vigil over the land of the Anars, hidden watchers ready to slay at a moment's notice. Their deadly skills were little used, the unforgiving mountains as much of a deterrent to any druchii interest as a wall of spears and a forest of bows.

With each year the memory of the Shadow King was celebrated with a hunt. The shadow warriors chased deer through the woods of the mountains, and offered up a share of their prey to Kurnous and the Shadow King.

With each year, Tharion tried to remember the Shadow King less and Alith Anar more, but it was difficult. His exploits were told around the campfires, and as bedtime stories to the youngsters. The elf who had been a legend while he lived quickly became a myth after his death. Some of those that lived in Elanardris did not even know that he had a name, calling him only by his title. Tharion tried to keep alive the memories of the elf behind the myth, but he sometimes felt like he was swimming against the tide. These people were desperate and a character out of fable was more comfort to them than a mortal of flesh and blood who had once dwelt in the lands they now occupied. It gave them succour to believe that some spirit watched over them. The more knowing of their number declared that the Shadow King was a wolf not a shepherd, more likely to be bringing vengeance in Mirai than he was to be watching over a flock.

It was a harsh existence but the folk of Elanardris endured, listening for news of the wider war while they kept themselves hidden. A stability of sorts grew in the area, the shadow society developing new traditions and codes, new beliefs and practices. Nobody knew who first coined the phrase Aesanar – the New People of Anar – but it helped that they had a name for themselves. Tharion was bestowed the title First Lord of the Aesanar by the people he ruled, his position a regency for when a new claimant to the title of Shadow King would emerge. Pragmatic and resourceful, the Aesanar healed and grew, waiting for the day when one would arise to lead them back into the war; waiting for the day the shadow war would begin anew.

In the thirteenth year of the civil war, nine years since the flag of the Anars had fallen at Dark Fen, that day came.

By firelight the shadow-walkers met once more in the shadows of the old manse. Tharion had called them together at the request of Casadir. The shadow-walker had been reluctant to explain why, saying only that he had met a messenger with important news that they should all hear. Casadir explained this briefly to the assembled shadow-walkers, and impressed upon them the need for secrecy.

All turned as one as a dark figure led a horse into the circle of light, a cloak of raven features upon his back.

'This is Elthyrior, the raven herald,' announced Casadir. There were scattered whispers; Elthyrior was part of the Shadow King legend. Many present had met him before, but several had not.

'Tell us of what you have heard,' said Casadir, sitting down and waving a hand to the space on his right. Elthyrior whispered something to his steed, which wandered out onto what had once been the grand lawn of the summer garden, and then the raven herald sat cross-legged next to the shadow-walker.

'A new power reigns in Anlec,' the raven herald announced, a statement greeted with gasps of shock. 'The druchii talk with reverence of him, a ruler they call the Witch King.'

'Who is this Witch King?' asked Tharion.

'I do not know,' said Elthyrior. 'None that I have questioned or overheard can say for sure. Some believe it is Hotek, the renegade priest of Vaul that fled Caledor several years ago. Others believe Morathi has adopted Prince Alandrian and granted him rule in return for his slaying of Alith Anar.

'I am told that he is blessed by all of the cytharai. I have heard that no weapon can harm him, and he learnt sorcery from Morathi herself. Some of the druchii say the Witch King will be the scourge that wipes away their foes and hails the great victory of Nagarythe.'

Elthyrior's emerald gaze swept across the shadow-walkers, each of them intent upon his words.

'We all know that reality and myth can sometimes be blurred, but I have heard grave claims about this Witch King,' Elthyrior warned. 'Perhaps a more telling question would be "what is the Witch King?". "His gaze shreds skin and flesh from bones", one captive told me. "He burns with the fire of our hatred", said another. All say one thing: he is the true ruler of Nagarythe and soon he will reign over all of Ulthuan!'

'Camp tales and fireside stories, no doubt,' said Tharion. 'Perhaps Morathi fears the war has turned against her, and has conjured up this Witch King to instil fear and obedience in her troops.'

'While there may be some truth to that, I fear the best we can hope for is exaggeration,' said Elthyrior. 'So widespread is this rumour, and so vehemently is it believed, I have no doubt that some new druchii lord has emerged to lead the armies of Nagarythe.'

'What can we do about it?' asked Anraneir. 'Tharion, would you lead the shadow army against this new tyrant?'

'If it is agreed that we will act, then I will lead,' said the First Lord. 'But I am no Shadow King. I do not claim to have the strength and the cunning to outwit such a foe.'

'Without the Shadow King, are we truly the shadow army?' asked Yrain, newly granted the title of shadow-walker. She looked at her comrades with an impassioned expression. 'The Shadow King has power, to rally the weak and put terror in the hearts of the druchii. Does it matter who bears the title?'

'It matters if he cannot deliver,' said Casadir. 'I would not take up that mantle. To be a leader is one thing, to be a ruler is another. The Shadow King must be more than these things. He must be wrath and vengeance, unyielding and eternal. To be a living symbol, an incarnation of what we all fight for, what we all believe in...'

'Is there any elf here who could be such a thing?' Tharion asked. For a moment Casadir smiled, a flicker of amusement that soon disappeared. He shook his head, dismissing any claim he might make.

None answered, each looking at his companions to see if any volunteered. A few shook their heads, either disappointed by this reaction or dismissive of the idea that a new Shadow King could be found.

Elthyrior stood up suddenly, hand reaching to his sword. His gaze was fixed upon something outside the light of the fires, close to the manse building. Some of the shadow-walkers readied their weapons; others looked around nervously.

The flames of the campfires flickered, losing strength. One-by-one they died until only a single flame remained, barely lighting Tharion and those close to him.

'What is it?' hissed Anraneir.

Rustles and panting could be heard coming from the darkness. Golden eyes flashed in the starlight. The shadow-walkers turned this way and that, seeking ghostly shapes that appeared and disappeared in a blink of the eye.

The clouds above the mountains broke, bathing all with the silvery light of Sariour in full bloom. Where there had been darkness and shadow, now stood a figure swathed in black, face hidden within a deep hood. It stood immobile, arms crossed, head bowed.

All around the camp, wolf howls split the air.

'Who are you?' Tharion demanded, sword in hand. 'What do you want?'

'I am the Shadow King,' said Alith Anar, pulling back his hood, 'and I want vengeance.'

TWENTY-FIVE

Return to Anlec

UPROAR ERUPTED, CRIES of disbelief mingled with shouts of celebration and exclamations of shock. The shadow-walkers crowded close, mobbing Alith. Gigantic wolves prowled the periphery, their barks and yaps adding to the noise.

Elthyrior stood apart, watching the proceedings with suspicion. He caught Alith's eye and the Shadow King waved away his followers, telling them he would speak shortly. As Alith strode through the long grass, the shadow warriors set to relighting their fires, the air alive with the hubbub of surprise and elation.

'A trick?' said Elthyrior when Alith reached him.

The Shadow King shrugged and smiled.

'A new myth,' he said. 'Only Casadir knows the truth.'

'And what is the truth?' asked Elthyrior, expression stern. 'It is not right that you deceive your followers in this way.'

Alith indicated for Elthyrior to walk with him and the two left the camp. The Shadow King and the raven herald picked their way along an overgrown path of marble and sat in the charred remnants of the summer house.

'It is a necessary deception,' Alith said, plucking the bloom from a moonwreath that was growing over the remains of the outbuilding. 'One that I did not begin.'

Elthyrior raised a doubtful eyebrow.

'Truly,' Alith continued. 'I was set to confront Alandrian and his Khainite witches, but Khillrallion struck me over the back of my head. Dazed, I could not stop him taking the moonbow and masquerading as me. Casadir had me halfway up to the roof before I regained my senses. Khillrallion and the others bought my freedom with their lives. It would have been dishonour to have thrown away that which they had so willingly given, and so I ran with Casadir. He is the only other soul that knows what happened.'

'That does not explain your disappearance for the last seven years,' said Elthyrior. 'You abandoned your people.'

'I did not!' snapped Alith. He closed his eyes, forcing himself to relax. 'The tide was turning against us, my people needed a calmer head to rule. Tharion had already suggested to me that we create a new haven in Elanardris and I had agreed. I could not have built what he has built. He has given us a future, one that I could not. Though I did not plan it, my death gave us that opportunity, the pretence for peace we needed. The druchii would be all too ready to believe the shadow army was no more. My death gave my people space to recover, to start a new path. Had I lived, Alandrian would have continued his hunt. Twice he nearly caught me, and both times it cost lives, lives very dear to me. I watched Khillrallion cut down and I realised that the greatest danger to my people was me, and the druchii's hatred of me. I am a symbol, but that works both ways. I am defiance personified, and that rallies the brave to our cause. It also riles the druchii, who lust after domination and control.

'I decided to disappear. I returned to Avelorn for a while and ran with my brothers and sisters again. It was a carefree time, I will admit. But duty nagged at me, and year-by-year I knew I could not find peace, and that while the Shadow King had to die, he could not remain dead forever. I returned to Elanardris last winter and contacted Casadir. He told me of everything that had happened, and only this morning he passed on to me the news that you had arrived.'

'So why return now?'

'You know that answer already,' said Alith, standing and walking to the fallen wall at the front of the summer house. He looked westwards.

'The Witch King,' said Elthyrior.

Alith nodded, not turning around.

'I too heard of this creature. As far as Cothique and Chrace his coming is being proclaimed as the great awakening of the Naggarothi. He fills them with dread and awe in equal measure. I have never heard such devotion uttered amongst the druchii, save for those hopelessly corrupted by the cults. No elf I know could command such loyalty, yet the Witch King rules Anlec and Morathi supports him. I must find out who he is.'

'I fear that we shall all know that before too long,' said Elthyrior. He stood and joined Alith. 'I am glad that you are not dead, Alith Anar.'

'Me too,' the Shadow King replied with a grin.

ALITH REQUESTED THAT his return be kept secret for the time being. He declined to make any comment on what had happened to him and flatly refused to answer questions regarding his death and resurrection. He simply assured his followers that he had returned to lead them to new victories, still as hungry to punish the druchii as he had always been. There were those that wanted to proclaim his triumphant return across Nagarythe, but Alith bade them to keep their tongues.

'All of Ulthuan will soon know that the Shadow King lives again,' he told them, smiling knowingly but keeping silent when they pressed for further detail.

Alith gave instruction also that the shadow-walkers were to begin restructuring the army, making the shadow warriors ready again for war. This was to be done under the pretence that Tharion was considering launching an offensive against the Witch King, but to be kept quiet to the wider populace of the Aesanar. The shadow army was to meet Alith at the ruins of the manse. When asked when the rendezvous would happen, Alith gave another cryptic reply.

'You will have no doubt when the time to march has come.'

ANLEC HAD NEVER looked so forbidding. Alith had thought it a terrifying fortress the first time he had come here. The druchii had taken its foundations and heaped upon it their warped aesthetic and cruel design. The towers soared higher than ever, the walls hung with silver chains bearing rotting corpses and sharp hooks. Heads were displayed upon long spikes above the gatehouses and the ramparts themselves had been fashioned like rows of slender fangs. Flocks of vultures and crows circled constantly, settling to peck at the disfigured remains on display.

Amongst the purple banners of Nagarythe fluttered standards of red and black, displaying symbols of the cytharai, bedecked with the skulls and bones of those that had displeased the city's rulers. A thousand fires burned in braziers upon the walls, casting a pall of smoke across the whole fortress.

The sound too was awful. The clamour of gongs and bells and drums sounded constantly alongside the caws of the crows and the screeches of the vultures, as the temples performed their bloodthirsty rituals. Shrill cheers and drawn-out screams could be heard through the din. A stench of charred flesh hung on the breeze. Dark magic seethed, creating a palpable air of evil that made Alith shudder. He wrapped his plain blue cloak tighter around himself, filled with a supernatural chill.

Alith took a deep breath and ventured forwards, passing through the western gatehouse.

He had come seeking answers: to know the identity of the mysterious Witch King. But he had another purpose, far more personal. For most of his life the druchii had taken from him: his family, his friends, his love and his lands. They had heaped upon him one more insult that he could not allow to pass. They had taken the moonbow.

Her whispers had disturbed his sleep through the long summer nights in Avelorn. While he had hidden out in the shrines to Kurnous in the Annulii, the moonbow's distant cries of torment plagued his thoughts. He had not spoken of this to Elthyrior, but this was the true reason he had returned. His family were gone. His friends were dead. His lands were wilderness. All of those things he could not bring back. But the moonbow… That he could reclaim.

Within the city, Alith's confidence returned. With a calm assurance, he made straight for the palace of Aenarion. He wasn't sure where the moonbow was being kept, but he knew it was in the citadel somewhere. He would take it from under the nose of Morathi, and in that gesture he would announce the Shadow King's return.

The stair up to the main gates were stained red with blood and guards stood every few steps, cruelly hooked halberds at the ready. Despite the sentries, the doors were thrown open and a steady procession of druchii made their way in and out of the palace. Alith joined the line waiting for entry, ignoring the grim-faced warriors stood to either side. Step-by-step the line moved forwards until Alith passed into the shadow of the citadel.

* * *

The majority of visitors continued along the central stairs, no doubt seeking audience with one or other member of Anlec's ruling court. Alith stepped aside, watching not for soldiers but for servants. His time in Tor Anroc had taught him that it was more often the servants' passages that allowed free and easy movement in such palaces. It was not long before he saw a flustered page appearing from behind a tapestry depicting Aenarion riding atop his dragon Indraugnir. Alith wondered if Aenarion had ever known the demented creature he had married, or might have ever guessed the cruelty he would unwittingly inflict upon the world.

Crossing to the concealed entrance, Alith looked up at the huge portrait. Clad in golden armour, the first Phoenix King was every part the noble lord and warrior legend held him to be. Yet there it was, in his right hand, the Sword of Khaine. Even represented in silver and red thread, that grim weapon exuded death. Caledor Dragontamer had prophesied that Aenarion had cursed himself when he drew that fated blade. Perhaps, Alith thought, he cursed us all.

Alith slipped behind the tapestry and found a slender archway. Beyond a set of steep steps led upwards. Alith followed their winding path, not sure where he was heading but content to allow instinct to guide his hand. When he thought he was about two-thirds of the way up the towering bastion of the citadel, he left the stairwell and found himself in a broad gallery lined with alcoves. The alcoves housed marble statues of the princes that had fought with Aenarion. Some of them were defaced, their features chipped away, crude messages scrawled on them with blood. Some were intact, those that still continued to serve the new powers of Anlec. Most of them Alith did not recognise, a few were familiar to him.

He came across one that made him stop. Its features were as his, and it was only after a moment's thought that

Alith realised it was a depiction of a young Eoloran Anar. Bloodied nails had been driven into its eyes. Eoloran was dead to all intents, and he was only one of many victims of the druchii that Alith would avenge, yet the reminder of his grandfather stirred something within Alith.

He had come here to reclaim the moonbow, to take back that which had been stolen from him. Was it possible that he could snatch away something else while he was here? Was the real Eoloran Anar still alive? Was he somewhere close by, locked in some dungeon of Anlec? Alith decided that he had time enough to investigate. Turning around, he headed back to the stairwell and descended into the bowels of the citadel.

Alith had expected a hellish scene, full of agony and torture. In contrast, the dungeons of Anlec were well lit with golden lamps, and silent. He saw no guards, and as he wandered the narrow corridors he found the cells clean – and empty. Not a soul was to be found. Confused, Alith headed back to the main stairs and sought out the servants' quarters, a few levels above the dungeon.

It was a twisted scene of everything he had encountered in Tor Anroc. Maids and pages hurried to and fro, many of them bearing scars and other signs of abuse. Some wore amulets of the darker gods, some dressed in the flamboyant robes of the pleasure cultists. They snarled and sniped at each other in passing, and cringed when their masters swept past bellowing orders and lashing out with whips.

Alith grabbed the arm of a young maiden slinking past with an empty silver tray. She looked at him fearfully as he pulled her to one side.

'Lay a finger on me and you'll answer to Prince Khelthran,' she said, with more dread than threat.

Alith released her immediately and held up his hands.

'I am new here,' he said. 'I don't understand what's happening.'

The maid relaxed, tossing back her raven hair and assuming an air of importance. Evidently he was not the first newcomer to have made such a mistake.

'Which lord do you serve?' she asked.

'Prince Alandrian,' Alith replied quickly, the first name that came to him. The girl nodded.

'You should do well,' she said, indicating with her head that Alith should follow her.

She led him into a storeroom, its shelves empty, dust upon the floor.

'Watch out for Erenthion, he has the cruellest temper of them all,' the servant told him. Alith nodded gratefully. 'And never turn your back on Mendieth, he's a sly one and will stick a knife in you without even knowing your name.'

'Atenithor,' Alith said with a smile, but received a frown in reply.

'The less people that know that, the better,' said the maid. 'Names attract attention, and attention can be very bad for your health.'

'I fear I may already have caught the gaze of some,' Alith confessed, his face a mask of worry. 'I have been set an errand but I know not how to fulfil it.'

'What is it that you've been asked to do?'

'I have a message for... For Eoloran Anar, from the prince,' Alith said quietly, his eyes flicking nervously to the closed door. 'I went to the cells but they are empty!'

The girl laughed but Alith could not judge whether from scorn or humour.

'No prisoners are kept in the citadel!' she giggled. 'They all go to the temples for sacrifice.'

'Then it is a prank?' Alith asked, keeping hidden the knot of worry that tied his stomach. 'There is no such prisoner?'

'There is an Eoloran Anar,' said the girl and Alith nodded with relief. 'But he is not a prisoner. His apartment is in the western tower.'

Not a prisoner? Alith put his confusion aside long enough to ask for directions and then excused himself.

ALITH WAS AGAIN surprised by the lack of guards in the western tower of the citadel. He guessed the druchii were arrogant enough to believe that no one would dare infiltrate the heart of the capital. Following the instructions he had been given, Alith quickly made his way to the floor where Eoloran Anar was said to live. He found himself outside a plain black door, half-open. He knocked and received no reply. With a glance around to check that he was not observed, he opened the door a fraction further and slipped inside.

The room was plainly furnished, lit from a wide window that led out to a balcony. Alith could see a figure sitting in a chair of woven reed, facing the sun. After checking the adjoining bedroom, Alith cautiously made his way outside.

Eoloran Anar sat with the sun on his face, eyes closed. He seemed to be asleep. For a moment Alith was taken back many years, to a time before all of their woes. He remembered sitting in the gardens of the manse, his grandfather taking the sun just like this. Alith would play with his friends until their noise roused his grandfather and he would gently chide them for disturbing him, before rising from his chair to join in their games.

Flames and dark smoke consumed the memory, leaving behind a vision of blasted Elanardris and the bodies of his friends nailed to the manse walls. Alith growled unconsciously as the memory faded away.

'Grandfather?' whispered Alith, crouching next to the ageing elf.

Eoloran stirred, a wordless mutter issuing from his lips.

'Eoloran,' Alith said, louder than before.

His grandfather turned his head, brow creased, eyes still closed.

'Who is that?' he asked, his voice a hoarse whisper.

'It is Alith, grandfather.'

'Begone with your tricks,' Eoloran snapped. 'Alith is dead. You killed them all. Take your apparitions away.'

'No, Grandfather, it really is Alith.'

The Shadow King laid a hand on his grandfather's and gently squeezed it.

'I'm going to take you out of here,' Alith promised.

'You will not trick me this way,' said Eoloran. 'You can blind me but you cannot make me a fool.'

'Look at me, Grandfather, it really is Alith!'

Eoloran turned his head and opened his eyes, revealing two white, lifeless orbs.

'Do you still take pleasure in your handiwork, daemon?' he said. 'I did not give you the satisfaction of my cries when you took my sight, and I will not give you the reward of my dashed hopes now.'

'I'll find you healers, Grandfather,' said Alith, tugging at Eoloran's arm in an attempt to pull him from the chair. 'In Saphery, the mages will be able to give you back your eyes. Come with me, I cannot stay long.'

'You would like me to leave wouldn't you, fiend?' said Eoloran, softly pulling his arm away from Alith's grip. 'How many souls was it that she promised you if I left? One thousand and one? Their deaths will not be on my conscience. You can threaten me, goad me, tempt me like this, but I will not allow you to seal that infernal bargain.'

'You have to come with me,' Alith said, tears in his trembling eyes. 'Please, you have to believe me, it's Alith!'

'I do not have to believe anything. It is torture enough that you keep me in this vile place, where I can smell the sacrifices and hear their screams. You leave open my door and tell me I can leave any time that I wish, but you know I could never do that. My spirit remains pure and when I am taken to Mirai I shall not be haunted by the shades of elves murdered for my freedom. I would stay here a thousand years longer and endure whatever torments you can devise rather than allow that to happen.'

Alith stepped back, quivering from sorrow and rage. He could take Eoloran forcibly, but if what the old elf said was true, his grandfather was not willing to pay the price for freedom that Morathi had set. Alith pulled free the knife hidden in the waistbelt of his robe, thinking to end the old elf's misery His hand shook violently as he reached towards Eoloran's throat, and then he snatched it back. He couldn't do it. Though it tore at his heart to do so, Alith could only do as he had been raised: respect his grandfather's wishes. He bent forwards and kissed him on the forehead.

'Goodbye, Grandfather,' Alith said, voice choked with emotion. 'Die with peace and dignity.'

One more humiliation to be avenged, Alith thought, his grief becoming the cold fury that had sustained him for many years.

Using the same clandestine means by which he had located Eoloran, Alith learned that the moonbow was kept on display alongside many other trophies taken by the druchii during their conquests. Alith's search led him to a semi-circular gallery overlooking one of the main halls. The chamber below was empty, but several dozen druchii thronged the gallery to view the exhibits. There were several soldiers positioned around the display, looking bored.

Alith loitered in the crowd for a while, looking at the standards of Bel Shanaar ripped from the halls of Tor Anroc; a cloak made from the pelt of a white lion torn from the back of a Chracian prince; the Sunspear, once carried by Prince Eurithain of Cothique; the charred bark stripped from a treeman of Avelorn. Alith hid his disgust at the grisly relics on display, pushing his way around the gallery until he came upon the moonbow.

It was laid upon a purple cushion, the metal dull and lifeless. A plaque beneath read: *Bow of the so-called Shadow King, slain by Hellebron, priestess of Khaine*. Alith stared for a moment, shaking his head. A soldier stood not far to his right, examining his fingernails. Alith weaved through the druchii and came before the warrior.

'I'll just borrow this,' said Alith. His hand flashed to whip the soldier's sword from its scabbard. Alith plunged the blade into the druchii's gut, giving a twist before pulling it free.

Chaos erupted around him as the druchii shouted in alarm. Some tried to grab hold of him and Alith cut them down savagely, kicking aside their bodies as he forged towards the moonbow. Others tried to run but Alith lashed out at any within reach, hacking them down without mercy.

Reaching the moonbow, he snatched it up, feeling it spring into life in his hand. Its warmth seeped up his arm and a chorus of gentle voices hovered on the edge of hearing.

The other guards were closing in with bared blades and Alith leapt to the wooden balustrade that lined the gallery. He was about to drop into the hall below when something caught his eye.

At the apex of the gallery was displayed a simple band of silver and gold, a gem-studded star set upon it: the crown of Nagarythe. Alith ran along the balustrade, leaping over the swing of a guard's sword as he closed in on the crown. Turning deftly, he parried the next blow and sent his sword through the warrior's throat. He spun and kicked another druchii in the face before leaping over him and driving the sword through his back. Alith swung with the moonbow to parry the attack of the next soldier, his sword cutting a thin ribbon of blood across the druchii's face. Alith hammered his shoulder into the warrior's midriff and drove his sword point into his side as he fell.

'I'll take this as well,' Alith laughed. Slinging the moonbow over his shoulder, Alith pirouetted past the next attack and snatched up the crown of Nagarythe in his free hand. He flipped the crown onto his head and ducked as a sword swung for his face. A kick to the knee sent his attacker reeling back and Alith followed up swiftly, showering blows upon his opponent's sword until his defence gave way. Alith drove the sword through his prey's chest and then jumped back onto the balustrade.

With a final flick of his sword, he sent the last soldier stumbling back before somersaulting from the rail. Landing lightly, he raced to the doors, hoping that they were not locked. They were not, and Alith burst out of the hall to find the long antechamber a scene of pandemonium. Servants and druchii nobles were pushing at each other to flee the fracas, while armoured warriors tried to battle their way through the crowd, fighting against the tide of elves.

Alith spied another servants' entrance to his right and jumped nimbly onto the shoulder of a servant. As the elf buckled, the Shadow King jumped again, using the head of a screeching noblewoman as a stepping stone, before throwing himself through the air towards a long banner hanging from the ceiling. Alith grabbed the pennant in one hand and swung above the throng, releasing his grip to send him sailing over the heads of the oncoming guards, breaking his fall with a roll.

Alith ripped down the concealing tapestry as he darted through the archway, flinging the canvas at his pursuers. He dashed down the steps beyond the doorway, ducking through archways and running across landings in a haphazard fashion. He had no idea where he was heading, so it made no difference whether he turned left or right.

Bursting through a double door, Alith found himself in a vaulted reception room, a naked couple writhing upon one of the couches. At the far end was an open window through which Alith could see the roofs of Anlec.

As he ran to the window, Alith drove his sword between the shoulder blades of the rutting male, pinning him to the elf beneath. He could hear the clatter of feet behind him but Alith did not turn around. Letting go of his sword, Alith pulled his thick cloak over his arm and head and lunged through the window at full speed, crashing out onto the tiled balcony beyond.

Alith vaulted one-handed over the rail and swung underneath, feet seeking purchase on the wall of the palace. There was none. Alith dropped another storey, breaking his fall with a roll, his ankle twisting painfully as he landed. Biting back the pain, Alith jumped again, disappearing into a forest of spires that crowned one of the citadel's many minarets.

In a few more moments he had vanished, descending swiftly into the crowds of Anlec.

THE CAPTAIN OF the guard was virtually prostrate as he entered Morathi's chambers. He kept his eyes firmly fixed on the floor as he crawled forwards, shuddering like a beaten dog.

'We found this, your majesty,' he said, proffering a roll of parchment. 'It was pinned by an arrow to the chest of one of my soldiers.'

Morathi strode forwards and snatched the parchment from his quivering hand. She turned away and then stopped.

'Stand up,' she hissed, not looking back. 'The city is sealed?'

'Yes, your majesty,' the guard whispered back. 'The search continues.'

Morathi rounded on the captain, her eyes holes of pure darkness.

'He's already gone, you imbecile!' she shrieked, slapping the captain across the cheek.

Dismissing her soldiers' incompetence, Morathi turned her back on the captain again and opened the parchment. Behind her the captain slunk towards the door, one hand held to the weal on his face, where Morathi's rings had struck him. Where the blood oozed from the wound it turned black and the captain stopped at the doorway, horrified. A dark bruise spread across his face, bloating his features, dark blood filling up his eyes. With a wet gasp, he fell to his knees and clutched his throat before slumping sideways, a trail of black slime dribbling from his lips.

Morathi read the letter:

Dear Morathi,

Not dead yet, bitch. Send your new thug to Elanardris if you dare.

Alith Anar, Shadow King.

It was signed in blood with the runes of shadow and vengeance.

TWENTY-SIX

The Witch King

SNOW CRUNCHED LIGHTLY underfoot as the shadow army gathered amongst the ruins of the ancient manse. It was a grisly scene, the blackened stones still littered with the bones of the dead druchii, while the scorched earth where Alith had built the pyres was still bare. A tree grew in the middle of what had once been the great hall; ivy and thorny bushes climbed their way into Alith's bed chambers.

For six days the shadow warriors had mustered here on Alith's command, dispersing by night for reasons of safety. Alith felt sure that this day would be the last. Scouts had brought word in the night that a druchii army was camped in the foothills, larger than anything seen for a decade. It had to be the Witch King's host.

Seven days ago, word had reached the Shadow King that Anlec was emptying of its army. At first Alith had thought this host would head south to Tiranoc, perhaps to assault Caledor. The following day he learned that it marched eastwards, towards the mountains.

The time had come to confront this foe. Alith could feel it in the air. The snows were light, the clouds grey over the mountains. There was a strange calm in the wilderness. Dark magic tugged at the edge of Alith's senses. Yes, he told himself, today he would know the truth.

Mid-morning brought shouts from the east, where a rider had been spotted coming down from the mountains. Alith sent word that he was to be allowed to approach, knowing that it would be Elthyrior. He would not be anywhere else on such a momentous day.

Sure enough, the raven herald rode into the ruins, his steed picking its way nimbly though the tumbled stones and hummocks of earth that concealed so many of the dead. His hood was thrown back, revealing his pale, pinched features. In his right hand he carried a spear, but something was bound along half its length, wrapped in a waxed canvas shining with water droplets.

Elthyrior spied Alith and directed his steed towards the Shadow King.

'I see it is not only my enemy that I have brought out of hiding,' said Alith as Elthyrior dismounted.

'The time has come to return this,' said the raven herald, handing Alith the bound spear shaft.

'What is it?'

'Cut free the bindings when the Witch King comes,' said Elthyrior, 'and you will see.'

'Do you know who the Witch King is?' asked Alith.

Elthyrior shook his head.

'You have far more eyes and ears than I, Alith,' he said. 'Besides, did you not venture into Anlec to find out?'

'I got distracted,' Alith replied, though he had the decency to blush while he said it. 'I am glad that you are here.'

'There are few of us left, and I do not think the raven heralds will survive this war,' replied Elthyrior. 'Our time has passed.'

Alith was disturbed by this. If there had been one constant throughout his turmoil of so long, it had been Elthyrior. The raven herald had been many things – a guardian, an ally and companion – though never quite friend.

'The Shadow King watches over Nagarythe,' said Elthyrior with a lopsided smile. 'Morai-heg gives way to Kurnous, and moves her all-seeing gaze upon others.'

Alith could think of nothing to say, and so the two of them stood side-by-side in silence, looking to the west. It was not long before the druchii army could be seen, marching along the road from the north-west, cutting across the foothills in ribbons of black. Alith scanned the skies, searching for sign of dragon riders or manticores, but there was nothing. It seemed that Alith's plan had succeeded: the Witch King would confront him personally.

FOR ALL THAT he had experienced, Alith felt a slight twinge of nervousness as the druchii army spread out across the hills. Their number was inconceivable, more than a hundred thousand at a rough guess. Where had so many warriors come from Alith had no idea. Had Morathi hoarded so many troops all of these years, perhaps waiting for the right leader to emerge?

Some distance away the army halted, out of bolt thrower range. The intent was clear: Alith was to feel no immediate threat and stay where he stood.

Whispers and shouts of alarm caused Alith to look at his shadow warriors. They pointed to the skies, where a dragon appeared through the clouds, descending slowly. It was the largest beast Alith had seen, half-again as big as the dragon that had carried Kheranion. Alith was about to call for his army to flee to the hills but stopped as the dragon circled back towards the druchii army, landing in front of it.

A tall figure dismounted, dropping to the ground beside the monster. The air shimmered around him, a haze of dark mists and rising heat. Alith watched closely as the Witch King approached.

He was far taller than any elf, and clad in an all-encompassing suit of black armour. He carried a shield adorned with a gold relief of a hateful rune that burned Alith's eyes when he looked upon it. The sword in his right hand was enveloped by blue flame from hilt to tip, casting dancing shadows on snow.

It was the armour that caught Alith's full attention. When the Witch King was less than a hundred paces distant, striding purposefully up the hill, Alith could see that it was not wholly black, but a ruddy light glowed from within. Wisps of steam swirled around the warrior. Alith realised with horror that the plates and mail of the armour smouldered, every joint and rivet still hot as if recently forged. The Witch King left molten snow and scorched earth in his wake while the air itself recoiled from his presence, streaming away from his body in whirling vortices.

The shadow warriors watched the Witch King carefully, bows in hand. Alith had ordered them not to attack until his command; he needed to know who dared call himself ruler of Nagarythe. Having seen the strength of the Witch King's host, there was no doubt that this warrior commanded the loyalty of Anlec.

As the Witch King advanced through the tumbled remnants of the old gate, Alith's gaze was drawn in by his eyes. They were pits of black flame, empty and yet full of energy. Nothing could be seen of his face save those terrible orbs; the Witch King's head was enclosed in a black and gold helm adorned with a circlet of horns and spines made from a silvery-grey metal that reflected no light.

Remembering Elthyrior's gift, Alith drew his knife from his belt and cut away the cords binding the canvas around the spear in Alith's left hand. He shook the shaft to dislodge the bag, which fluttered away in the wind. Stirred by the breeze a flag snapped out from the shaft, tied with gold-threaded rope.

The banner was tattered and stained, ragged with many holes and frayed stitching at its edges. It had once been white, but was now dirty brown and grey. The design upon it was indistinct but Alith recognised it immediately as a golden griffon's wing: the standard of House Anar.

Alith felt a surge of courage flow through him, dispelling the dread surrounding the approaching Witch King. The banner had flown in this place since the time of Aenarion and Alith drew on its strength, on the power of centuries that even the blood of the Anars could not wash away. Emboldened, Alith stared at his foe.

'By what right do you enter these lands without the permission of Alith Anar, lord of house Anar, Shadow King of Nagarythe?' Alith demanded, raising the ragged banner above his head. 'If you come to treat with me, hear my oath to the dead. Nothing is forgotten, nothing is forgiven!'

The Witch King stopped half a dozen paces away, the heat from his body prickling at Alith's skin. His infernal gaze moved up to the flag. The Witch King sheathed his sword and gestured at the banner, a mere flick of a finger.

The standard burst into black flames and disintegrated into a flutter of charred flakes that were quickly taken away by the wind, leaving Alith holding a burnt staff. He let the smoking wood drop from his fingers.

'House Anar is dead,' intoned the Witch King. His voice was echoing and deep, as if coming from a distant hall. 'Only I rule Nagarythe. Swear loyalty to me and your past will be forgotten, your treachery forgiven. I will grant you these lands to rule as your own, your fealty owed only to me.'

Alith laughed.

'You would make me a prince of graves, a custodian of nothing,' he said. He grew serious, eyes narrowing. 'By what right do you demand such loyalty?'

The Witch King stepped forwards and it took all of Alith's nerve to hold his ground. Strange voices hissed at the edge of hearing – spirits of sacrifices bound within the armour. The heat was near unbearable, causing Alith's eyes to water, his skin cracking with dryness. Alith licked his lips but his mouth was also parched. Worst was the crawling, filthy sensation of dark magic that leaked through Alith, drawing the life from his blood, chilling his heart.

'Do you not recognise me, Alith?' the Witch King said, bending close, his tone quiet, swathed in a charnel aura of burning and death. 'Will you not serve me once more?'

The voice of the creature in front of Alith was cracked and hoarse, but the Shadow King recognised it. A lifetime ago it had spoken words upon which Alith had hung all his hopes and dreams. Once, in the distant past, that voice had sworn to Alith to set Nagarythe free from tyranny and he had believed it. Now it called for him to surrender.

It was the voice of Malekith.

ABOUT THE AUTHOR

Gav Thorpe has been rampaging across the worlds of Warhammer and Warhammer 40,000 for many years as both an author and games developer. He hails from the den of scurvy outlaws called Nottingham and makes regular sorties to unleash bloodshed and mayhem. He shares his hideout with Dennis, a psychotic mechanical hamster currently planning the overthrow of a small South American country.

Gav's previous novels include fan-favourite *Angels of Darkness* and the epic *Malekith*, first instalment in the Sundering trilogy, amongst many others.

You can find his website at:
mechanicalhamster.wordpress.com

TIME OF LEGENDS

NAGASH THE SORCERER

The undead will rise...

MIKE LEE

UK ISBN 978-1-84416-660-2 US ISBN 978-1-84416-556-8

TIME OF LEGENDS
HELDENHAMMER
The Legend of Sigmar
GRAHAM McNEILL

UK ISBN 978-1-84416-689-3 US ISBN 978-1-84416-688-6

•KNOWLEDGE IS POWER•
WWW.BLACKLIBRARY.COM
NEWS • LIMITED EDITIONS • BLOG • MULTIMEDIA